# TO THE
# TOWER BORN

ALSO BY ROBIN MAXWELL

*The Wild Irish*
*Virgin: Prelude to the Throne*
*The Queen's Bastard*
*The Secret Diary of Anne Boleyn*

# TO THE
# TOWER BORN

## ROBIN MAXWELL

*wm*

WILLIAM MORROW

*An Imprint of* HarperCollins*Publishers*

The book is a work of fiction. References to real people, events, establishments, organizations, or locales are intended only to provide a sense of authenticity, and are used fictitiously. All other characters, and all incidents and dialogue, are drawn from the author's imagination and are not to be construed as real.

HarperCollins books may be purchased for educational, business, or sales promotional use. For information please write: Special Markets Department, HarperCollins Publishers, 10 East 53rd Street, New York, NY 10022.

FIRST EDITION

*Designed by Stephanie Hantwork*

Printed on acid-free paper

Library of Congress Cataloging-in-Publication Data

Maxwell, Robin, 1948–
    To the tower born / Robin Maxwell.—1st ed.
        p.    cm.
    ISBN 0-06-058051-8 (acid-free paper)
    1. Elizabeth, Queen, consort of Henry VII, King of England, 1465–1503—Fiction.
    2. Richard III, King of England, 1452–1485—Fiction.    3. Edward V, King of England,
    1470–1483—Fiction.    4. Richard, Duke of York, 1472–1483—Fiction.    5. Caxton,
    William, ca. 1422–1491—Fiction.    6. Tower of London (London, England)—Fiction.
    7. Political prisoners—Fiction.    8. Great Britain—History—Richard III,
    1452–1485—Fiction.    I. Title.

PS3563.A9254T6 2005
813'.54—dc22                                                                2004063571

05    06    07    08    09    WBC/RRD    10    9    8    7    6    5    4    3    2    1

*For the Windsor princes,*
*William and Harry*

## ACKNOWLEDGMENTS

First and foremost I must thank my old friend and writing partner, Billie Morton, for the original idea to write a brand-new twist on this oft-told story, and for seeing me through to the end.

My beloved agents, Kim Witherspoon and David Forrer, went far beyond the call of duty during the writing and rewriting (and rewriting) of this book. For their brilliant ideas, daily support, and unflagging belief in me, I am eternally grateful.

From the beginning, my editor, Carolyn Marino, held a clear vision of this novel. Though I struggled down the road to completion amidst obstacles and detours, her vision proved ultimately correct, and for that I am deeply indebted.

Fellow author, historian, and dear friend Vicki León was teacher, coach, and midwife of this project and, as always, kept me laughing.

My mother, Skippy, and my husband, Max, are the two steadfast pillars of my life. They hold me high above the raging tempest of everyday living so I am free to write. My love for them knows no bounds.

THE JUDGE'S EXPRESSION was one of seething disapproval. "You are saying that you wish to retain your given name, that which was yours previous to this marriage?"

"I do, your lordship."

"And what, for the record, is that name?"

"Elizabeth Caxton, though I've long been known in my trade as Nell, and would request——"

The judge turned to the court scribe. "Record that on this day of Our Lord, twenty-three April, 1502, one Elizabeth Caxton, daughter of William Caxton, has been granted by the courts a divorce from the aforementioned Gerard Croppe, on the grounds of——"

"Desertion," Nell finished for him in a firm but even tone.

"Silence, Mistress Caxton."

"And fornication many times over," she added, ignoring the judge, whose nose, crisscrossed with veins, had turned an alarming shade of purple.

"Silence!"

Nell held the judge steadily in her gaze. *He dislikes women,* she silently observed. *The entire species of them.*

"If this display is any indication of your disobedience and

rebellious nature," the judge said, "then I can only commend your husband for his desertion."

"And his adultery?" asked Nell, smiling mildly.

"Out of my court!" he shouted.

"With pleasure," she said, then turned from the bench, where a scraggly assortment of crooks, prostitutes, and battered housewives sat. There she found her friend Jan de Worde, looking the prosperous businessman he was, amongst the crowd of spectators. The native Dutchman had come to witness the dissolution of Nell's marriage to a man about whom Jan had stringently warned her after first meeting him. Knowing Jan, there would be no recriminations. He was the kindest person alive.

"I'm well rid of him," said Nell.

"Your father would have been pleased."

They walked out of the precinct hall into the spring morning. Nell was a free woman again. The sun on her face and a warm breeze delighted her senses, but all round her on the London streets were disturbing reminders that all was not well.

As they walked a brisk pace down Fleet Street, they were struck by the sight of every house and every shop swathed in black crepe. It was even draped cross the narrow roadways, strung from window to window, a grim reminder of a loss, at once public and, for Nell, personal.

Her godchild, Arthur, Prince of Wales, heir to the fledgling Tudor dynasty, lay dead, struck down suddenly at the age of sixteen, his shining future as King of England no more than a fading memory. The somber period of his mourning had, however, two weeks after his death, been rudely punctuated by a scandal of sorts. *No,* thought Nell, *'tis more like the ripping open of an old wound.*

A man named James Tyrell had just died a brutal traitor's death at Tyburn for crimes against England and his king, Henry the Seventh, and few had taken notice of his death. But yesterday all round London had been posted the man's confession—not of the crimes for which he had been hanged, drawn, and quartered, and his head stuck on a pike on London Bridge. What James Tyrell had confessed to was a crime he said he'd committed eighteen years before—the murder of the little princes Edward and Richard of York. He had named not only his accomplices in the crime—the men who had actually suffocated the boys with their feather beds and buried their bodies under a stairwell in the Tower—but his master at the time, and instigator of the foul killings.

He named the long-dead King of England, Richard the Third.

Jan de Worde, the most prominent printer and publisher in the country, heavily patronized by the present-day royal family, had, in fact, produced the broadsheets of the confession, hundreds of which were now nailed at every street corner, church, bath-, and public house in London.

Nell and Jan paused at the Hound and the Fox pub, where a group had gathered to read and argue the content and merit of the posting.

"Well, of course he did it, crook-backed, wither-armed old Richard!" cried a housewife, her market basket hiked on her hip. "I was but a girl back then—"

"If you was a girl, *I* was the Archbishop of Canterbury," declared a man beside her.

The crowd, all neighbors, laughed and hooted at the gibe.

"You were thirty-five with seven brats in 1483."

"What*ever* my age," said the housewife indignantly, "I remember it as if it were yesterday."

There was a general murmuring of agreement in the gathering.

" 'Twas as sad a time as it be today," said another.

"Sadder," said a robed priest who stood at the back of the

crowd. "Our beloved Prince Arthur was taken by God's will to his bosom. But those poor children were taken in a crime so unnatural, so wicked, that God and his angels cried in heaven."

"Aye, remember the great rains that followed?"

"The Lord and his minions weeping," the priest told his parishioners.

"Aye, aye," murmured the crowd.

"A terrible thing."

"Richard of Gloucester is burning in hell for his sin."

"And will be for all future and eternity," the man of God assured them.

"Come," said Nell to Jan. "I've heard enough."


THEY WENT ONTO the north end of London Bridge, where above them ravens were still having their way with what was left of James Tyrell's head, and strolled down the bridge's ancient roadway, both sides of which were closely lined with the shops of textile and clothing merchants—mercers and haberdashers who, with their families, lived above their establishments in gilt and gabled houses, the upper stories leaning precariously out over the lower.

"I hope you understand that I had no choice but to publish the broadsheet of Tyrell's confession," said Jan.

"Of course I do," Nell assured him. "If my father was still alive, he would have been bound to do the same. When your patron is the King of England—"

"More to the point, the king's *mother*," her friend added.

"Indeed, when your patrons are the bloody Tudors, you watch every step, every breath, every word." She patted his arm. "We do what we must to survive, Jan. When Margaret Beaufort wishes something done, we do it. That said, I have come to the

end of my tether with 'the Venerable Margaret' and her ridiculous restrictions. I'm going to see the queen today if I have to
chew the old cow's head off to get in."

The door of Caxton's Mercantile and Haberdashery brought
them into the mercer's first, a large shop of high shelves, these
brimming with the largest selection of domestic and imported
textiles in all of London. There was, of course, English wool,
cotton from the Low Countries, velvet and satin, taffeta and
brocade from France and Italy. Silks in every conceivable hue
from the East.

Through an archway was another world. Polished wood panels and Turkey carpets on the floor made luxurious London's
finest haberdashery. There were dressing cubicles, comfortable
seats, and full-length looking glasses for the customers to watch
as a staff of cutters, tailors, silkwomen, and seamstresses catered
to the city's elite, and those who sailed in on the River Thames
from all parts of the known world.

At first sight of Nell, her employees greeted her cheerfully.

"Peter," she said to a broad-faced young man, "will you see to
Master Worde's order? The black fustian doublet and leggings."

"Yes, ma'am."

"There will be no charge," she told the tailor.

"Nell—" Jan started.

She fixed her friend with a look that silenced his argument.
"Would you like to ride back to Westminster with me when
your fitting's done?"

"No, thank you. I've business at the Tower."

Nell and Jan embraced and he took his leave.

"I shall be at home for the better part of an hour should you
need me," she told Peter.

Nell climbed the wide, polished wood staircase and entered
the first floor of her living quarters, a fine apartment that

spanned the width of her shops below. In her great room, a long row of new, glass-paned windows looked east down the Thames and flooded the place with morning light. She loved the view of the splendid watercourse now teeming with greatships, barges, and wherries, the river without which England would have remained a marshy Roman backwater. Instead, by its grace, London was today civilization's most renowned city, the center, some said, of all the world.

Nell Caxton was a prosperous businesswoman, and her house reflected her wealth, as well as a fascination with strange and exotic artifacts gathered from her buying trips to distant ports—skins of African animals gracing her floors, an intricately painted ceiling panel from a Turkish sultan's harem, a wall hung with the gold- and silver-shot silk panels from India that now fluttered in the breeze from her open river window.

She had made a good life for herself as a *femme sole*—a businesswoman in her own right. Her ill-fated marriage was now, legally, a thing of the past. There was much to be done and she was altogether happy to be doing it alone.

The very next order of business was a ride to Westminster Palace. Since the death of Prince Arthur, the king's mother, Lady Margaret Beaufort, had prohibited all visitors from seeing her daughter-in-law, the boy's grieving mother. Nell had received no letters from the queen, her dearest friend in all the world. It was not like Bessie to stay silent, even in times of heartache—*especially* in times of heartache. They'd been through too much together for Nell to believe that the lack of correspondence was Bessie's choice.

The silence would be broken today. Nell chose an appropriate kirtle and gown, black on black, long sleeves buttoned tightly at the wrist, and a high pleated neck. She took up the wrapped gift she'd prepared—several yards each of the finest black brocade, silk, and satin that Bessie might use for her year of mourning—and went off to see the Queen of England.

Passing through the high-walled gates of Westminster, Nell was struck, as she always was coming here, with nostalgia. On the short row of stores just inside the gates was her late father, William Caxton's, old establishment, its dignified frontage still, as it was famously known, "under the sign of the Red Pale." The printshop and bookstore now belonged to his beloved apprentice, later associate, and finally partner, Jan de Worde. Behind the storefront and separated by a small garden was the house they'd lived in from the time she and her father had returned to their native country from the continent in 1477. She'd been thirteen when, under the patronage of the royal Yorks, Caxton had set up the first printing press in England and published the first-ever books in the English language.

It had been in the early months of their homecoming from Burgundy that, with both their families' hearty approval, the printer's daughter and the eldest princess of England had met and become fast friends. With the printshop within the very walls of Westminster, the teenagers—Bessie just two years younger than Nell—had done much to-ing and fro-ing twixt the two residences.

*This is so like coming home,* thought Nell as she gazed round her. Yet today there was less joy in it, for her dear friend had lost her firstborn child, the all-important heir to her husband's throne. Whilst Nell had been named Arthur's godmother, as she had to Bessie's other children—she'd seen little of the eldest, he sent off like all Princes of Wales to be raised in the Welsh Marches at Ludlow Castle.

God had never seen fit to give Nell children of her own, and she suspected that this had been her husband's greatest complaint. A barren wife was more than an embarrassment. She was a liability. Strange as it seemed, Nell herself had refused, to her husband's fury, to pray constantly to Saint Anne for fertility, wear Saint Waudru's girdle for the same purpose, or subject herself to the apothecary's repulsive and sometimes barbaric remedies to stimulate conception.

Why could Gerard not be satisfied with a loving, lusty wife? A *wealthy* wife at that, one who was godmother to all the princes and princesses of England?

Well, she was best shed of him. And if he came back begging after two years' absence, he could go to the devil. Next time she would listen to her trusted friends when they warned her about a man. Even her father's gentle words of caution had gone unheeded in the blush of love.

Now William Caxton was gone, and there was nowhere an emptier place in Nell's soul than that left by his death. He had been her friend, her inspiration, her collaborator. He had provided her freedoms no girl of her time or station had been allowed. He'd left her a very wealthy and independent woman. Her education was as brilliant as that of a royal prince, and that, of all his gifts, had been the finest. He'd been gone since 1491—eleven years—yet the pain of her father's loss, whilst its razor-sharpness had been dulled by time, was as deep and lonely-making as it had been when she'd placed her hand on his face and gently closed his eyes.

Now Nell moved with confidence through the Westminster Palace corridors, her face familiar to all the courtiers, guards, and servants. To reach the queen's apartments she was forced to cross an inner courtyard—a pretty garden abloom only with rosebushes—the bloodred of the Lancaster line, pure white of the Yorks. The two families, linked by a common ancestor,

Edward III, had fought thirty years for supremacy—the "War of the Roses"—before Bessie had married Henry the Seventh and brought peace to England's nobility. Now, though it did not exist in this garden or in nature, King Henry Tudor had commissioned the artistic rendering of the "Tudor Rose," a white center surrounded by red petals, and this new dynastic symbol was painted upon walls, carved into columns, and embroidered into tapestries in every royal house in England.

Taking their ease in the courtyard was a sight strange even to Nell's worldly eyes. Here amongst the roses was a troop of human oddities—a hideous lizard-skinned woman, another so fat that Nell wondered how she could fit through a doorway.

*Ah,* thought Nell, *another of King Henry's bizarre diversions.* There was a man whose whole face was covered in thick fur, speaking to what appeared to be a tall, well-dressed gentleman standing with his back to her. But as Nell came abreast of the group, smiling politely to the lot of them, she saw that out of the tall man's belly a second small "twin brother" was growing. His twisted torso and dangling, withered appendages were dressed in a matching outfit to his brother's.

"I tell you, evil times are upon us," said the fat lady. "A fish *ninety feet long* beached itself at Dover!"

"You're a doom monger, Annabel," said the wolfman. "Not twenty miles up the coast, the face of the Virgin was seen in the clouds, on the *same day.*"

"One cancels the other out," Nell heard the tall man say as she passed. He was caressing his twin brother's tiny slippered foot.

"Good lady!"

Nell turned back and saw another of the weird troop, a man who squatted on his haunches with his back to her, examining the rosebushes.

"Was it me you were addressing, sir?" she asked him.

" 'Twas indeed," he said, at the same time standing and turning to face her.

He was an ordinary sort of man, of average height and weight, brown hair hanging about the shoulders of his simple tunic.

But he had no eyes.

Where they once had been were two dark, puckered holes.

"How did you know I was a *lady?*" asked Nell, sincerely curious. "My scent? The sound of my skirts brushing past? Were my footsteps lighter than a man's?"

"None of those. You wear no French perfume. Monks and priests wear skirts. And your footfall"—he paused to correctly fashion his answer—"is strong and decisive, as a man's would be."

"Then how——?"

"I need no eyes to see what I see."

Nell regarded the man closely. His friends might have signaled him her sex, and so far, even his observation that her gait was more a stride than a dainty, ladylike tread told Nell nothing of the man's true gifts.

Nell, like her father before her, was skeptical of superstition. The mysteries, terrors, and portents that pervaded everyday life were meaningless to her, and she had little patience with the gullible.

"I foretold the coming of the comet with the long, wispy white beard," said the eyeless man.

"As did the learned astronomers at Oxford," Nell countered.

"I predicted the death of Maximilian to the hour."

"And what do you 'see' in these roses in the royal garden?" she demanded to know.

The man cocked his head at the question. Then he held his palm over a bloom on one of the white rosebushes. He stayed quietly thus, as if feeling it through the skin of his hand. "The York blood is stronger than most know."

*How did he know that the bush was a white one, for the Yorks?* Nell wondered. Then she remembered that white and red roses gave off their own distinctive fragrance. Surely the man was a charlatan.

The man snatched his hand away and tilted his head in Nell's direction. If he'd had eyes, he surely would have been gazing directly into her own. *"Most,"* he repeated pointedly, "though *you* know the strength of the Yorks, mistress." The other hand he now held above a bush of red roses. The same long silent moment passed. "Madness flows in the Lancaster line."

"You're speaking treason, sir," said Nell, and, suddenly uncomfortable, began to move away.

" 'Tis the *Tudor* rose which blooms in no man's garden that most haunts my visions," he said, just loud enough for Nell to hear.

Looking round her carefully, she moved back to the sightless man.

"What do you see of the Tudors?" she whispered.

"Mixed blood of the Yorks and Lancasters is the most vital. The Tudors will reign in peace for a hundred years. Great queens as well as kings."

"One hundred years is a very long time for a dynasty to rule," said Nell, her skin beginning to crawl. "And as for peace—"

"You mark my words!" he insisted, then laughed ruefully. "But how will you know I am right? You'll die in the year 1542."

"Really?" said Nell, unsure whether or not she was amused. "I shall be an old woman by then. Will I outlive my children?"

"You *haven't* any children," he answered, "nor will you ever."

Shaken and quite speechless, Nell reached into the leather purse at her waist. The seer's hand opened, palm up, the instant before she dropped the coin into it.

"Thank you, good lady. God be with you."

"And you, sir," she said.

She turned and left him. Without her realizing it, her pace and length of stride quickened, and she found she was relieved to be away from the blind seer and his freakish friends.

Once she arrived at the queen's apartments, the two unfamiliar guards, their long-handled halberds crossed before Bessie's door, stared straight ahead, refusing to meet Nell's eye. When she moved forward to knock, their weapons suddenly crossed lower. If she'd not pulled her hand back quickly, her wrist would have been cracked by their handles.

She felt her fury building. Was Bessie a prisoner now? "Let the queen know her friend Nell Caxton is here," she demanded of the guards in a voice that sounded more fearless than it was.

"We have our instructions, madam," said one of them.

"The devil take your instructions!" Nell cried.

With a loud creaking, the double doors of the apartment opened inward and there stood the Queen of England. Bessie was thin as a reed and her normally pink, creamy skin was oddly translucent. Her sky-blue eyes were red-rimmed and lines of grief were etched into her still-beautiful face.

"Nell, you've come! Let her through," she ordered the sentries.

"But Lady Margaret—" one objected.

"Am I the Queen the England?" Bessie asked him with rare tartness in her voice.

"Yes, Your Majesty. But—"

"Then do not risk my displeasure."

The halberds uncrossed smartly. Bessie reached out and, grabbing Nell's hand, pulled her inside. Together, before the guards could do so, the two women slammed the double doors shut behind them. Then they fell into each other's arms laughing.

Soon, though, Nell felt Bessie's shoulders begin to quake. Her laughter had turned to sobs. Nell held her friend as she wept, trying to murmur words of comfort through her own tears. After a time, the queen straightened and composed herself. She sniffed back her grief and attempted a smile.

"Come, sit," Bessie said, leading Nell to two chairs by a window.

"You look to need a lie-down, friend," said Nell.

"You're right. Come on."

They left the presence chamber and, moving through a doorway, entered the queen's bedchamber, a place of almost obscene opulence. Its centerpiece was the Bed of State, hung with red velvet, and covered, all eleven square feet of it, in the softest ermine.

*In this bed,* thought Nell, *have been conceived each of Queen Bessie's twelve children, only two daughters and two sons of which have survived infancy.* But it was here too that the women had whiled away many happy afternoons, talking, laughing, reading, commiserating, and conspiring. With more than twenty-five years of shared history, there was not a secret between them, a single subject unexplored, a single emotion unexpressed.

"Go on, put your feet up," Nell ordered, a mother hen. She tucked a pillow behind Bessie's back so she sat comfortably against the gilt headboard. Then Nell kicked off her slippers and climbed up beside her. They had often joked that Bessie much preferred Nell in that spot than her husband.

Indeed, Henry Tudor was a dreadful man, with a demeanor as sour and severe as his countenance. By his subjects he was feared rather than loved, or even respected, and his avarice was legendary. Through the work of his two unholy tax collectors, Henry Tudor had amassed a fortune off the blood and sweat of the peasantry, craftsmen, and merchants. The noble class felt his sharp pincers too, but their wealth was so great that the king's taxation was hardly an inconvenience.

After winning the crown from King Richard the Third, Henry Tudor had carefully observed European royalty and the economies of all the world's greatest kingdoms. He concluded, quite rightly, that *wealth equaled power*. Though first in his line—perhaps *because* he was the first in his line—he determined that he would become the most powerful prince in Christendom. Hence his lust for gold. Indeed, after seventeen years on the throne of England, he was well on his way to attaining his goal.

Bessie had always complained to Nell that all but a few grams of her husband's passion were spent on his quest for money and power, and the rest on devotion to his mother, Lady Margaret. Whilst still married to her third husband, Lord Stanley, that lady had taken the veil, but she had not retired to a nunnery, as Bessie's own mother—once Queen of England—had done. The Venerable Margaret instead had seized control of her son's court. Along with King Henry, she was—like one of his human oddities—one half of the two-headed beast that ruled England.

With her son's full consent, she pushed her daughter-in-law, Queen Bessie, aside, and oversaw every detail of daily life, including, and especially, the royal children's education. She advised the king on matters domestic, worldly, and religious. To the outside world she seemed to live an exemplary life, pious and virtuous to a fault. Her generous patronage to charities, from convents to the college at Cambridge, had earned her the moniker "the Venerable Margaret." She wore a hair shirt under her nunlike gowns. This torturously coarse garment, worn next to the skin by religious ascetics to "mortify the flesh," as well as her daily praying that sometimes surpassed six hours, led many to believe that she was a saint.

In truth, all four feet and eight inches of her were as fearsome as Saint George's dragon.

By Lady Margaret's displacement of her daughter-in-law, it appeared to all that Bessie was queen in name only.

Nell and Bessie knew better, but as they had always done, they kept their council. Moved in secret and mysterious ways. Together navigated through, and ruled, a world unseen. It was how it had been for most of their lives together, and whilst in the court's eyes Queen Bessie's status was humiliatingly low, the friends had their private reasons for preferring it that way.

"I noticed yet another troop of oddities in your rose garden," Nell said, choosing to ignore her conversation with the blind seer.

"Ah yes. Henry's second attempt at cheering me."

"I worry to ask of the first," said Nell.

"Oh, you *should* worry." Bessie sighed. "The king has grown stranger every ycar, but I fear Arthur's death"—she hesitated, as though it might have been the first time she'd uttered aloud that terrible phrase—"may have unhinged him altogether. I must say, he grieved for Arthur with a passion he never displayed for life," Bessie went on. "He'd even shown me rare moments of kindness, but more often he was flinging himself from meeting to meeting, lashing out at courtiers, ambassadors, and bishops. Even, to his mother's horror, he railed at God Himself for taking his precious treasure."

"So what was his first attempt to cheer you?"

"He decided that nothing would do the children and me more good than a bearbaiting, but instead of a bear he brought in a lion from the Tower menagerie and had it chained to the stake. The four mastiffs set on him, quite unexpectedly took the poor beast down." Bessie's eyes clouded. "But rather than reward the dogs for their victory, my dear, deranged husband insisted they be *hung* 'like the traitors they are.' Right before our eyes the executions were carried out." Bessie sighed. "You see, the lion was the Tudor symbol. When the 'common curs' had ripped the king's precious cat to pieces, they had, in effect, defiled the Tudor crown." Her face crumpled and tears began silently coursing down her cheeks. "I miss my sweet Arthur," she whispered.

"Ah, Bessie . . ." Nell grasped her friend's hand and brought it to her lips.

"I cannot believe that only six months ago we were celebrating his wedding so happily. How beautiful was Arthur's Spanish bride. Mary and Margaret so lovely."

"And little Harry on the dance floor . . ." Nell remembered. "The way he kicked and twirled and leapt like a young stag through the steps."

Bessie smiled through her tears. "And how proud was Arthur. On the morning after his wedding night, he came out to his men and called for a large cup of ale. He was thirsty, he said, for he'd been 'in the midst of Spain that night.' " Bessie sought Nell's eyes. "I'm yet blessed with three perfect children. How can I complain to you?"

"That I have no children is no excuse for you not grieving in front of me. 'Twas not my destiny to be a mother, save *god*mother. And that is what I am to all your children, Bessie . . . to the great consternation of the Venerable Margaret."

"Sod the Venerable Margaret," Bessie said.

The women laughed at that, the pain beginning to lift somewhat.

"Mother?"

Nell and Bessie turned at the small voice from the doorway. There stood Prince Harry, tall and leggy at ten, with a wild mop of red-gold hair framing a cherubic face.

"Mother, are you all right? Have you been crying?" He saw her friend sitting next to her on the Bed of State. "Nell!" he cried, and, after greeting his mother with a great embrace, came round and hugged his godmother with equal ferocity. "How is it you're here?" he demanded of Nell, genuinely perplexed. "Grandmother is letting no one in."

"Then how did *you* get in, Harry?" Nell inquired with a wry smile.

"I told them I would be King Henry the Eighth one day, and if they displeased me, I'd not forget and *whack* off their heads for their disobedience!" He laughed merrily, then went back round to Bessie's side. "Look what I've brought you."

Harry produced a twisted wreath of flowers and herbs— what sweethearts called a love knot—something that was given as a token of affection.

"I went to Apothecary Coke this morning, and he helped me with it. I thought that if made with healing plants and herbs, it would prove medicinal, and if you laid it beside your pillow"— he looked suddenly shy—"you might inhale its comforts with every breath."

"'Tis beautiful, Harry," the queen said, and sniffed it. "Do I smell motherwort and barberry?"

"Yes, yes!" he cried, then launched into an impassioned explanation of each of its floral stems and the purposes of every flower and herb.

Nell knew that whilst the queen had loved Arthur with a feeling mothers reserve for their firstborn children, she shared a special bond with Prince Harry. Unlike Arthur, Harry, the second son, had been kept close to home at Westminster.

The king had shown scarce attention to Harry, bestowing what little affection he had for his children on his heir. Arthur had been strong and healthy. He'd been trained from earliest childhood to shoulder the mantle of kingship—Tudor kingship. The firstborn of Henry the Seventh of England had drawn a marriage with a princess of *Spain*. What prestige, what power lay in Arthur's lineage, future. What promise would spring from his loins!

Little Harry had been destined for the Church. He'd make a fine cardinal, it was oft repeated. To the great merriment of his clergy, his father had fantasied Harry, bright and pious as he was, one day wearing the "shoes of the fisherman." "Imagine," his father would say, "the first English pope."

Bessie and Nell both knew how Harry loathed such thoughts, how awful it would be for him to leave London and live in Rome. He loved England and had no wish to be the Holy Father. The three of them had commiserated together at the thought of Harry as pope, with his starched red robes and the stifling Italian summers. Whilst he sincerely mourned the death of his brother, Nell thought, Harry could not but be celebrating the death of his father's dream of the papacy.

Here, then, in the shade of a glittering court, mother and son had found private joy and comfort in each other's company. Only in the past weeks had the shift toward Harry occurred, now that it was clear that *he* would inherit Henry the Seventh's throne, as Henry the Eighth. His father was lavishing time, if not affection, on his only remaining son. The bond between Harry and Bessie, however, was altogether unaffected. He was not a fickle boy. He loved his mother deeply and resented the treatment she had long received.

The door from the presence chamber to bedchamber opened without a knock. The three sitting comfortably on the Bed of State knew instantly who would dare walk through the door without invitation.

A black-clad, black-wimpled woman blew into the room

like a tiny hurricane. Her long, thin, wrinkled face was more than stern. Bessie always said that Margaret Beaufort proudly showed on her face the discomfort of wearing a hair shirt as a constant advertisement of her piety. Her voice was thin and sharp as a blade as she acknowledged Bessie and Harry with a nod, then said, "Good day to you, Nell."

Nell came off the bed, came round, and curtsied to the queen mother. "Good day to you, madam." She lowered her eyes. "I'm very, very sorry for your loss."

" 'Tis yours as well," said Margaret.

"How very kind of you to acknowledge."

There was no love lost between the queen and the queen mother, but Bessie had long ago learned the way to deal with Margaret Beaufort. She was outwardly compliant, even obedient, so that it might never be said the queen was defiant toward the king's mother. But Bessie's words to her mother-in-law were always mildly caustic, sometimes cynical, with healthy doses of wicked humor tossed in for good measure.

Nell was much more careful, keeping conversations with the woman light and respectful. After all, Lady Margaret had, at her son's accession, become William Caxton's greatest patron. Dozens of books in the English language had been published by her good graces and financial largess. Till his death, Lady Margaret had virtually kept the shop under the sign of the Red Pale in business. When Nell's father had died, Margaret had transferred her patronage to Jan de Worde.

She had tolerated Nell's friendship with Queen Bessie, though it had rankled when Bessie had named Nell godmother to the royal children. Still, Lady Margaret had reserved her displeasure, if not out of respect for Nell, then for her abiding regard for the man who had forever changed England with his press.

At this moment, however, Lady Margaret appeared at the

limit of her reserve. "I do think your visit premature," she added pointedly to Nell. "I believe I denied your requests and you are therefore here—"

"I wrote Nell asking her to come," said Bessie, interrupting her mother-in-law.

"But you are in mourning, my dear," said Margaret.

"And nothing will do me better than the sight of my dearest friend in the world"—she put her arm round Harry's shoulder—"and my sweet son."

Margaret was beginning to seethe at the subtle attack on her authority, though her ability to hide signs of anger was finely honed. "But, Elizabeth"—Margaret Beaufort insisted on calling Bessie by her given name—"you are in a very delicate condition. If you do not rest, you will become ill, and this family cannot bear another tragedy."

"Thank you for your concern," Bessie replied in the most even of tones. "But I have borne twelve children in my life. Have no worry that I can determine the safe length of a friendly visit."

For a fleeting instant Nell observed on Margaret's face a fury so hideous that it might, like Medusa's gaze, turn the three of them into statues of stone. A moment later it was gone, replaced by a tight-lipped smile.

"Nell, do tell Master Worde that his broadsheet on the Tyrell confession was most appreciated by the king." Then, with something close to supernatural restraint, Margaret Beaufort quietly pulled the door closed behind her.

In the next moment there was a deep and unanimous exhalation of breath from the trio, followed by a fit of hilarity that Bessie attempted to stifle lest her mother-in-law hear it. Finally they calmed themselves.

"Mother?"

"Yes, sweetheart."

"I saw Master Worde's broadsheet. I read it through."

Nell and Bessie exchanged a concerned look.

"It said," Harry continued, looking with distress at his mother, "that the man Tyrell, who was just beheaded, confessed to the killings of your brothers—the princes in the Tower—and that my great-uncle Richard paid him well to do the deed. Is it true?"

Nell and Bessie were silent, unbalanced by the question.

"There is no simple answer to what you've asked, son."

Harry was perplexed.

"In life, there is truth and there is deception," Nell said. "Sometimes deception is a necessary evil."

"But truth is always better," Bessie added.

"So is Master Worde's broadsheet truth or deception?"

Nell and Bessie sought each other's eyes. In the silence that followed, a flood tide of memories and emotions were loosed, and a decision made.

"Harry," his mother began. "One day you shall be King of England. The story behind James Tyrell's confession is the story of your family, your ancestors." She glanced at Nell, who nodded encouragingly. "I think you deserve to know the truth."

Nell went to the large window overlooking the river. She turned back to her friend. Bessie's expression was taut, even fearful. Yet they both knew the story needed telling, a full and truthful telling to an open, eager mind. To the one person in all the world who most needed to hear it.

Harry was only ten. It would shake his world to the core. But when he was grown and sitting on England's throne as Henry the Eighth, he would remember it all, every detail, and from it he would glean invaluable lessons. Kingly lessons.

Bessie, sitting silent beneath the canopy of the Bed of State, was thinking the same. Nell was sure of it.

"Harry," said the queen, her gaze fixed on Nell, "if we tell you the story, the *true* story, will you promise that it will be our secret?"

"Of course, Mother!" His eyes were shining, as though he were a great adventurer setting out on an epic journey.

"This tale, which is not so much a tale as a *history*," Nell began thoughtfully, "involves not simply the little princes who disappeared from the Tower, and their uncle Richard. It involves your grandmothers and grandfathers, aunts and uncles and cousins."

"Really?" Harry was incredulous.

"But the story begins in 1483," Bessie continued seamlessly, as though the friends were sharing one mind, "with Nell and with me."

"With *you*, Mother?"

She nodded. "In fact, Harry, it started with me and *my* mother in this very room. Well," Bessie corrected herself, "just outside the door."

# BESSIE

WITH A WINK TO the guards standing sentry at the entrance of the royal bedchamber, Princess Bessie tiptoed past. She hoped desperately not to be seen or heard by her mother, Queen Elizabeth Woodville, whom Bessie glimpsed sitting before her looking glass.

"Take a guard with you," her mother called out through the door.

*God's blood!* Bessie swore silently. *The woman has eyes in the back of her head.* "I'm only going to Caxton's!" she called back.

"Come in here, Bessie."

The girl sighed and pushed open the door to her parents' opulent inner sanctum. A maid was brushing out the luxuriant fall of golden hair for which Queen Elizabeth was famous. The magnificence of her alabaster skin and perfectly sculpted features never failed to amaze Bessie. Despite sharing the pale hair and complexion and the ice-blue, heavily lidded eyes, the eighteen-year-old princess knew that all who insisted she was as lovely as her forty-six-year-old mother were exaggerating. No one was as beautiful as the Queen of England.

"Why must I take a guard, Mother? The printshop is *next door*. Within Westminster's walls! I doubt there are kidnappers lurking in the shadows to snatch me. I'm only going to Nell's."

"See if there are any new French romances come in," said the queen.

"Yes, Mother."

"And tell Master Caxton that I wish to order a second copy of *The Canterbury Tales*."

"I will."

Bessie turned to go, but the queen's voice stopped her in her tracks. "Why must you wear that old rag?"

" 'Tis no such thing." Bessie felt color rising in her cheeks. Her mother took great pleasure in provoking her. "There's no need to wear silks and satins for a morning walk."

The queen turned and glared at her daughter. "I don't want to hear that the two of you have been traipsing round outside Westminster walls. Shopping on Totehill Street."

"I'm going to Caxton's printshop." Bessie enunciated precisely to underscore her annoyance. "Then I'm coming home."

"See that you do."

Bessie was finally out the door.

"And don't forget my romance!" she heard the queen call. But the princess had escaped her mother's clutches and made her way down the main staircase. She was passing Westminster's great hall when she heard her name called.

Music was wafting from within, and when she poked her head inside she found her sisters Mary, sixteen, and Cecily, fourteen, together with her nine-year-old brother, Dickon, having a lesson in the saltarello with their Italian dance master. They looked tiny, the four of them in the enormous chamber, and the music of drum and pipe echoed in the high-vaulted ceiling.

"Come join us, Bessie," called Dickon. He was tall for his age—most of his height in his long legs. He was a handsome child and, like his beautiful sisters, shared the yellow locks and blue eyes of their mother and father. She adored the boy for his sweet disposition and playful spirit. Indeed, she found more pleasure in his company than in that of her sisters, who seemed all but obsessed with their marriage plans and the latest fashions.

"Another day," Bessie called back to Dickon. "I'm off to visit Nell."

Dickon abandoned his dance partner, Cecily, in midstep and ran to the door. "May I come? Oh please. I *hate* these lessons."

"I could barely get permission from Mother for myself to go out. We'll go another day."

"Can we go to the market? I must be old enough by now."

Bessie tugged at his long curls. "I'll talk to Mother about it."

"Do you promise?"

"I promise. Now go back to Cecily. She looks very silly leaping round without a partner."

A few moments later Bessie was outside in the palace courtyard.

"Princess Bessie! Good morning to you!"

"Aren't you looking lovely as this lovely spring day."

Bessie smiled as she called back greetings to the men and women of the base courtyard. There were so many of them, from cooks to scullions and laundresses, to stonemasons and gardeners and coal carriers. It took thousands of these workers to run her father's London castle. Westminster, a very grand castle it was, befitting a great king—her father, Edward—and Elizabeth, her mother, who was said to be the most beautiful queen England had ever had.

*And the most hated,* thought Bessie. *I hope I shall never be as hated as my mother.* These same people who greeted Bessie with such sincere friendliness could manage nothing more for Queen Elizabeth Woodville than grudging respect. That was fair, thought Bessie, as the woman treated her servants with nothing more than icy hauteur.

The princess slowed in her tracks at a stone house set squarely in the middle of the base court. 'Twas the bakery, its gorgeous yeasty fragrances trying to draw her within. She could take a beautiful white *manchette* loaf to Nell and her father. But no, she was too eager to be going to stop at the bakehouse.

It felt good to be alive, Bessie thought. Soft warmth of a spring day on her cheeks. Rounded cobbles under her slippers. Beautiful smells from the bakery. And she hurrying to see her best friend in the world.

Several old men sunning themselves in the almshouse yard smiled and waved at Bessie. She would not stop to see them today either. She liked these men enormously. The once-hardworking laborers, now supported by the abbey, were Bessie's friends, though if her mother knew how her daughter fraternized with these poor commoners, she'd have her head.

As she rounded the almshouse wall, Caxton's came into view. It was the largest shop on the short, narrow street leading out Westminster's front gate. The castle, main and base courts, the soaring abbey, and this string of businesses lay within a thick wall. Beyond the gate lay Totehill Street, one of London's major east–west thoroughfares, lined with every variety of shop and enterprise.

Caxton's red-striped wood sign, THE RED PALE, swung in the slight breeze, and beneath it the door opened. A woman carrying a parcel in her arms came out, the parcel the size and shape of several books.

Bessie smiled. Surely her friend Nell was inside working her trade as a bookseller. She was good at it. And liked her job. It was one she was not forced to do, for her father was a wealthy man, but did for the pleasure of it. This seemed to Bessie a great blessing. Sometimes she envied Nell for her *usefulness* in the world. *What is a princess useful for, besides the marriage bed and baby making?* But no, she would not dwell on such things today.

As Bessie pushed the shop door open, she anticipated the heavy clanking of the cowbell above her head. It was a bit of a joke, that bell, for most shops had something small and tinkling above their doors to announce customers. But Caxton's shop with its crashing printing press was such a noisy place that a cowbell had been needed to be heard above the din. This day, to Bessie's surprise, Caxton's was blissfully quiet. The bookshop at the front was as silent as her father's library. Through the archway in the back Bessie could see that the press was still. Jan de Worde, the printer's brawny-armed apprentice, was carrying a heavy box of type down the steep wooden steps from above. The smell in Caxton's, Bessie thought, was like nothing she had ever known—still-wet inks, papers and vellum, leather, and the oil that lubricated the presses. Nell always said the smell was as natural to her as baking bread to a kitchen maid.

There was her friend standing with a customer, reverently turning the thick pages of William Caxton's fourteenth-century illuminated manuscript, *Deeds of Alexander the Great*. Anyone who came into the shop, themselves no doubt interested in volumes popular, religious, and rare, would be granted a peek at the great book, a gift from Caxton's old friend Burgundy's Philip the Good. Everyone marveled at the gem-encrusted cover, the gold leaf and painted illustrations, and letters twined with flowers and vines and mythical beasts. Once a person was gorged with the wonder of that book, Nell would lead them cleverly to the tables and shelves of newer books that were for sale. Some had been imported from the continent, many in French—the language that the educated English read from most often. There were scholarly tomes in Latin and Greek and several in Arabic, the flowing letters of which fascinated Bessie, who wondered how anyone could possibly read them.

But the true pride of the bookstore were the books printed

by Nell's father on his press. Books translated from the French and Greek and Latin to *English*. It was new, this reading of the printed word in the native tongue. A revelation. A novelty. And Nell's father had invented it. Not the press, of course. Printing with movable type was thirty years old. Every man of learning had in his personal library a copy of the first book ever printed on Johann Gutenberg's press—the Bible.

Bessie marveled to realize that in the six years since Caxton had come from the city of Bruges in Burgundy to set up shop in Westminster precinct, great numbers of his countrymen and women had been learning to write and read English. So customers for the translated works were becoming plentiful, and enthusiasm was growing.

Add to that a pretty, twenty-year-old girl, brilliantly educated, who listened with the greatest apparent fascination to her customers' interests and desires, who would point them to just the right volume, and you had the most famous and beloved bookstore in all of England. Sometimes Bessie found it hard to believe that her friend was at the very center of such momentousness and influence.

William Caxton himself was generally too busy to serve book buyers, what with his presses running day and night to turn out a growing number and variety of printed matter. He trusted that the store was in the best of hands with his daughter, the love and light of his life—he a longtime widower with no other children to dote on.

Nell looked up then and saw her friend. A grin cracked her face wide open, and with a whisper to her customer, she came round the table and indulged with Bessie in an excited and mutual hug.

"I've never heard it so quiet in here," said Bessie.

"Father and Jan are setting type for a new book. Enjoy the silence. It's about to end."

"I nearly stopped at the bake house to bring you some bread, but I couldn't wait to tell you—"

The cowbell clanked again and both girls turned to witness the entrance of a surprising trio of royals. Surprising, as Richard of Gloucester—Bessie's father's only living brother—came so infrequently to London. She realized she had not laid eyes on her uncle Richard, his wife, Anne, or their nine-year-old son, Ned, for nearly four years. Of course Bessie knew they were arriving shortly to join the royal progress out to Wales, but the sight of them in Caxton's shop was unexpected and somehow incongruous.

Upon recognition, there were many exclamations and embraces. Bessie marveled loudly at how much Ned had grown, all the while thinking secretly that he looked too small and frail for a boy his age. She was reminded of her brothers, Edward and Dickon, the two princes—tall, leggy, golden lads exuding life. This pale, large-eyed child, Bessie thought, would never reach adulthood. The burning core that fueled a person's body, in Ned's frame burned with too feeble a glow to sustain life. Anne was petite and prettier than Bessie remembered. She was aging well. Perhaps birthing only one child had benefited her. Though, thought the princess, her mother the queen had borne nine and was no more worse for wear.

It was Richard, though, who took Bessie most by storm. She'd stepped back to allow Nell her greetings and obeisances to the Gloucesters, who, like every other member of the royal family, held William Caxton as their friend. Bessie had never remembered Richard so darkly handsome. Brooding brown eyes. Luxuriant black hair worn long. A clean-shaven face made all of angles. And a slow smile revealing straight white teeth.

"Does my father know you're here?" Bessie said to Richard, suddenly worried that she was staring at him.

"I've only just sent word to him," Richard replied. "We arrived yesterday. We're staying at your grandmother Cecily's."

Bessie was aware that when he spoke to her his eyes never left hers. It was strangely discomfiting, but suddenly she realized that it was as much his height as his attention to her that caused her feeling. All the men of her family were tall. Her father was a very *giant* at six feet and four inches. Her mother's brother, Lord Rivers, and her father's brother, Uncle Clarence, when he was alive, were both large, well-made men.

Compared with them, Richard was short. His arms and shoulders were, however, unnaturally muscular from fighting with sword and battle-ax from his twelfth year. So whilst his torso was powerful, his normal-size and -shaped legs appeared more spindly than they were.

"Bessie dear," said Anne with the sweet smile she was known for. "Will you tell your mother that the suit of clothing she had made for Ned fits him perfectly?"

"I will, Aunt Anne."

"You're looking so beautiful, Bessie," Anne said. "I think in looks you've the best of both your parents, and your grandmother Cecily's lovely manner."

Bessie kissed Anne's cheek for the welcome compliment. She was a beautiful woman herself.

"What can I show you, then?" Bessie heard Nell say to her uncle Richard.

"Well, 'tis a gift for a boy," he replied. "Your friend's brother, Prince Edward."

"You'd best not let Edward hear you call him a boy, Uncle," said Bessie. "Lately he fancies himself a man."

"Does a boy become a man at thirteen?" Ned piped in. He was a serious child. "That's how old my cousin Edward is, is he not?"

"I think it depends on the boy," his mother answered. "We

haven't seen young Edward in nearly four years. He may well be very manly at thirteen." She regarded her husband warmly. "Your father had already fought in his first battle at thirteen."

"I think I have just the book for the Prince of Wales," said Nell, her eyes mischievous. "I'll be right back." She hurried from the bookstore through the arch into the printshop.

Bessie and the Gloucesters all began browsing silently amongst the books that lay everywhere on tables, and were set—spines out—on shelves round all sides of the small room.

A moment later Nell returned carrying in her hands a large volume, followed by her father, William. He was beginning to show his age, thin hair falling in a ring round a balding pate. He stood of middling height but, like Richard, was brawny of chest and arms, in his case the result—he liked to say—of carrying heavy trays of typeface and working the presses himself.

"Gloucester!" he cried, then, seeing Anne and Ned, greeted them one by one with a hearty embrace.

William Caxton, thought Bessie, was equally loved by everyone in the royal family. It was no surprise, as the man's loyalty and assistance had, ten years before, made it possible for the exiled King Edward to retake the throne that had been stolen from him. Truly, there was no common-born Englishman alive who was more highly regarded than Caxton.

"My Nell tells me you have need of a special book for a special boy," he said. "I have just the thing." He motioned to Nell and she placed the volume she had carried in on the counter before the family.

It was bound in green leather edged with gold, making it look very regal indeed. Bessie crowded in, peering over Aunt Anne's tiny shoulder as Anne turned the cover back to reveal the title.

" 'Jason and the Argonauts,' "Richard read. "In English! Brilliant!"

"See who translated it," Nell suggested.

Aunt Anne read, " 'Written by Raoul Lefèvre, translated by . . . William Caxton'!"

Nell's father was beaming. "There's more," he said. "Read the dedication."

Richard read silently, then looked up, incredulous. "You've dedicated it to Edward, Prince of Wales."

"He should be pleased," said Caxton.

"More than pleased!" Richard exclaimed.

"It's perfect," Anne said, and grasped her husband's hand. She turned and shared a private look with him that was at once intimate and conspiratorial.

The gesture, to Bessie's amazement, made her heart lurch unexpectedly, and she found her eyes stinging with threatened tears. She turned away quickly, pretending to gaze at the illuminated manuscript, trying to control herself. She forced herself to logic—the best antidote for rampant emotions, her tutor liked to say. Bessie had to admit that, more times than not, she was a victim of her emotions. *Why,* she wondered, *can I not be more like Nell, who though warm and kind is ruled first by her head and afterward her heart?*

But why had the sight of her uncle Richard and aunt Anne's private moment clutched at her so desperately. Was it jealousy? *Logic. Logic,* she commanded herself. The two of them had been deciding on a gift for Edward. When they'd seen the volume of *Jason,* their shared look said, "We've found the rare and perfect treasure we've been searching for."

Then, in passing, Richard caught Bessie's eye again and he smiled at her. She began to blush and had to turn away.

*What was happening to her?*

"Should I wrap it up, then?" Nell said. Relief flooded Bessie. The Gloucesters would be gone soon and her runaway emotions, like a wild horse, could be reined in.

Thankfully the transaction was made quickly, the book wrapped in soft leather, and the family sent on their way. William Caxton excused himself and hurried back to his printshop.

"What's wrong with you?" Nell demanded as the cowbell jangled at the Gloucesters' exit.

"Nothing," Bessie lied.

"I don't believe you. You've gone a funny color. And I know you have no earthly interest in that illuminated manuscript you've been studying like an Irish monk."

Bessie tried to speak but ended up stuttering. Nell laughed and grabbed her friend's hand. "Come on, then. We're going up to my room and you are going to tell me exactly what you're thinking."

Bessie tugged halfheartedly in the other direction. "I promised Mother I'd find her a new romance."

"I have just the one," said Nell. "We'll get it later. But right now you're coming with me."

Bessie allowed herself to be led through the archway into the printshop. Bessie was always struck by the sight of Caxton's famous printing press, a strange framework of timber, iron, and worm screws, a mechanism that, many commented, resembled a cheese press.

Just now Jan de Worde was dunking into a huge ink pot a fat, soft cotton inking ball mounted on the end of a stick. The apprentice was waiting for his master's final approval of the frame, set in the press's center, filled with small letters made of lead.

It was the first page of the new book to be printed. Caxton examined the lines of type carefully before giving the signal. Then the boy began daubing the assembled page with his ink ball.

Nell and Bessie had paused on their way out, for the printing of a book's first page was always a moment of pure celebration at Caxton's, and a privilege to be present.

"What is it today, Master Caxton?" Bessie asked.

*"Pilgrimage of the Soul,"* he said.

"Another unholy tome," she joked.

It had not always been easy for William Caxton, bringing the press to England. The Church considered the machine as an "ungodly instrument," and anyone who practiced the trade the devil's own.

Too, there'd been much opposition by the London Guild of Stationers, who felt that machine-made books would eliminate the need for scriveners and text writers who copied books by hand. It was purely the support of Bessie's family that, in the early days, had kept the angry mobs from storming the shop to destroy "the evil within." Or so William Caxton liked to say. Sight of the royals and their noble friends frequenting the Red Pale soon turned the tide.

William Caxton oversaw the swabbing with an exactitude that had earned him a reputation for perfection. Too much ink would leave smudges, too little and words would be unreadable. An imperfect page was always thrown away, and with paper as expensive as it was, mistakes were costly.

The printer nodded to Jan. A sheet of clean paper was laid down on the form. Then the apprentice stepped away. Normally Caxton would pull the lever on the inaugural page. This day he smiled at Bessie. "Princess," he said. "Will you honor us by printing the first page?"

"I'm the one honored, sir." She stepped forward and, feeling suddenly shy, allowed Nell's father to help place her hand on the lever, just so. He whispered a few words in her ear and stepped back.

With a long, firm stroke she brought the handle down, feeling the friction of wood and metal and paper.

"Good!" said Caxton, and came forward with Jan.

Bessie stepped back and watched as the apprentice carefully peeled the printed page from the press. They all gathered round to view the result.

"Perfect!" Caxton exclaimed. "Excellent work, my boy," he said to Jan de Worde, and clapped him on the shoulder. "And a firm, clean stroke from our girl!" He beamed at Bessie, who was glowing with delight. "I shall make sure you receive the first bound copy."

"Thank you, Master Caxton!" Bessie reached up and gave the elderly man a hug.

"Come on, then," said Nell. "Let's leave the men to their work."

The girls moved through the back room, where William Caxton designed and made his own type. He had become well known for typefaces that showed artistry but were, at the same time, easy to read.

Nell and Bessie moved out the back door through the small garden that shared its beds of herbs and flowers with Caxton's crates of paper and great bottles of printer's ink. They climbed the stairs of the residence, a modest-size but richly appointed half-timbered house.

Nell had a lovely room of her own with a canopied bed, a writing table, and a chair by the window, large and comfortable enough so that she could sit for hours by daylight and read to her heart's content.

"Now tell me the truth, Princess." Nell suppressed a smile. Bessie hated it when her friend addressed her so. "What caused you to turn several shades of violet down there?"

"I did no such thing! You are a dreadful creature, Nell Caxton." Bessie tossed a pillow at Nell, who ducked and laughed. "But did you see the look that passed between my aunt and uncle?"

"There were several," said Nell with a wry grin. "To which do you refer?"

Bessie tried to form her thoughts into coherent words before she spoke. "The one that was rife with love and devotion and . . . understanding and . . ."

"Lust?"

"Nell, be serious."

"I'm perfectly serious. The pair of them are *steeped* in lust." Nell regarded her friend carefully. "You're blushing again, Bessie."

Bessie gave an exasperated sigh and found herself at a rare loss for words.

"You're not in love with him, are you?" Nell asked.

"Of course I'm not! He's my *uncle*."

"What has that to do with it? He's very handsome."

"Do you really think so?" Bessie asked, suddenly eager to hear confirmation of her own opinion.

"Perhaps not to every woman's taste. But yes, he's got a beautiful face."

"Beautiful and brooding," Bessie insisted. "His eyes . . . did you notice the way he looked straight at you when you talked together, holding your eyes with his. Deep, dark pools . . ."

"You *are* in love with him," said Nell, with a maddening matter-of-factness.

"I'd wager he hasn't any mistresses," said Bessie, without trying to refute Nell's accusation. "And only two bastard children, born *before* he married Anne."

"Does that make you love him more?"

Bessie thought for a long moment. "I think it does."

"You're mad! You love him more because he's faithful to his wife? My God, the future Queen of France—"

"Don't remind me."

"—would be her uncle's mistress."

"I would not! I never said such a thing. And don't be horrible. I only mean that—" Bessie shook her head. "I don't think I know another man who is faithful and still adores his wife after so many years of marriage. All my uncles and cousins and stepbrothers—"

"And your father."

"Particularly my father," said Bessie, not needing to finish her thought.

"I've heard something recently," said Nell, tantalizing her friend with the teasing come-on.

"Well, *out* with it."

"Do you promise not to be cross with me? I'm only the messenger."

"I swear I shan't be cross."

"Your father has a mistress named Jane Shore."

"I know that, Nell. All of London knows that."

"Well, does all of London know that he shares Mistress Shore's intimate favors with Lord Hastings?"

"My father's best friend?" Nell's eyes widened with real surprise.

"*And* Lord Grey."

"My stepbrother!"

"The very one."

"And my father doesn't mind?"

Nell shrugged, herself perplexed at such an idea—a king who shared his favorite concubine with other men.

"Does my mother know her firstborn son is swiving her husband's whore?" said Bessie.

"You mustn't be rude about Jane Shore," said Nell, only half jesting. "She's not a whore, but a true courtesan. She's said to be lovely and bright and companionable. A very fine woman indeed."

"It's still horrible," Bessie insisted.

"No more horrible than the thought of you swived by Richard of Gloucester."

Bessie began pummeling Nell playfully.

"Where do you hear such tawdry street gossip?" Bessie demanded to know, falling back on Nell's bed.

"I keep my ears open here at the shop," Nell answered. "My father's couriers come in from everywhere. But where I learn most everything is on Totehill Street. The shopkeepers are best for juicy tidbits, but the prostitutes are helpful, and the cutpurses know much more than you would imagine. I think," Nell continued, "that if you asked your friends the almsmen what they *really* knew about the inner workings of Westminster, they would tell you a sight more than stories about the old days as hide tanners or royal dog keepers."

"I never considered such a thing," said Bessie, turning on her side and propping her head on her hand.

"By my reckoning, there is an entire *world* of intelligence lurking beneath the one we see. A network, of sorts. Imagine the intricate crisscrossing of avenues and buildings in London." Nell was warming to her subject. She sat down in front of Bessie, her eyes glittering excitedly. "Westminster—the palace and abbey, and our little street of shops inside the wall. And without, Totehill Street and the alleys jutting from it—St. Paul's, the Strand, the Tower of London. The wharves and docks and warehouses. The Thames itself with ships sailing in and out, to and from the whole world. 'Tis like"—Nell closed her eyes, and her hands in front of her moved slowly apart—"a great and intricate web that you can see with your eyes. Very coarse and solid and dirty and filled with clamor. But underneath it all"— she opened her eyes again—"is a second web. *Invisible* to the eye. But just as real."

Bessie was transfixed, enthralled by her friend's description.

"This is the web of intelligence. Wherever there is a person along the web, there is a small repository of information. Two women talking across the backyard fence share their information with each other, a tidbit they heard from a friend who works as a laundress at the palace. One of those women will tell it to her husband, who will go to the alehouse that night. By next morning the tidbit—its details likely changed along the way—will have spread through an entire neighborhood, with every husband telling every wife, who, in turn, spreads the word at the baths, or the well, or the Wednesday market on Totehill Street. Not only do the shopkeepers hear, but farmers from the surrounding countryside who've come to sell their wares. *That* is how news moves through London and beyond its walls."

"And I presume you are the 'Mistress of the Web,' 'Lady Spider,' who creeps along the gossamer strands gobbling up every tidbit of intelligence."

"Come, don't be unkind, Bessie."

"I'm not at all unkind. What you say is altogether sensible. I simply marvel that my best friend *thinks* in such a way. Oh!" Bessie cried, suddenly sitting up. "I never told you why I've come here in such a hurry today. You are invited on Progress to Wales to see my brother."

"I am?" said Nell, her jaw slack, her eyes twinkling. "I *am?!*"

"Yes, yes!"

Nell crushed Bessie in a hug.

"Oh my goodness," said Nell, suddenly sober. "How can I go? Who'll mind the store? Who'll mind Father?"

"Nell, there's a whole staff to make sure he's fed, and dressed in clean linen. And Jan de Worde can see to the bookstore. Your father will want you to go. You know he will."

"He will. Yes. Oh goodness!"

Nell jumped up and stood silently at the bedside, though

Bessie knew her mind was a whirlwind. She could not help but smile, seeing her friend so excited. "Do you have enough to wear?" Bessie asked.

"I don't know." Nell raced to her cupboard and flung open the door. It was crammed with gowns, some plain for work-days, some pretty for coming to court. She pulled out a tawny kirtle and a moss-green overdress and held them up to herself. "How many outfits will I need?"

"Quite a few." Bessie stood next to Nell, examining the contents of her wardrobe. "Why don't we look at them one by one and see what you have?"

I T HAD BEEN the most glorious spring Bessie could remember. One, she was sure, that would always be fixed happily in her memory. Now she walked along the long line of the Royal Progress, which had stopped, for the moment, to water the horses and the small herd of cattle that fed the members of the train as they traveled along the rutted road west to Wales.

She'd left Nell behind in their conveyance, having been summoned to see her parents in theirs. The mile-long procession of carriages, carts, and chariots, shaded and decorated with colored silk canopies, was a sight to behold. It was no wonder farmers and their families came out to wave and gape at the magnificent sight, though Nell had quite rightly observed that the unfortunate nobles who lived along the four-day route and were forced to feed and entertain the thousand-person Progress might be crying behind their welcoming smiles.

She passed the long line of soldiers uniformed in blue and gold, steel helmets so highly polished their glinting blinded the eye. Some members of the party—royals, courtiers, clergy, and servants—had emerged from their vehicles to stretch their legs.

Bessie arrived at her parents' conveyance—a fabulous enclosed caravan, its gilt sides and arched roof glittering, a hundred gay banners fluttering from a hundred poles atop it. A footman helped Bessie step up inside. It was dark and warm, the down-filled opulence of plush velvet cushion and tapestry. The air was rich with smells of candle wax, her mother's French *parfum,* and her father's wine-reeking breath. The king and queen were on opposite banquettes. Bessie curtsied to them one at a time, her father first, then her mother.

Queen Elizabeth, her back straight as a ramrod, greeted her daughter with the wary smile of a woman who cannot tell whether the one approaching is a friend or foe. For two years past they had been engaged in an endless domestic battle, the queen expecting her strict authority to be honored, Bessie maddeningly defying that authority at every turn. Bessie knew that no one beside herself could provoke the queen to such paroxysms of shrill fury. But she did not care, for she misliked her mother. Not for the rampant ambition that drove her, or the careless use of her power to enrich her large family of brothers and sisters, and the sons of her first marriage. She misliked the queen for the ice that coursed through her veins. The shallowness of even her most valiant attempts at motherly affection.

Her father was easier. Once an unsurpassed warrior, a fearful force on the world stage with which to be reckoned, who had gone soft in recent years, sodden with drink and debauchery, he was yet a cheerful, warmhearted parent. His once fine-skinned cheeks and nose were crisscrossed with broken red veins. Now he reclined like a great, beached whale amidst down cushions, cradling his skin of wine in the crook of one fat arm.

"Come, girl, sit by me," he said to Bessie.

She sat near his feet and tried not to stare at the wrinkles in his hose or feel pity for what he had been and, now, had sadly become. Moving with drunken languor, he lifted the wineskin and sprayed a stream of it down his throat.

"We've had some news, Bessie," he began.

"Dreadful news," her mother amended. "Dreadful."

"What is it? What's happened?"

"Your father's treaty with France has fallen to pieces."

Bessie was immediately alarmed. The king's treaty with Louis the Eleventh had kept England from going to war with France and, for the past eight years, brought her father's treasury fifty thousand crowns a year—a not insubstantial sum. Many at court, however, including her mother, had believed the English king weak for accepting money instead of a sure military victory over their ancient enemy.

"Will the payment—?" Bessie began.

"We have received our last payment," the queen said, and glared at her husband.

"There's more, I'm afraid," he said. He was slurring his words. 'Twas not two in the afternoon, but the drink had taken its toll. "You shall not be marrying the French dauphin."

Bessie suppressed an urgent desire to whoop with joy, but instead retained a sober expression. "I'm very sorry to hear that," she said.

"You're thrilled," said the queen, skewering Bessie with a vindictive stare.

"Why is the marriage canceled?" Bessie asked her father, ignoring her mother entirely.

"Louis has determined that an alliance with Spain is of greater value than an alliance with myself. Maximilian has a daughter. She's the dauphin's new bride. They have already married." With great effort the king pushed himself to sitting, reached over, and patted his daughter's arm. "Not to worry, sweetheart. We'll find you a good husband."

"Who?" the queen shot back. "What prince is there on the continent that is of any value to us? This is a disaster!"

"Now, Elizabeth . . ." he said, but lay back down in the pillows, finishing his sentence with nothing but incoherent muttering. Then fell silent.

In the dim candlelight the queen bristled so violently that Bessie was forced to bite the inside of her lip to keep from laughing aloud.

"I pray that all will be well, Father," she said finally, "and I trust that you and Mother will find me a suitable husband."

"She's mocking us, Edward." Elizabeth's voice was pure venom.

"Come, Elizabeth," he chided. "She's neither said nor done anything untoward." He looked at Bessie from under hooded eyelids. "Have you, sweetheart?"

"Nothing, Father." Bessie glared back at her mother. "I wish for nothing but what you wish for me."

"Liar," her mother said.

Bessie's face flushed hot with fury, both at her mother's insult and at the truth of her accusation. "May I have leave to go?" she said.

"Of course," the king replied. He pulled a braided silk cord that hung from the ceiling and a moment later the caravan door opened.

Bessie rose and, again curtsying to them both, walked out into the daylight.

THE WELCOME TO Ludlow had been splendid. As the castle came into sight, Bessie and Nell, their heads poking out their carriage windows, watched the king's harbinger riding ahead and shouting loudly that His Majesty and the court approached and that all should make ready for them.

The first blasts of trumpets could be heard from Ludlow as the gates were thrown wide open and the vanguard of soldiers, first in line, clattered across the moat bridge into the large courtyard. One by one the conveyances followed. This day the windows of her parents' caravan were thrown open to show the royal couple displayed like two precious jewels in an ornate setting.

As Bessie and Nell's carriage crossed the bridge, they beheld a most joyful scene. There were drums and pipes and singing. Every cook, laundress, and scullion, every house soldier, clerk, and steward, stood in the yard cheering and strewing thousands of rose petals—all white, signifying the York family flower— over their heads and onto the carpets upon which the royals would soon be treading.

Prince Edward's master tutor, Bishop Alcott, with terrible pomp and ceremony, marched forward to meet the caravan, holding before him on a high pole King Edward's crest with its symbolic "Sun in Splendor," cast in solid gold.

"Who are *they?*" Nell asked, pointing to a row of well-dressed male courtiers, trying to maintain their dignity whilst clearly wishing to rush from their formation and greet their visitors.

"They're my brother Edward's council, most of them my mother's Woodville relatives." Bessie thought for a moment. "*All* of them my mother's Woodville relatives."

"They look as though they're ready to spring at us," Nell observed.

"My parents allow no women in Ludlow Court, in order to keep the men pure around my brother, and they're bored beyond belief out here in the middle of nowhere. Every one of them wishes to be in London. The Progress coming to them is the next best thing." Bessie leaned even farther out her window. "There's my brother! How handsome and grown up he looks!"

Edward Prince of Wales was, Bessie thought, a larger version of Dickon—the same long legs and yellow locks, sky-blue eyes and sweet disposition. He was standing with proud dignity in a gorgeous purple tunic, edged and fitted with silver trimmings. But as the royal caravan came to a stop, try as he might to restrain his joy, he broke from his dignified pose and raced to the caravan door, waiting breathlessly for it to be opened. He flew into his mother's arms and she, momentarily unfrozen, laughed delightedly and opened them again so that Edward's father might embrace him too. As the king, queen, and their first-born son emerged a golden triumvirate into Ludlow Court, a cheer went up from the well-wishers.

A strange couple were next to emerge from their covered chariot—a potbellied, florid-faced man, Lord Stanley, and his diminutive, tight-faced wife, Lady Stanley, known by most as Margaret Beaufort. They hurried from their coach so that they would be waiting when the doors opened for the Gloucesters, whose fine carriage followed. Bessie's uncle Richard was helped down by Lord Stanley, his steward. Lady Margaret was there to respectfully greet Richard's wife, Anne. Little Ned followed his mother out.

After the four youngest princesses emerged from their carriages, Dickon, frantically relieved to be released from his coach prison, began running wide circles round the group, whooping with unbounded joy.

"Dickon, calm yourself," cried Queen Elizabeth. But it was in vain. There would be no stopping him for several minutes more.

A tall, well-made man looking to be just past forty went to meet the queen, and they embraced with true affection.

"Who is *that?*" Nell asked of the man. "He looks familiar."

" 'Tis my uncle Antony Woodville, Lord Rivers. My mother's favorite brother. He's my brother Edward's governor—indeed, Governor of Wales."

"I *know* Antony Woodville. Have known him since childhood. He's my father's dear friend."

"Of course," Bessie said. "Was he not the translator of the first book your father printed in English?"

"Indeed. I've not seen him since I was a little girl. Certainly not since Father and I returned from Bruges. Father and he have been working via courier."

"That doesn't surprise me. Uncle Rivers has been here with Edward for years. And when he's not, he's off on one pilgrimage or another."

The door of their carriage was opened, and as Bessie and Nell were helped down by the footman, young Edward spied his favorite sister and came to greet her with many kisses and enthusiastic hugs. Finally they separated.

"I do not think you know my friend Nell Caxton," said Bessie.

Nell curtsied to the boy. "Your Grace."

"Of course. You're Master Caxton's daughter. I've heard of you from my sister. She says terrible things about you."

Bessie pinched Edward's ear and he yelped.

"Welcome to my court at Ludlow," he said, and bowed smartly to Nell. "And you too, sister." He eyed Bessie closely. "Funny, I remember you as prettier."

"Edward!" She grabbed his slender waist and began tickling him. He shrieked with laughter.

Nell, wide-eyed, surveyed the roiling throng of nobles. She had been to Westminster Court many times with her father, but they had been staid and decorous occasions, filled with rigid protocol and ceremony.

This was promising to be the event of her lifetime.

IT WAS A SWEET afternoon in Ludlow's east meadow. Workmen sawed and hammered, constructing the risers that, later that week, would seat an audience of a thousand. Bessie and Nell were dressed for the country in pretty day frocks, their hair loose about their shoulders, secured round their foreheads with circlets of flowers. They stood side by side watching as Lord Rivers instructed the Prince of Wales in the ways of chivalry.

The muscles in Edward's right arm trembled violently as he attempted to lower the long wooden lance with slow control toward the fluttering handkerchief held in Bessie's outstretched hand.

"Steady, steady, Edward." Lord Rivers had a soothing voice that seemed to give the boy on horseback the last draft of courage he needed for the final few inches of descent. "Good."

Bessie draped the kerchief over the tip of the lance.

"Now lift," said Rivers. "'Tis not so difficult as lowering."

"But needing more strength," Edward croaked. He was perspiring and red-faced, a vein throbbing in his neck. The seven-foot lance rose in a less-than-graceful arc, but finally it rose straight above the prince's head, and held steady like a soldier's pike.

"Now release the kerchief," insisted Rivers. "A slight jiggle should do."

"What if, on Sunday, the wind takes it?"

"Your uncle Rivers shall make sure there is no wind that day, Edward," said Bessie.

Rivers smiled the smile that charmed the whole world. Despite her contempt for the queen, Bessie adored her mother's brother. A moment later the white linen square fluttered down, Edward plucking it easily from the air.

"Good. Now touch it to your heart," Rivers said.

With his eyes fixed on his uncle, Edward did as he was told.

"And now to your lips. Tuck the kerchief into your sleeve. On Sunday 'twill be a gauntlet."

"Brilliant, Your Grace," said Nell to Edward. "You are the perfect picture of chivalry. Whatever lady you choose to champion will surely swoon at your efforts."

"You tease me, Mistress Caxton. As badly as my sister does." Edward dropped his lance into Rivers's hands; then, with a cherishing hug round his horse's neck, he flung himself out of the saddle.

Bessie put her arm around him. "Edward, Nell was not teasing. You must learn how to graciously accept a compliment. Sometimes 'tis harder than accepting criticism."

Edward turned to Nell and executed a handsome bow. "I thank you, Mistress Caxton, for your kind compliment."

She bent over and whispered in his ear, "You may call me Nell."

As Edward's groom came to take his horse, the quartet left the tilt yard, heading for Ludlow Castle.

"We've spent far more time today on your martial arts than is prescribed," said Rivers to his nephew.

"For good reason," Edward rejoined. "I think my father would approve of us breaking his rules that I might make a good show of myself on Sunday."

"Our father *never* approves of breaking his rules," said Bessie with a grin. She referred to the strict commandments King Edward had established that regulated every moment, waking and sleeping, of the Prince of Wales's existence. It was said that it was only the king's great love for his elder son that had caused him to write these ordinances, requiring all in his household to memorize them and always obey them—from waking and bedtime rituals, to religious attendance, education, and recreation. His uncle Rivers was charged with the task of keeping from the boy's presence all swearers, brawlers, backbiters, common hazarders, or adulterers, all to the purpose that nothing should steal "God's precious gift, the king's most desired treasure" from him.

"Perhaps I should skip my dancing lesson to catch me up," Edward suggested, with as much seriousness as he could muster.

"Perhaps, if you mean to catch up your day," Bessie teased, "you should skip dinner instead."

"Aaugh!" shouted Edward, playfully pummeling her arm. Bessie and Edward walked ahead, leaving Uncle Antony and Nell to follow.

# NELL

S O TELL ME," he said to her. "How does my dearest friend?"

"Father is very well," Nell answered with a shy smile, delighted to be alone in Rivers's company. "How could he not be? He lives an idyllic life, he tells me often. He lives an arm's length from the seat of power. He may be old, but he is strong and healthy of heart and mind. He's wealthy, works in a respected trade, and enjoys the love of the whole royal family, with Lord Rivers his best and most loyal friend in all the world."

"And a beautiful daughter who dotes on him," Rivers added.

Nell found herself blushing furiously at Rivers's compliment, and said quickly, "And who slaves in his bookstore."

Rivers laughed, a rich, mellifluous sound. When the man smiled, Nell thought, he was the handsomest gentleman in the world. A Greek god.

"So business is good?" he asked.

"Excellent. My father insists that the location inside Westminster you helped him secure is the key to his success. Virtually everyone of importance at the palace or abbey is forced to pass beneath the sign of the Red Pale on the way *anywhere*."

"He's too modest," Rivers insisted. "William Caxton's success lies in his foresight—to have known that the English would one day wish to read books in the English language. And his industriousness, of course."

"*Your* books are selling very well," Nell told him.

Now it was Rivers's turn to flush with pride.

"Particularly *The Dicts and Sayings of Philosophers*," said Nell.

"I would guess 'tis not the subject matter that entices readers to it, as the novelty of it."

"Of course. 'Twas the first book printed in English, but your translation was brilliant."

"Nell Caxton, you flatterer!" He put his arm round her and hugged her to his side. Thus they walked companionably across Ludlow's moat bridge.

Up ahead, Bessie was still teasing Edward mercilessly when their brother Dickon exploded out the residence door and came running across the yard to meet them. Now the king and queen emerged from the same door, and attending on them were Lord Stanley and his wife, Lady Margaret. The boys began wrestling playfully before their parents, and their shouts of laughter echoed in the castle yard. As they rough-and-tumbled, the little princes seemed a pair of golden Olympians. They were sweet and fresh and joyful, and they cheered every soul who saw and heard them.

A commotion at the gates drew the family's attention there. A large contingent of soldiers wearing not the king's livery of blue and gold, but red jackets and red-plumed helmets, came thundering cross the moat bridge, filling the yard. Now to the fore came riding the column's leader—a tall, arrogantly handsome man. Nell felt Antony Woodville bristling at her side.

"Who is that?" she whispered to him.

"Harry, Duke of Buckingham. He's married, quite unhappily, to the queen's sister Catherine."

Even before Rivers stepped forward, Nell could see there

was trouble brewing. The crowd quieted, and everyone silently noted that Buckingham had not bothered to unhorse, leaving him that much higher than Rivers, who was on foot—a rude gesture by any measure.

Nell noticed Bessie's father quietly pulling the queen with him, to hide themselves, back inside the doorway. Perhaps he wished to witness the exchange between his men—perhaps a contretemps—objectively, without affecting its outcome.

The sound of the yard being filled with the mounted troops had brought Richard of Gloucester to his second-story bed-chamber window and he too watched with interest.

"How does my Lord Rivers?" Buckingham inquired with cordial grace. He looked round him. "I see the royal party has arrived."

"It has indeed, Lord Buckingham." There was sharp formality in Rivers's tone. "And I see that you have brought with you an army to greet your king and queen."

Buckingham's laugh was derisive. "You've exaggerated my small column of men into an army."

"You know very well that the mustering of any soldiers not of the king's colors is illegal."

"Do you not mean 'Lord Rivers's colors'?" This was a stinging retort, though Harry Buckingham managed to keep the smile plastered on his face.

"I am the governor of Ludlow, my lord. And the governor of the Welsh Marches too." Rivers was bristling now. "But I am always aware that *my* governor is King Edward, something that you have managed to forget. Therefore, by the order of the king, I command you to disperse your troops immediately. When that is done you shall be welcomed into the royal circle."

It seemed to Nell that Buckingham was, by sheer will, keeping his expression sanguine, for it was clear that beneath the placid smile and uncreased brow he was raging. She wished desperately to whisper a comment to Bessie, but her friend was halfway across the courtyard.

"May I not be allowed to greet my good aunt Lady Stanley?"

Prince Edward glanced at Margaret Beaufort to see her narrow face locked in an impenetrable expression.

"Of course you may, Harry," said Rivers mildly, "*after* you've dismissed your illegal army."

That was Buckingham's limit. High color rose from neck to cheek to forehead in the space of a breath, and Nell heard Dickon stifle a laugh. Edward elbowed the younger boy, which had the opposite effect than desired. Dickon uttered a single bark before his older brother could clap a hand over his mouth.

At the moment of threatened explosion, King Edward and the queen stepped out from the doorway into view, making their presence known, to Buckingham's very great surprise.

"Your Majesties!" Buckingham was off his horse and down on bent knee in humble obeisance with almost comical haste. The queen nodded to him, but made little attempt to hide her cool contempt for her brother-in-law.

"Rise, Harry. Let me look at you," said the king.

He clapped a brotherly arm round Buckingham's shoulder and walked with him to a quiet corner of the yard away from curious ears. They spoke softly, their heads tilted toward each other's. Buckingham's shoulders seemed to settle, and Nell guessed that the king was speaking comfortable words into his ear. Buckingham was, after all, the highest-ranking peer in England, Edward's brother-in-law, and, whilst a Lancastrian by birth, had been for many years loyal to the Yorks.

A few moments later, when they had circled back to the head of his troops, Buckingham was once again smiling, his color normal.

"Then you will give my sister-in-law our regards," Nell heard the king say.

"I will, Your Majesty."

"And will you two come to the tilt on Sunday? Elizabeth will want to see her sister."

"Yes, of course." Harry Buckingham bowed grandly to the king. "A good day to you." He turned to the queen and the other onlookers, careful not to meet Rivers's eye, and bowed to them as well. With impeccable grace, the duke mounted his horse and brought it round. Then, with the merest wave, he signaled his uniformed column to follow, and they thundered from the yard.

Looking round her, Nell saw everyone sag with relief. Bessie's father might not look the magnificent king he once was, but he nevertheless retained his kingly authority and charm. He and the queen went on their way across the courtyard to the chapel. Richard of Gloucester disappeared from his window. Lord and Lady Stanley, without a word, slipped back into the castle. The two boys were all over their uncle Rivers, plying him with excited questions.

Bessie and Nell were blessedly alone in the courtyard. They walked toward each other quickly.

"You must tell me what just happened," Nell demanded.

"Well," said Bessie, "when my brother was sent here to rule as the Prince of Wales, he was only three. Naturally he needed a guardian. A governor. My mother convinced my father that her brother Rivers was the perfect choice. He *was,* in fact. There is no one in England—you know this, Nell—who is more learned or pious or thoughtful or brave than Lord Rivers."

"Just so," Nell agreed.

"Well, until that time, Harry, Duke of Buckingham, had been the high lord and master of the Welsh Marches. He was already at odds with my mother for forcing him to marry her sister Catherine. He always thought himself very grand indeed, and looked down his nose at the match with 'Queen' Elizabeth Woodville's kin. 'Twas far beneath his station."

"But Buckingham is of *Lancastrian* descent," Nell said.

Bessie nodded. "As you saw, he is Lady Margaret's nephew. If the Yorks were ever to fall to the Lancasters again—"

" 'Twill never happen," Nell insisted.

"But if it did, Margaret Beaufort would be first in line for the English throne."

"Lady Margaret!"

"Shh," Bessie cautioned. "Did you know she's already the wealthiest woman, in her own right, in all of England?"

"I didn't."

"But the thing is," Bessie went on, "Margaret has no wish for the crown herself. 'Tis her son, Henry Tudor, she would champion."

"But Henry Tudor has been in exile in Brittany for years."

"Seventeen years. Exiled for rising up against the Yorks."

"In that case, why does your family keep Lady Margaret so close?"

"Better to know exactly where your enemies stand than to have them lurking about, out of your sight. And besides, since she married Lord Stanley, she's proven quite faithful."

"I do find her fascinating," said Nell. "So tiny, yet so . . . resolute. She seems to have a rod of steel in her spine. I think she terrifies her husband."

"She terrifies *me*." The girls laughed.

"Come," said Bessie, "let's go find our room."

S UPPER THAT EVENING was the best Nell had ever in her life eaten. The Ludlow cooks had surpassed themselves with beastings pudding, moor fowl smothered with red cabbage, and lamprey pie garnished with crayfish on gold skewers—offerings that, for the king's pleasure, bordered on gluttonous. His appetites, along with his girth, had grown famous, and he insisted that all enjoy their food with the same gusto as he did. Indeed, thought Nell, the king was altogether jolly this night, though he was sober as a monk. Nell remembered Bessie saying that her father was so intent upon keeping his elder son happy, and serving as a model of decency, that on these visits to Wales, he drank little and whored not at all.

The seating arrangements had come as a pleasant shock to Nell. Whilst she'd been separated from Bessie, who sat at her brother Edward's right hand, who was likewise at the king's right hand, Mistress Caxton had been granted an equally privileged chair at the left hand of Lord Rivers, who was at the left hand of his sister the queen. To Nell's other side sat Lady Margaret Beaufort. Both of her dinner companions sought Nell's conversation. At first it had been frivolous, everyone commenting and chuckling at the jugglers who'd been more silly than proficient, dropping their colored balls and tripping foolishly on the rushes. The skinny contortionist in his spun-silver costume had wrenched gasps of disbelief from his audience. Musicians were setting up their instruments for the dancing that would come after the sweet course.

"Nell—" It was Lord Rivers turning back from his conversation with the queen. "Tell me, how good is your Latin?"

"Truthfully?" she asked with mock seriousness.

"Only the truth," he said.

"Better than yours."

He laughed at her audaciousness, then said, "With whom did you study in Bruges?"

"The same man who taught the king's sister Margaret of Burgundy. Master Talbot. He said he'd never had a student whose double translations were so perfect as mine. He liked to say I had the mind of a man."

"Did you find that complimentary?" Rivers asked.

"At first I did. Then I chafed at the notion. Most of the women I knew, I told him, were far more clever than their husbands, most of whom were brutes who knew of nothing more than making war and keeping horses happy."

"Surely there are exceptions to that rule," Rivers insisted, suppressing a smile.

"Of course. My father, for one." Suddenly Nell's boldness failed her, and she had to look away when she added, "And you, my lord."

"I have a proposition," said Rivers.

Nell felt herself fluster suddenly, for Rivers's words immediately led her to thoughts of a carnal nature. But when he continued, unaware of her lewd thoughts, the proposition proved to be of a far more innocent kind, though just as surprising.

"Prince Edward's Latin tutor has taken ill and he is currently without one. A new man has been hired from the continent, but it will be several months before he can arrive. Would you like the post? Temporarily, of course. Women have no place in the Ludlow Court."

"Then how can you offer me the position? I may have the mind of a man, my lord—"

"I've already secured the king's permission."

"But my father—"

"If you write to him, we will send a courier to London and have an answer back in less than a week. Come, Nell," said Rivers, placing a gentle hand on her arm. "How could you possibly refuse such an honor?"

"I haven't said I refuse."

"Good. I'll be delighted to have you here. You're right about the intellectual capacity of most men." His gaze swept the dining hall and the Ludlow courtiers. "Even my relatives." Suddenly Rivers lost his aplomb. "We shall spend many happy hours debating Pliny—Major and Minor."

"Well, I—"

"So you'll write your father tonight."

Nell was now quite convinced that Rivers's interest in her was more than professional. But according to Bessie, though his wife did not live at Ludlow, he was a married man. And he was her father's dearest friend! Before she could answer him, a short trumpet blast drew everyone's eyes to the center of the hall. Richard and Anne of Gloucester, and little Ned, were approaching the dais, the boy holding a prettily wrapped package in his arms. *It has to be the book I sold them,* she thought. All three made their obeisance to the Prince of Wales, and Ned held out the package.

The place quieted so that all were able to hear when Richard said, "Take it. 'Tis a gift from our family to you."

Nell could see the Duke and Duchess of Gloucester smiling warmly. Edward reached out and took the package from Ned. At once he knew what it was.

" 'Tis a book, is it not?"

Gloucester nodded and Nell leaned forward, eager to see Edward's expression. He untied the leather thongs that held the wrapper closed and found the volume. Breathless, with the carefulest of fingers, he turned back the cover to reveal the title.

"*Jason and the Argonauts*! In English!" he cried, genuinely delighted.

"Read on, Edward," his aunt instructed. "I think you'll be pleased."

Edward read silently, then looked up. " 'Twas translated by

William Caxton himself!" Now it was Edward trying to find Nell and catch *her* eye. She returned his beaming smile. She and Bessie, just beyond him, shared a conspiratorial look.

"Do read on, Edward," his uncle urged. "Go to the dedication."

He did as he was instructed. " 'For Edward . . . *Prince of Wales*'!" Edward whooped with surprise, and his eyes twinkled as he continued. " 'Accept *Jason* from your humble servant . . . and subject.' He's dedicated it to *me*. A book of my very own." He looked up. "Thank you, Aunt and Uncle! Thank you, Ned!"

"He'll think it a bribe." Nell heard the whispered voice next to her. She turned to Lady Margaret, whose tight-lipped mouth was cynically pursed.

"I beg your pardon?" said Nell.

"The Prince of Wales may like his gift, but he suspects 'tis a bribe for his affection. He loathes Gloucester." Margaret was taking close note of Nell's reaction to her bold statement.

Nell was at once flattered and suspicious of the woman's motives. The correct response and tone were essential. She kept her voice low. "Prince Edward *wrongly* believes Gloucester was responsible for his uncle Clarence's execution."

"Do you not think it curious," Lady Margaret said, clearly pleased with Nell's engagement, continuing the conversation as though the two women were equals, "that the king has not made his *own* complicity in Clarence's execution clear to his son? That it was *he* who ordered it. Why would he wish the boy to so mislike his only remaining brother?"

Nell thought carefully before leaning close to Lady Margaret's ear and speaking softly. "Perhaps the king has given it no thought."

"Does he not care that Prince Edward's hatred of Gloucester deeply grieves his brother?" Margaret persisted.

"Perhaps he is *unaware* of his son's perceptions," Nell suggested.

"Unaware? But how can a King of England be so blithely ignorant?"

Nell was suddenly conscious that she was being led into a subtle trap. The answer, if she were to utter it, was that King Edward was so sodden with drink and debauchery that his faculties were suffering. And *that* idea spoken aloud was treasonous. Nell had caught herself in time, but wondered at Lady Margaret's ambush.

"Ignorant? Not at all," said Nell. "Gloucester has himself refused to burden his brother with the problem. And the prince has not complained openly. Those around the king may have reasons of their own for perpetuating this misunderstanding."

Lady Margaret regarded Nell closely and her lips twisted into something that might have been called a smile. "You are a very clever girl, Mistress Caxton."

"Thank you, Lady Margaret."

The musicians struck up the first chord of a pavane, and with that, the older woman turned away, finished with Nell, and began speaking with her husband, Lord Stanley, who sat at her left.

Nell was quite overcome. First an offer of employment to tutor the future King of England. Now a mental challenge and a compliment from the shrewdest woman in England. Oh, how she longed to speak to Bessie!

"Nell."

She turned to see Lord Rivers standing behind her with his upturned hand outstretched. "Will you dance with me?"

She exhaled once to calm herself, then took his hand. " 'Twould be my pleasure."

. . .

WHILST NELL HAD been Princess Bessie's close—nay, *insep-arable*—friend since the return with Nell's father from Bruges six years before, and whilst Mistress Caxton had been many times invited to Westminster Court, she had never experienced the magnificence and excitement of a royal family gathering such as this. Indeed, she had never dreamed of being so warmly embraced by the Yorks. Besides Bessie, the king, queen, the princes Edward and Dickon, and Lord Rivers had treated her like nothing less than royalty.

Since their arrival in Wales, Nell had partaken of hunts, both on horseback and from blinds. Even a "wild-goose chase" with everyone racing on their mounts single file through the Ludlow Greenwood. Every meal was eaten together, dinners and suppers, each a sumptuous feast, invariably accompanied by music and dancing, jugglers and acrobats, and all manner of entertainments.

Every night the girls, happily exhausted, would retire to Bessie's bedchamber. They chattered about the day's events as maids undressed them, slipped nightgowns over their heads, and they never stopped talking as they were tucked into the luxurious canopied bed laid with the finest lawn sheets and richest lace-and-velvet coverlets. They chattered for so long and so incessantly that sometimes the sun was rising before they'd finally fallen asleep.

"Your father does love his brother Richard well," said Nell one night. "Have they always been so close?"

"Since they were young boys. My grandfather's death brought them closer still."

"Your grandfather, the Duke of York?"

Bessie nodded.

"Now, *there* was a powermonger," Nell observed.

"No more so than Lady Anne's father, Warwick," Bessie

added. "First he was my father's 'kingmaker,' then turned round and tried to dethrone him."

"Do you never wonder how Richard, who is so loyal to his brother, can be married to the daughter of the man who thrice sought to destroy him?" Nell asked.

Bessie sighed heavily at that, and Nell realized the subject of Anne and Richard of Gloucester was still a sore one with her friend. "Perhaps they're not as happy together as they seem," Nell said, hoping to soften the heartache.

"They're deliriously happy and you know it." Bessie looked miserable. "Everyone knows it."

Nell pushed the hair back from her friend's brow. "Best not to dwell too long on what can never be, Bessie. You've an exciting future ahead. Think of that."

"Exciting? I may have escaped having to marry the pimply French dauphin, but Jesus knows who my parents will choose for me next."

"Jesus be *praised*! Whomever you marry, you will become a queen. The highest lady in the land."

"But a *foreign* land," Bessie replied, turning her face away. "Ah, Nell, I don't mean to whine and complain. Surely I'm the luckiest girl in all England. But that's my point. I love England. I don't want to leave her." She turned back and gazed at her friend. "I don't want to leave *you*."

"Perhaps the pope will grant a dispensation so you can marry your brother," Nell quipped with a straight face.

"Nell!" Bessie laughed. "You're a dreadful girl!"

Under the covers a sharp poke was delivered to Nell, who squealed. The maids, still hanging their mistresses gowns, giggled.

"Seriously, though," said Nell, pulling the covers up around her neck, "to be a queen is a marvelous thing."

"I suppose it is."

"Think of a chessboard," said Nell.

"A chessboard?"

"Which piece on the board is most powerful? Not the castle. Not the knight. Not the bishop. Not even the king. 'Tis the queen that moves the farthest *and* in every direction. You may have no say in whom you marry, but once that crown is on your head, no woman—or most men, for that matter—wields greater control. Look at Queen Margaret of Anjou. Look at your father's sister, Margaret of Burgundy. Your own mother! These are women who have forged their own destinies, directed armies. Ruled in the absence or dereliction of their husbands. Bessie, without a queen there is no kingdom!"

Bessie was smiling shyly. Clearly, she'd taken Nell's words to heart. "Will you come and visit me where I live?"

"I might," Nell teased.

"I could hire you as my spymaster."

"Oh, I like the sound of that," said Nell. "The court of a queen of your stature will certainly be *steeped* in conspiracy and espionage."

Bessie laughed delightedly. "How do you always manage to make me feel so much better?"

Nell was suddenly serious. "Because I see you more clearly than you do yourself. And I remind you of all that you are capable of accomplishing in this life."

"Which is no more than yourself," Bessie insisted.

"True," Nell agreed, and with a sly grin added, "though I cannot pop little kings and queens out my cunny."

"Nell Caxton!" Bessie cried, pummeling her friend in mock outrage. Their shrieks of laughter grew so loud and uproarious that they echoed through the Ludlow courtyard and made smile everyone who heard them.

. . .

For two days now it had been cold and rainy, and whilst the family was quite used to indoor amusements, there was a worry that Sunday's tournament would be ruined by inclement weather. Despite Prince Edward's attempt at lightheartedness, and Nell and Bessie's repeated assurances that the skies would clear, the boy could think of nothing else.

Today they had all gathered in Ludlow's high-ceilinged great hall, and a fire blazed in the massive hearth. The women sat amicably round a large, gorgeous-hued tapestry, and were gossiping as industriously as they were stitching.

The three cousins, Edward, Dickon, and Ned, were doing battle with wooden swords, and Nell noticed that the stronger two—the princes—played fairly with Ned. They were careful not to injure a boy they knew to be more frail than themselves, whilst fighting hard enough that Ned would not feel patronized.

Nell and Bessie had seated themselves closest to the men, who were gathered in council—the better for the girls to hear what was being said. The first order of business had been Prince Edward's maintenance, but that was dispensed with easily, as Lord Rivers and the other Woodville relatives kept a staid and orderly household for the boy. He was growing up well, and the king had nothing but adulation for his brother-in-law Rivers.

When the girls heard the word *Scotland* uttered, they exchanged a furtive look and listened as intently to the men as was possible over the chattering females. Besides making his brother Constable of England for life, the king had given full powers over Scotland and the northern borderlands to Richard of Gloucester. Now Gloucester was giving report over those territories. It was clear from his words that he had done well there.

Battled for, and secured, the Scottish borders. Won the siege of Edinburgh. All to the pride and joy of the king.

"There's good reason why they call you 'Lord of the North,' brother." From the corner of her eye, Nell saw Bessie's father throw an affectionate arm about Richard's shoulder. Then she glanced at her friend, who was watching the moment quite openly. Bessie always said that above all, Gloucester craved his elder brother's love, perhaps even above his wife Anne's. She saw Bessie's lips curl into a smile, and knew the girl was quietly happy for her uncle Richard.

"Lord Stanley." A serving boy had entered the great hall unnoticed and handed Richard's steward a folded letter.

Stanley moved to the slitted window to read by the gloomy light. He looked up and spoke to the men. "My son Lord Strange has broken his arm."

"Damn!" Nell heard Rivers mutter.

Stanley addressed Rivers. "He sends his deepest regrets, my lord, for he wished very sincerely to meet you on the jousting field on Sunday."

"What is it, Father?" Prince Edward approached, no doubt sensing something was amiss.

"I'm afraid your uncle Rivers is without a jousting partner for Sunday's tilt."

The prince's face collapsed utterly into disappointment verging on despair. "What will you do, Uncle?" he said, his voice cracking with emotion. "There's no one suitable who could be sent for in time for Sunday. No one who would dare challenge *you*. The games will be ruined!"

Whilst Edward's sentiments were those of an adoring nephew, they were not without some truth. Rivers was, by reputation and in fact, the finest jouster in England. Indeed, on the continent as well.

"Go on, Hastings," the king enjoined his friend, "*you* meet my brother-in-law on the field."

"Pigs will fly first, Majesty," Hastings replied with all seriousness, causing the men to roar with laughter.

"I have it," said Rivers, trying to keep a straight face. "I'll send a challenge to Harry Buckingham."

There were more whoops of hilarity from everyone, except the Prince of Wales, who looked near to tears. The lack of a jousting partner for Rivers was no laughing matter.

"I challenge you, Rivers." It was Richard of Gloucester speaking.

The room went silent as a tomb. Prince Edward's eyes were saucers, and his jaw hung slack. The ladies looked up from their stitchery. Nell could feel Bessie, sitting next to her, straighten in her chair.

"It has never been my pleasure to joust," said Richard, finally breaking the silence. "I have always found the sport . . . frivolous. But I am a man-at-arms. I believe I can deport myself proudly at the tilts. I shall do so in honor of my brother the king."

Richard's words seemed reasonable enough. But then Nell caught sight of Lady Anne's face. It was a mask of incredulity and fear. Nell was afraid to glance at Bessie, for everyone in the hall knew that Gloucester's overproud challenge might have been a blunder . . . perhaps a fatal one.

Nell felt the light prick of a needle on her arm. Bessie was trying to get her attention. When she turned, her friend had an imploring look in her eye. Both girls remained silent and ladylike, but within moments had found reason to excuse themselves from the sewing circle.

The rain had let up momentarily, so Nell and Bessie ran outside and hurried to the privacy of the tall hedge maze, and wove through the living green walls. But when they arrived at the center they found themselves unnaturally tongue-tied. The reason was Gloucester's challenge to Antony Woodville. It was a strange and uncomfortable moment, for each of the girls held a forbidden fondness for one of the challengers, and for the first time in their lives, they had been thrust into opposition with each other.

"Will your father allow the joust?" Nell said to break the uncomfortable silence.

"I don't know," Bessie answered. "He seemed unconcerned."

Nell was reminded of her conversation with Lady Margaret, and the woman's intimating that King Edward was perhaps losing his strength and capability. Nell had mentioned nothing of this to her friend, and stayed silent on it now.

"Perhaps we should get back," said Bessie, "before it starts to rain."

"Let's do," said Nell, and as they found their way back out, running into blind corners, back to where they'd started, laughing at their utter confusion, all discomfort between them faded.

The girls were nearly through the maze when they heard voices on the other side of the hedge wall. Clearly, others of the family had taken the rain's letup as an opportunity to walk out in the overcast afternoon.

"Why have you done this, Richard?" they heard Bessie's aunt Anne say. Her voice was low but clearly angry.

Nell and Bessie froze in their tracks and, with their eyes, agreed to silence. In fact, they had agreed to eavesdropping.

"You could be badly injured. Killed!" Anne said.

"I will be neither injured nor killed," Gloucester replied. "I promise you."

"But why? Why!" she cried. "No, let me tell *you*."

Bessie and Nell were barely breathing.

"You shall risk your life and limb," Anne continued, "chance to leave your son fatherless, your wife a widow, because you *loathe* Antony Woodville."

Richard was silent, as though he was unable to refute his wife's words.

"How could you do such a thing!"

"You speak as though I have no chance against Rivers."

"You have seen him on the jousting field, Richard. You *have* no chance against the man."

"And *I* have seen him on the battlefield! I am a hundred times the soldier he is. The king has called him a coward in war."

"No. The king took issue with Lord Rivers's choice in making a pilgrimage too soon after winning back England after my father's rebellion. The joust is an art, Richard. And you have never studied it."

" 'Tis another form of armed combat," Gloucester argued.

"He is a head taller and two stone heavier," said Anne.

"Inch for inch, pound for pound, I'm Rivers's match."

"And you're stubborn as a mule!"

"Let us be finished with this, Anne."

"No."

"No?"

"Not until I hear you admit the true reason for this folly." When Richard remained silent Anne said, "Then let me tell *you*. Despite the revulsion you claim at seeing your brother's gluttony and decadence, you crave his love and admiration like a child craves sweetmeats."

Nell felt Bessie clutching for her hand. It was extraordinary to be privy to such intimate family intelligence.

"It annoys you beyond measure," Anne went on, "that Edward has placed his 'precious jewel' into the trust of Lord Rivers, because you despise the man every bit as much as you do his sister the queen. You think him an overrated scholar, and you find his famous piety insincere—"

"His pilgrimages are a sham."

"And you mistrust his loyalty to the king, though he was the only man besides you and Hastings that sat out a painful exile with Edward during my father's coup. In short, you are jealous of Edward's affection for Rivers, and now you are willing to risk your life to prove to the king that you are a better man than your brother-in-law!"

Richard was silent.

"Maybe you believe that the royal blood you have coursing through your veins imbues you with magical powers," Anne said. "Or that all your recent victories with the Scots are insignificant proof of your loyalty. Or maybe you simply believe that *whatever* the outcome, your challenge—so foolishly mismatched and against your favor—proves courage and greatheartedness that Edward has forgotten you possess."

"Are you through?"

"I am." Suddenly her voice softened. "Richard—"

"The challenge cannot be rescinded, Anne."

"I know that."

"I will live through it," he said gently.

"You'd best do." Her voice was stern, but their argument was clearly over.

"Lady Margaret," the girls heard Gloucester say.

"Lord Richard. Lady Anne," the female voice replied deferentially.

It was obvious to the girls that Margaret Beaufort had approached the couple. Nell and Bessie strained to hear every word.

"I'm glad I found you," said Margaret. "Have you all the linen you need?"

"I think we do," Anne answered.

"I understand your hairdresser's fallen ill. I would be glad to send mine over."

"I'm all right today," Anne replied. "If Mary's no better tomorrow, I may well avail myself of your woman."

"Very good," said Margaret, and was gone.

A moment later Richard said, "She is a strange woman."

"She is Lancastrian," Anne replied, as if that explained everything.

"Married to a loyal Yorkist," Richard amended.

"Who has not *always* been loyal to the House of York. There's never been a nobleman with as ambiguous a history of loyalty as Lord Stanley—fighting for the York in the fifties, my father in the sixties—"

"He hasn't fought on the Lancastrian side since 1471," said Richard.

"By that time, York supremacy had been unmistakably *proven*," Anne argued.

"Stanley's been a faithful servant to my brother Edward for so long that I do trust him," Richard insisted.

"My darling, loyalty is so deeply ingrained in your soul that you believe it must naturally be so in others."

"So you do not trust Lord and Lady Stanley?" Richard asked.

"I reserve my judgment on him, but she is someone to watch very, very closely."

The Gloucesters finally moved from their place in front of the hedge maze. Flattened against the inside wall, the girls saw the couple pause at the arched maze entry.

Richard gazed adoringly at his wife. He stroked her cheek with his finger, tracing the outline of her delicate jaw. "The voice of reason," he said quietly. "What would I do without you?"

"You'd brood yourself into a black lump of coal," Anne answered with a smile.

He laughed at that and enfolded her in his arms. Nell pretended not to see Bessie's pained expression. A moment later Richard and Anne were gone.

The friends exchanged a look that spoke both of their embarrassment at such blatant eavesdropping and delight at their amazing good fortune to have done so.

"Did you know how deeply Gloucester loathed your uncle Rivers?" Nell began.

"Not in the least. I must be blind or stupid. Or both."

"But how could you know?" Nell responded. "You've told me that neither uncle is ever at court."

"True." Bessie was thoughtful. "Do you believe my uncle Richard is right? That your Lord Rivers's piety is false?"

"He is not 'my' Lord Rivers," said Nell with unconvincing indignance. "But 'tis possible. My father always says that a person's deepest relationship with God is a mystery, most especially to the person himself. And that for nobles, the number of pilgrimages traveled and the sums given as charity to the church are as likely political acts as religious ones. I personally believe Lord Rivers—"

"Your *beloved* Lord Rivers," Bessie teased.

"—is sincerely pious," said Nell, ignoring her friend's mischief. "But of course I've no substantive proof."

"Perhaps you'll gather some in the next few months at Ludlow," Bessie said with a wicked grin.

Nell had written to her father asking his permission to stay on as Prince Edward's tutor. Everyone knew he would happily give it.

"I might," said Nell, blushing at the thought of the glorious spring that lay ahead of her. There was the challenge of teaching Edward. And there was Antony, Lord Rivers, who seemed every day more smitten with her. "I will miss you, Bessie."

"And I you," said the princess, throwing her arms around Nell in an embrace. They felt the first drops of rain on their faces.

"Back to our needles," said Nell.

"And idle gossip," said Bessie.

They grinned like two conspirators, then ran back through the gathering storm to Ludlow Castle.

# BESSIE

THANK CHRIST FOR the fair weather," said Bessie to Nell. They, with the rest of the royal entourage, were following a winding pathway that had been specially cut through the jonquiled meadow to the east of the castle. "Edward would have been crushed had the games been ruined by rain."

"Tell me about Lord Rivers's wife," Nell whispered suddenly.

"Living or dead?" Bessie replied. She wondered why it had taken Nell so long to inquire about the man with whom she was clearly in love.

"Living."

Bessie thought before she answered. Though she too loved her uncle, she'd spent little time in his presence for the last ten years. "You know he'd been a widower for nearly five years."

"Yes."

"Well, after his wife died, it took my mother no time at all to begin her matchmaking. At first she was positively determined to marry him to the Scots queen. Those negotiations went on endlessly—three years, I think."

"So he would have become King of Scotland?"

"That was my mother's plan."

"Did Antony . . ." Nell corrected herself. "Lord Rivers—"

"Come, Nell," Bessie chided. "With me, at least, you must call him what you do in your heart." Bessie shot her friend a sideways glance and saw she was smiling shyly.

"Did Antony wish for the new marriage? For kingship?"

"Neither. He'd not been particularly attached to his first wife—an arranged marriage—and was enjoying bachelorhood. And he balked at the thought of leaving England."

"But all the pilgrimages he made . . ." Nell began.

"Pilgrimages are different. Despite the way he looks—elegant and worldly, and contrary to what my uncle Richard thinks— Rivers is the most sincerely pious man I know. He even risked my father's extreme displeasure going off on one of his pilgrimages too soon after the Warwick rebellion. But to be the King of Scotland would have meant leaving England for the rest of his life. And he hated that thought."

"Like you," Nell said.

Bessie glanced at her friend and knew her mind was racing.

"It never occurred to me that a *man* could be a marriage pawn," said Nell.

"With my mother plotting and scheming, *anything* is possible."

"But he didn't marry the Scots queen," Nell observed.

"No. Thankfully the idea was abandoned, and Uncle Rivers breathed a long sigh of relief. But not long enough. Last year his sister foisted another marriage plan on him—this time not for dynastic purposes, but strictly financial reasons. The lady in question was substantially older than my uncle and quite cantankerous, but almost as wealthy as Margaret Beaufort. Nothing Rivers could say or do moved my mother from her plan. All of his pleading fell on deaf ears. So he married the loathsome woman, but under the condition that he would never have to bed her, or even live under the same roof with her."

Nell was silent as she walked, but her features had settled into something resembling happiness.

"Do you not think it is ironic," said Bessie, "that we've both fallen in love with men we cannot have?"

"Brutally ironic." Nell smiled sadly at her friend. She grabbed Bessie's hand. "At least we have each other."

Bessie squeezed Nell's hand. "Till death," said the princess.

"Till death," said Nell.

They emerged into a large clearing where the splendid tournament grounds had been erected. Already, the risers were filled with a raucous crowd composed of the castle staff, Ludlow villagers, and farmer families from the farthest reaches of the Welsh Marches, eager for the day's pomp and pageantry. At the center of the risers was a raised, canopied box, this carpeted and hung magnificently with tapestries and fluttering China silk. Bessie viewed the jousting field beyond, its low wooden tilt wall, on either side of which the opposing horses would run at one another, and at each end of which had been erected a stable, their facades appearing as miniature castles.

"This is my first joust," said Nell.

"I wish you could sit with me," Bessie said.

"I shall be quite happy with family friends and withered old clergymen."

They hugged, and Nell left her friend to find a seat in the riser closest to the royal box.

To a blasting fanfare the King and Queen of England and their brood emerged onto the platform. The crowd rose for their entry, and a great roar of approval shook the morning air. Bessie was not unaware of the vision they presented. The Yorks were the richest family in England, attired in their holiday finery, a dozen handsome heads of golden hair made even more dazzling by the day's sparkling sunlight.

Bishop Morton stood and delivered a droning benediction over the tournament. Then, with a great blast of trumpets, the games began.

Two riders in the Prince of Wales's livery galloped in suddenly, one from either "castle," this to announce the grand entrance of the prince himself. Bessie's heart leapt at the sight of the small, proud figure encased toe to head in gleaming armor, tall lance upended, riding forward on his high horse that was trapped out in matching plate. Edward's face was hidden behind his helmet and visor, but she imagined it flushed with pride, this perhaps the finest moment of his childhood.

Prince Edward caused his horse to dip into a graceful bow before his mother and father, which caused more applause by the crowd. Then, lifting his visor, Edward trotted to the place below where his sister sat and bade his horse to kneel, just as he had done for the King and Queen of England. When horse and rider rose, the prince extended his lance in Bessie's direction and cried out, "If you please, a token from my lady!"

Bessie stood and draped her French lace handkerchief over the tip of Edward's lance. She held her breath, praying that the lift of his lance would prove steady and graceful. It was. Then, with the slight jiggle his uncle Rivers had taught him, Edward released the kerchief, which fluttered down to his hand. He pressed it first to his heart and then to his lips. The spectators came to their feet with applause and whistles.

In the next moment the Prince of Wales wheeled about and rode along the partition wall to the far end. During the time he'd been acquiring Bessie's token, a wooden quintain—a target mounted on a horizontal pole—had been wheeled out to the far end of the lists. Edward trotted to the opposite end of the tilt wall, and at the drop of a red flag, he spurred his horse to action and raced the whole length of it. The armor must have weighed heavily on his child's body, but his spine was rod straight, and the movement of mount and rider was strong and seamless. At the last moment the lance, with great control and steady aim, was lowered toward the quintain. If hit with accuracy, the target would swing harmlessly aside. Should Edward strike it off center, however, the heavy arm would swing round and ingloriously knock him off his horse. To everyone's delight—for all present wished the boy well in his solitary game—each of Edward's six runs proved a perfect bull's-eye, and with each success the cheers grew louder.

When the quintain was removed, replaced by six gold circles suspended on cords, Edward "rode at the rings" and carried five of the six off on the tip of his lance. With one final, triumphant bow to his parents and Bessie and a wave to the cheering crowd, the demonstration came to an end, and Prince Edward rode off.

The jousts were next. Pairs of knights, each with fresh horses for each of four rounds, rode full speed at each other with lowered lances. Dozens of weapons were shattered upon their opponents' shields, making points for the rider with the broken weapons. Though lance tips were blunted—to save England's finest from death and injury—jousters nevertheless fought as if their lives depended on it. Bessie found herself unaccountably thrilled by the thundering hooves and crashing steel. She shouted encouragement loudly, and jeered her disappointments like one of the common crowd.

"Bessie," her mother hissed. "Quiet yourself. You sound like a fishwife."

"Leave the girl alone, Elizabeth," Bessie heard her father say. " 'Tis a joust. Yes! *Yes!*" he shouted as two knights collided with a resounding crash.

The queen glared at her husband and defiant daughter, neither of whom was in the least perturbed by her fury.

The morning hushed suddenly, and Bessie knew that all were anticipating the match between her two uncles. Ludlow had lately been abuzz with the challenge, for it was an event of historic proportions—the king's beloved brother riding against the king's beloved brother-in-law. Lord Rivers, being the local governor, was the common crowd's favorite. Few had ever seen the king's brother.

Richard of Gloucester came first to the field, emerging from his castle as the "Black Knight" in dark-burnished armor, his attendants leading three more armored mounts behind him. Upon a sixteen-hand horse encased in that massive metal suit, Richard's stature belied his smaller size. His high posture and the ease with which he carried his lance proved his strength beneath the steel plate, and Bessie felt a strange pride that the bearing of her uncle was so regal.

A moment later a rumbling in the crowd, then a roar, grew as the opposite castle door opened. All eyes turned to find a strange and riveting sight. A "hermitage" had been built over a horse, entirely covering it. It was a wood-framed structure of white velvet, with four glass windows on either side, a cross of Saint Antony mounted at its top, and a ringing bell above that. Once it had come full center, attendants rushed to all sides of the simulated building and with practiced hands removed it to reveal a horse trapped in tawny satin and gold plate. It was ridden by a robed and deeply hooded "White Hermit." Now with a great flourish, the hermit's robes were pulled away, and there, resplendent in full silver armor was Antony, Lord Rivers, the visor open, a fist raised as if triumph was already his.

In an age-old ritual so beloved by the people, each jouster now came forward to receive a token from his lady, who could be anyone *not* his wife. The woman would be expected to swoon with delight that such a gallant knight would ride, at peril of his very life, for her honor.

But when the "Black Knight" rode up the ramp to the royal box and Gloucester dipped his head in Bessie's direction, she was stunned and began blushing madly. The feelings she bore for her uncle Richard were so new and unsettling. *So forbidden,* it had never occurred to her that they might in any way be returned. She gathered her wits quickly and stood smiling demurely.

But she was without a token, she realized, having given her handkerchief to Edward. After a flustered moment of indecision, she tugged at a ribbon holding her sleeve together and, pulling it away, laid bare her whole arm. Bessie heard her mother gasp, but the gesture was appreciated by the crowd, for it perfectly evoked the romance of chivalric love. Bessie dared not look at Lady Anne, fearful that the Duchess of Gloucester might recognize the love for her husband that was seething in her niece's heart.

Bessie saw her mother straighten in her seat in anticipation of her brother, the "White Hermit," prancing his horse up the ramp to demand one of her jewels as his token. But to everyone's delight, and her mother's horror, Rivers trotted his mount to the stand next to the royal box and lowered his lance to Nell Caxton.

Bessie could see her friend blushing madly. But smiling delightedly, Nell lifted from her neck a small jewel on a gold chain and hung it over the lance tip. The crowd cheered their approval of his choice.

As Rivers and Gloucester galloped onto the field, Bessie sought Nell's eyes as they silently congratulated each other on their honors. The jousters made for opposite ends of the tilt wall, calming and staying their horses beneath them in the moments before the signal.

Then the flag dropped and Bessie was riveted by the sight of one white and one black knight riding hell-bent toward a terrible clash, evoking Armageddon itself.

Impact! Rivers's lance broke clean on Gloucester's shield, but her uncle Richard stayed firmly seated, wavering in his posture not at all, as though a gnat had grazed him. Cheers went up in the risers, where all were on their feet, shouting their approval and calling bets and jovial insults.

The jousters rode back the way they'd come. They were helped down from their mounts on wooden steps by their "seconds" and a cadre of grooms, then up into the saddles of the next set of horses.

Bessie could hear in the risers closest to the royal box women laughing great belly laughs and calling out lewd exchanges about the challengers on the field. "I like my men small and hard."

"Give me long and strong."

"Just give me a man!" But clearly the White Knight was the favorite of this Ludlow crowd, and they began to shout his name, the sound flowing into a chant.

"Rivers! Rivers! Rivers!"

The second round began. The thundering hooves, the terrible moment of contact. A shrieking sound and the sight of wood exploding above the combatants' heads. A broken lance—nay, a *splintered* lance—fell slowly to the ground. It was revealed as Gloucester's weapon! He had won the round soundly, the many slender shards of wood a testament to his strength and fury.

Bessie cheered wildly for her champion, ignoring her mother's disapproving stare. Her uncle Rivers was unhurt, riding away waving at the crowd from whom a loud murmuring could be heard. *Was their favorite lord defeatable?*

When the third pair of horses began clattering down the

lists, there were now two names shouted from the fickle crowd.

"Rivers!"

"Gloucester!"

"Rivers!"

"Gloucester!"

When they met this time Gloucester received a good jolt, but Rivers's lance remained intact. Neither man had scored. With only one round to go, Gloucester might still come good, defeat Rivers! The crowd was stamping now, rocking the risers, shrieking deliriously, for, they knew, it was the fiercest match they would ever in their whole lifetime witness.

The final charge began and the roar round Bessie deafened her. Her whole body was trembling. It was a blur of galloping beasts, flashing colors, glittering steel. Impact! And a sight unbelievable to her eyes.

*Richard of Gloucester was aloft!* Time stilled, and for an eternity his body was balanced, his shield upon the tip of Lord Rivers's lance. Gloucester's horse—its rider suspended above it—galloped on. Then he fell, heavily, a pile of dark crashing metal. He lay motionless.

Bessie froze, though chaos howled all round her. She turned to see the king on his feet, he, tightly clutching Lady Anne's white-knuckled fingers.

On the field, Gloucester's second and his grooms rushed to their master's side. His helmet was lifted gently from his head. There was blood at the corner of his mouth.

Bessie could hear Lady Anne groan piteously.

"There is no blood from his ear," she heard her father say to Anne. "Thank Christ, none from his ear."

Silence descended on the assembled. Six men were gathered round Richard of Gloucester's supine form. Lord Stanley strove to remove Richard's chest plate. A leg moved. A cry went up from the crowd! An arm rose feebly, but the man's eyes were still closed. Without warning, the lifted arm arched violently, the metal gauntlet smashing his groom hard across the cheek and nose. The man fell back with a cry, bloodied. But now Richard was stirring, coming back to life. They helped him to sitting.

Even from where she sat, Bessie could see confusion still clouding Gloucester's eyes. He was raised up by his men, all groaning metal joints and parts straightened as well as possible. *How quickly they put him to standing,* she thought, then realized that standing dazed was far more comely for a proud knight than—for one moment more than necessary—lying helpless and supine in the center of a jousting field. An armored knight on foot was a clumsy, clanking sight, and Gloucester's defeated walk from the tilt yard was horrible to watch. Another cheer went up from the risers. It was sincere enough, thought Bessie, for it was not a bloodthirsty crowd, this. Her uncle would live down the shame of the fall and defeat at Rivers's hand. The pathetic flailing arm giving injury to his groom would be far harder for him to bear.

But few eyes were following Gloucester now.

Lord Rivers was the great and glorious victor of the day. Helmet held proudly under one arm, he rode his prancing horse for a second time before Nell Caxton. In his metal fingers he clutched her jeweled pendant, then raised it high as the approving roar grew louder. Now he touched it to his lips, then his heart.

*Nell must be swooning,* Bessie thought. There'd be no sleeping tonight.

Then, with a graceful swivel of the beast underneath him, the champion began parading before the adoring crowd, the chant of his name, "Rivers! *Rivers!* RIVERS!" sundering the bright afternoon.

Never, thought Bessie, had she ever felt so torn, both joyful for her dear friend Nell and miserable for her defeated and disgraced uncle Richard.

THE WEDNESDAY WESTMINSTER market was a great living beast, thought Bessie as she and Dickon, followed by four guards, picked their way through the crowded thoroughfare. The castle and abbey together were the beast's head, Totehill Street its long torso, the small lanes and alleys jutting from it, its writhing limbs. Farmers had traveled many miles the night before to bring their produce, meat, and fowl to the makeshift stalls. They were careful to leave clear the windows of the permanent shops, or else face loud, angry protests from those merchants whose displays might be compromised. But all hawked their wares with equal fervency.

"Wet fish here, caught this morning with me own hands!"

"Fresh bread, brown and black, and *manchette* white as snow!"

"Cabbages, onions and cabbages!"

"Fat hens here! Duck eggs! Chicks for sale!"

All who saw Bessie recognized her as their princess and not only called out friendly greeting to her, but bade her send their regards to her friend and theirs, Nell Caxton.

Westminster precinct itself was a thriving corridor, what with the royal residence housed next door. Totehill Street ran east, paralleling the river, to the Tower of London, where much government took place, and therefore much traffic passed through. Rich traffic at that. When Parliament was in session everyone prospered, from the greengrocers to the silkwomen to the cutpurses. Gold- and silversmiths grew positively rich.

Bessie had not been out for a day of shopping since the family's return from Ludlow, but this morning she had begged her mother's permission for the outing. Dickon had insisted on joining her. It was his first foray out onto Totehill Street, and the queen had demanded that four burly guards come to protect them.

"From what?" Bessie had demanded with irritation. "I've encountered nothing but love and respect from everyone I meet outside the walls."

"There are whores and cutpurses and rapscallions in the streets," her mother had insisted.

"Well, I'd say the two of us are amply protected with a quartet of armed soldiers."

"Keep your eyes on your brother. Make sure he doesn't speak with any ruffians," the queen instructed her daughter.

"I shall personally introduce him to a very nice murderer I know."

Now Bessie smiled, remembering the look of fury on her mother's face. She knew she was defying God's commandment, the one that admonished children to honor their parents, but surely God had never counted on Elizabeth Woodville.

They'd made a stop at the brewery, as Nell had asked Bessie in her last letter to pass a message along to Maggie Brown the brewer. She was a manly sort of woman, stout, with large square hands and a square, wide-mouthed face. Whilst Bessie was well known at the brewery from her visits with Nell, Maggie had never before laid eyes on the little prince.

"Your Grace," she said, and dipped into a low curtsy that was comical in light of her masculine demeanor. "How honored I am for your visit."

Dickon glowed. Although the obeisance was customary, he'd never received a greeting so sincere and enthusiastic outside the court. He struggled briefly for a fitting reply, then said, "Your husband's brewery is very fine."

"I haven't got a husband, Your Grace."

"Then your father . . . ?"

"Sadly deceased," said Maggie.

"*You* are the brewer?" he said, perplexed.

"*Femme sole,* that's what I am."

"A woman has rights to do business without a man, Dickon," Bessie explained to her brother. "There are many such women in London."

"How does a lady become such a thing?" the boy asked Maggie.

"Well, first, m'lord, I am no lady. But in my case my husband died. I'd always helped him at the shop, and when he passed away I chose to run the business."

"I see," he said, with so adult a tone that Bessie was forced to bite her lip to keep from smiling.

They continued through the market, filling Bessie's basket with vegetables, a round of cheese from the white meats store, and an array of sweet confections Dickon had carefully chosen from a long case at the bakery. A dozen goose eggs were had from the poultry stall managed by a brawny young man, handsome but for his toothless visage. Dickon found it difficult to tear his eyes away from the gummy pink smile and finally asked, "How did you lose your teeth, sir?"

"Football," he replied with a great grin. "Every Sunday after church. We love the game, my mates and me. They've tried to outlaw it, the clergy has, but nobody listens. I got kicked in the face a time too many. I still have my *back* teeth, see?" He pulled away his gums to reveal a number of intact choppers. "I can chew just fine."

Dickon's face was aglow. "I should like very much to learn football." He turned to his sister. "Do you think Mother would allow me?"

"You would grow horns and a tail first," she replied.

When their baskets were full, the royal children and their guard proceeded back along Totehill Street market and in through Westminster's walls. Bessie dismissed the soldiers at the almshouse, where she had stopped to visit her friends who lived there.

Dickon surprised Bessie, wishing to visit with them as well. She knew her brother could hardly wait to bestow the baked gifts he'd bought for his family, and he had never before shown an interest in the twelve old men. Yet he insisted on following her through the gate of the pretty, gardened courtyard surrounded by a dozen cottages. The Church supported these pensioners, retired from their trades, each who lived in his own simple but comfortable home till his death. The prince and princess were greeted with the greatest warmth by the men, who, by their own admission, were the most grateful individuals at Westminster. They were grateful, they said, for they were poor men spared the humiliation of beggary in old age by the charity of Westminster's abbot.

Bessie watched Dickon handing out their offerings of meat and eggs, bread and cheese, for their larders, and was warmed by his sincere interest in them, and their delight that the little Duke of York was showing concern for them.

Dickon even accepted an invitation by their father's retired dog keeper, Tom Wilson, to come in and see his humble hearth and home, and "the oldest dog in England," his favorite hound, who never left the fireside.

Bessie was proud of her little brother, who was displaying, even at his tender age, true princely behavior.

When she saw one of the day's escorts hurrying toward the almshouse garden, Bessie sighed. The guard had a look on his face that said he'd been savaged by the queen, perhaps for failing to bring the young royals all the way back to their mother's presence.

"Princess," the guard began, most agitated. "You must come quickly. Where is your brother?"

"I'll get him," she said, and made for Master Wilson's cottage to fetch Dickon. "Tell Mother we'll be there presently."

"Yes, Princess." The guard hurried away.

Nell was right about one thing, thought Bessie. There were benefits to marrying a foreign prince, the first being that she would never again have to take an order from Elizabeth Woodville.

# NELL

**M**Y *LIFE,* thought Nell as she gazed at the pretty, golden-haired boy sitting across the desk from her, *has become a long, sweet dream.*

Her posting at Ludlow through the spring of 1483—a slow, warm season in a verdant pastoral, embraced by the royal family and housed in luxury, had merely been the setting for the true jewel of her existence. Nell had fallen in love twice over. First with her student, the thirteen-year-old Prince of Wales, whom she now thought of as the brother she'd never had. He was so dear and precocious a child that tutoring, a wholly new profession for her, had proven a natural and joyful endeavor. This was a strange and wonderful phenomenon—*work become play*. Edward openly reciprocated her affection, and every day Nell was the recipient of some small but dear token of his love and respect. A bouquet of wildflowers he had picked himself. A pair of doeskin gloves he'd had made for her from the pelt of his latest hunt. The sharing of daily letters he'd received from his family at court.

Of course there were cheerful ones from Bessie, but there were also letters from his mother, replete with domestic gossip—the childish exploits of Edward's brother and sisters—as well as missives from his father, these of a more serious nature. The king had recently, to Edward's delight and pride, begun keeping his son apprised of state business. Treaties forged and broken. Matters pertaining to the treasury, Royal Navy, trade, and taxation. All of this, Nell ingested, then digested, as great feasts of knowledge. She realized to her surprise that, as to the affairs of England, she had become very well informed.

Her other love—and she hardly dared to call it such—was that which she shared with Antony Woodville, Lord Rivers. To this point, theirs was a passionate affair of hearts and minds only. As she had come to know him better, Nell had learned that Antony's reputation as England's most learned, cultured, and pious man was entirely deserved. His erudition on a wide variety of subjects was nothing short of breathtaking. He had traveled extensively and studied deeply. He loved the classics and was particularly fond of Socratic and Platonic dialogues—a favorite of Nell's as well. These they studied and discussed endlessly, discovering nuances and even humor in the ancient texts.

Antony was openly charmed by Nell and particularly valued her intellect, which, on alternate days he claimed was second only to her beauty. On the other days he swore the reverse was true—that she was the loveliest creature in all England. He marveled at her fascination with political affairs and was intrigued by her unique concept of the invisible "intelligence web" existing in London. Never was there a hint of disapproval for her "manly interests."

But to this date their romance had not proceeded beyond an intense incarnation of chivalric love. Courtly love. They might sit side by side for hours, poring over a Latin translation. When they spoke together, debated, laughed, punned, their eyes were locked together, as if searching for a way into the other's soul.

She knew his eyes so well. The gray-green sparkle of them, the small golden flecks in the irises. How often he blinked. The pattern of the crinkles at the corners—the right different from the left. She knew the contours of his face as well, that beautiful face. The aquiline nose, the full, sensual lips. The perfect teeth, the chiseled jaw. And the laugh. Nell supposed that was what she loved best about Antony—the deep, throaty laugh that she was so frequently capable of eliciting from him.

Yet, she thought, they had never so much as held hands. If they chanced to touch, skin brushing skin accidentally, thighs touching under the desk through the fabric of her gown, his tunic and hose, it was like a sharp jolt, one of equal measures pain and pleasure. She would feel it at the point of contact, but the shock would travel through her body from limb to torso. The heart would pound. Stomach churn. Cunny tingle. There was always a moment of mutual embarrassment when such a thing occurred, and Nell was certain Antony was feeling the same thrill as well.

Her dreams of him had been torrid and seething things, and for days after one of them she could barely look at him without turning bright primrose pink.

But they had, without speaking of it, refrained—heroically refrained—from any physical indulgences that spring—for one simple reason. It was not Lord Rivers's marriage that impeded them, for that was nothing but a sham. It was not Nell's virginity, for she had long wished to lose it like other girls of her station, and to delight in the carnal pleasures Master Chaucer had written of in his *Canterbury Tales.*

The reason for Nell and Antony's restraint was simple—the king's "commandments" that prevailed at Ludlow to protect the Prince of Wales. The overseer of those rules was Lord Rivers himself. It was incumbent upon him to assure that Edward's environment was pure and sin-free. That no one at his court disobeyed those rules. If Lord Rivers himself were to flaunt the commandments, the very gates of hell would fly open, and heads would surely roll.

Nell and Antony both counted their blessings for such elevated positions in the scheme of things, and also respected King Edward too deeply to break his commandments and betray the trust he'd bestowed upon them. Truly, Nell and Lord Rivers were the keepers of the king's most precious treasure. Denying physical pleasure was the sacrifice they had painfully accepted.

It was doubly ironic that Prince Edward not only knew of their romance, but approved of it. One evening before bedtime when Nell and Rivers were together reading aloud with the boy from Malory's *Morte D'Arthur,* he told them how alike he believed Camelot and Ludlow were to each other.

"How do they compare?" Rivers had asked.

"First, they are both set in the west, in Wales," Edward answered, happy to have his theory given an airing. "The courts of both are very grand and wonderful, though there is danger all round about. I am Ludlow's Arthur"—Edward chuckled at that—"or at least one day I will be, and I am surrounded by the bravest knights, though we've no Round Table. We might have one made. Could we, Uncle?"

Rivers had strived to remain serious in order not to dampen his nephew's fantasy. "That might be arranged," he'd said, straight-faced.

"Yes, well, of all the knights, the greatest is Lancelot, or in Ludlow's case, Lord Rivers." Edward beamed at his uncle, who could not help but be charmed and flattered by such a comparison.

"Of course I'm not married," Edward had added, suddenly shy, "but beautiful Queen Guinevere of Ludlow is Mistress Caxton."

Nell, enchanted by Edward's storytelling, had been caught short by the last comparison.

"In Camelot," Edward had continued, warming to his story,

"Lancelot and Guinevere become lovers and betray the king, but I do not think——"

"Edward, 'tis far past your bedtime," Rivers said, interrupting the boy. "We shall continue reading *Morte D'Arthur* tomorrow evening." He'd had a hard time controlling his smile, and Nell blushed furiously.

Even now, as she watched Edward dutifully working on his double translation of Tacitus, her face reddened, remembering.

When the door opened, Nell and her pupil both looked up and called out happy greetings as Lord Rivers entered. Not only Antony's form, thought Nell, but his bodily grace as he moved through the world thrilled her, and today she did not bother to hide her joy at seeing him. His even more frequent presence during the prince's lessons convinced her that the Governor of Wales shared her deepest feelings.

"Good morning, good morning!" he called out to them, closing the door behind him.

"Has the London courier arrived?" Edward asked.

"Not yet," said Rivers.

"He's very late," the prince observed.

"Are you eager for a particular piece of mail, Edward?" Nell inquired.

"Dickon promised to write me about an African lion they've recently delivered to the Tower menagerie. The old one died. He was withered and toothless and slept all day and night. This one, I hear, is young and very fierce. Have you seen the menagerie, Mistress Caxton?"

"No," she said. "In fact, I've never had the occasion to visit the Tower of London at all, except of course to peer into the yard through the gates."

"Oh, 'tis my favorite place in all of London," the prince said.

There was a sudden pounding on the schoolroom door.

"Enter!" Rivers called out.

The door swung open and they saw this day's London courier standing still as a statue, his face ashen, at the doorsill.

"What is it, man? Speak," Rivers commanded.

Edward rose from his bench and in that moment the courier's eyes found the boy. The man strode across the room and without warning fell to his knees before him.

"The king is dead!" he cried, and gazed up at Edward. "Long live the king!" As if finally remembering, he thrust a sealed parchment at Lord Rivers, who stood, stunned at the announcement. Gathering his wits, he took the parchment and, thanking the messenger, dismissed him. Slowly he pulled open the letter.

"This is from your mother, Edward. Written to me. 'This day, nine April, 1483, Edward the Fourth died most suddenly and unexpectedly. My son, Edward Prince of Wales, is proclaimed rightful King of England. You, brother, are herewith ordered to bring him in all haste to London for his crowning. Bring with you as great an army of loyal men as you can gather in the next days, but hie to Westminster with no delay. Your loving sister, Elizabeth.' "

Nell, reeling with the news, yet unable to grasp all of its ramifications, found herself rising to her feet and moving toward her charge. *My life is a dream,* she thought once again as she executed a low and reverent curtsy that brought her to one knee before the thirteen-year-old boy—a child whom she loved and who loved her in return.

"Your Majesty," she intoned. "Long may you live and reign."

Nell was aware of Rivers coming to her side and himself falling to his knees in front of his nephew. She chanced a sidewise look at him. There were tears brimming in his eyes as he took Edward's hands in his and kissed them. "My king," he said. "Deepest condolences on the sad death of your father. I am, as I have always been and will always be, at your service and plea-sure. God will surely grant you a long and glorious reign."

Nell felt a small hand on her shoulder. She looked up to see that Edward had placed his other hand on his uncle's head.

"My friends," he said, his voice tremulous. "What has hap-pened is both terrible and great. I am at a loss what to do. What to say. May I depend on you both to help and guide me?"

"Yes, Majesty," Nell answered quickly. "I am your most happy servant."

"I live and I die for you, Edward," Rivers pledged with terri-ble gravitas.

Thus began the reign of King Edward the Fifth of England.

I T WAS THE GREATEST army—two thousand strong—that had ever traveled the road 'tween Ludlow and London. Besides the troops were carts of goods, and peopled carriages and coaches of the household Progress. Nell and Rivers rode on horseback, flanking young King Edward on his high horse, just behind the long procession's vanguard. She marveled at the speed and ease with which Rivers had mustered the army and the Royal Progress within days of his sister's letter. All these armed Welshmen came quickly, eager to serve under their new king. Along the road, passing through villages and farms, every man, woman, and child within fifty miles had come out to wave and cheer, call out their good wishes and "God save the king!"

Nell's heart was close to bursting to see the warmth and joy with which they welcomed the boy. On the day of their last lesson at Ludlow, Edward had announced to her with a strange mixture of pride and modesty and disbelief, "I am the King of England. My father is dead, and I am Edward Quintus. Blood of royal blood. God's own general on earth."

Of course he had planned for this day, Nell knew, but in that vision Edward had been a grown man altogether ready to assume the mantle of kingship. He had assiduously studied a thousand years of the English monarchy and knew full well the fate of boy kings. Chaos and civil strife accompanied all such successions, and he repeated to her the old saw "Woe to the land whose ruler is a child."

His uncle Rivers had tried to reassure him. He would stay by Edward's side, he promised, to guide him through the coming days and months and years. Though his father was gone, Rivers would provide all the manly example and paternal love that a boy and king could ever need.

"Soon you'll be crowned, Edward," Rivers had said, "and the people will love you. There are not so many years between the present and your majority, and no earthly reason that with a wise council to steer you, the long peace your father negotiated should not continue unabated."

Much had been said between the three of them, and now they rode in companionable silence.

Nell saw a cloud of dust on the road ahead, and a moment later a man she recognized as Rivers's courier came riding hellbent. He reined in his horse before them and, dipping his head to the king, stopped before his master. He thrust the parchment he carried at Rivers, who ripped it open and began to read.

"What is it, Uncle?"

Rivers waved the messenger off, then looked at Edward and Nell. "Richard of Gloucester shall be meeting us at Northampton, just before we reach London."

"Uncle Richard," Edward murmured to himself. It was almost as though the thought of Gloucester had not shadowed his mind till this moment. But now Nell could swear she saw the king's face darken at mention of his hated uncle. She wondered if there would ever be a time when Edward would soften toward the man.

"Is . . . is anything wrong, my lord?" Nell said to Rivers.

"No, nothing is wrong." He looked at Edward. "But your mother and Gloucester may be slightly at odds with regards to certain of your . . . arrangements."

Edward became alarmed. "What 'arrangements'?"

"The date of your coronation, for example. The queen wishes for the soonest date. In his letter Gloucester has written his concern that he mayn't arrive in London in time for the crowning."

"Then he should have left more time for traveling," said the boy, clearly relieved.

"That's a good lad, Edward." Rivers smiled. "You needn't worry about anything."

"What did you call me?" said Edward, suddenly serious.

"I called you Edward," Rivers replied, straight-faced.

"Do you not think, my lord," the boy said imperiously, "that 'Your Majesty' would be more in order?"

Nell watched as Edward's lips clamped shut and his face began to twitch madly. A moment later he roared laughing, and with a snarling grin Rivers reached out and gave him a good clout on the head. Then on a silent signal the pair spurred their mounts, and in perfect accord took off racing to the head of the vanguard.

Nell watched them go, warmed to her core. There was so much happiness around her. So much anticipation for the future. She was traveling home to her dear father, and Bessie, and her friends on Totehill Street. A new young king was the hope and pride of England, and a beautiful man was in love with her. What more, she wondered with a deep, satisfied sigh, could a woman ask for than that?

. . .

MIDDAY ON 29 APRIL, having just passed through the village of Northampton, Nell rode at the head of the Royal Progress. At his own pleasure, King Edward was riding behind with the rear guard. Now Lord Rivers galloped to join her at the fore, and called a halt to the long column. He turned to Nell, his brow furrowed.

"I'm afraid Northampton is unsuitable for a stopping place," he said. "It suffered a severe drought last summer, the town fathers just informed me. Should so large an army as ours impose itself for even one night, the meager stores of food they are portioning out to last them till the fall harvest will be dangerously depleted." He looked round him, then skyward. "'Tis still early in the day. I think we should press on. Stony Stratford is fourteen miles closer to London."

"But you promised Lord Gloucester we'd meet him at Northampton," she said. "He's already worried about joining up in good time with the king. It might try his temper if you were to ride closer to London without his permission."

"I have no need of his permission, Nell. My sister the queen is Edward's protector, and we ride under her orders. Gloucester's temper is not my problem . . . nor yours." He brought his horse side by side with her mount and reached his hand out to stroke her cheek.

Antony, during the five-day Progress, had become bolder and bolder with his open affection toward Nell. It was as though with the death of his brother-in-law, the authority of the king's Ludlow "commandments" had dissolved. And whilst Rivers naturally and enthusiastically protected his nephew from all harm, he no longer felt constrained in his personal behavior with regard to Nell. She could not count the times he had kissed her hand. Gently stroked her shoulder. Even pushed a strand of hair back from her face. He was unconcerned whether anyone from the Ludlow Court observed his affectionate displays, and he was particularly warm, almost intimate with her, in the presence of the young king, who, Nell could see, heartily approved of his uncle's attentions toward his tutor.

Whilst they had not spoken of such things aloud, she wondered if Rivers was contemplating a divorce from his wife. But they were in transit, and everything was happening so fast. Nell had not been able to write to Bessie since leaving Ludlow, and had received no letters from the princess since her father's death. She felt for her dear friend at so terrible a time, but she selfishly wished to pour out her heart to Bessie about Antony— her suspicions of his intentions. Her hopes. Her fears.

It would have to wait a few more days, Nell knew, till they reached London. Oh, the reunion with Bessie would be sweet! And sad. And exciting too, for her friend's brother was now King of England, and Nell herself had, in the past months, become like another sister to the boy.

"Besides," Rivers continued, snatching Nell from her reverie, "we have no way of knowing how far from Northampton Gloucester and his troops still are. I'll leave a messenger in Northampton Towne, and when they arrive, he can ride to us at Stony Stratford and let us know. Don't worry yourself, my love," he added, then wheeled about and rode off.

*My love.* Nell's heart lurched in her chest. *He called me his love!* It was odd, for Nell had never thought of herself as a love-struck girl, like her friend Bessie, all atwitter over the unrequited amour with her uncle Richard. But here Nell was now, shuddering with delight at Antony's first uttering of an endearment. What was next? she wondered. How much better might her life become?

Nell smiled to herself, her mount swaying a pleasant rhythm

beneath her, gazing up through the leafy maple boughs lining the road to Stony Stratford. *Heaven itself is the limit,* she suddenly realized.

T HE REST OF the journey to Stony Stratford had proven uneventful. Antony had found wide-open fields to encamp the troops and servants, and a fine inn in town to house the king and his courtiers. They'd not yet settled into their rooms when the messenger left behind at Northampton rode into camp to say that Richard and company, a mere three hundred gentlemen retainers—hardly an army—had arrived at the original rendezvous.

Rivers quickly decided it would be politic to ride back and greet Gloucester, personally explaining the change in plans to avert any hard feelings, should any exist. To her delight, Antony invited Nell to ride back the fourteen miles, as he was eager for her company in relative peace and quiet. All that would be accompanying them would be a small guard—twenty men—and they could enjoy the long, lazy afternoon and evening, the sun not setting till nearly ten.

She'd accepted the invitation instantly, though jesting that her saddle-sore rump would be bruised and raw by the time they arrived.

Antony's eyes twinkled. "Then I shall have to kiss it and make it better."

Nell had laughed aloud. He was growing bolder by the moment.

Now they were riding back to Northampton side by side at an almost leisurely pace. The small guard, split in two, was well before and behind the couple, allowing them what was perhaps the closest thing to privacy they had ever known.

At first they had ridden in a pleasant and comfortable silence, enjoying the warm sun on their backs, and a cooling
breeze that wafted in from the greenwood on either side of the
road. When Rivers finally spoke he kept his eyes straight
ahead.

"What do you suppose your father will say when I tell him
I'm in love with his daughter?"

"Well, I doubt he'll be surprised," Nell answered, "as I've already made it quite plain in my letters to him that I feel the same
for you."

Rivers was clearly pleased and much relieved. "Does he approve?"

"Of his daughter loving a married man? 'Tis an unwelcome
complication. That I am in love with the nobleman he most ad-
mires and respects in the whole world? He applauds my good
taste."

Rivers smiled. "I have already taken the liberty of speaking to
our young king." He paused thoughtfully before continuing.

Nell was barely breathing.

"I asked if he would be so bold as to overrule the protector,
his mother, just this once, and insist that my marriage to Lady
Philbin be annulled . . . so that I might marry you, Nell. Edward enthusiastically agreed."

Tears stung Nell's eyes and she found herself speechless. Her
silence was so prolonged that Rivers turned a perplexed gaze on
her. "Do you not wish to be my wife?"

"Antony, good heavens, of course I do!"

He was visibly relieved. "The process may be long and somewhat complicated."

"There's no rush, my love." The words were out of her
mouth before she knew she'd said them. The idea of being
Antony, Lord Rivers's wife had hardly permeated her conscious

mind. But Nell was joyful in the entire breadth and depth of her soul.

"I've promised Edward that no one should know our plan."

"Of course. Antony—"

He turned to her, but again Nell found herself tongue-tied, flummoxed.

"I know what you're thinking," he said.

"Tell me what I'm thinking."

"That you wish the guard would suddenly disappear. That I would sweep you off your horse, drag you into the wood, and ravish you. Repeatedly."

Nell laughed. "That is *precisely* what I was thinking," she said. "When did you begin reading my mind?"

He looked away then, but Nell could see there were tears in his eyes.

"When you called me love," he said. "When you called me love."

THE SUN SHONE a huge golden coin as it set over the Northampton field where Richard of Gloucester's troops had made their camp. Rivers spotted the Yorkshireman first and called out to him.

"My Lord Gloucester!"

Nell and Rivers's horses walked the final distance between them and came side to side with Richard.

"Rivers. Mistress Caxton. How goes it?" Gloucester smiled cordially, and Nell quietly sighed with relief.

"The king's cavalcade made better time than anyone expected," Rivers said.

"I'm pleased to hear."

"We reached Northampton by ten this morning, but I could

not see that the town could support so large a contingent of soldiers as ours, and the whole household as well. So we traveled on and found Stony Stratford the perfect stopping place."

"How is my nephew?" Richard asked.

"Edward sends his warmest regards to you and looks forward to joining up tomorrow for the ride into London."

"Good." He eyed Nell. "And how are you, Mistress Caxton?"

"The rump is sore, but I am otherwise well."

She appraised Bessie's uncle closely and could easily see the attraction.

"I hope you'll dine with me tonight at Northampton's inn. I've arranged lodgings for myself, and I'm sure they can find two more rooms for you. Surely you'll not wish to ride back to Stony Stratford tonight."

"That's very kind of you, Gloucester," Antony said.

Nell noticed Richard's three hundred gentleman soldiers setting camp. Their paltry numbers added to her relief.

"I'll be a while yet getting my men settled," said Richard. "Why don't you ride ahead and see about your lodgings."

Rivers and Nell turned their horses. "At the inn, then," Rivers said.

Gloucester waved. "We'll dine."

A T A CORNER TABLE of the crowded Northampton Inn, Nell, Rivers, and Gloucester had been drinking wine together for what seemed like hours, and the food had not yet come. Upward of a hundred of Gloucester's northern gentlemen were packed cheek by jowl in the noisy common room, tired from the long day's ride, and drinking copiously as they too waited for their supper.

The inn's owner, rotund and pig-faced, had donned his Sunday best for the greatest occasion he and his establishment would ever host. Every quarter hour "the new king's two uncles" had been subject to his good-natured groveling. He would approach the table and, smiling a black-toothed smile, recount with delight, and far too many details, why the meal was so long in coming, making promises that the victuals, specially prepared for his honored guests, would be well worth the wait.

Of course Nell and Rivers gave no hint of the intimate nature of their relationship. Nell was simply the king's most honored tutor—William Caxton's daughter—who had kept Rivers company on the journey back from Stony Stratford to Northampton. If Richard suspected their liaison, he gave no hint of it. And Nell, who, hours before, had felt a foolish girl in love, had reverted to a cooler head, her observant faculties brought sharply to the fore.

She found herself harboring suspicions about Gloucester. His cordiality and good humor seemed odd, considering the humiliation he had received at Rivers's hand on the jousting field at Ludlow not two months before. There was the brusque tone of his recent communiqués to Rivers, and what would have been an unpleasant surprise—that without his knowledge, plans had shifted, leaving the king's party fourteen miles closer to London than he and his small army were. Nell could swear she detected a note of shrillness in Richard's laughter, one too many shifts of his eyes toward the inn door. She could not shake the feeling that something was amiss.

Maddeningly, Antony seemed blissfully unaware, and there was no way to communicate her worries to him. Perhaps, thought Nell, she was giving Rivers too little credit. Perhaps he too suspected Richard's geniality. But her lover had drunk several cups of wine too many and was verging on tipsiness.

Dinner had finally arrived—large steaming portions of roasted meat and crusty kidney pies. The hubbub in the common room rose to a deafening crescendo as hungry gentlemen fell on their food. Nell, Rivers, and Gloucester dug in at once and didn't notice Harry Buckingham enter until he was looming over their table.

"Good evening!" he boomed above the din. The trio looked up to see the large, handsome nobleman who, to Nell's eye, exuded an almost excessive vitality. She glanced at Richard, who stood to clasp Buckingham's hand. She watched Gloucester's face and saw him smile at Buckingham, a smile that Nell perceived to be both relieved and conspiratorial. Indeed, Buckingham's presence here was curious, and that Gloucester had clearly been expecting him—all those glances toward the door—was worrying.

But Buckingham greeted Nell with respect, and congratulated Rivers on his beloved nephew's accession. To Nell's relief, Antony had quickly sobered with Buckingham's appearance. Without invitation, the man squeezed in with them at the table, declaring his exhaustion from the long ride in from Wales. Then, spearing a chunk of roast on his knife, he chewed it voraciously. He washed it down with a long quaff of wine and sat back with an air of complete satisfaction.

Gloucester called for another round of drinks and Harry began regaling the party with entertaining stories of his adventures on the road. Nell marveled at the man, and it even occurred to her that there was something magical about Harry Buckingham's presence. Here was a man who, not two months before in Ludlow's courtyard, had been publicly challenged by Lord Rivers, yet here he was laughing and joking with him, clapping him heartily on the back as a friend does a friend.

Gloucester and Buckingham had got Antony talking about his most famous pilgrimage, the one distinguished not by acts of extreme piety, but by his party's violent assault by highwaymen outside Rome. Rivers seemed relaxed in the men's presence, and Nell prayed that despite his levity, he was watching his companions' behavior with a cool and dispassionate eye.

Perhaps, Nell thought, Buckingham was simply thick-skinned. Perhaps that conspiratorial look she believed she'd seen pass between Gloucester and Buckingham had been imagined. *Am I just an overly suspicious and ridiculous girl, dreaming up trouble where there is none to be found?* she wondered.

By midnight all the food was eaten and everyone was desperately road-weary. The common room was nearly empty, all the gentlemen having gone up to their beds. Good nights were exchanged with promises to meet before dawn for the ride down to Stony Stratford, where they'd join with the king and his army for the final ride into London.

The inn's owner insisted on personally showing Nell and Lord Rivers up to their accommodations—climbing a central staircase to the second floor, then to opposite ends of the sprawling establishment, dropping Rivers at "the Dormer Room." The innkeeper beckoned Nell to follow him, making it impossible for her and Rivers to say a proper good night to each other. With a longing smile she followed the waddling man down the long hall to "the Rose Room," a tiny but surprisingly clean single-bedded place under the eaves, with a single window opening onto the inn's yard.

Once the innkeeper had shut the door behind him, announcing his intention to show the others to their rooms, Nell collapsed on the bed. The mattress was lumpy and, under the coverlet, was likely crawling with unmentionable vermin. She was considering sleeping atop the blankets when she heard two familiar voices wafting in from outside. She was forced to climb to the corner of her bed to put her ear to the window, where now the sounds from the courtyard below had become very clear.

It was Gloucester and Buckingham speaking quietly, unaware that their voices were being funneled and magnified into Nell's hearing.

"Some decisions need to be made, and they must be made quickly," said Harry.

"Go on," said Richard.

"Rivers must be taken down at once."

"Taken down?" Gloucester sounded mystified.

"Arrested," said Buckingham. Clearly Gloucester was hesitant. "Arrest him, Richard. For treason."

Nell felt as though the breath had been knocked out of her. But she pushed closer still to the window, not daring to miss a word.

"Disperse all the troops he's brought with him from the Welsh Marches." Buckingham's voice was pure vitriol. "Send a strong message to our sister-in-law the queen."

Gloucester spoke then. "All Rivers's troops are in Stony Stratford. He came back to Northampton with only a small guard."

"They've been seen to," said Buckingham. "Even now my men—I brought three hundred Welshmen—are surrounding the inn. There's no escape for Rivers."

Desperation surged like a great wave over Nell. She wished to rush immediately to Antony's room to warn him, yet she could not afford to miss a syllable of this conversation.

"You look surprised, cousin," said Harry Buckingham. "I wrote and told you I was your man. Completely and utterly at the protector's command. I am here to serve you. See that your brother's will is carried out, and that England can rest easy during Edward's minority."

*The "protector's" command? Nell's mind raced. What was Harry Buckingham saying? Queen Elizabeth was the king's protector, just as she had been during Warwick's rebellion when Edward the Fourth had been exiled on the continent. Now Buckingham was calling Richard of Gloucester protector! Something was horribly, horribly wrong.*

Nell flew out her door and raced down the long hallway toward Antony's room.

It was too late.

A small company of soldiers wearing Harry Buckingham's distinctive red livery had reached the top of the central stair and was heading straight for Rivers's door. There was nothing she could do. She stood helplessly as they pounded on it and shouted for him to come out lest the door be broken down. Yorkshire gentlemen in their nightclothes emerged from their rooms to investigate the ruckus, crowding the hall and making it nigh on impossible for Nell to see Antony as he emerged from behind his door.

The first glimpse she got of him was as he was being marched down the staircase. Their eyes locked briefly, and he had only time to mouth "I love you" before he was gone.

Nell followed the red-uniformed soldiers down the stairs, but they had already hustled Rivers out of the inn's front door.

In the empty common room she found Gloucester and Buckingham. They were not yet aware of her presence.

"Tomorrow we'll ride to Stony Stratford with our six hundred men," said Buckingham. "Arrive at dawn."

Richard seemed more confident now. A man ready to take charge. "We shall take possession of the king's person. Set him properly on the throne."

Nell saw Buckingham smile a slow smile. "You'll assume the protectorship, Richard, rightfully yours. A new day is dawning in England, and a York son is rising in glory."

"My lords." Nell had managed to find her voice. The men turned to see her standing there.

"Mistress Caxton," Richard began. "I'm very sorry for the disturbance. Lord Buckingham and I have been forced to right a terrible wrong."

"Why has Lord Rivers been arrested?" she asked, trying to keep a steady tone.

"He and his sister, and the other members of the Woodville family—in particular her son, Lord Grey, have attempted to usurp the protectorship," Richard explained.

"But the queen *is* England's protector," Nell argued.

"She was, Mistress Caxton, until her husband added a deathbed codicil naming *me* to that title," said Richard. "The queen knew this, but failed to inform me. Indeed, she failed even to inform me of my brother's death."

This was stunning news. Nell's face must have reflected her dismay.

"Do not worry yourself about it, Mistress Caxton," Buckingham said in a decidedly condescending tone. "Everything is well under control." Dismissing Nell, he turned to Richard. "Come, we've much business to attend to." Buckingham threw an arm round Gloucester's shoulders and began walking him away.

But Richard turned back and spoke to Nell in a kindly tone. "Do try to get some sleep. We ride for Stony Stratford before dawn. I'm sure the king will be in sore need of your friendship."

"Yes, my lord." As the two men left the common room, Nell could not be sure if she had uttered the words or only thought them, for her body and mind seemed altogether paralyzed. In the space of a few moments, her heaven on earth had collapsed entirely. The man who was her future had been taken from her, accused of treason. The king—the means by which

Antony might be released from his marriage—was now under the control of *whom*? Richard of Gloucester? Harry Buckingham?

What must the queen be thinking? How would poor Edward respond to the news of his dearest friend's arrest? And where was Bessie? What on earth was her friend going through at this moment?

With leaden feet, Nell climbed the central stairs and returned to the Rose Room. She sat on the bed, her back straight, her hands folded in her lap. *I must pull myself together,* she thought. *Use logic and deduction and reasoning. I must find a way to help Antony. Stay strong for Edward. Be very, very brave.*

But all Nell could do was weep.


THERE HAD, IN THE END, been no possibility of sleeping, so when Nell deemed it a proper hour—it was still dark—she gathered the few things she'd brought with her to Northampton Inn and tiptoed down the central staircase. A few of the northern gentlemen had begun stirring. Most were still in their beds, catching a few final moments of needed rest.

Nell was beyond exhaustion. Trying desperately to think straight so as not to further worsen the situation, she had finally decided that she must attempt to see Antony again. She must find where Lord Rivers was being held, all the time praying that he had not yet been sent away.

Outside the inn's front door she spotted two of Buckingham's soldiers. Certainly they were meant to be standing guard at the lamplit door, but they had clearly just woken and were still rubbing sleep from their eyes, downing the day's first rations of beer and biscuit. She approached the soldiers with forced cheerfulness.

"Morning, lads," she said, "or is it even morning yet?" Nell flashed them a pretty smile.

"Not the way I feel," the taller one grumbled.

"It durn't matter how much sleep Walker gets," the shorter, pudgy guard offered. " 'Tis never enough."

"Do you know when we'll be setting out for Stony Stratford?" Nell asked.

"Soon, by my reckoning," the tall guard answered. "My Lord Buckingham plans to join up with the king before dawn. And 'tis fourteen miles' ride."

"I'd say they're striking camp as we speak," Pudgy added.

"Where is it you've camped your army?" Nell asked.

"With Lord Gloucester's men, in the meadow north of town," said the tall guard.

Without taking her eyes from the red-liveried soldiers, Nell slowly withdrew a tiny pouch from her bodice. Their eyes, however, were drawn unself-consciously down to the soft round tops of her breasts and lingered there as she took two small gold coins from the pouch. Only when they saw metal glittering in lantern light was their attention drawn away from her flesh.

"The king's uncle Lord Rivers was taken into custody last evening by your company," Nell whispered in a husky voice. "Do you know the gentleman's whereabouts?"

The soldiers were suddenly alert to the bribe and the danger.

The pudgy guard was also alert to the opportunity. "We might know his whereabouts, miss."

Nell observed the taller soldier's eyes darting, his breathing grow shallow as he prayed his cohort would strike a profitable bargain. She slowly, seductively, plucked two more coins out of the purse.

"They put 'im in the bakehouse," the tall soldier blurted out.

Pudgy gave him the evil eye, having hoped to do some further dealing. But Nell was massaging the purse in her palm, and the man's eyes grew hopeful again.

"If I wished to speak to the gentleman unnoticed . . ."

"I saw a window round the back. No guards there," Pudgy offered, having decided this was the limit of the young lady's needs and the extent of her purse.

Nell placed three coins in each soldier's hand and said, "You've done a good deed, lads. I thank you."

"Thank *you,* ma'am," said Pudgy.

"Approach from the south," the tall one said. "And keep your voices low. Very low."

With a smile, Nell left the guards and picked her way round the back of the inn. The bakehouse wasn't far, but she was forced to move behind a copse of trees to its south in order to approach without being spotted by the pair of soldiers standing sentry at the bakehouse door. In the moonlight she was able to see the window in the back, and with all the stealth her rustling gown and the sucking mud under her slippers would allow, she crossed to the small stone building.

The window had been left slightly ajar, and Rivers's jailors had thankfully left their captive a single candle burning. She could not see him anywhere amidst the floury worktables and sacks of grain, nor near the round-topped oven.

"Antony," she whispered in the lowest of tones.

He popped up so suddenly at the window, she gasped.

"Shh!" he warned.

"You startled me."

"I was sitting on the floor just under the window. Oh, Nell—"

"My love, have they told you anything?"

"Not a word since my arrest. Neither Gloucester nor Buckingham has been to see me."

"Antony . . ." Nell hesitated, finding the words hard to say. "You have been deceived by your sister. She wrote to tell you of the king's death and instructed us to come quickly to London with Edward, but she failed to mention that on his deathbed, your brother-in-law named Gloucester as protector."

"What?"

"She also failed to mention the fact to Gloucester. Or even news that the king had died."

"Oh, sweet Jesus!"

Distress marred Rivers's features. "Gloucester must have assumed that I knew. Assumed that I was conspiring with her."

"I'll tell him the truth!"

"No, Nell. You mustn't involve yourself. Firstly, they will never believe you. And if they know we are close"—Nell could see Rivers was thinking on his feet—"not only will you be in danger, but young Edward—"

"He is the king," Nell argued. "They wouldn't—"

"We have no idea of their intentions. We have no clue what other mischief my sister the queen is up to. That she deceived Gloucester in this way, that she has betrayed me . . . I fear that Elizabeth, in her desperation, is capable of anything."

"What should I do, Antony?"

He put his hand through the window. She grasped it with her own.

"You did well coming here to see me. 'Twas very brave. But you must be braver still. Pretend we are both simply servants in the household of the king. Pleasant friends. Show only dismay that someone close to the king has come under suspicion of treason. Say *nothing* in my support."

"But—"

"Not a word. When they take me away—"

"Oh Antony, no!"

"—you ride south with Gloucester and Buckingham. Stay very close to Edward. You'll be the only trusted friend he has."

"I shall contact Bessie the moment I reach London."

He was thinking hard. "Do that. Bessie is a clever girl. Learn as much as you can from her of the goings-on at the palace. You must write me what you know, through letters from Edward to me. Surely the king will be allowed to correspond with me, but you cannot be known to be writing me yourself."

"What if they open Edward's letters to you?"

Rivers was silent for a long moment. Suddenly the candle flickered out and Nell could no longer see his face.

"You must devise a code."

"A code. But, Antony, both sender and receiver must understand the code."

"Just devise one, Nell, and I will decipher it."

They heard rustling at the bakehouse door.

"You must go," he whispered urgently.

"I don't want to leave you."

"Nell—"

"Please tell me all will be well."

He squeezed her hand and pain was palpable in his voice. "I cannot promise you that. I fear we have fallen on very evil times. But know that I love you, Nell. That had circumstances allowed, you would have been my wife."

"In my heart, I *am* your wife."

The bakehouse door was being unlocked.

"Tell your father that I love him."

"I will." Tears were coursing down her cheeks.

"Thank him for bringing his press to England. And thank him for giving me you. Now go!"

He snatched his hand back quickly, and as the door creaked open, Nell withdrew behind the wall. She heard the soldiers enter and roughly manhandle Antony out of the bakehouse. The sound of clanking manacles and chains on his feet broke her heart, and she wondered miserably how so high and proud a man could have, in so short a space of time, been brought so low,

When she found the way was clear, she stepped out into the yard and into plain sight, as though nothing on earth were amiss, and made for the stables to find her horse.

THE RIDE SOUTH in the gloomy hours before dawn to Stony Stratford was as soul-sickening as the same stretch of road the day before had been magical and filled with light. Nell rode just behind Gloucester and Buckingham. Behind her were their two armies of three hundred each, in one long column. Whilst Nell could hear but occasional snatches of conversation between the two noblemen, she observed them closely, the way Harry Buckingham leaned deferentially toward Richard. How after a long speech in rousing tones by his cousin, Gloucester would sit taller in his saddle, as though Buckingham was buoying him up with potent words of encouragement. There was even laughter between them, which Nell particularly resented. How dare they laugh when, even now, Antony, in chains like a common criminal, was being transported to the far north of Yorkshire?

They arrived at the Stony Stratford Inn just at dawn as the king, his army and entourage were saddling up for the march into London. The cavalry and foot soldiers were making ready for departure, and in the field beyond, the chariots and coaches, now decorated with fluttering silk banners, were being placed in order of the final procession.

Nell spotted Edward and his groom waiting to give him a leg up onto his horse. She watched as the young king waved the man away. Nell imagined that Edward wanted no help into the saddle on the day he would ride triumphantly in through Londongate, letting his people—*his subjects*—see their sovereign for the first time. See that he was only thirteen, but man enough to take to his horse himself. She watched as Edward flung himself up to sit tall on his favorite chestnut mare and gaze out at the salmon sky, the sun just peeking over the eastern horizon.

His head snapped round as shouts heralded coming riders. As they neared, Nell could see Edward spotting her, then trying to catch sight of his uncle Rivers. Instead, it was his uncle Richard and Harry Buckingham, leading a small army, some of them in Buckingham's livery.

Gloucester and Buckingham approached the king, allowing Nell to follow. They came off their horses and at once fell to their knees before Edward.

"Your most Gracious Majesty," the Duke of Gloucester intoned reverentially. "I place myself humbly and completely at your service."

Buckingham repeated the pledge, adding, "And most grievous condolences on the death of your father."

"Thank you, my lords. I . . . I accept you into my service." He looked to Nell, who, try as she might, could not suppress her alarm and misery. Edward attempted and failed to keep the tremulousness out of his voice. "My Lord Gloucester . . . Do you know the whereabouts of my uncle Rivers?"

Gloucester rose, then said softly, "I think we must talk, Edward. May I help you down from your horse?"

"I can do it myself." Edward had gone very pale.

"Let us go back to the inn," said Gloucester. "We can talk more comfortably there."

They were walking side by side now—King Edward the Fifth and his uncle Richard. Buckingham came just after, and Nell trailed along behind him. As they made their way through the army that had escorted him here, Gloucester could not have been more outwardly deferential, directing all the men whom they passed to drop to their knees in reverence to the new king, but the boy's world was collapsing all round him, and Nell could see that he knew it.

Once inside, the two dukes bade Edward sit, and he did, without argument, take a chair. Though Harry Buckingham pretended the same deference as Richard, it was easy to see a cold anger emanating from the man, a gritting of the teeth behind the false smile. The boy locked eyes with Nell, who tried desperately to remain strong and steady.

"I'm sorry to say," Gloucester began, "that your uncle Rivers has been placed in our custody."

"*Why,* my lord?"

"Obstructing the will of your father, the late king," Richard replied.

"But he is my *governor.* My friend. I trust him with my life! And my mother the queen is even now making plans for my coronation."

"Your mother"—Buckingham fairly spat the word, confirming Nell's worst suspicions of him—"has no rightful authority in this. The ruling of the land is reserved for men, not women."

Nell bristled, deciding in that moment that she loathed Harry Buckingham—a low cur, and treacherous in the extreme.

"You see, Edward," said Gloucester more gently, "your father added a codicil to his will on his deathbed, and in that codicil he named me, and not your mother, as your sole protector."

"*You,* the protector? But my father always entrusted my mother and her family with my care. She was once made regent in his absence."

"That is true. But think on this. For whatever his reasons, the protectorship was placed in my hands before your father's death, yet your mother did not, nor did Lord Rivers, inform you of my protectorship. Worse still, the queen never even informed me of the king's passing. This must be considered a conspiracy." Richard paused to gather his thoughts. "Your Majesty, you are very wise for your age, and you are my sworn sovereign, so I will attempt to explain the changes in circumstance."

Edward's face had set into a hard and very cold expression.

"There are two factions at court," Richard began. "First, those noblemen and clerics who support your mother and the Woodville family, of which she is the undisputed matriarch. They are content to allow the queen to rule your fate till your majority—"

"Queen *dowager,*" Buckingham dared to correct him.

"Indeed, now that her husband is dead, your mother is no longer Queen of England, but queen dowager. In any event, a second faction, of which your father's dearest friend in life, Lord Hastings, is the leader, is determined—like myself and Lord Buckingham—that your father's will be carried out to the letter. It was Hastings who had the sense to send a message to me at York about my brother's passing. This faction understands your father's intent in his deathbed codicil—that only one man in the kingdom has the proven strength to govern England until your maturity. Only one man in whom he could place his entire trust. One man of the York blood. That man is I, Edward. I say with pride and certitude that I was, and remain, your father's most devoted servant." Richard's face contorted with anger. "Your mother and her family began plotting against him the moment he drew his last breath."

"Or before," Buckingham added. "And we've reason to believe that an attempt will be made by them on the Duke of Gloucester's life."

"In any event," Richard continued evenly, "they attempted to seize control for themselves, and deny the king's will." He paused and held Edward's eyes. "Where do *you* stand, Your Majesty? For or against your father's wishes?"

Nell saw Edward rub his forehead. She wished she could go to him. Comfort him. Give him counsel. But she knew if she uttered a single syllable she would be ejected from the room.

"Of course I will obey my father's will and wishes," Edward managed to utter.

"Then 'tis decided," said Richard quickly.

"But what of my Lord Rivers?" Edward demanded.

"He defied the king's will," said Buckingham sharply, "and that is why he has been arrested for treason."

"Treason!" Edward cried. "Treason . . . no, Uncle, please . . ." He implored Gloucester now.

"It had to be done, Edward."

"But I am the king and I command you to release him!"

"Do calm yourself, nephew," said Gloucester.

"Where is he? Where is my uncle Rivers!"

"He's been taken to Yorkshire and will be held there until your council is chosen and a determination can be made as to his punishment. Your mother's son, Lord Grey, also a conspirator, has been taken into custody as well. I must also inform you that the army that accompanied you from Wales is, even now, being disbanded and sent home."

"I want to send word to my mother," Edward said with all the authority he could muster.

"Of course. Buckingham," said Richard in a calm aside to his accomplice, "will you have writing materials brought to His Majesty?"

Buckingham bowed deeply and backed away.

"Mistress Caxton," said Richard in the politest of tones. "Would you leave us? I need to have a word in private with the king."

Nell's mind raced, trying to find a word to say, a plea to stay with Edward, but she knew it futile. With a curtsy to the boy and a look that spoke of her commiseration, she turned and left the room.

*How has it come to this?* she thought to herself. *And what in God's name will happen now?*

# BESSIE

Princess Bessie could hardly believe her eyes. Stone dust was flying as workmen with massive sledgehammers pounded away at a common wall connecting Westminster Castle and the sanctuary tower of Westminster Abbey. Piled up nearby were all the goods of the queen's household—boxes and crates of clothing, plates, hangings, and even furniture. Arriving from the Tower of London every few minutes were cartloads of treasures—jewels, caskets of gold and silver coin.

There was panic in the air. Two of Bessie's youngest sisters, toddlers Katherine and Bridget—were standing by, crying, Dickon attempting to comfort them, though he himself appeared disoriented by the scene of confusion. Stewards and maids, cooks and laundresses carrying the tools of their trades, were making even more piles to either side of the workmen. Though it seemed impossible, they were all waiting for a hole to be knocked through the sanctuary wall.

*Sanctuary,* thought Bessie. *The royal family is being forced to take sanctuary in Westminster Abbey!*

With a great cry, one of the brawny wall-bashers broke through, and soon stones were being pulled and knocked away, the hole widened enough that the goods could be carried through.

"Quickly!" The palace steward clapped his hands twice. The

treasure went in first, then the gold plate. Bessie saw four men struggling with the enormous canopy of the eleven-foot-square Bed of State. She waited for a break in the parade of servants carrying goods. Then gathering up her brother and sisters, she bustled them through the opening.

There awaited an even more alarming sight. Her mother, the once-proud Queen Elizabeth Woodville, now sat upon the rushes on the floors, a desolate and dismayed expression distorting her still-beautiful face.

Bessie went to her quickly, worried that the pathetic sight would further frighten her brother and sisters. "Mother, come, get up. Let me find you some cushions." But Elizabeth shook her head and, with glazed eyes, stubbornly refused to budge. The pale, brown-robed friars of the abbey were now coming to peek into the sanctuary, where their new guests were setting up household.

The panic had begun the day that Bessie had taken Dickon with her to the Totehill Street market. When the guards had found her at the almshouse, distributing food and gifts to her pensioner friends, and begged her to come quickly back to the palace, she'd not immediately realized that something was terribly wrong.

Bessie had arrived at her parents' apartments as the physicians were leaving, shaking their heads hopelessly and murmuring amongst themselves.

"What's happened?" she'd demanded of Dr. Argentine, the physician she knew best, called most often for the royal children. He had always been a font of information, which he proffered with great good humor. That day his expression had been pained. He'd grasped Bessie's arm.

" 'Tis the king. He is not long for the world. You should be with your mother now."

"What! Dr. Argentine, what has happened?"

With a look of sadness and dread, Dr. Argentine clamped shut his mouth and turned away, following his cohorts out the apartment doors.

In the royal bedchamber's anteroom Bessie had found her mother, not as she might have expected—prostrate and weeping quietly—but upright and in constant motion, dictating to a scribe and giving orders to the stream of servants and messengers flowing in and out of the room.

"Mother—"

The queen looked up, saw her daughter, and, barely acknowledging her, went back to the scribe to whom she was dictating. Bessie had not been deterred. She moved closer.

"Gather as many troops from Ludlow as you can find," she'd heard her mother say to the scribe. "Four to five thousand minimum, and hie to London promptly with my son."

"Mother, you must answer me!" Bessie had cried. "What's happened to Father?"

The queen's face when she addressed her daughter was hard and angry. "The king caught a chill whilst fishing. They've brought him home. Put him to bed. There's nothing more that can be done for him. He's in there dying." Elizabeth thrust her chin at the bechamber door.

"But—"

"He brought his council together round his bed not an hour ago, and amended his will." Elizabeth Woodville tried hard to remain calm. "Whereas I had previously been named your brother's protector until his majority, the new codicil names as Edward's sole protector . . . your uncle Richard."

Bessie had been confused. "Why did Father do such a thing?"

The queen's fury had grown. "How should I know! What I *do* know is that his decision cannot be allowed to stand."

"I want to see my father!" Bessie had cried, tears stinging her eyes. "Mother, you must let me—"

"Listen to me, Bessie. Your father has not even called *me* to his bedside. His council has been called. His 'friend' "—she spat the word—"Lord Hastings is in there now. But he's not called to see his wife." Tears had threatened in the queen's eyes, but she refused to let them fall. "Go to your sisters and brother and comfort them as best you can."

"Mother—"

"Just go. I'm busy here. Can't you see!" The queen had turned back to the scribe. "Are you finished?"

"Almost, Majesty," he mumbled, head still down over the parchment.

"Wait. I wish to amend what you've written. Just say to bring 'as great an army of loyal men as you can gather.' Change that. Be quick about it, and send the letter to Lord Rivers by our fastest courier." She beckoned to a servant just entering. "Tell my son Lord Grey to attend me, and Bishop Morton as well."

Head spinning, Bessie had stumbled from the royal chamber. Her dear father lay dying within, and she was barred from seeing him. *How can this be happening?* she'd wondered. A chill on a fishing trip! It was not possible. *And why had Father so disrespected her mother?*

Her brother Edward would, at the moment her father drew his last breath, become King of England. Soon he'd be in London. And Nell. She'd be returning too. Once again Bessie had been racked and torn by opposing emotions—the crushing pain of her father's imminent loss, and joy at the return of two people so near and dear to her heart.

Later that day her father, a mighty and beloved king, had passed away. His body had been stripped and washed and anointed with holy oil. Then, naked but for a cloth covering his lower parts, he had been laid on a bier in Westminster Abbey for all to see he was indeed dead, and to prove he had died of no violent causes.

In the days following, Bessie had kept her eyes and ears open, just as she knew Nell would have wanted her to. Indeed, she began writing everything down, every detail, every smattering of gossip, every overheard conversation, though she knew there would be no way to communicate with Nell until her return to London.

She learned through the abbot—virtually their only visitor in sanctuary—that Uncle Richard had seized control of the king, claiming himself sole protector. Her mother's brother Edward Woodville—surely on the queen's orders—had quietly made off with much of England's treasury and all the ships in the Royal Navy—a circumstance that seemed, even in Bessie's political naïveté, a desperate act, and one of which her father would not have approved. Her stepbrother, Lord Grey, had been taken into custody, but most disturbing was news that her uncle Rivers had been arrested by Gloucester and sent to a prison in Yorkshire. Poor Nell must be frantic.

Her uncle Richard, thought Bessie, was acting like a man possessed either by the devil or by the certainty of his rightness. She was fraught with terrible images, uncertainties. All the worst that could happen. And all at the hands of the man she loved. Bessie was sick with the thought that her mother, so often ruthless and self-serving, had somehow done wrong during the transfer of power after her father had died. Now this scene from hell—the frantic rescuing of the family fortune, the sheltering in sanctuary, and her mother sitting disoriented in the rushes—was confirmation that her fears were justified.

And what of Edward? What must he be feeling, now in the charge of a relative he already blamed for the death of his beloved uncle Clarence? His stepbrother, Lord Grey, was arrested, but worse, his adored uncle Rivers was en route to a northern prison, charged with treason. Here Edward was, the king, and perhaps the most unhappy child in all of England.

She needed desperately to talk to Nell. That steely mind of hers would be clearer than her own. If only they could meet. Somehow they would devise a plan. Make things right again. Bessie was a *queen,* Nell had told her—or at least one day would be a queen—the player with the greatest reach and power on the game board. She must stop acting like a mere pawn and begin asserting her will. Otherwise, thought Bessie, she deserved to be tossed and battered by the Fates.

She gazed with loathing at her mother, sitting glaze-eyed amongst the rushes, and saw the soul price Elizabeth Woodville paid for her evil ways. In that moment, Bessie swore to herself that whilst she would steer her own course and destiny in life, she would harm no one and strive always to retain her dignity.

Now if she could only find a way to meet Nell.

# NELL

THE BLAST OF TRUMPETS was deafening, so deafening, Nell realized, that the drums and shouts of men and women, thick upon London's walls just ahead, could not be heard above the din. She thought in that moment of Jericho, the city besieged by Joshua, its walls blown down by loud trumpeting. Today, this city's vanquisher was England's protector. He was Richard of Gloucester, riding in the somber black of mourning at the right hand of King Edward the Fifth, the boy clothed in royal-blue velvet as he prepared to enter the capital, to the great joy of his subjects. To Edward's left rode Harry Buckingham, also in black, but somehow managing by the haughtiness of his posture and expression to appear more proud and resplendent than either king or protector. Behind them were members of the Ludlow Court, of which Nell rode as one, and six hundred gentlemen of Yorkshire and Wales.

*What a vainglorious man Harry Buckingham is,* Nell thought as she trotted along behind him. Since that terrible night at Northampton Inn, he had clung to Richard's side like a barnacle to a boat's hull, whispering in his ear, urging him to ideas and decisions that he allowed Richard to believe had been his own. Buckingham had also begun flaunting his much-despised marriage to the queen's sister Catherine Woodville. Before, it had been a curse. Now it allowed Buckingham to call himself "the king's uncle."

Nell clearly saw a great gaping wound in Richard's heart at the loss of his brother, and a sincere deference to his nephew. It was also clear that Gloucester honestly believed that, by his actions, he was honoring the dead king's will. With Buckingham, these were altogether false sentiments—a devious man acting sad, humble, and indignant, somehow managing to be believed. So whilst Nell inwardly raged against Gloucester's imprisoning of Antony, she knew—for she had heard it with her own ears— that *Buckingham* had been the instigator.

Nell watched as the great London gates swung open and a fabulous procession came out to see them through. It was the mayor and the alderman, followed by London's most prominent citizens. They, and their horses too, were dressed and caparisoned in matching fur-trimmed scarlet satin.

When the royal procession had passed through Londongate, the crowded city streets within exploded with cheers and cries of "God save the king!" and "Good King Edward, long may ye live!" As they approached Westminster, Nell felt her heart beating faster, for the thought of seeing her dear friend Bessie, surely on the palace wall, there with her family to wave as her brother passed, had been her greatest anticipation, greater even, she thought guiltily, than the sight of her father.

But as the cavalcade reached Westminster's wall, she could see many noblemen and women standing atop it, cheering and crying out, but Princess Bessie was not amongst them. Nor, in fact, was any member of the royal family—not the queen, nor Dickon, nor the princesses, nor any of the Woodville relations.

The situation, bad as it had seemed, Nell realized, was far more grievous than she ever could have imagined.

"Nell, Nell!" The sound of her name being called roused her

from her grim torpor. She turned to see Jan de Worde waving madly at her from the roadside. There beside him, a sight so welcome it brought instant tears to her eyes, was her father. The expression on William Caxton's face was indescribably complex. It spoke of his great relief at her return. It confirmed Nell's most dire fears of the present circumstances, and promised her a loving haven from which to weather what would surely be the catastrophic storm to come.

I T WAS TO THE TOWER of London that Edward was taken—"for his protection," his uncle Richard proclaimed—before the boy's coronation. Nell Caxton, begging no one's permission and barred by no one's decree, accompanied him there. Openly she was the king's Latin tutor, but in a silent agreement between the two of them, she stayed as his nearest friend in the sad absence of their mutually beloved Rivers.

True to Edward's word, the Tower was a luxurious royal home, much more than Ludlow—a mere provincial castle— had been. Ancient and foreboding though the outer bastions and the White Tower in the center of the yard were, the royal residences, as well as the chapels, and the immense great hall where all meals were taken, had been renovated by England's two previous kings. The place was therefore filled with carvings on every pillar, with tall expanses of stained glass in chambers and chapels, and sumptuous wall hangings. The ceilings glittered with golden stars, painted lions of red and green, and flowers of every hue and description.

The inner wards of the walled fortress were bustling and festive, more so now that the official court had been moved from Westminster. That palace was now a somber and lifeless place, what with the remains of the royal family hidden away in the abbey's sanctuary. On Tower Green were dozens of tents and awnings, stables and wooden stalls, with fishmongers, pie makers, mercers, and millers hoping to obtain large orders from the palace steward.

Scurrying importantly from round the Tower grounds were all manner of household functionaries, all under the supreme command of the Constable of England—and therefore the Tower— namely Harry Buckingham. Below him was the chamberlain, Lord Hastings. There were Knights and Squires of the Body who saw to the personal needs of the king, some sleeping on pallets in his room and helping him dress and undress. There were Yeomen of the Crown, and Grooms and Pages of the Chamber, and even a special servant who saw to the cleaning up of the messes made by the castle dogs.

The nighttime ritual required two squires at the foot of the bed, and two at the head, a man to carry in the bedclothes, and one to hold back the curtains. But before Edward was allowed to climb in, the sheets, cotton blanket, and ermine counterpane were laid out and smoothed *just so,* the pillows beaten, and holy water sprinkled on the final product.

When the king dined, each dish was presented with high ceremony. Always in attendance at meals was a servant with towel and basin, a "Doctor of Physique" who stood behind the boy advising him what and what *not* to eat, thirteen minstrels to play throughout the meal, and a jester to make Edward laugh so his food would properly digest.

Despite the attention paid him, Edward had remained so gloomy since his arrival that every day Nell would coax him out of his quarters to visit the dairy or pigeon loft, the bakery or forge. She'd expected him to enjoy the menagerie more than he did, but he claimed that seeing the great cats and bears and long-legged ostriches caged reminded him of what he saw—splendid as it was—as his own imprisonment. She tried to have him view his stay here as but temporary. That soon after his coronation he would be returned to Westminster and surely reunited with his family.

But Edward was haunted first and always by the thought of his uncle Rivers alone and imprisoned in Yorkshire. The passing of letters between them was permitted, but whenever Edward asked his uncle Richard about Antony's fate, he was told only that as long as Rivers stayed far from any of the queen dowager's plotting and conspiracies, he was safe.

The ruthlessness of his uncles Gloucester and Buckingham in that affair filled the boy with a dread of them, a mistrust from which he could not be dissuaded. Nell had attempted to draw a distinction between the two men, giving Richard more credit for honesty and good intentions. But there was the fact of Edward's prior loathing of Gloucester in the matter of his uncle Clarence's execution, which had never been resolved. In the king's eyes, Richard was untrustworthy and sinister, and Nell's words fell on deaf ears.

Besides Rivers, the boy missed his family horribly, particularly Bessie and Dickon. Edward's favorite occupation was writing letters to them. Nell and he would sit on opposite sides of his writing table, and these were some of the only happy times they had. They shared the lead inkwell, laughing when they sought it at the same moment, sometimes having silly duels with their quills. And despite the anger at his apparent powerlessness, he took great pleasure in signing his letters "Edward Quintus."

There was much news to write to his family—how Edward's coronation plans were forging ahead, with endless fittings for his robes and Nell's gowns. Knowing how sorely his nine-year-old brother must be suffering in the confines of the grim, windowless Sanctuary Tower, Edward spent particular effort in buoying Dickon's spirits. He related anecdotes about his new court jester, whose after-dinner banter was far more ribald than their mother would have approved of, and promised that after the coronation, they would visit the Tower menagerie as often as Dickon pleased.

Resuming communication with Bessie and her father had felt to Nell like the first rush of spring. In the past dark days she'd forgotten how airy and optimistic was her friend's spirit. And despite Bessie's severely reduced circumstances, indeed confinement, there was not a mote of anger or cynicism in her letters. Nell's father also knew instinctively to delete any hint of politics or opinion out of his letters to her. They were newsy and filled with gossip from Westminster precinct, the printshop, and Totehill Street. But for both Edward and Nell, there were terrible constraints at all times hindering them. They could never be sure if the letters they sent or received were opened and read by the protector, or his "incubus"—as Edward called Harry Buckingham.

Had the king and his tutor felt they had a freer hand, they would have described to their loved ones the strangeness of the new court, Edward's new council cobbled from both the Gloucester faction and Woodville supporters, and how the loyalties of the two flowed in and about each other like the waters of an estuary—salt and fresh.

They would have observed that not only was Buckingham's influence on the protector vast, and Richard's rewards to his protégé generous—some said overgenerous—but that everyone was aware that Harry Buckingham's spies were everywhere. Nothing happened in the Tower, in London, or anywhere in the realm without his knowledge. Despite his continued deference to Gloucester, many wondered where the true power in England's government lay.

Also present, and prevalent, at the new court were Lord and Lady Stanley. Nell remembered the Duchess of Gloucester's assessment of Lord Stanley with his ambiguous loyalties, and her outright mistrust of Stanley's Lancastrian wife, Lady Margaret Beaufort.

In a position so obviously close to the young king, Nell was treated with extreme deference by Lady Margaret. It made her feel queer to have so highborn and powerful a lady treating her so, and she could not help but believe it false. Yet the woman commanded respect, and Nell was strangely awed and humbled in her presence.

One untoward element in Lady Margaret's orbit was her personal servant, Reginald Bray. Edward had whispered to Nell that the man's long face and large, square teeth reminded him of a donkey, and that his name was all too fitting. From that moment on, Nell was unable to see the man without imagining a braying ass. Beyond that, though she did not mention it to Edward, Nell found Reggie Bray a sinister character. Why, she could not say. Perhaps it was the way he looked at her—rather, *leered* at her. She sensed above all *disapproval,* that one of her sex should have such intimacy with the new king.

Edward's and Nell's joint letters to Lord Rivers were the most difficult of correspondences. Edward was careful to say nothing that would worsen his uncle's plight. Nell struggled to devise a code whereby she could clandestinely intersperse Edward's thoughts with her own sentiments of love and continued devotion. Whilst she was never entirely satisfied with her efforts, she was sure that Antony would comprehend her meaning, no matter how clumsy the attempts. Antony's letters back to Edward—and secretly to Nell—were similarly bland and cryptic. It was not much with which to hold on to their love, but for the moment it was all they could hope for.

A bright note was the late king's friend Lord Hastings. Whilst being "guilty" of having alerted Gloucester to the queen's plotting, he had shown himself to be, first and foremost, loyal to young Edward, making many pleasurable visits to the royal residence, sometimes bringing gifts, but more often coming to chat easily and reminisce about their dearly missed friend and father. Even Nell found Hastings a comfortable companion, and whilst he shared the dead king's reputation for womanizing, he showed her nothing but kindness and respect.

For her part, Nell, also forbidden to leave the Tower confines till after Edward's crowning, found many friends amongst the Tower staff, even meeting some of her Totehill Street friends doing business within the palace walls.

Much could be accomplished, she soon realized, with a few well-placed confidants in the kitchen, in the laundry, or in the gardens. Nell took particular care to learn the names of every gate guard and sentry and, with utter discretion, took Edward to meet them as well. They were delighted and deeply honored to make their young sovereign's acquaintance, and he took great interest in learning something personal about each of his new "subjects."

Therefore, the weeks passed with a combination of pleasure and pain, some small, some great. But the solace that Nell and Edward found in each other's company made everything bearable.

# BESSIE

THE QUEEN DOWAGER, thought Bessie, had much improved since the frantic day of moving from Westminster's palace to the abbey's sanctuary. Her mother was back to her shrewd, icy self, brimming with plots and plans to wrest control back from her unpleasant brother-in-law Gloucester. There was hardly time for the children, who were clearly suffering from their confinement in the dark tower, its few windows mere slits in the thick stone walls. Her four sisters were slightly more content with indoor pastimes than Dickon, for the boy's favorite games were out-of-doors. Bessie, seeing the queen's mind elsewhere occupied, took it upon herself to mother her brother and sisters, engaging the girls in bright conversations as they stitched at a family tapestry. She even allowed Dickon to give her gentle lessons in swordplay so that he would have a sparring partner of sorts.

At first it had been well nigh impossible for the queen to receive news from the Tower of London, where all government business was taking place . . . without her. It rankled that even the queen's men—like her loyal cleric, Bishop Morton—were silent. She was thankful that her eldest brother had made away with the Royal Navy, and enough of the English treasury, to help launch a rebellion against Richard of Gloucester when the time came. But she worried most for her son, Lord Grey, and her brother Antony, who languished still in Richard's northern prisons.

Little King Edward, the queen was sure, was fine.

Bessie had shown her brother's letters to her mother and found herself quietly angry that the queen dowager seemed to worry so little about the boy. He was well enough taken care of, she said whenever Bessie expressed concern. The detested Richard of Gloucester was many things, but he would do no harm to his precious brother's son, she'd insisted.

On a warm evening in June, when the airlessness of the thick-walled Sanctuary Tower had kept Bessie tossing sleepless in her bed, she heard a commotion coming from her mother's tiny chamber—a room adjoining Bessie's own. She crept from her bed and watched as her mother hurriedly threw a wrapper over her nightdress.

Careful not to be seen or heard, the princess, on tiptoe, followed her in the dark, placing herself where she could observe the faces of her mother's visitors flickering in candlelight. Visitors who had arrived clandestinely in the middle of the night.

It was Lord Hastings, with Bishop Morton in tow. Her mother, thought Bessie, would be elated by such high drama and secrecy. Indeed, it was soon apparent that a conspiracy was brewing, though at first the queen was sharp with Hastings, mistrustful. For it was he, prematurely alerting Gloucester to the king's death, and laying bare her overthrow of the protectorate, who had foiled her original plot. Bessie watched with amazement as Hastings fell to his knees before Elizabeth Woodville and begged her forgiveness.

"Majesty," he implored. "You cannot fault me for wishing to adhere to my dearest friend King Edward's will. At his death it seemed as though you were intent upon an opposite course."

"I was, Hastings. And I'm not ashamed to say so."

"Now I can see, madam, that you were right all along."

" 'Tis very clear, Your Majesty," intoned Bishop Morton with the utmost gravity, "that the Duke of Gloucester means to destroy the succession entirely."

"What do you mean?"

"It began with the raising of Harry Buckingham to dizzying heights," Hastings answered. "Titles, land grants, power almost equal to the protector's own. He is not simply Constable of the Tower of London, but Constable of England itself. We have all marveled at the trust Gloucester has placed in this arrogant Welshman, who had, until two months ago, played *no* part in government whatsoever."

"You're jealous, Hastings," said the queen, unable to hide her amusement. "Richard has acted ungratefully to you."

He bristled. "That may be so, but 'tis not what brings us here, madam."

"Tell me," she demanded.

Bishop Morton leaned in to the queen, and Bessie was forced to creep closer into the shadows so that she could hear his voice. "Do you remember a man named Stillington, Your Majesty? He is now the Bishop of Bath and Wells."

"Of course I remember Stillington."

"He has been to see the protector. Gloucester and Buckingham met with him alone," Morton said.

From her place in hiding, Bessie saw her mother clutch the table behind her to steady herself, though Morton and Hastings were unaware.

"We believe that on Gloucester and Buckingham's word, Stillington means to revive the rumors of adultery of our late king's mother, Lady Cecily."

"To what purpose?" the queen demanded, panic rising in her voice.

Bessie could see that her mother was trembling. The queen sought a chair and sat herself down. Something was very wrong.

"Perhaps the same as the Duke of Clarence's when he made the same accusation about his mother eight years ago," said Morton. "To denounce the legitimacy of your children and claim the throne for himself."

Bessie's heart began pounding. She tried to move closer, but feared detection.

"That is nonsensical," Elizabeth rejoined Morton. "If the rumor is true, then my brother-in-law Richard is a bastard too."

"Gloucester is a clever man, Your Majesty," Hastings continued. "The rumor could be 'revised.' Few remember the details. 'Proof' could be provided—"

The queen interrupted him. "How long was Stillington closeted with Gloucester and Buckingham?"

" 'Twas a brief meeting," Hastings replied. "So said the tailor who informed us of it."

"Brief?" said the queen.

"How long does it take to plant a treasonous thought in a man's ear?" said Morton.

Bessie's mother sagged visibly. She was relieved by something that had just been said. That much was clear to her daughter.

Hastings went on, quite oblivious to the change in the queen's posture. "We believe Gloucester and Buckingham will move within days. Disseminate the gossip, furnish their proof. But I have a large army of loyal men at my disposal, madam," said Hastings. "Lord Stanley will stand with us as well."

Bessie was startled to hear that Lord Stanley would so easily betray Gloucester, but remembered Aunt Anne's suspicions of him.

"We have met several times in secret," Hastings continued.

"All it will take is my word, and the protector can be deposed . . . and otherwise 'removed,' backed by my forces. You, madam, will again be in command of your child's fate."

Now the queen was peering at Hastings very closely. "You have no evidence of Gloucester's plot. Just a report from a court tailor of a 'brief ' meeting between Gloucester and a discredited priest."

"But Buckingham——" Hastings began.

"Why should I trust *you,* my Lord Hastings?" she said. "You betrayed me once already. I may loathe my brother-in-law Richard of Gloucester, but I trust his motives toward my dead husband's son more than I trust yours."

"Your Majesty——" Hastings implored.

"No, you listen to me. I watched helplessly for years whilst you encouraged my husband's debauchery. You *shared* women with him. And you hated me, always. Heaven knows what ridicule you heaped upon me, gleeful at my humiliation. He loved you so much. Before his death, the king requested that *you* should be buried beside him. He said nothing of me. You are hoping that in displacing Richard, you will also displace Buckingham. With them gone, a great void at the highest places in government will need filling, and you are hoping that I, controlling my son's destiny, will allow *you* to fill that void."

"Your Majesty," said Morton, interjecting. "You are most correct with regard to Lord Hastings's past behavior, and perhaps even"—he looked at his cohort—"even his future desires. But why else would Stillington——"

"Is my brother-in-law proceeding with the coronation plans?" the queen interrupted.

"Outwardly it appears so, but——"

"Do nothing, then. And pray that the crowning goes on as planned." Her tone changed slightly when she added, "Do watch carefully to see if Stillington returns. If he does, send a message to me at once. And prepare your troops to move. Until then, my lords"—the queen stood, tall and imperious—"a good night to you."

As the men departed, Bessie scurried as quietly as she was able through her mother's chamber back to her own. She waited for the sound of her mother retiring as well, but it never came.

Bessie lay awake the rest of the night whilst Queen Dowager Elizabeth Woodville, her head filled with conspiracies, sat silent and contemplative until well after the sun rose over the June morning.

# NELL

PLEASE, IF YOU WOULD, lift your arm, Majesty."

Nell, looking up from the writing table, saw King Edward sigh deeply and raise his eyes heavenward. The tailor had sworn he was nearly finished with the fitting, but that had been three quarters of an hour ago. She marveled at the boy's patience and good nature through the endless fittings for his coronation raiments. There were close to a dozen robes and tunics and capes, hose, slippers, and caps that would be worn over the space of the weeklong festivities, and despite the upsetting circumstances of his accession, Edward knew that he must appear very grand for his coronation. He had admitted to Nell, though, that he was more eager at the thought of seeing his family again than even at the thought of Saint Edward's crown being set upon his head.

Princess Bessie had written that the royal family too were having their fittings, the queen dowager having agreed that they would all, herself included, come out of Westminster Sanctuary long enough for the occasion. It was incomprehensible that Elizabeth Woodville would not come to see her son crowned king. She believed there was little risk that Gloucester would do violence to her with all of England's nobles watching. After the ceremony, Bessie said, they would hurry back to seclusion, for their future was still uncertain.

Bessie's letters had grown very serious since the family had gone into sanctuary, and Nell sensed that her friend was maturing quickly, her worldliness and sense of politics growing more sophisticated with every passing day. There were some, Bessie wrote, who agreed with her mother that Richard of Gloucester's protectorship should end with Edward's coronation, no matter his age. But any fool could see, Bessie added, that the intent of her father's deathbed codicil could not have been to place his devoted brother in power for a mere month or two.

Nell knew Edward was similarly aware of this circumstance. He wished it wasn't so. He wished to be reunited with his family, with his uncle Rivers. Come back under the authority of his mother. But as he repeated to Nell many times—as though to convince himself of it—he was king now, and could no longer indulge in childish thinking and boyish daydreams. There were serious matters at hand, and whilst he was rarely consulted on such matters now, the manner in which he disported himself in these early days of his reign would nevertheless be remembered in the long history of kings that he had once studied. Now *he* was someone to be studied by future men and monarchs. He wished desperately that he would be remembered for his courage and dignity in the face of adversity.

Just now Nell was writing to Bessie, wondering why there had been a break in her daily letters. She'd not had one for several days and was beginning to worry. The usual courier who delivered letters from Westminster Sanctuary brought the king correspondence from his family, but recently the packets had held none from the princess to Nell. She prayed that Bessie was not ill, but took pains in her missive not to sound alarmed.

"Just the hem, Majesty," Nell heard the tailor say, "and then we are fini—"

Shouts and a loud scuffling outside on Tower Green silenced

the tailor, and with a wondering glance at Nell, with the other two he moved quickly to the window. Nell knew at once what she was seeing, but the horror of it paralyzed her. She felt Edward clutch at her hand. His father's dearest friend, Lord Hastings, was being dragged forcibly through the milling crowd on Tower Green by four guards. Following behind, walking side by side, were Uncle Richard and Harry Buckingham, their expressions black and scowling. A small company of soldiers followed to keep the tradesmen and castle servants from crowding the small procession.

*No!* thought Nell. *This cannot be. There is no good ending to this scene.* Indeed, the guards with their struggling prisoner had stopped at a thick log that lay separate from a pile of such logs, not yet milled for the building of a new bakehouse. The soldiers forced Hastings to his knees before it, and the foremost of the guards turned back to the dukes, who had stopped a dozen yards behind, waiting for the signal. *The signal. They are going to execute Hastings, right on Tower Green!* A sword was drawn, but Gloucester was clearly hesitating. There was still time . . .

Edward began crying, "No, no! Stop, I command you!" He pounded on the glass so forcefully that Nell, fearing he would break it and slash himself, stayed his hand. The tailor, alarmed by the scene, fled. Edward's voice, his royal command, could not be heard outside, since the glass window was fixed closed.

"Nell, what can we do? What can we do!"

She looked round the room in desperation and spied the iron inkwell on their writing desk. Crossing the room she retrieved it and rushed back to the window. She could see Hastings's body, still whole, lying prostrate, his neck stretched across the log. Edward grabbed the heavy inkwell and with a final "Nooo!" smashed it against the glass, shattering it.

The sound of his plaintive cry finally reached his uncle Richard, but the silvery blade was already slicing an arc through the air. Nell saw Gloucester swivel to detect the source of the cry.

It was too late.

Edward's loyal servant, once his father's dearest friend, lay in two parts, his neck spurting an obscene fountain of crimson.

Edward doubled over and was sick, fouling his coronation robes with vomit. Nell crumpled to the floor, stunned by the horror of the scene. But a worse horror was dawning in her head.

The execution of Hastings meant that conspiracies were afoot, or at least suspected. And if any of them could be traced back to Lord Rivers, his life was in peril. Never had she felt so sickened or so utterly helpless. Edward collapsed next to her and, resting his head on her shoulder, began to weep.

Nell wept with him.

# BESSIE

BESSIE'S MOTHER WAS BRISTLING with indignation, but there was, underneath it, all-encompassing fear. News of Lord Hastings's horrific execution for plotting the protector's downfall had unnerved her. Clearly Richard of Gloucester was capable of anything. And now he had come to Westminster Sanctuary demanding an audience.

"What can I do but see him?" she said to Bessie as she checked her image in the looking glass. "If I do not, he will break the sanctity of the church, breach the walls, and come in by force."

But Bessie had heard the other side of her mother's logic. Afraid of the Duke of Gloucester as she was, she trusted him in one important respect. She believed that Richard would do *anything* to place his brother's son on the English throne. And was that not what she herself wanted above all?

Bessie had begged her mother to allow her to be present at the audience, and appraising her eldest daughter quickly and finding the eighteen-year-old as much of an ally as she was likely to find, the queen had agreed.

"Let him come in," announced the queen dowager.

And in he came.

Bessie had not seen her uncle Richard since the games at Ludlow. They had locked eyes momentarily when she'd draped her ribbon over the tip of his lance, and now, as he strode into their chamber, she found the pull of his gaze irresistible. Indeed, he acknowledged her with a nod even before he bowed to the queen dowager. Bessie wondered if he had the merest inkling of her feelings for him.

"Madam," he said to Bessie's mother. "I pray that you and your family are well."

"Well as can be expected in this dreary prison."

"You are here by your own choice. In fact, that is why I have come. To beg you to leave sanctuary and come out into the world."

"I will not," she said, and turned away to calm herself. The queen was trying desperately to bring a semblance of evenness to her features and steady her trembling limbs.

Bessie thought that aside from that terrible night of the move into sanctuary, she had never seen her mother so distraught as she was now.

"I will not force you to come out, Elizabeth," Richard said gently.

The use of her given name seemed a further affront to the queen, and Bessie saw her mother's back stiffen.

"But I must insist that you give me Dickon," Gloucester went on. "His brother is in sore need of a companion. 'Twill be good for them to be together. They can celebrate the upcoming coronation. They can enjoy boyish games. Laugh. Feel a family again."

Elizabeth remained still and silent. Clearly she was relieved not to be held complicit in Hastings's plot. Bessie wondered if her mother was even thinking about Richard's demand to take Dickon.

"Please," said Gloucester. "Let me take the boy."

"I understand you've brought troops with you."

"I have."

"Then you mean to take him with or without my permission."

"What I am told by the lawyers," Richard said, "is that a child who has broken no law has no need to seek sanctuary. Therefore taking him from sanctuary breaks neither the edicts of men nor God."

"Mother," Bessie said, and went to her. She spoke quietly in the queen's ear. "Let Dickon go with your blessings. He will be safe in Uncle Richard's care. You know that."

Elizabeth Woodville was trembling with fury. First Edward taken from her control. Now Dickon. She was to be left with nothing—girls. But what choice did she have?

"I will not wait all day for your answer, madam."

It was the first hint of anger Bessie had heard in Richard's voice.

"Oh, take him!" Elizabeth cried. "Take him and be done with it!" With an angry flourish she swept from the room, leaving Bessie alone with her uncle. She felt suddenly shy.

"Bessie—" Gloucester's voice was gentle now. As gentle as it had been harsh a moment before. "Will you prepare your brother for coming to the Tower?"

"I will, my lord," she said.

He placed his hand on her arm. His look was imploring. "I shall do him no harm."

"I know that, my lord. Tell me, how is Edward?"

Richard looked pained. "He is not ill, but I cannot say he is well. He's not spoken a word to me since Lord Hastings's execution. You must believe me, Bessie, the man was plotting treason against me."

"I know he was," she said quietly, unable to meet his eye.

"How brave you are to be so honest. I'm very grateful." Bessie forced herself to look at her uncle.

"Your friend Nell Caxton is a great comfort to the king."

"Thank you for saying so."

"And I promise you this," he said. "Dickon's company will greatly improve your brother's spirits."

This made Bessie smile.

"If *you* wish to come out of sanctuary . . ." he began.

"No, my lord. Thank you, but I will stay here with my mother."

He dipped his head, respectfully acknowledging her loyalty.

"I'll fetch my brother now," she said.

"Thank you." The dark eyes were unexpectedly warm.

Bessie turned away so her uncle Richard would not see her blushing.

# NELL

A S THE HEAVY WEST gate of the Tower swung open and the first of Gloucester's guard marched through, Nell could feel Edward, standing by her side, barely able to resist rushing forward to meet them, or more specifically, the little prince whom they were escorting. The look on the king's face as he saw Dickon break from the procession and run toward him was as ecstatic as the little Duke of York's loud whoops of joy. The boys kissed and embraced fervently, but, aware that much of the Tower staff were watching, they refrained from tears and quickly regained the stately demeanor demanded of two brothers of royal blood.

Nell could see Gloucester and Buckingham coming through the gate now, watching the joyful reunion. Richard looked genuinely pleased, but Harry Buckingham's face was stiff, unreadable. Nell could not help but see sinister motives in that bland expression. Handsome and magnetic as he was, she found him the most loathsome of creatures, and her blood chilled in his presence.

Edward and Dickon, arm in arm, were making for the royal residence. The king turned back to her.

"Nell, come with us!" he cried. We'll have a celebration." They slowed to let her catch them up. Each boy put an arm round her waist. "I shall call for a splendid supper in my rooms. Just the three of us. And my jester."

"And a juggler," Dickon insisted. "And an acrobat."

"Several kinds of sweets," Edward added.

"*Only* sweets," Dickon suggested. "I've always wished to eat a meal with neither fish nor fowl nor meat nor vegetables—only sweet pies and marchpane and pudding."

Edward and Nell exchanged an indulgent smile.

"Any other requests, brother?" said Edward.

"After dinner, I should like to go to the menagerie."

"Done," Edward agreed.

"Oh, I almost forgot," Dickon said, turning to Nell. "This is for you. From my sister." He handed her a sealed letter.

Nell, with a queer feeling, tucked the parchment inside her sleeve. "How is Princess Bessie?" she asked the younger boy.

Dickon, his initial excitement suddenly sobered by the true circumstance, looked into Nell's eyes. "Troubled," he said. "And missing you a great deal." Then he brightened again, just as suddenly. "As I have missed my brother. But no more. We're together again."

Edward was smiling broadly. The pain and weariness had left his face and he looked for a moment a happy boy again. "Together again," he said. "I shall call for the juggler."

THE BOYS' HAPPINESS and enthusiasm had been infectious. Over their meal of sweets alone—the cooks had taken their king's command to heart—and with the unremitting hilarity from the fool, a spate of jugglers, minstrels, and contortionists, there had been so much laughter and silly banter that Nell had been able to forget for a few brief hours her troubles and fears.

Now back in her room, she slid Bessie's letter from her sleeve, broke open the seal, and read it by the light of a candle.

*Dearest friend,*

*I write this in haste so that Dickon may carry it with him to the Tower. How do I begin? With outrage? With pity? Despair? I was privy to the plot that Hastings tried to hatch with my mother—one that for all her earlier conniving, she had nothing at all to do with—the one that lost him his head. I wrote to you about it on the very night I learned of it, fearful of its consequences. But so worried was I that the letter would be intercepted and our communication then forever disallowed, I gave it into the safekeeping of not our usual courier, but Master Thomas, the old pensioner at the almshouse, whose daughter Helen is your friend at the Tower kitchen. I thought it a safer and more clandestine route to you.*

*Alas, with the most miserable of luck, poor Master Thomas was set upon by thugs that sprang forth from a Totehill Street alley. They beat him unconscious and took the few pennies he had. The letter he carried they cared nothing about, and it was probably trampled in the mud. 'Twas several days before I learned of the man's condition, for he lay in hospital, dead to the world, no one knowing his name or residence, and by the time he returned, black-and-blue and limping to Westminster, Hastings was already found out and cut down.*

*Oh, Nell, I am heartsick! My uncle Richard has grown insane with his fierce protection of my father's legacy for my brother. 'Tis true that Hastings was plotting to bring Gloucester low and reinstate my mother as protector. But could there not have been a proper trial for the man? And we have heard also that poor Edward witnessed the atrocity with his own eyes. How awful for him!*

*Now, as you know, Richard has taken Dickon from us. Part of me feels misery at losing him from our sight—he's a lovely,* merry boy—but another part revels with him at his freedom from his grim sanctuary, more a prison than a safe house. He shall have the company of his brother the king, the company of my dearest friend in the world, and run of the fabulous palace that is the Tower of London.

As I was readying him to go with his uncles Gloucester and Buckingham, he talked endlessly about the wild animals he would visit every day at the menagerie. He seemed very happy to be going.

Mother is in such a state of fury at her impotence that she can hardly pass a civil word with anyone. I know 'tis a sin to dishonor a parent, but I can say to you in all honesty that right now I hate the woman. Never has there lived a more selfish and self-serving person in all the world as Elizabeth Woodville. You must promise to tell me if I ever begin demonstrating those traits. If I do, then you have my permission—no, my command—to slap me silly and shout at me to come to my senses.

As for my ill-fated love for Uncle Richard, I have nothing but doubt and confusion and fear. I try desperately to forget him, to hate him, but the vision of his beautiful face swims before me, both waking and sleeping. I'm guilty of a further sin, to covet another woman's husband, but as time goes by I find myself a girl rife with sinfulness and shame.

The only ray of pure sunshine is the prospect of seeing you at the coronation. I can almost feel the warmth of your arms about me, see the sparkle in your eyes, for I know that in all the world, you are the one person who loves me as sincerely as I love back.

So on that light note (they have been very few and far between, I fear) I shall end this letter with hopes of receiving the same from you in the next day or two.

Your dearest friend and confidante,
Bessie

. . .

"N ELL." It was Edward's voice calling from outside her chamber door. She was still abed, even at seven in the morning, though lying awake as she had the whole night through. Sound sleep had evaded her since Lord Hastings's execution, and a shroud of worry lay heavy over her heart and mind.

Now King Edward the Fifth was tapping at her door. "Nell, are you awake?" His voice was feeble, yet she knew it was the voice of doom. Knew it with great certainty. Yet she must call him into her chamber. Call horror to herself. Agony.

"Come in, Edward." For some time now the two of them had, in private, ceased the formality of "Your Majesty" and "Mistress Caxton." They had lived through terrible times together. Held each other trembling. Wept together. They were family.

The door creaked open and Edward entered. The ravaged, tearstained face was all she needed to know the worst had come to pass. She struggled to sit up in bed and opened her arms for the boy to come into. He moved with the pace of a funeral procession, for that was what this was.

News of Antony's death. His execution.

Edward reached the bed and, sitting heavily, folded himself into her arms. He was silent, and all his tears had dried. She wondered if he refrained from open weeping now for her sake. It would be like him, so magnanimous and compassionate a young man. *I must stop calling him a boy,* she told herself. He was King of England, and here he was coming to bring her both dreadful news and comfort, on the death of her beloved Antony. Edward himself must be dying inside.

Nell too remained dry-eyed, but her body began to tremble violently in great waves that rushed over her, then receded.

"Oh, Antony," she heard herself moan aloud. "Oh, my love."

Edward pulled from her arms so that he might see her face, allow Nell to see his. See pain mirrored in each other's eyes. Share the grief. Begin to feel their loss.

"I'm so sorry, Edward," she finally whispered.

He leaned to kiss her cheek.

"As am I," he said. "As am I."

N ELL WAS RAW, as though her skin and soul had been flayed. Since news of Lord Rivers's death had been made public she had dropped all pretense that they had been merely friends and cohorts in service to Prince Edward at Ludlow. News had also come that the queen dowager's son, Lord Grey, had been executed at the same time.

Reckless though she knew the action to be, Nell marched, the next day, into Richard of Gloucester's office unannounced, and demanded his attention.

"I wish to know why Lord Rivers was executed," she said, doing all she could to keep her voice steady and emotionless.

Richard answered in a mild and respectful tone, one that he might use with a peer of England, not with a commoner, a woman. A young woman at that.

"'Twas necessary, Mistress Caxton, for the good of the realm. He was a traitor. The Hastings plot—"

"He was hundreds of miles from the Hastings plot!" she rudely interrupted Gloucester. "He had no contact with Hastings or Lord Stanley or Bishop Morton!" These were the others who had been arrested that fateful morning in the midst of a council meeting at the Tower from which Hastings was unceremoniously dragged to his beheading on the Green. "Or do you have *proof* that he was part of that conspiracy?"

Richard remained calm and dignified throughout Nell's tirade, and she was conscious and very grateful that Buckingham was nowhere in sight. Was that, she wondered, the reason she felt she could speak so boldly to the protector?

"You are correct in that I have no direct proof of Lord Rivers's involvement in the Hastings plot. But he was warned, as was his sister, that any conspiracy involving any member of the Woodville family would provoke the severest consequences for himself."

"But the queen dowager took no part in the plot!" Nell cried, realizing too late that she had revealed information she had no business knowing.

Gloucester looked at her with more interest now. His small, wiry body seemed to tense, and he came to stand directly before Nell.

"How is it that you are so sure of the queen's innocence?"

"I . . . I . . ." Nell's brazen confidence suddenly failed her.

"And did you really believe that no one knew about your love affair with Antony Woodville?"

Nell felt her body go rigid with anger.

"The truth, Mistress Caxton, is that Rivers did not die so much for his part in the Hastings plot as for his involvement in the original Woodville treachery when my brother died. The queen attempted a coup against myself, and against her own husband's will."

"But Antony knew nothing of the original plot either!"

Now Richard was genuinely surprised.

"The queen simply wrote and told Lord Rivers to bring the king to London, quickly, with a large army. I saw the letter," Nell continued, her voice trembling with passion. "She *never mentioned to Antony* that you had been named protector in her place."

Gloucester looked suddenly stricken. He sat on the edge of

his desk and was silent for a long moment, his eyes darting as he considered the shocking information that he was clearly hearing for the first time.

"So you are saying," he finally began, "that his own sister allowed Rivers to step into the deadliest of situations without even a warning?"

"That is precisely what I am saying."

Gloucester was clearly upset. "Thank you for coming, Mistress Caxton. You have . . . you are . . ."

His stuttering unnerved Nell. Angry as she had been on her arrival, now she could see that Richard of Gloucester was grappling with the most horrifying mistake—what he had previously viewed as a justifiable state execution was little more than murder.

"I wish to see my father," Nell said, more a demand than a request. "Lord Rivers was my father's dearest friend, and he will need my comfort."

"Yes, of course. But a day. No more." Gloucester had gone very pale.

Clearly the man had a conscience, thought Nell. There was decency in him. But neither Gloucester's conscience nor decency would bring Antony Woodville back to life.

One of the greatest men that England had ever produced was gone forever.

I T WAS LATE when the carriage finally clattered to a halt beneath the sign of the Red Pale. Nell stood on the cobblestones, still as a statue, numb and staring. It wasn't until the coach had rumbled out of Westminster Gate that she realized the bookstore and printshop were brightly illuminated within.

*What can be happening?* she wondered. Her prudent father,

unlike some merchants, never wasted candle wax lighting the shop windows after business hours, and he never worked but by the light of the day, as the smallness of the type sorely tested his old eyes. But now Nell could see the place was ablaze with light, like a castle hall lit for a Christmas ball.

She crossed the cobbles to the door. Her alarm grew when she found it unlocked, and the cowbell clanking above her head seemed, for the first time, ominous, a very death knell. The candlelit bookstore was empty and silent, as was the printshop, except now, as she drew closer to the archway between the two, she heard the faint click of metal on metal—type being set. A moment later her father, whose presence she had not enjoyed for almost five months, came into view.

He looked a man possessed.

Somehow, even in the utter silence, he had not heard the cowbell, as though he were existing in another world, with its own sights and sounds and smells, quite apart from the one in which Nell moved. She could see that William Caxton was carrying a long, narrow box—a line of type—which, with the greatest of care, he set into a larger oblong box in the middle of his press—a page about to be printed. When he turned again, she saw that tears glistened on his cheeks and wet his beard.

Her sob of pain at the sight wrenched the printer from his solitary world. As though with sudden recognition of an angel standing before him, he opened his arms, and without a word, Nell went into them. All his love and joy at seeing his daughter flowed into her, warming and comforting her. Yet his steely grip told the story of his wretchedness. They parted reluctantly.

Then, steeling himself against further emotion, Caxton picked up the inking ball and began to swab the finished plate.

"What is this, Father?" Nell was staring down at the broadsheet, a public announcement.

"On the table in the back" was all he said, continuing his work.

In the back room, Nell found a parchment covered with her father's writing surrounded by a halo of candles just next to his boxes of lead type. Here was where her father had transposed the handwritten word to the printed word, finally to become the published word. She leaned down and began to read.

*This day of Our Lord, 25 June, 1483, we have heard news of a most tragic death. Antony Woodville, Lord Rivers, has been executed in the yard of Pontefract Castle, York, at the pleasure of England's protector, Richard of Gloucester.*

*My Lord Rivers was a man of intellect divine, of beauty in face, form, and soul. A shining knight of chivalry, worldly charms, private piety.*

*We will ask ourselves in the coming months and years why he died. What evils coalesced to consequence the obscenity of his unnecessary death. Are we not inured to deaths in all forms—by accident, illness, old age? Do we not take in stride the passing of parents, brothers and sisters, most especially the loss of children at all ages. These are expected occurrences, and whilst painful, are borne patiently, as the true nature and progression of things.*

*'Tis only needless death that is unbearable. It robs the mind of equanimity, the nights of sleep, and the soul of peace. 'Tis a monster that haunts us ceaselessly.*

*Why did Antony Woodville die, his head shorn from his body in Pontefract Castle's yard? Whose betrayal caused this? Whose jealousy? Whose hatred set the blade swinging? What petty lies built that scaffold?*

*Nothing is so frightening as power in the hands of a tyrant. Our protector—perhaps more the minions round him—blazes with his strength, wielding it like a great sword. Limbs bleed, heads roll. Fortresses are lost and won with a splash of ink on parchment. We, the people of England, have been powerless in the shadow of these few dark creatures called noblemen.*

*But now perhaps this blessed machine will crush the despot's sword 'tween its metal frame and plate of leaded words. Will press, for posterity into the pages of books and broadsheets—finally readable by masses of Englishmen and -women—knowledge, ideas,* truth.

*Behold the printed word! 'Tis a weapon in our hands, and before our eyes! Soon a man will not die for imagined treason with no one the wiser of its folly. We shall read on a street corner, or in a history, the mad machinations of kings and counselors and bishops, their unbridled suits for power and more power still. Their rivalries, their revenges, their stupidities and outrages.*

*Antony Woodville's royal murder is one such outrage . . .*

Nell could not go on reading. She turned to see William Caxton at his press, standing rigid, with his hand on the lever, the first clean sheet of paper waiting for its imprint.

"Father," she said quietly, though she knew he could hear. "Father, you cannot print this."

"I can," he insisted, his voice quavering with defiance. "I will print it, and treason be damned!"

Nell walked slowly to her father, but before she reached him his arm descended forcefully. When the press top lifted, Nell could see the sheet had been perfectly printed.

As though utterly spent, Caxton sat heavily on a wall bench. His shoulders sagged visibly.

"I shall print it," he said dispiritedly, "though I can never publish it." He looked up at Nell with a father's loving eyes. "I care too much for your life to make it public." A rare bitterness creased his features. "Once again our Fates are ruled by the few."

His fisted hand smashed the bench beside him. "Fie on their claims of royalty! The 'chosen of God on earth'! I say God *cries* seeing our famous sovereigns. Idiots! Monsters and idiots!"

"Father, come, please." Nell put out her hand and he let her help him up. "We'll go back to the house. Talk there. Let us put out the lights in the shop. They're a beacon that can draw nothing but suspicion."

"They killed Antony," he said, distraught, refusing to move. "The finest intellect in England. My friend. Your beloved."

"I know, Father, I know——"

"Nell?" It was Jan de Worde. He came up quietly behind her.

"Jan," said Nell, relieved for the help, "extinguish the candles. I'm taking Father home. Pull the sheet out of the press and bring it back to the house. But first disassemble the tray."

"What is it?" Jan asked. "What has he printed?"

"Our death warrants," she said.

"YOU WILL ORDER a thousand barrels of ale for the city's taverns," Nell heard Richard of Gloucester say through the partially opened door to an anteroom adjoining his office. She had just scooped up a pile of documents Edward was meant to sign, when Richard and another man entered the outer office. They were yet unaware of Nell's presence.

"We cannot appear to be stingy at Edward's coronation," the protector insisted.

"No, my lord. 'Twill be a splendid occasion, and long remembered" came the deferential answer.

It was Lord Stanley, Nell realized with no little amazement. It had taken hardly a week after Stanley's arrest for his part in the Hastings plot, as it was now known, for Richard's steward to regain his master's trust. Though most were outraged by

Hastings's horrific killing and, like herself, saddened by Rivers's execution, some whispered that the protector had treated far too leniently the other members of the conspiracy.

Bishop Morton had been sent to live in Harry Buckingham's Welsh home at Brecnock.

Thomas, Lord Stanley, was placed under house arrest in one of his own houses. Gossip had it that Margaret Beaufort had added a few mea culpas of her own, admitting that she and her husband *had* been loyal to Hastings, but only because they believed that *he* was faithful to Richard's brother the king. That their heads had been turned by Hastings's clever tongue, and the frightening assertion that Richard was planning to usurp young Edward's throne.

Now here, a week later, was Stanley groveling at Richard's feet. Nell guessed the wily conspirator was back in the protector's service, more for need of his help than because of Richard's belief in his apologies. Stanley was the finest administrator in London, and organizing to perfection a weeklong celebration for the coronation of a king, done in a manner befitting both the memory of Richard's brother, Edward, and the honor of his nephew Edward was no small matter.

Nell, still unnoticed by the men, was moving toward the adjoining door when she heard a third voice join Gloucester's and Stanley's.

"Richard."

It sounded like Harry Buckingham. He was the only man left in London, Nell knew, in whom the protector placed his complete trust.

"Can it wait, Harry?" said Gloucester. "I must finish London's provisioning—"

"It cannot wait," Buckingham said with what Nell perceived as excitement.

"What is it?"

"Will you leave us, my lord?" she heard Buckingham say to Stanley.

Nell could not see, but as the office door shut, she was sure that Stanley would be seething with indignation at his dismissal by his arrogant nephew.

"What *is* it?" Gloucester demanded as soon as Stanley was gone.

"Stillington is back. The Bishop of Bath and Wells must have a private audience with you."

Quiet as a cat, Nell moved closer to the anteroom door.

"I sent him away once—politely," Nell heard Richard say. "I have no interest in hearing false claims about my mother's adultery. This time—"

"This time," said Harry Buckingham, "you must not send him away at all."

Now Nell heard the office door open again. Someone was being shown in.

"My Lord Protector." The voice sounded old and feeble.

"Bishop Stillington," Richard greeted him. "Come, sit."

"Show him what you have," Buckingham instructed their visitor.

Nell heard the sound of a parchment being unrolled.

"Is that your brother Edward's signature?" Stillington demanded in a querulous voice.

There was a long moment of silence in which, Nell imagined, Gloucester examined the document Stillington had brought.

"It is, yes," Richard finally answered.

"Then your brother the king was already a married man when he took Elizabeth Woodville as his wife," Stillington said with a tone of authority tinged with disapproval. "This is a precontract of marriage with Lady Eleanor Butler."

"I beg your pardon?" Richard sounded thoroughly confused.

"Elizabeth Woodville," Stillington continued, "was apparently not the first woman to withhold her favors from King Edward until a marriage contract had been offered."

"But this would mean"—Richard was momentarily silent—"that Edward and Elizabeth's marriage was *void*."

"Precisely. Moreover," the bishop added in the gravest of tones, "all the children born of that marriage . . . are illegitimate,"

"Richard." Harry Buckingham's voice was thick with urgency. "Your nephew Edward is *not* the true King of England."

Nell's knees felt watery and her head was suddenly light. She hardly dared to breathe for fear of missing even a syllable of the conversation in the next room.

"Does the queen dowager know?" Gloucester asked.

"Of course she knows!" said Stillington. "She has known since the time before the Duke of Clarence's execution. She knew because I told her! She feared more than anything that Clarence would learn of it, for if he did, he would *use* it against her. She went so far as to have me imprisoned to silence me! And before I could be freed, Clarence was sent to the Tower on charges of treason, and executed," the bishop added indignantly. He pointed to the document. "This," he said, referring to the document, "is the *real* reason Clarence died."

"I always believed that Elizabeth was angry at the accusation of my mother's adultery," said Richard, "that Edward and I were bastards, and *he* not fit to wear the crown."

"That is what the king and queen wanted you to think," said Stillington. "But here is proof of nothing less than *royal bigamy*. If you agree this is your brother's signature, then you've no legal right to, next week, crown his bastard son the King of England!"

"Do you realize what this means, Richard?" Buckingham said, unable to control the excitement in his voice. "*You* are next in line for the succession. My lord, you are the true King of England!"

Nell's head was spinning. Surely this could not be happening.

"Edward, deposed by a signature on a parchment?" she heard Richard mutter. "Bishop Stillington, we *must* find Lady Eleanor. Make her swear——"

"The lady is dead, my lord," said Stillington. "But I myself stood at their betrothal. See my signature there, right under your brother's? What further proof do you need?"

"My God," Richard uttered, at a loss for words.

"Richard." It was Buckingham, even more urgent. "I'll gather the council. They must hear what Bishop Stillington has to say. See the precontract with their own eyes. Immediately."

"I must speak to Anne," Nell heard Gloucester say with much urgency.

There was silence from Buckingham and Stillington. Nell felt currents of anger, fear, and power pulsing through the door.

Finally Gloucester spoke, his voice frantic. "How can I be king?" he said.

Buckingham was calm and sure. "How can you *not,* my friend?" he said. "How can you not? Come now and we'll——"

Richard cut Buckingham off. "Do what you will, Harry. I must speak to Anne!"

"Very well. Meet me back here at noon," Nell heard Buckingham say. "I'll have the council assembled."

But there was no reply from Richard of Gloucester. He had, Nell suspected, already left the room.

"A moment please," said Buckingham to the bishop.

Nell panicked, realizing from the sound of footsteps that Buckingham was approaching the anteroom she was in. She quickly slipped behind the heavy door and when it swung open as the man entered, it came within a fraction of an inch of her nose. She prayed her crushed skirts would not betray her presence. But a few moments later he was gone, pulling the door closed behind him. Nell sagged with relief, and her jittery fingers dropped the sheaf of papers they held. Heart pounding, she gathered them quickly and, when she surmised all was clear, fled for the privacy of her room.

I T WAS SEVERAL HOURS later when Nell reached the hallway leading to the king's chamber. She had a long letter she'd written to Bessie tucked into her sleeve, recounting the conversation she had overhead in Gloucester's office. The writing had been a painful experience, even as Antony Woodville's death had been painful. But whilst his ending was heartwrenching and irrevocable, news of Edward, Dickon, and Bessie's bastardization seemed to Nell only the beginning of something much worse. And though the intelligence gained in the protector's anteroom was burned into Nell's brain, she knew she must not take it upon herself to speak the dreadful news to the king.

The first—and indecently speedy—consequence of young Edward's demotion became apparent as Nell approached his apartments and found that the set of guards who regularly stood sentry at the outer chamber door were entirely absent. She pushed open that door, praying that within would be standing the pair of soldiers who guarded the inner door. These sentry posts were also empty. Indeed, the door stood slightly ajar.

From inside she could hear the two boys speaking together in normal tones. No alarm. No hysteria. They were yet unaware of the change in their circumstances. Nell walked into the room, trying valiantly to suppress every emotion that threatened to spill from her. The king sat at his writing desk, with Dickon hovering over him impatiently. They noticed her entrance, but Nell's presence had become so natural to them that they continued their conversation unself-consciously. She busied herself with an imaginary task, her back to them, trying to gather strength for the terrible moments ahead.

"Edward, hurry. I want to go see the lion while he's being fed."

"A moment more, Dickon."

"What is taking so long?"

"I'm writing to Bessie."

"May I write something to her as well?"

"You take forever with writing, Dickon. Tell me what you want to say, and I'll say it for you."

"All right, tell her . . . tell her that we're very, very sad about Uncle Antony."

"I've already told her that," Edward replied, pain evident in his voice.

"And that we're exceedingly angry with Uncle Richard."

"I've told her that too."

Though he lowered his voice now, Nell could hear Dickon say, "You didn't tell her that I cried, did you?"

"No, Dickon, I didn't."

"Good. Crying is for girls."

"Well, you cried," Edward said quietly, "and so did I. What else would you have me write?"

Dickon's voice returned to a normal pitch. "Have you told her all the fun we're having exploring the Tower?"

"Some."

"You must tell her about the armory and the treasury, and the *dungeon!*"

"Give me a minute," said Edward.

"What about all the animals in the menagerie? The lion and the white bear. And the black-and-white-striped horse?"

"Dickon! How can I write when you never stop talking? Why don't you go outside," Edward suggested. "I'll catch you up at the lion's cage."

"And shall we play ball on the green after?"

"Yes, Dickon, we'll play ball."

Nell took this opportunity to intrude upon their conversation and turned to face them. It was with awful irony that she curtsied formally to the king and addressed him as "Your Majesty." She performed a smaller obeisance to Edward's brother.

"Nell." Edward spoke her name with incredible warmth. Dickon smiled shyly.

She noted that Edward had moved the little table with the new inkwell replacing the old one so it faced away from the window on Tower Green. It was the one from which he and Nell had witnessed Lord Hastings's execution. The broken glass had since been repaired, but the boy king could no longer bear to gaze out that window. It still haunted him, he'd told her, the vision of spurting blood, the lifeless torso. And now to that was the added thought of Uncle Rivers, who had died the same way, so far from his family and friends, alone in a Yorkshire castle yard. Edward could only imagine his death, and Nell was sure his imagining was worse than the real thing. Rivers had been such a greathearted man, Edward reasoned once to Nell, that the fountain of his blood must have spurted farther and longer than Hastings's. She begged him not to dwell on such gruesome thoughts, but the boy claimed he was helpless from preventing them coming into his head.

And the hatred that welled up in his soul for "that foul creature Gloucester," as Edward now called him—he could barely call him uncle—was so violent that the king confided to Nell that he worried it would damn his own soul. This fury was so overwhelming that Edward dared not even confess it to his chaplain, and apologized to Nell for burdening her with it.

Revenge was brewing in Edward's head, Nell suspected. He had only to wait for the right time. Unconscious of his sister's feelings for Richard, Edward had written Bessie that once he'd taken power as king, Richard, Duke of Gloucester, would feel cold steel at his own neck. That that eventuality was the only reason Edward relished the thought of his coronation. It brought him that much closer to taking his revenge.

"Mistress Caxton," said Dickon, bringing Nell's attention to the younger boy. "Will you not convince my brother to come outside?"

"I shall do my best," she said, and forced a smile.

Dickon took his leave. So intent upon play and a sunny afternoon that the little prince, on walking out the door, failed to notice the absence of the guards. Nell and Edward were alone.

"I'm just finishing a letter to Bessie," he said.

"Excellent," said Nell, trying to keep her features even and her demeanor calm. "I have one for her as well. Perhaps your courier will take them both. Edward," she said carefully. "Are you aware that you are . . . unguarded?"

"How do you mean?"

"Look outside your door."

The boy stood and moved to the doorway. He looked puzzled. "The outer door?"

"There's no one there either."

"How peculiar."

"Why don't you seal your letter and give it to me. I'll take it to my friend at the Iron Gate."

"No worry. I'll call my courier and he'll take them both." Edward gazed at her. "You have the strangest look on your face. Are you entirely well?"

Before she could answer, voices were heard outside the door.

"There are the guards returning now," he said.

But the door opened and Dickon, looking angry, walked through, followed by his uncle Richard.

Nell could see the king's hackles rise. He sensed something wicked was afoot.

"Would you excuse us, Mistress Caxton?" Gloucester said.

"No, Uncle. She stays. Whatever you have to say to me"—he regarded his brother—". . . to *us,* may be heard by Mistress Caxton as well."

Richard began to speak—bravely, Nell thought—and re-layed the worst news that Edward, in his whole life, would ever hear. His face was rigid and ashen. Dickon wept quietly. Nell stood still as a stone.

When he was done Richard asked gently, "Nephew, do you understand what I've just said?"

"No, my lord, I do not," Edward replied smartly. "For you have told me I am king no longer. Have never *been* king. Just a bastard boy, like my poor brother, whom you have made to weep."

Edward put a hand to his ear that had been sore of late. Then he went to Dickon, placing an arm round his brother's quaking shoulder.

"This was not my doing," Richard said. "You must believe that."

"So you will take the throne in my stead?"

"It has been offered to me."

"And *that* is not your doing either?" Edward added harshly.

Nell saw Gloucester wince, and for a moment she believed she saw true remorse in the man's expression. She remembered that Stillington's revelation had at first evoked horror in Richard.

"The law is the law," he said. "All are convinced—the council, the clergy, the lawyers—that the precontract is valid. Edward, your own mother does not deny this."

"Our mother who was never queen," Edward replied bitterly.

"No one planned this, I swear it."

"Get out."

"Please, Edward . . . Dickon."

The younger boy began to sob.

"Just leave us!" Edward commanded.

Gloucester stood and covered his eyes with his hand. He stood that way, unmoving, for several moments. The he swiveled on his heel and was gone.

"Nell?" Edward's voice had lost all of its authority. He was terrified. Confused. "What are we to do?" he whispered.

Nell gathered the two boys together and hugged them to her. She prayed for a modicum of control and evenness. "We'll think of something," she finally managed to say.

"But who is left to help us?" Dickon pressed her. "Everyone who loves us is dead or confined to sanctuary."

"It's all right, Dickon." Nell's heart broke as she heard the king summoning strength and courage back into his words. "Everything will be all right," he said. "I promise. I promise."


SEVERAL HOURS LATER the Tower staff was yet unaware of Richard of Gloucester's usurpation of Edward's throne. Nell, unable to stay still or remain in her room, had come outside and now strode about the grounds trying in vain to ease her raging emotions. The walled fortress suddenly felt a grim, even sinister place. Whilst she wished desperately to speak to her friends there—gatekeepers, cooks, stewards—she was certain that she must remain silent until a formal announcement had been made, or face the most serious of consequences.

Her sense of isolation and dejection grew when she passed the royal residence and chanced to look up at Edward and Dickon's window. Heaven only knew what depths of loss and grief they were feeling now. Her own loss she refused to dwell on, or risk losing her ability to function altogether. Without that, she would be unable to bolster the boys and that, thought Nell, was her God-given duty. Wandering round the Tower yard was pointless, she finally realized, and climbed the stairs to her room. Upon entering, she was startled to see a man standing by her desk with his back to her. He appeared to be rifling through her things.

"Sir!" she said sharply.

He turned and she saw it was Harry Buckingham. He did not bother to greet her even with a false smile.

"Mistress Caxton."

Nell found herself livid at the sight of him. "What right have you to be in my room, examining my belongings?"

"I am Constable of England, and what goes on within the walls of every royal castle in the kingdom is very much my business."

"Have you found what you were looking for?" she inquired in her most caustic tone.

"Not really. But then, I have no need to discover incriminating evidence against you for my purposes."

*Incriminating evidence? What is Harry Buckingham up to now?*

"And what are your purposes?"

"To inform you that your services to Master Edward are no longer required."

The message he had delivered, whilst unpleasant, came as no surprise to her. What struck her with greater force was that Buckingham seemed to take such great pleasure in calling her royal charge by the much-diminished title "master."

"I believe, my lord," she said in the most haughty tone she could manage, "that even the illegitimate son of a king is your superior."

Buckingham's face grew red and hateful. He took a menacing step toward Nell, but she stood her ground and held his eye.

"You have two hours to gather your things and be gone from here. Do not attempt to see the boys again, or I will have you arrested. Do I make myself clear?"

"Your motives have been clear to me since the first moment we met at Northampton Inn," she said. "You've a transparent mind, my Lord Buckingham, and whilst Richard of Gloucester may be blinded by your false brilliance, others can see what I see. Many others."

"A guard will be at your door to escort you out in two hours' time," he said. "Be ready."

Buckingham turned on his heels and slammed out of her room.

Indeed, well before the two hours had passed, Nell heard a sharp rapping at her door. She was packed and ready, though she'd not had time to write more than the briefest note of farewell to Edward. This she had slipped into a pile of dirty linen, one she knew would be collected by Nan, her laundress, and discreetly delivered to the boy.

The four red-liveried guards who collected her—as though one was insufficient to escort a lone woman across Tower Green—spoke not one word to her during the walk from her quarters to the West Gate. As she approached the postern she heard her name called.

Nell turned to see Lady Margaret, diminutive and compact, her features set in a somber and rigid expression. Nell knew at once that Margaret Beaufort was privy to news of Gloucester's coup. Nell said nothing, waiting for Lady Margaret to speak first.

"Circumstances change with the speed of lightning," she said in a voice that seemed too low and modulated for such a tiny woman. "To survive, one must be ready to shift with the same such speed."

Nell thought the sentiment odd, but remained even-toned. "That seems a sensible piece of advice, Lady Margaret."

"In light of the changing circumstances," the older woman went on, "would you consider a position in my household, that of secretary?"

Nell was dumbstruck. King Edward's deposing was not two hours old, neither public nor official, yet this brazen woman was offering the poor boy's closest companion her next job! Nell's first instinct was to shout at Lady Margaret that she was heartsick and angry and could no more consider a new post at the moment than she could dance on her mother's grave. But a cooler head prevailed. Nell inhaled deeply and released the long breath before her reply, and she found that her voice was surprisingly calm and even.

"How very generous an offer, good lady. But I am being rushed from the Tower by Lord Buckingham's guard just now, and I have no time to give it proper consideration. I hope you'll forgive me. I must go."

"I'll visit you at your father's establishment," Margaret Beaufort said, unfazed. Thick skin shielded her from insult and insolence. "I assume that is where you shall be returning now. We can discuss my offer in a few days' time."

"Of course," Nell agreed, finally out of clever, evasive retorts. It had been a day filled with horrible surprises. Such days, it seemed since the evening of Antony's arrest, had become not the exception, but the norm.

When, she wondered, would it ever end?

# BESSIE

ESSIE SLIPPED QUIETLY out of the ground-floor door of the Sanctuary Tower and joined the throngs surrounding and pouring into Westminster's walled compound. As she moved toward the cathedral's entrance she could see that it was the greatest gathering she'd witnessed in her lifetime. Of course, she'd missed her brother's entry into London and that, she'd heard, had been a fine and massive congregation.

This was different. This was the crowning of the king himself, and that man was not the one expected, the one for whom preparations had been in the making for more than three months. Today the nobles, city fathers, guildsmen and merchants, all dressed in their richest finery, were wary, subdued, whispering amongst themselves, and the mood of the crowd was different than one would expect had the crowned head been that of the young, golden lad, son of a beloved king. Instead that head was darker, older, and the result of an unnatural order of succession.

Certainly there were some who were grateful that their new king was not a child ruled till his majority by a grasping and despised woman, but a seasoned soldier, long trusted by his brother. It was the way in which Richard had come to this day that had left everyone uneasy. Just a week before, Harry Buckingham had stood in the pulpit of a London church after Sunday sermon and publicly exposed her father's precontract with Lady Eleanor Butler and, in a passage shorter than a psalm, nullified King Edward's marriage with Elizabeth Woodville, making bastards of all their children.

It had shocked and dismayed virtually everyone that the council had offered the crown to Richard of Gloucester. It was not that he was hated, but that he was known to so few. Bessie's uncle had stayed very much to himself in the north, and in the months of his protectorship had gone ahead very quietly with state business in the young king's name. For Richard to suddenly usurp Edward's throne and ascend it himself was altogether unheard of, unsettling.

Yet here they all were, the highest and mightiest of Englishmen and women, foreign ambassadors, cardinals, bishops, and priests in gaudy church vestments, and tonsured monks in their modest brown robes. Heads of state from the continent were here as well, having made their way to London in the past weeks, expecting to see the boy king crowned.

Conspicuously absent was the newly dishonored royal family. Bessie's brothers in the Tower had refused to attend the crowning of King Richard the Third, and their mother, having lost the title of queen dowager through her husband's bigamy, had not even bothered to refuse the invitation when it arrived at Westminster Sanctuary.

In attending the coronation, Bessie had boldly defied her mother. The former queen had forbidden her daughter to go, but such was the chaos that ruled their house, and the misery that afflicted Elizabeth Woodville, that Bessie had dressed and quietly slipped away unnoticed.

Was it perverse of Bessie to wish to see her uncle Richard crowned king? she wondered. Had it been Edward taking the throne, it would have been a joyous day, despite all the confusion and death preceding it, for it meant that the future, if not the present, was assured. Now it seemed there was no future at all for Bessie and her family. The boys were no longer princes—simply royal bastards—and the girls were hardly marriageable.

The real joy of this day for Bessie was the long-awaited reunion with Nell. Their plan—for Bessie to meet her friend under Caxton's sign of the Red Pale—was obviously untenable, she now realized, what with the river of humanity flowing toward the cathedral and away from the printshop. Nell would perceive the problem and would surely find Bessie where she was standing, at the right side of the cathedral's great doors.

She could not very well keep her head down, for she wished Nell to easily find her, but thus exposed, anonymity, invisibility, proved impossible. Everyone entering the soaring church chamber saw her, and all knew her. She had been "Princess Bessie," beloved daughter of a beloved king. Now she was merely fodder for gossipmongers. She heard the pitying whispers all round. Titters. This made her angry, and strangely proud. Bessie lifted her head and thrust out her chin, remembering the posture she had taken as a royal princess amidst her father's subjects. She would not be cowed by their cruelty. Bastard or not, she was still the daughter of a great king.

Her eyes scanned the crush. There was Nell! She was flanked by her father and his apprentice, Jan de Worde, and she too was searching the crowd for her friend. Bessie began waving, conscious of the commotion she was causing, and ignored the annoyed stares of the clergy lining the steps of the cathedral. *Damn them!* thought Bessie. *I'm not a princess anymore. I shall do as I please.*

It took Nell and her small party more than ten minutes to reach the door, and such was Bessie's anticipation and excitement that the time seemed an eternity. When the girls were finally in each other's arms, the kisses, hugs, and laughter were sweet. William Caxton looked on with delight.

"Jan and I will find our places. You two will want some time together, but do not tarry too long or someone will fill your seats."

"Yes, Father," Nell said, and the men disappeared inside the cathedral.

Bessie and Nell found a quiet niche between two stone buttresses and just stared at each other for a long moment. Then they burst out in relieved laughter and embraced again. When they finally pulled apart Nell looked deeply into her friend's eyes and spoke with the gentlest irony.

"Lady Bessie."

"Indeed. Princess no longer."

"Is it awful?" Nell asked.

"What is awful is living with my mother. She's taken to her bed and ceased speaking to anyone, though the fury festering inside her needs no words to infect the household with poison. My sisters sit and cry, and the letters I get from Edward and Dickon make *me* cry."

"I know," Nell agreed. "I hear from Edward regularly too. I most worry about his infected ear."

"I wish we could get them home."

"I've thought of a way to see them," Nell said, her voice dropping to a whisper.

"Oh, Nell!"

"Next time we meet, I'll explain."

"I've something to tell you as well," said Bessie.

Nell moved closer.

"Do you remember me writing to say that my mother had been approached by Hastings to be part of his plot, but had refused to be involved?"

"I do."

"What I did not know till now is that she'd *always* known about my father's precontract with Eleanor Butler. Indeed, she'd gone to extreme lengths to hide it. At the time Stillington told my parents—five years ago—she'd had him jailed. My uncle Clarence learned of it, and she had him silenced."

"You mean *executed*."

"Some would say murdered." Bessie thought back for a moment. "When Lord Hastings and Bishop Morton came to sanctuary trying to involve my mother in their plot, it was the *precontract* she feared Bishop Stillington had revealed to Gloucester and Buckingham the first time they met."

"There was a meeting with Stillington previous to the one I overheard?" Nell asked, surprised.

"Apparently. My mother was very nervous when Hastings and Morton mentioned that Stillington had come to see Richard, but the moment she learned that the meeting had been *brief,* and that plans for my brother's coronation were continuing as before, she visibly relaxed."

"She must have realized that Stillington could not have divulged your father's bigamy, or the meeting would have gone on longer."

"Yes. That was when she realized 'twould be neither necessary nor safe to join Hastings's plot to overthrow Richard."

Bessie noticed Nell's shoulders slump at her last words. Realizing the melancholy thought she had evoked in her friend, she put her arms about her. "I'm so sorry about Uncle Antony. Oh, Nell—"

Her friend accepted the comfort for only a moment before straightening. "I mustn't think about that. If I do, I shall weep myself into a puddle. Now it's time to go see your uncle Richard crowned King of England."

Bessie shook her head in disbelief. "I can hardly comprehend that it's come to this. We were at Ludlow just a few months ago celebrating as a happy family. Now Father and Rivers, Lord Grey and Hastings are dead. My brothers are prisoners in the Tower of London, and I am a commoner."

"There's nothing about you that's common," Nell said with great matter-of-factness.

Bessie clutched Nell's hands. "Everyone should have a friend as good as you are."

Nell smiled bravely. "We'll see this thing through together, you and I."

"Right."

Linking arms, the pair pushed their way back into the throng and entered Westminster Cathedral. The summer heat, the press of a thousand bodies, and the smoke of incense had already made the place oppressive. As they walked down the nave's central aisle, Bessie could feel that all eyes were on them. In silent agreement, they kept theirs straight ahead, seeking Nell's father. Bessie could see him waving them to his place to the right of the altar near the front. They took the empty seats William Caxton had saved for them, and Bessie concentrated on the scene before her.

It was the first coronation she had ever witnessed, a scene she had long imagined, not just for her brother Edward, but for herself, for she had been meant to be crowned queen of *some* realm, as Nell had always reminded her she would be. That, of course, would never happen now. Now, thought Bessie, she'd be lucky to be married at all. She could very well end up in a nunnery—an awful thought, but altogether possible.

Her eyes sought the gilded pew once habited by her family— and found to her astonishment that in it sat one person alone. Little Ned, future Prince of Wales, was clearly uncomfortable in such resplendent attire. He looked small and lost without his relations surrounding him. His cousins, aunts, and uncles were all either dead now, in exile, or in sanctuary.

To the plaintive sound of Gregorian chanting, Ned's mother and father, humble and barefoot, were making their way down the cathedral's long aisle, first Anne looking lovely in white tissue and cloth of gold, her dark hair flowing long about her shoulders. Anne's train was carried with haughty formality by Margaret Beaufort. Her husband, Thomas, Lord Stanley, walked behind the queen, carrying the royal scepter.

Then, accompanied by his "kingmaker," Harry Buckingham, and two archbishops, came her uncle in a gown of purple velvet— Richard the Third, moving with grace and dignity toward the altar.

Bessie was instantly riveted to the sight of his face. She had never, she thought, seen a man more broodingly beautiful. His black eyes shone and his olive skin glowed. The sharp cut of his jaw—Bessie stopped herself. *I should loathe this man,* she thought. *He has stolen the crown from my brother. All of my family curses him, yet I admire him.*

The Archbishop of Canterbury began intoning a benediction, and incense wafted to Bessie's nostrils. Richard and Anne, kneeling side by side, bared their breasts for the anointing with holy oil. The crown of Saint Edward was held high overhead, and Bessie could see Richard, chin lifted, following it with his eyes.

*What must he be thinking?* she wondered. *He never wished for this.* The crown was lowered slowly to a droning prayer. In the moment before it touched his head, he turned and, with quiet desperation, sought Anne's eyes. She was waiting, with her face turned toward him. Richard's shoulders sagged, a barely perceptible gesture. But Bessie had seen it—*his relief. Anne is by my side. Anything is possible!*

A sob escaped Bessie's throat and hot tears crowded her eyes.

The glittering crown was set carefully onto Richard's thick black hair and settled heavily on his head. The monks' plainsong rose and filled the arched cathedral. *An honorable man is made King of England,* thought Bessie. *God save the king!*

# NELL

THE COURIER FROM the Burgundian Court arrived under the sign of the Red Pale with little pomp and less ceremony. " 'Tis just like his mistress," Nell heard her father say when the messenger presented him with a sealed letter and a fat purse from his old friend Duchess Margaret of Burgundy. Rich and powerful as she was, and ruler of the most splendid land in Europe, Bessie and Edward's "aunt Maggie" was modest and well considered in all things.

Indeed, Margaret had had the foresight to become William Caxton's very first patron. It was *she* who had encouraged him to change professions, from "governor" of the Merchant Adventurers Company—the most wealthy and influential English businessman on the continent—to printer, at a time when printing was an almost unheard-of profession with no promise of remuneration, save her patronage.

Nell enjoyed hearing her father tell the story of his years in Burgundy as a merchant adventurer, and his early ties to the royal York family.

"Margaret was a rare beauty back then," he said. "The only one of the York children besides Richard who was small and dark-haired. She'd hated her marriage to Philip the Good, who despised her for her infertility."

"Unfortunate for royalty, a barren womb," Nell observed.

"She was very, very lonely and suffered badly from the lack of English company so far from home."

"Till you became her friend," Nell offered.

"Yes." Caxton's eyes grew clouded. "Your mother had recently died and Duchess Margaret learned that I was alone with a young daughter. She befriended me and I her."

"I remember when her brother, King Edward, came to Bruges," said Jan. "I was a small boy, but there was great excitement—the King of England exiled on our shores!"

"Margaret offered her brother and the few faithful who'd escaped Warwick's rebellion refuge. That was when she introduced the king to me."

"And that was how your fortunes came to be made," Nell added. "When he needed a large sum of money to return to his kingdom to wrest the throne back from his usurpers, *you* raised it."

Now Caxton smiled, remembering. "When I returned home with you, Nell, and you, Jan, thinking of bringing the first printing press to England, the royal family awaited us with open arms."

"A shop and a house within shouting distance of Westminster Palace," Nell added. "Every grateful royal an enthusiastic patron."

"What days those were, when sanity reigned," said Caxton with a rueful smile. "Well . . ." His eyes softened. "Lovely Margaret. She still counts me as her friend."

Jan held up the bulging purse her courier had delivered. An avid reader, and proud of her role as instigator of the English-language press, Margaret always purchased a dozen copies of every book Caxton printed. This was the reason for today's bulging purse.

"May we hear the letter, Father?"

As he always did, Caxton read Duchess Margaret's letters aloud to Nell, and recently to Jan de Worde, who was shaping up, in her father's estimation, to be something more than a mere apprentice. Jan was as clever and industrious a young man as Caxton himself had been, and her father confided to Nell that one day, when the time had come to give up the press to retirement, Jan de Worde would likely take it over.

" 'Dearest William,' " he began reading as Nell and Jan puttered about the bookstore, dusting and rearranging the volumes on their shelves. " 'I would begin with the usual greetings, and the wish that all is well with you and Nell, but I am too heartsick for such pleasantries. Here I sit, helpless on the continent, whilst in England my family is being torn asunder.' "

Caxton's face grew dark with the words he was speaking, for the letter was a reminder that the turmoil all round them stretched far across land and sea.

" 'I had not yet recovered from my favorite, though wayward, brother Clarence's execution when Edward died suddenly," Caxton read on. "It seems impossible that only a few months have passed since then, and it seems every day a messenger arrives at my court with new and horrible tidings from London. I cannot say with whom I am most angry. With my brother Edward for dying, with my brother Richard for usurping young Edward's throne, or with my sister-in-law Elizabeth for setting in motion such evil circumstances with her greed and perpetual scheming. Now my nieces and nephews will pay the price for their elders' follies. Of course, I worry most about the boys locked in the Tower of London, with Harry Buckingham holding the key. And poor Bessie. She is a sweet and beautiful girl, but who will want to marry her now? I will attempt to make a match for her in Burgundy. Since it cannot be for dynasty, then perhaps a love match. There are worse things, after all.

" 'Enough of my complaints. I would be most grateful if you would provide me' "— Caxton broke off as his eyes scanned the rest of her letter with the names of requested books. "And it goes on." He looked up at Nell. "There she is, ruler of a great and powerful country, and as helpless as we are to change the Fates."

Sobered and silenced by the thought, they were startled when the shop doorbell clanked and Bessie entered.

She regarded them all with alarm. "Has someone else died?"

The question struck the Caxton trio as somehow comical, and they burst into simultaneous laughter.

"No one has died," William Caxton answered. " 'Tis a letter from your aunt Maggie. And whilst reminding us of our losses, it thankfully reports no new ones."

Bessie relaxed and smiled.

"There's something about *you* in it," said Nell.

"Tell me!"

"Your aunt is trying to find you a love match in Burgundy."

Bessie rolled her eyes. "I dread her idea of a love match."

"I hear the men are quite large and virile in Burgundy," Jan piped in unexpectedly. With his Low Countries accent, it became "larch and vurl," and this sparked another round of hilarity.

When the laughter finally ceased, Nell grabbed Bessie's arm and announced, "We're off. My last day of freedom, and I'm going to spend it carousing on Totehill Street with my best friend."

"Enjoy yourselves," said Nell's father.

"We shall be sure to keep an eye out for large and virile men," Bessie added as they went, laughing, out the door.

Once the girls were on the street and out Westminster Gate, their merriment was short-lived. It was a gray, overcast day, and the truth was, Nell and Bessie were out for neither a day's shopping nor for pleasure. Their errand was far more serious. A dozen shopkeepers, vendors, and streetwalkers called out their greetings to the pair, but the girls never stopped to chat with a one of them, instead waving back with friendly smiles.

"I argued with Mother again about the family coming out of sanctuary," said Bessie. "She will not budge."

"And her reason?" Nell asked.

"She insists we are all in danger. From whom I cannot say. Uncle Richard, every week, requests my sisters' and my presence at court. Every week my mother says no. I'm convinced she *prefers* sanctuary. She is more private that way. Able to do her business without prying eyes behind fifteen feet of stone wall."

"Did she forbid you to come out today?"

"As always. She says I'm a dreadful girl to disobey her so blatantly, but how can she keep me locked away? We're no longer royal." Bessie was starting to fume. "She just wishes to control me."

"Well," said Nell, "*I* shall soon be under the wing of an even *more* controlling woman, if that can be imagined."

"Do you think Margaret Beaufort is more of a fiend than my mother?"

Nell thought for a moment. "'Tis hard to say who is the greatest powermonger, but they are certainly cut from the same cloth." She was struck suddenly by an uncharacteristic jolt of uncertainty. "Was it horribly disloyal to have taken the post? Should I have said no?"

"Certainly not!" Bessie cried. She stopped in her tracks and forced Nell to look at her. "In the past months you've learnt how it feels to be at the very center of things. You've such a good mind for it, Nell. And sad as it is, there's nothing that can be done to put my brother back on the throne." She grasped Nell's hands. "What an extraordinary opportunity—secretary to Margaret Beaufort. It would be for anyone. But for a woman . . ."

"With you and your mother still confined," Nell added, " 'tis important to have a friendly ear at court."

"Don't think Mother hasn't thought of that already. But honestly, Nell, you needn't make excuses. I'll wager that if you stayed home, you'd miss the excitement of it all."

"Admitted." Nell was thoughtful. "I just somehow feel I shall have an unparalleled education under Lady Margaret's tutelage."

"You no doubt will. And then," Bessie said with a grin, "you can pass it along to me."

They continued walking and kept up a brisk pace for half a mile till they reached a row of goldsmiths' shops. Here, the coach Nell had arranged for them was waiting. They hopped in and the two girls were off.

It took the carriage more than an hour, passing Fleet Street and Temple Bar, and finally down Thames Street, to traverse the five miles to the Tower of London. Bessie paid the driver and they alighted near the West Gate.

Nell, looking round quickly, pushed Bessie into Gresham's Mercantile, a three-story building that sat in the Tower's shadow. This dry-goods and sewing establishment was the main producer of uniforms for the Tower staff.

As they entered, Nell inhaled the rich fragrance of the cloth and textiles as one would perfume—the smells from her earliest childhood and her father's own mercantile shop. They were greeted by the store's owner, George Gresham. Tall, lean, and the picture of a prosperous London businessman, he was an old friend of William Caxton's, one whom Nell knew could be trusted.

With hardly a word spoken between them, Gresham led her and Bessie to a locked door of his shop's back room, and there began the prearranged disguising. There were two outfits laid out, each of appropriate size to the girls. Off came their rich and refined gowns, and on went the simple, coarse garments of serving women. Nell was transformed into a laundress, Bessie into a kitchen maid.

Bessie stood staring at herself in a long looking glass. "This reminds me," she said as Nell laced up the back of her bodice, "of my aunt Anne and uncle Richard."

"*Everything* reminds you of your uncle Richard," Nell teased her gently.

"No, no, have you not heard the story of how, when Uncle Clarence tried to keep Anne from marrying Richard, Clarence hid her from him by disguising her as a kitchen maid and putting her to work in a country house?"

"This is a true story?"

"On my honor true, and highly romantic. Richard, you see, was determined to have his childhood sweetheart despite his brother's greedy attempts to keep them apart. He cleverly ferreted out Anne's whereabouts, snatched her away from her potato peelings, and married her in secret before Clarence could steal her again."

"You do have an interesting family history, my friend."

"Too interesting," said Bessie, and sighed. "Well, how do I look?"

"All you need is a pot and ladle. And I?"

Bessie appraised Nell's appearance. "I'm afraid the ruby earbobs will give you away."

Nell pulled them off, then said, "Let me see your curtsy."

Grabbing her skirt on either side, Bessie bent a knee.

"A bit deeper," instructed Nell, "and lower your eyes. In fact, 'twould be a good idea if we were to keep our heads down as much as possible. It wouldn't do for either of us to be recognized."

"I'm afraid, Nell."

"So am I. But I have it on good intelligence that Harry Buckingham is never at the Tower on Mondays. He's hardly there at all. He spends all of his time with the king at Westminster Court."

"We should go," Bessie said.

Nell patted down Bessie's gray fustian skirt. "Your brothers await."

T HE GIRLS HAD AVOIDED the Tower of London's West Gate, as it was the one most used by nobles and government officials, who might recognize Lady Bessie. Instead they entered at the Iron Gate at the Tower's southeast corner, where Nell's friend, Rob Fiske, stood sentry. It had taken Rob a moment to recognize Nell, and a brief whisper in his ear to allow them passage into the Tower yard.

"What did you say to him?" Bessie demanded to know.

"Head down," Nell reminded Bessie as they hurried across the mostly deserted Green outside the royal residence. Now that court had moved back to Westminster, the Tower yard was a quiet, somber place. Nell leaned close to Bessie and answered, "I simply said, 'Sod Buckingham.' The Tower staff all hate him so," Nell continued. "They loved the royal family. But Buckingham was always arrogant and unkind, especially to the lower servants. They do not easily forget such treatment."

The disguises seemed to be working. A clerk, a steward, and several stonemasons took no particular notice of the girls. Even a pair of laundresses hurrying past were none the wiser. Nell and Bessie grew confident enough to lift their chins so their faces could be seen by all. Attired thusly, they found themselves wholly unimportant, and therefore invisible to anyone of "importance."

"Let's go to their rooms first," said Nell. "It sounds as though Buckingham lets them roam the Tower grounds very little these days."

Bessie was gazing round them. "I've been here many times, but today I find the place menacing somehow."

" 'Tis just the darkness of the day, Bessie." Nell was trying hard to keep her friend's spirits high. "I promise you, 'twas a cheerful place when court was here. And you know how lovely the royal residence is."

When they arrived at the residence, Nell, instructing Bessie to hang back, strode up to one of the door guards.

It took a moment for Matthew Kingston to make sense of the familiar face in such unfamiliar garb. " 'Zat you, Nell?" he said, eyes narrowing with suspicion.

" 'Tis I, Matthew."

"I won't ask what you're up to."

"That's a good friend."

"You're lookin' pretty as ever." He winked at her. "Say, were you not banished from the Tower precinct?"

"I was. By Harry Buckingham."

"Sod Buckingham! What can I do for you?"

"Let me and my friend in to see the boys."

"I would, but they're not here."

Nell stifled her alarm. "Where have they gone?"

"The Garden Tower. They were moved last week."

Nell was thinking fast. "Who guards them now?"

"Markham and Ladd."

"Thank goodness." She sighed, relieved. Had their sentries been strangers, this day's adventure would have been in vain. "Thank you, Matthew. Are your sons well?"

"Eatin' us out of hearth and home, and outgrowin' their breeches every week."

"Send my regards to Mary."

"I'll do that." He grinned at her and eyed Bessie. "Maybe on your way out you and your friend can bring me somethin' from the kitchen."

Nell returned to Bessie, trying to hide her concern. "They've been moved," she told her friend.

"Moved from the royal residence?"

"Despite the cheerful name, you'll find the Garden Tower much less grand, but nothing to be—"

"Damn Harry Buckingham's eyes!" Bessie cried. "Edward may no longer be king, but my brothers are still his nephews."

"By marriage only," Nell reminded her. "And a hated marriage at that."

Bessie sighed. "Has my uncle Richard any control over this man whatsoever? Is this shameful treatment *his* will or Buckingham's?"

Nell could see Bessie's lip begin to quiver. Her friend did not wish to think ill of Richard, even now.

" 'Tis my guess," said Nell, "that our new king is so busy with affairs of state and trying hard to win his people's love that he leaves certain details to his right-hand man. That man, whether we approve or not, is Buckingham. And Lord Harry, as constable, has say over all that goes on here. But let us not waste another moment moaning about your brothers' accommodations. 'Tis time we could be spending with them."

Nell glanced up to see a familiar face and called out, "Nan!"

A plump young laundress in her gray dress with starched white collar and cuffs turned at the sound of her name. She squinted at Nell and Bessie and recognized Nell at once. She came hurrying over.

"Oy, Nell, what are ye doin' dressed like me?"

"Trying to *be* you" was Nell's reply.

"'Ooze yer friend from the kitchen, then?" Nell asked, eyeing Bessie. "The queen?"

"Actually . . ." Nell whispered the answer in Nan's ear.

The girl's eyes went wide and she stared at Bessie. Nell put out a hand to stay the laundress from dipping into an automatic curtsy.

"Here, take me bundle of linens so's ye look the part," she said to Nell, then turned to Bessie and spoke confidentially. "Ye know, I love yer brothers like my own. And I know they say you're not the princess anymore, nor Edward the king, nor Dickon the Duke of York, but sod them. And sod Harry Buckingham!"

Nell, looking very official with her pile of clean lawn sheets, led Bessie across Tower Green. They passed the menagerie, where Dickon's favorite beast, the young African lion, paced back and forth and back in his small cage. He seemed to have lost some of the proud bearing he'd had when he'd first arrived. Nell could hardly look at him now. Suddenly the animal's confinement seemed cruel.

When they reached the Garden Tower, a square, squat building on the riverside, overlooking the constable's garden, it took only a few words and a smile to her friends at the door to gain her and Bessie's entrance inside.

"Oh, Nell . . ." Bessie's tone was desperate from the moment she set foot on the Garden Tower steps, for this felt a desperate place. Unlike the royal-residence staircase, cheerful and welcoming with its fine tapestries, colorful family crests, and banners adorning its walls, this was cold bare stone. Only a few wall torches lit their way up the steep stairwell. The smell of mildew and urine was strong and unpleasant.

Three stories above, the girls followed a dark hallway, empty but for a pair of door guards now squatting near a wall, engaged in a game of dice. They barely looked up as the laundress and kitchen maid entered the chamber of the boy who, till a few weeks past, had been King of England.

They saw Dickon sitting alone, close to the slit window, trying to read by the day's gray light, the room's torch having not been lit. It was a clean but otherwise sparsely furnished outer room with a door, Nell supposed, that led into a bed-chamber.

When he heard the outer door creak open and shut, Dickon looked up quickly. *Ah,* thought Nell, *he is still hopeful. A sign of good spirits.* And when he saw the faces of the two "serving girls," there was not a moment of confusion or misrecognition. The nine-year-old leapt to his feet and went to embrace his sister.

"Oh, Bessie, you've come!" He turned with moist eyes to Nell. "Was this your doing?" He knew instinctively to whisper.

Bessie answered. "We have the cleverest friend in the whole world."

Dickon hugged Nell then, and she was gratified to feel strength and life in the boy's embrace.

"Is Edward within?" Bessie asked, nodding toward the inner door.

Dickon's face sagged. "He is, but he is not himself."

Nell saw Bessie fight against panic at the news, keeping her voice calm and even. "How is he not himself?"

Dickon dropped his eyes. "He prays all the time. On his knees."

Bessie bit her lip. "What does he pray for, Dickon?"

"An end to his suffering. His ear is very infected. His whole head aches terribly and his pillow is sodden with pus and blood every morning." Now Dickon seemed on the edge of tears. "He prays fervently for his immortal soul. I think . . . I think he believes he may die soon."

"Oh no, Dickon, no," Nell said in her most reassuring voice. "Your brother may be in terrible pain, but I promise you, he is not going to die."

"Dr. Argentine comes to see us every few days," he said. "And yesterday he put an evil-smelling potion on Edward's ear, saying 'twould draw out the infection. Perhaps it has not yet begun to work."

"That's right," said Bessie. "Such things take longer than a day to take their effect."

Nell had wandered to the slit window and found what Dickon had been poring over when they'd entered. It was the green leather volume of *Jason and the Argonauts* that William Caxton had dedicated to the Prince of Wales, the one presented to Edward at Ludlow by the Gloucester family.

Dickon said, "Edward has been reading it to me every day . . . when he is not praying . . . or weeping. The stories cheer us. There's been little else for that . . . till now." His face crinkled into a smile. "I quite like you as a cook, sister." And with a chuckle he said to Nell, "And I see you've brought us clean linen. Very good."

"I must see Edward." Bessie had lost all semblance of levity. With a fearful look to Nell she pushed open the inner door. They could see it was dark, and in the gloom a single candle flickered at a makeshift altar. Kneeling before it was Edward, his back to them. Even from where they stood looking in, they could see he was thin, his tunic hanging off two bony shoulders. His head was tilted at an odd angle, and this sight, above all, forced a small gasp of pity from Nell's lips.

"Edward. Turn round and look at me," said Bessie. " 'Tis your sister."

"Bessie?" he cried without turning, then struggled to his feet. She went to him and caught him as he teetered off balance, but then their embrace was fierce and, for both, openly tearful.

Nell was forced to look away, so painful was the sight, but when she saw Dickon's red eyes and wet cheeks she went to him, and held the little boy to her for comfort.

Thus the four of them remained for a time, till all tears had fallen and dried. Then Nell lit several wall torches and they gathered on the bed the boys shared, and talked quietly. It was difficult looking at Edward, for his skin, now unnaturally pale, was stretched over the bones of his face, and his blue eyes were dark-ringed and shone with obvious pain. Still, he was very cheered to see his sister and Nell. He pretended bravely that he was well, never mentioning his ear or headaches, or his frequent morbid praying. He refrained entirely from speaking of the dead.

"How is our mother?" he asked Bessie eagerly.

"Mother is . . . *Mother,*" she answered with a wry smile. "She drives me wild, Edward. I should like to throttle her with my bare hands."

Edward laughed at that, and Nell could again see the boy she'd taught Latin at Ludlow, the child brimming with life and good cheer. The king who had promised that she and Antony could be wed. Now it was Nell who fought back tears.

"Mistress Caxton," Edward said, teasing with his formality. "I understand this was *your* little adventure."

"Not so little," Dickon piped in. "Worthy of Jason himself, I would say."

"Indeed," Edward agreed, then looked suddenly concerned. "Should you be caught——?"

"We shall not be caught," said Bessie. "We have it on good assurances that the Lord Constable of the Tower never appears here on Mondays."

Now Edward's face creased with genuine worry. "That is generally true. But I had word that he would be coming today with papers for me to sign."

"Dear God," Nell muttered. Her heart began to thump in her chest. "Perhaps we should cut short the visit and come again another—"

A commotion outside the outer door silenced Nell. The four of them froze, straining to hear what the fracas was. But Harry Buckingham's angry voice was all too clear. "Lazy imbeciles!" he was shouting. "I'll kick you till you're bloody if I catch you off guard again! Now stand up and do your job!"

Nell gestured for Bessie to pick up Edward's dinner tray and whispered urgently to the boy, "Dirty linen?" He gestured to his pillow and she quickly ripped the case off it and grabbed a box filled with pus- and blood-caked bandages near his bed. "Head down!" she whispered to Bessie as the outer door opened and Harry Buckingham stormed in.

A laundress and a kitchen maid were both meant to curtsy to such a high lord as Buckingham, and it was the deep level of respect that they were expected to show that saved them. Heads bowed so low that their inconsequential faces could not be seen, they executed the obeisance quickly, silently, and, keeping their backs to the man as they gathered the tray and dirty linen, hurried from the room and past the chastised and upright guards.

They did not speak, or even look at each other, till they were taking great strides across Tower Green.

"I didn't get to say a proper good-bye," Bessie said, her face racked with misery.

" 'Tis all right. We shall come again." Nell cursed silently, for her words were so utterly unconvincing.

"Edward looked so ill. Oh, Nell—"

"Steady, friend. We need to leave this place unobserved."

When they reached the Iron Gate they quickly stowed the box and the food tray before making their escape, receiving a high sign from Robert Fiske.

Once outside the massive walls, Bessie collapsed into sobs. Nell just held her, silent, for she could think of nothing of comfort to say. Bessie's brothers were in dire straits, that much was clear. Releasing them from their circumstances seemed insurmountable. And tomorrow Nell was to begin her position a whole day's ride from London. There she would stay, living at Woking Manor all week, returning home on Saturday evenings, going back to work on Mondays. Again, she and Bessie would be separated, with only letters to sustain them, between Sundays.

A light rain began to fall, furthering their dismal day. They hurried back to Gresham's Mercantile and redressed in their finery.

Bessie hailed a passing farmer hauling his wagonful of onions into tomorrow's Totehill Street market and paid him from her purse for the trip back to Westminster. They sat crushed next to the man, who chatted amiably the whole way, but the girls were cloaked in a deep, unhappy silence.

NELL HAD LOOKED round her on her first day at Woking Manor thinking, *Sweet Lord, I have come to work in a very beehive. And Margaret Beaufort is queen bee.*

Lady Margaret's sprawling estate southwest of London was only one of her many splendid properties scattered round England and Wales, properties that had come to her through inheritance from her parents, and three previous husbands before Thomas, Lord Stanley. It was well known that Lady Margaret was a wealthy woman, but it was not until Nell had stepped through the massive stone doorway, and beheld the richness of the surroundings and the constant influx and outgo both domestic and international, that she understood her employer's stature in the scheme of international politics.

There were pages and couriers, noblemen and women seeking favors, bishops, bankers, guild runners, merchant adventurers, sea captains, and ambassadors, besides mysterious men and women who Nell supposed were spies, coming and going at all times of the day and night.

Lady Margaret herself was in constant motion, a tiny whirlwind. She slept but three hours a night, and prayed for three. She had to be coaxed away from her office to eat birdlike portions—much of which was left on her plate—perpetually distracted by this or that piece of business that needed handling. Supremely productive, demanding and exacting to a fault, her mind never ever ceased working. Nell imagined that her dreams must be mere continuations of her day. Indeed, her lady's maid, Lydia, told Nell that when Margaret Beaufort opened her eyes in the morning, she woke in midsentence, making mental notes to herself and letting fly with a stream of instructions for the coming day. Yet she never tired, and was generally even-tempered with her large staff.

Only when someone was foolish enough to tarry momentarily or make an excuse that a particular task was impossible to accomplish did Lady Margaret reveal her ire. She suffered neither fools nor slouches in her household, and more than one mistake or offense was reason for immediate dismissal. However—and Nell appreciated this—she offered praise for a job well done. Those she had carefully chosen to work for her seemed agreeable to her terms and not unhappy in her service.

Lady Margaret's own steward at Woking was in complete charge of domestic cares, the woman of the house having no time for such petty distractions.

That steward was none other than Reginald Bray.

Nell's first encounter with the man at Woking happened as she unpacked her things in the small but beautifully appointed room she'd been assigned on the third floor of the manor. Her door was ajar, and when she looked up, she found Reggie Bray leaning on the doorsill staring in at her. He actually smiled, showing the large horse's teeth, and Nell was forced to bite her lip so as not to laugh aloud.

"She's given you a very fine room of your own," he said.

"Yes, 'tis lovely."

"Much finer than the usual servant."

"Is that so?"

Nell wondered where Reggie Bray's bedchamber was, and if it was as elegant as her own. Part of her worried that it was not, and that his jealousy would mean trouble for her in the future. The other perverse part hoped hers was the richer.

"Did you wish a word with me?" she asked.

"I have no need to speak with you, Mistress Caxton," he replied in the rudest imaginable tone.

"Then, Master Bray," she said with equal contempt, "leave me to my unpacking, if you please. And shut the door behind you."

He just stood there and sniffed indignantly.

"You may shut it *now*," she said.

He slammed the door hard.

"Haw-hee-haw!" she said after him.

Behind a beautiful door intricately carved with angels and

demons and dragons, Margaret's headquarters themselves resembled a beehive, the central office "the Queen's Cell," with
a warren of smaller rooms surrounding it. A waiting room, a
scribe's chamber, a library, and a locked treasury complete
with counting table and chests filled with a fortune in coin,
plate, and jewels. There was an armory and a map room. And
a luxurious receiving chamber for Lady Margaret's important
visitors, which resembled nothing less than a royal presence
chamber.

On arrival, Lady Margaret had personally taken Nell on
a tour of the household and offices, and fully explained the position for which she'd been hired. The job of second correspondence secretary was to log all incoming letters, deeds,
documents, messengers, and audiences, and the same for all
outgoing, in addition to making arrangements for their couriers.

Whilst the first correspondence secretary was privy to the
*contents* of these materials and meetings, Nell was allowed only
to record their comings and goings.

It was hard to believe, she wrote Bessie after several days,
that so narrow a task could take up every moment of the working day. But narrow as the job was, Nell found it utterly fascinating. She had, in the past four months, lived in two royal
households, and Woking, aside from the absence of royalty, was
itself a miniature court.

Nell had been given a workplace in the scribe's chamber,
where two young men on stools hunched over their desks, each
requiring several extra candles, even on the sunniest days, to illuminate their never-ending piles of documents.

Nell's was a long, broad table, and it was always covered
with paper and parchment letters and documents, ledgers and
leather courier pouches. It astounded Nell how voluminous was
Lady Margaret's correspondence, and she became immediately

curious about the contents of each and every article she handled.

Of especial interest were the number of letters she sent and received from her son, Henry Tudor, an exile abroad in Brittany for more than fifteen years. Mother and son wrote to each other every single day, which seemed to Nell—herself a loving and diligent daughter—somewhat excessive.

There were regular, perhaps once weekly, letters from Margaret's husband, Lord Stanley, who was rarely at home. He lived at Westminster Court now, again in King Richard's favor—his steward. Nell, remembering the role he'd played in the Hastings plot, wondered if the king kept the man so close by him because he trusted Stanley . . . or because he *mis*trusted him.

Whilst no letters arrived from, or were sent to, Lady Margaret's nephew Harry Buckingham during the first week of her employment, Nell found a sheaf of old correspondence from him, tied with a leather thong. All she could surmise was that these letters were of some import to Margaret Beaufort, as they occupied a shelf close to letters from her son and husband. How she wished to lay her eyes on these!

Besides written correspondence, Nell was expected to schedule all of Lady Margaret's appointments, which she termed, to Nell's amazement, "audiences." The woman quite clearly regarded herself as royalty. She was, after all, descended from the same ancestor as the York kings, and only the tricks of fate and vagaries of military action during the War of the Roses had kept Margaret Beaufort and Henry Tudor from the throne.

Margaret was careful, however, infinitely careful, to prove her loyalty to the Yorks every day. Nell had guessed at this, but was granted confirmation the same evening Lord Stanley returned home after a long absence at court. Nell, still learning her job, had stayed in her office long after the scribes had gone to their supper. Indeed, the "beehive" was quiet, and Nell believed she was alone.

Margaret had, however, stayed behind as well, for shortly Nell heard two voices, one her employer's and another Nell recognized as Lord Stanley's. She quickly went to the scribe's door to tell Lady Margaret she was there. Nell had been told on her first day that sound carried very effectively down the corridors of Lady Margaret's offices. She had planned it that way, surely so that nothing that went on there escaped her.

It would not do to be found eavesdropping on her employer and Lord Stanley. But the moment Nell showed herself at the doorway, Lady Margaret, seeing her, made what appeared to be a signal to her secretary, behind her husband's back.

*Could it be?* thought Nell. *I must be mistaken.* Margaret had touched her ear as though to say *listen,* but, with a subtle flick of the same finger, waved Nell back behind the scribe's door. *There it is again! The same signal.*

Heart pounding, Nell silently stepped back out of sight, but the couple's voices carried with perfect clarity down the hall to her.

"Are you writing to Henry?" Lord Stanley asked.

"I am. Shall I send him your regards?"

"If you would."

"I only wish you knew my son," said Margaret wistfully. "'Tis been so long that even *I* have seen him. I wonder sometimes that if I came upon him without knowing it was Henry, I would even recognize him. Shameful, that."

"Not shameful, Margaret. Simply the price of exile."

"I suppose."

Nell heard the scraping of wood on stone, and she imagined Lord Stanley pulling a bench beside his wife, who had gone silent, probably back to letter writing.

"How does King Richard like our little gift?" Lady Margaret inquired. The inflection with which she spoke the monarch's name left no question in Nell's mind that he was despised by her.

"How can he not like one of the loveliest estates in Suffolk?" Lord Stanley answered. "Of course he knows the purpose of the gift is an apology."

Margaret's voice grew icy. "An expensive apology, Thomas, one that was unnecessary had you listened to me at the outset."

"I grant the Hastings affair was an unfortunate blunder." Stanley sounded like a boy being chastised by his mother. "But I think your nephew's suggestion of so overgenerous a mea culpa was unnecessary."

"Dear Harry Buckingham is uniquely positioned just now. He has the king's ear and the king's entire trust, both of which you sadly no longer possess."

"I intend for this to change."

"It had better. And soon."

"Watch your tongue, Margaret! And temper your scolding." Stanley was bristling. His wife was strong, but he recognized his own importance. "Remember," he cautioned, "why so high-and-mighty a Lancaster as you still sits so close to the York throne. Sits with her head still attached to her shoulders!"

"You're quite right," Margaret demurred. "You know that I'm very grateful."

Margaret might be grateful, thought Nell, and she was wise enough to keep relations with her husband cordial, but the woman knew very well who ruled this household.

"Richard has gone north to Yorkshire for a time," Stanley announced.

"He's left London after three weeks on the throne?" Margaret said with genuine surprise. "Is he mad?"

"It has gone well enough for him here. Protests against the usurpation have been minimal, and his policies are more than acceptable to his subjects, both noble and common."

"Then why is he leaving?" Margaret demanded.

"Our King Richard has a tough shell and a soft heart," Stanley replied. "He may be acceptable to Londoners, but he's keen to feel the warm embrace of people who *love* him. Only in the north can he find such people."

Nell could imagine Lady Margaret wearing the look she assumed whilst she was thinking hard. The eyes were open, as though staring into an abyss or, conversely, a vast cauldron of opportunity. Her fingers would drum on the document upon which she was working. A serpentine tongue would flick over her thin lips. "Will you go north with him?" Nell finally heard her ask.

"Yes, of course. I'll be leaving tomorrow."

There was yet another silence before Stanley continued. "Will you at least pretend that you'll miss me?" he said.

"Who would that fool, Thomas? But I do love you."

"In your way," he said.

"Is that enough?" Margaret Beaufort asked dispassionately.

"More than enough," he answered.

"Good." The single word was deliberate and final. Clearly it had ended the conversation.

Nell heard the stool scrape and footsteps retreat from the office. The heavy door closed.

"Mistress Caxton. Come in here, please," Lady Margaret called. Her tone was brusque.

*Oh, I am in trouble now,* Nell thought. *I must have misread Lady Margaret's signal. Two weeks on the job and I am finished. Disgraced for eavesdropping.*

Nell walked down the corridor to the main office, trying to

wipe what must have been a look of pathetic confusion from her face.

Margaret Beaufort looked up, a mild expression in her steely eyes. "Be assured, Nell, that there was nothing in my conversation with Lord Stanley that I did not wish you to hear." Lady Margaret executed that which served as her smile. "You are in my service now, and I expect your complete loyalty and utter discretion."

"You have it, Lady Margaret. I assure you."

"Why do you think I hired you, Nell?"

"Your previous second correspondence secretary—"

"It had nothing whatsoever to do with Master Childs."

"Why *did* you hire me, Lady Margaret?" Nell was relieved to have found her voice, and not left standing tongue-tied and stupid before her employer.

"Because your mind is sharp," Margaret answered. "Because you are brilliantly educated. Because you are a woman. But most importantly"—Lady Margaret looked Nell dead in the eye—"because I perceive that you can be useful to me."

"Thank you, Lady Margaret," said Nell, humbled by the answer. "I hope I will prove your trust and your very generous belief in my abilities."

"As do I," Margaret said, returning to her letter writing, thus dismissing her secretary.

Nell turned toward the scribe's chamber.

"Leave the work and go have your supper, Nell."

"Yes, madam."

Nell turned back again to find Lady Margaret gazing up at her. She smiled feebly at the noblewoman, aware of how insignificant she felt in the woman's presence. As she opened the office door to leave, she heard Margaret say, "Approach men with a fine balance of humility and boldness. This balance carefully achieved, they will never realize that you are in control."

Nell nodded to indicate she had heard the advice, then quietly shut the door behind her.

A T SUPPER THAT NIGHT Nell found she was able to adhere only to one half of Lady Margaret's suggestion.

The trestle table where the Woking office staff were eating Nell found almost altogether full. One empty place remained, and that was next to Reginald Bray. All had seen her enter and there was no choice, unless she wished to publicly offend the house steward, but to sit beside him.

She took her place and greeted the scribe to her left, then turned to her right. Reggie Bray was staring straight ahead, pretending Nell was invisible, voraciously gnawing on a beef bone and washing it down with long drafts of wine. She was rather pleased that he'd chosen not to acknowledge her and, when her meal was set before her, began to eat whilst engaging in pleasant conversation with the scribe.

She was quite unprepared for the feel of Reggie Bray's hand on her right thigh. Her mind raced. *What to do?* The scribe was bemoaning the scarcity of high-quality quills, and Nell forced herself to continue nodding in commiseration. As the hand moved up her leg, kneading and caressing it, she picked up her cup of wine and with the greatest control, took a dainty sip.

All of a sudden she shrieked loudly, and with a great lurch flung the wine cup to the right, tipping it so that its contents flew in a graceful arc, soaking Reggie Bray's face and doublet with the claret liquid.

Quickly she gave her molester a sharp kick under the table, then cried in the most apologetic voice, "Oh, Master Bray, forgive me!" She began dabbing his dripping face with her napkin, but furious, he pushed her away.

"You *must* forgive me," she begged. "'Twas a mouse ran over my foot and gave me a fright!"

Bray stood and pushed back his bench with such force that it fell with a great crash. Everyone in the dining hall was either tittering or trying not to titter, for they all loathed the man as much as Nell did.

"Vile rodent!" she cried, just before he stormed out.

When he was well gone, everyone fell about in great gales of laughter.

I KNEW SHE WAS an unusual woman, but I did not realize that she was extraordinary." Nell was on her father's arm as they strolled down Totchill Street on her Saturday evening off. Jan de Worde walked on her other side. They had dined shortly after the Woking driver had left her off under the sign of the Red Pale.

Now she, her father, and his apprentice were heading for the Kings Head Tavern to finish the night. Nell had hoped that Bessie would be joining them, but there had been an unusually large presence of troops surrounding Westminster when Nell had arrived home, and she suspected this was the reason her friend was not at liberty to come out.

Indeed, another company of soldiers in the royal livery were trotting toward the trio just now.

"What is all this about, Father?" Nell asked, indicating the guard as they passed. "Why so many soldiers when the king and queen are in Yorkshire?"

"I'm afraid my head was stuck in a translation all day. I cannot say."

"The soldiers guard mainly Westminster Sanctuary," Jan offered.

This alarmed Nell. "The Sanctuary?" she said. "What possible reason could Richard have for securing Elizabeth Woodville and her five daughters? They pose no threat to him."

William Caxton pulled open the door of the pub for Nell. "I think we shall know soon enough."

The Kings Head, normally abuzz with gossip on a Saturday night, was in a right uproar. There was not a table to be had, and men stood three deep at the bar. Everyone was talking—rather, shouting—at once. It took Nell but a moment to determine the jist of the excitement.

Rebellion was afoot!

A revolt against King Richard was brewing in the south of England, its purpose to restore the crown to King Edward. Nell felt the blood rushing through her veins to hear such a thing. *Sweet Edward released from horrid captivity and sitting on his rightful throne.*

But her elation was short-lived. The instigators of this rebellion, she learned, were none other than Elizabeth Woodville and her despised relations. That was the reason for the increased guard round Westminster Sanctuary. Poor Bessie must be wild with fury at her scheming mother.

Much was argued about the chances of such a revolt succeeding. It was not a *London* rebellion, after all. 'Twas only the country bumpkins of the south. And who, after all, would follow the lead of a woman? This was not France, where whole armies would rise up behind a fourteen-year-old female prophet named Joan.

"I won't be rising up for Elizabeth Woodville, but for the firstborn son of a true and beloved king!" a patron shouted out in drunken splendor.

"A *lusty* king," his friend added, "who had *two* wives. A man after my own heart!"

There was much laughter at that, and the arguing went on whilst Nell and her father queried the most knowledgeable men in the crowd for details. Which Woodville relatives were involved? Which southern parishes? How many had already risen up, and how many more were promised?

From the corner of her eye Nell saw the door open and Matthew Kingston enter. He was alone, and there was such blackness hanging about the normally jolly Tower guard that she quickly disentangled herself from the crush and went to him. He seemed rooted to the spot, his eyes glazed, and he appeared confused, as though he'd forgotten how to push his way through the throng, step up to the bar, and demand his grog.

"Matthew, what is it?" Nell said to him. He did not immediately answer. "Surely you've heard news of the rebellion in Kent?"

"I've heard," Matthew replied, but said no more.

Nell was suddenly alarmed. If such a revolt was under way, surely every last Tower guard would be on duty to prevent Edward's and Dickon's freeing by the rebels. Why was Matthew Kingston standing here at the Kings Head Tavern?

"Father! Jan!" Nell shouted in a voice loud and sharp enough to be heard over the hubbub. They were at her side within moments. Others, seeing Nell with the Tower guard, followed to surround them.

"Matthew," said Nell, "tell us what you know." She clutched her father's hand, for she felt in her bones that she would soon hear something terrible. She had no idea how terrible it would be.

The man was struggling to compose his trembling mouth, and tears had begun to form in his eyes.

"The boys are gone from the Tower!" he finally blurted out. "Their rooms are empty."

If the commotion had been frantic when Nell entered the Tavern, now it was violent. Men pushed and shoved to get closer for hearing.

"Who took them?" someone cried.

"Who else but King Richard!" someone shouted in reply.

"Are they dead or alive?"

"They must be dead!"

"No, no! They were just children!"

Nell, trying hard to keep panic from her voice, said to Matthew, "You must tell us all you know."

" 'Tis not much," he answered. "The princes—" He stopped, then assumed a defiant tone. "They were still royal to me. Prince Edward was ill, and young Dickon had ceased his daily visits to the menagerie."

"Aye," a woman said. "Of late, they'd been seen less and less playing ball on Tower Green."

"First the cooks and maids and grooms who had served them since their arrival were let go," Matthew continued.

"Reassigned?" Nell asked.

"Most were told to go home. Their services were no longer needed. The guards they let stay, and so we felt ourselves lucky and kept our mouths shut, believing it just the whim of some noble prick. Then yesterday, at the start of my shift, they told me 'twould be my last." The guard wore an agonized look on his face. Matthew had proudly held his post at the Tower for seventeen years. "There may be a few kept on, but most of us were sent packing. All I know is that the boys are gone."

"Murder!" someone cried.

"Poor infants!"

"Edward was dead the day Richard stole his crown!" an old man muttered.

Nell understood the sentiment. In the past, when English kings lost their thrones, they soon after lost their lives—some violently. Young Edward the Second had been reamed with a red-hot poker, and poor, simple Henry the Sixth was murdered by the York brothers, some believed by Richard of Gloucester.

The shouts and cries grew to such a roar that Nell fled to the street, her head throbbing. The cool evening air stung her red, perspiring face. A few moments later William Caxton joined her. He took Nell's arm and they began a brisk walk back to the shop.

"Bessie and her mother must be told," said Nell.

"Perhaps they already know," said Caxton. "Perhaps if Elizabeth Woodville is the organizer of the rebellion, she had them rescued."

"Not likely," Nell countered.

"Not likely," her father agreed.

"But why would Richard want them disappeared?" Nell asked. "He proved them illegitimate. What harm are they to him now?"

"The proof is in the pudding, Nell," her father said. "A rebellion has just been launched in Edward's name. As long as the boys live, they threaten the king's sovereignty."

Nell was racking her brain. "How can I get through to Bessie? All those soldiers—"

"You're not to risk tangling with them," Caxton said. "Your friend is safe in sanctuary now. Messages being sent in or coming out are precisely what Richard's soldiers will be looking to prevent. I don't have to tell you this is serious business, Nell."

"I promise to stay clear of Westminster Sanctuary," she answered.

But William Caxton had said nothing about the Tower of London.

IT HAD BEEN TERRIFYINGLY easy to gain entrance to the Tower, now that there was no one of consequence to protect inside. Just before midnight, at the West Gate, Nell had found Gerald Spencer, a man she knew, standing guard with someone she'd never seen before. Gerald looked decidedly down at the mouth. Nell approached him with a sad, knowing look.

"Bastards!" he muttered. "If I find who took those poor little boys, I'll rip their throats out."

"Do you think they're alive . . . or dead?" Nell had whispered.

"Who's to say? But they was sneaked out of their rooms in secret, no rebels storming the Tower to break them out into freedom. I fear the worst."

"Listen, Gerald," she'd whispered. "Let me in. I want to see if anyone inside knows anything at all."

"Go on, then," he said, pulling open the heavy gate. To the new guard who began to object, Gerald said, "Mind yer business and keep yer trap shut."

If the Tower of London had been a sad place on her last visit with Bessie, now it felt a proper graveyard. Hardly a light shined in any window. The Green was entirely deserted. It was eerie walking alone across the grassy yard where not three months before, when Edward Quintus reigned over his court, Nell would have had to weave her way through hundreds of noblemen and merchants, jugglers, musicians, and jovial servants finished with their shifts, ready for their first cup of ale.

Now she was alone, the yard dark and dead. She was at Garden Tower before she knew it. No one guarded the outer door. She inhaled deeply, smelling the fragrance of grass and river fog, preparing herself for the inevitable mildew of the stairwell and whatever horror lay ahead. Once she was inside, none of the torches was lit, and she groped about in the pitch blackness, clinging to the damp stone walls to guide her way.

The second floor was similarly deserted, and only a few slitted windows admitted dim moonlight for her passage toward the boys' last residence.

"Aaigh!"

Nell fell backward when a scuffling rat brushed her foot. She recoiled, realizing that several more of the repulsive, shadowy creatures were moving in and out the open door of the apartment she was now approaching.

That open door felt sinister to Nell, a symbol of all that was wrong with the scene. *Oh, how has it come to this?* she cried silently. *Where are the sentries, cheerfully guarding their beloved king? Where is the fragrant stairwell hung with tapestries and coats of arms? Where is the doorman to see me into royal suite, the shining faces of two young brothers, their glorious futures spread out before them?*

Nell steadied herself before entering the outer room, where she had last come upon Dickon poring over *Jason and the Argonauts*. She saw immediately that it was empty and that the door to the bedchamber too was flung wide open. Inside, the moonlight shone on a tray from the kitchen, one that had no doubt held the boys' last meal here. It sat on the floor, picked clean of all scraps, but the rats were busy elsewhere. Nell's hands tightened into fists to see them crawling busily in and out of the open box near the bed, dragging the last bits of Edward's bloody ear bandages away to their foul nests.

Disheartened as she was, she searched the room for clues to

Edward and Dickon's disappearance or, God forbid, murder. The place was in a shambles, blankets tossed about, the feather beds that the boys slept upon pulled out from the bed frames. Nell's heart sank when she admitted to herself that a struggle had occurred here. *A struggle, dear God!* In the wardrobe hung far too many clothes for it to seem that the boys had simply been transported with their things to another location.

Fighting tears, Nell retraced her steps. On the Green she strove to compose herself. *Someone . . . there must be someone here who knows more.*

Many of Edward's servants had been let go in the past days, so Matthew said. Surely someone must remain. Nell gathered her wits and stiffened her jellied legs. She took off across the yard and, reaching the servants' quarters, entered with no difficulty. It was dark inside, but Nell searched among the sleeping figures and found, to her great relief, the one she had come to see.

She leaned over and whispered, "Nan, rouse yourself! I must talk to you."

"Nell Caxton?" Nan rubbed the sleep from her eyes. She struggled to sit up, and when she lit the wall torch, the three other laundresses on their pallets were awakened, and grumbled with annoyance.

In the torchlight Nell could see Nan's eyes were red and swollen from crying. "Have you come about the boys, then?" she said with no hesitation.

"I have. Oh, Nan, you must tell me what you know about what happened."

The girl bit her lip and looked away.

"Are you afraid that if you speak——?"

"You would be too, Nell. I mean, if they can make off with a little boy who was once the King of England, what'll happen to a bigmouthed laundry girl? But I'll tell ye what I know, though 'tis not much."

"Anything is better than nothing."

"Well, you saw the state they were in a few weeks ago when you came with the princess." Nell nodded. "It didn't get no better. In fact, it got worse. Poor Edward's pain was excruciatin'. He cried and he moaned and prayed all the day and night. Little Dickon was beside himself, so lonesome and scared. All of us from the kitchen and laundry would do what we could to help when we went to their rooms—a sweetmeat, a warm compress for Edward's ear. Then four days ago word came down that all the boys' servants and guards were to be replaced."

"Yes, Matthew told me."

"Me, the bigmouth, asked why on earth did we need replacin', and who would be replacin' us? 'None of yer business,' they said."

"Who is 'they,' Nan? Who sent word? Was it King Richard?"

"He'd gone north, to Yorkshire, by then, though it could've come down from him, I suppose. But the one who so rudely said 'twas none of my business was the Tower's own delight."

"Harry Buckingham?"

"In the flesh."

Nell's mind raced. "He came here himself to give the order?"

"That he did. With terrible threats to anyone who disobeyed . . . or spoke of it. Our beloved constable stayed only long enough to see the first of us booted out. He'd brought his own maids and laundresses and stewards, and placed those boys in their care. Then he left and we haven't seen the smallest part of him since."

"That was four days ago," said Nell.

"For two days the new crowd was acomin' and goin' from the Garden Tower. Then last night the sentries were given their marchin' papers. There were plenty of Harry Bucking-ham's soldiers about, but none at the boys' door. All day it was unguarded, but we worried at disobeyin' the little ratbag. Finally I got up the nerve and climbed the stairs. There were no guards at the apartment door. I knocked, very careful like, but there was silence. Like a tomb of the dead." Nan's eyes welled with tears. "I went and they were just gone altogether. The room was . . . disarranged. A chair knocked over. The feather beds——"

"I know, Nan, I saw them."

"Someone took them, Nell. Took them. Dead or alive, I don't know. And we let it happen. We took the orders of that God-cursed man."

"So you believe 'twas Harry Buckingham?"

"Sure, 'twas his orders, but who ordered *him*?"

" 'Tis all over the London pubs," Nell said, "that a rebellion's been raised in the south of England to place Edward back on the throne."

Nan's eyes brightened. "Might it have been the rebels who took him?"

"Perhaps." Nell grasped the laundress's rough red hands. "Let us pray that it was." She stood. "You've no idea how helpful you've been. Thank you, Nan. And God bless."

"God bless you too, Nell Caxton, and speed your way."

DURING SUNDAY'S CHURCH sermon Nell's mind wandered. The heat, even in the morning hours, had grown oppressive and the air felt stagnant—too heavy to breathe easily. Everyone was fidgeting around her. Babies cried. The smell of all those bodies pressed close together made Nell feel faint.

The priest, stationed so close to Westminster, had chosen to avoid all mention of that which was running riot in every Londoner's brain, for by now news of the rebellion and the missing princes was known to all. In this very church, Harry Buckingham had first announced Edward's bastardy to the public, paving the way for Richard's accession. With the new king four days' ride away, there'd been no time for the priest to hear his views on the matter, and so it was prudent for the man of God to say nothing.

Services finished, the churchgoers fairly exploded from the doors, gathering into groups on the stairs and in the street to hear news of the recent events refreshed. As though to mimic events, great roiling storm clouds had gathered in the western and southern skies. *A rain is what we need to relieve the heat,* Nell thought. It was much worse than when they'd entered the church.

William Caxton, Nell, and Jan de Worde separated and moved from group to group listening for a voice that had, perhaps, come from Kent or Devon, where the rebellion had reportedly broken out.

"Nell! Jan!" It was Caxton. He had clearly discovered a prolific fountain of information. They joined him in a group surrounding a thin, wild-eyed man named Jenkins who smelt of perspiration and whose clothing was hardly church-fresh. He had ridden all night from Guildford, he said, where armed townsmen and farmers were gathering by the thousands.

"Thousands?" Caxton repeated. "How many thousands?"

"Two, p'raps," Jenkins said. "But that was just Guildford. As I rode from town to town, men were mustering everywhere in great numbers."

The crowd was growing round the self-sent messenger.

"Are they all for Edward?" Nell demanded.

" 'Tis hard to say, miss. For some say Edward is dead, murdered by King Richard. Others say he and his brother were snatched from the Tower by rebels and will be restored by this revolt. But one thing's for sure. Now our rebellion has a leader."

"Who is he?" Caxton demanded.

Jenkins looked around him. "Lord Buckingham."

The listeners were momentarily stunned into silence. *The kingmaker had turned against the king he had made!* Then the crowd hooted with excitement and pressed in round Jenkins, shouting questions.

"You're saying the king's best friend betrayed him?"

"Is Harry Buckingham for the boy?!"

Nell strove to keep the shock of the news from blunting her senses.

"I wish I could say," Jenkins replied. "First reports were, he would return Edward to the throne. By the time I left to come north, 'twas said that Buckingham wished the crown for himself."

There were derisive shouts and hisses. Buckingham was less popular in London even than King Richard.

"People don't know what to think," Jenkins continued. "But they're arming themselves, and they're ready to fight!"


LATER, AT THE KINGS HEAD, the tables were filled but the talk was subdued. Such widely diverse news was disquieting, confusing. Clearly a revolt was under way, but that was all that was sure. The fate of the "little princes"—that was what they were now called—was uncertain. Were they dead or alive? Most believed they had somehow perished at King Richard's hands, though some held out hope that they lived, and that Edward would take back the throne from his usurper. As the day passed, more messengers from the south arrived in London and word spread fast, making its way into every pub, where nearly the entire population of the city had gathered for hearing the latest news.

*Harry Buckingham was heading a rebellion against Richard.* But who was willing to fight behind Harry Buckingham?

"Anyone's better than Richard," one man said.

"Anyone other than Buckingham," said another.

"The poor infants," Nell heard a teary-eyed woman say. " 'Tis pure evil to murder children."

"Richard done it for sure!"

"I hear he's grown horns and a tail!"

"Why would he kill them? The boys were bastards under law. What threat did they pose him?"

"Satan needs no threat for his actions."

Nell looked up to see her father, head down, scribbling notes, recording all he heard. Later that evening, he and Jan would return to the printshop to set type for a broadsheet, recording all the news they'd heard that day. They would work the night through, and tomorrow these would be distributed and posted at every tavern and church and market in London. Someone who could read would stand on a box and shout the news at the top of his lungs.

Nell marveled at the thought. *The printed word in England, still damp from her father's press, would inform the populace of unfolding events!*

But now Nell found herself eager to return to Woking. She was sure Margaret Beaufort would know something of her nephew's revolt.

She stood and kissed the top of her father's head. Caxton did not look up from his writing, but spoke to her nevertheless. "Be mindful of yourself, Nell. Anything can happen when rebellion is afoot."

"I will pray for your safety," Jan added, suddenly appearing at her side. "I wish most heartily that I could accompany you to Woking myself." His eyes were downcast. Shy.

"You're better served working with my father tonight," she said. "But I do thank you, Jan, for your care."

Nell picked her way through the still-crowded tavern and made for the rendezvous with the driver from Woking.

A light drizzle had begun.

O N THE ROAD west out of London the drizzle gave way to a cloudburst. The driver, named John—the same sturdy young man who had driven her into the city—carried on a steady stream of conversation with his passenger through the window between his seat and the coach's interior. Rain splashed off his hooded oilcloth cape and dripped onto Nell, yet she engaged him, for he spoke not just about the weather, which was worsening with every moment, the rebellions, and the missing boys, but about his position with Margaret Beaufort, gossip from the Woking household, and the reason for his mission to London.

"Dr. Argentine is Lady Margaret's physician," he informed her. "The old man's made up some concoctions for her, and I picked them up. Female troubles, or so says Lydia, her lady's maid. Lydia and me are sweethearts." John was silent momentarily. "I hope to ask Lady Margaret's permission for her and me—I mean Lydia, not Lady Margaret—to be married next year. Do you know Lydia, Nell?"

"I've met her, but we've not had much time to talk."

"That's Lady Margaret for you. She's a fair employer, as employers go—not that I've had many employers before. Lady Margaret's my first. But you must work yourself silly and make no mistakes."

"She's hard on servants who make mistakes?"

"Ach! Thomas Cockburn, my friend, was her footman. He fell asleep on a job, and that was the end of him. Well, it *was* an important job. Transporting gold from the manor. You don't fall asleep when gold is involved."

"Where was the gold going?" Nell asked, careful to sound nonchalant.

"To the coast. Dover, I think. 'Tis a regular thing. She has a son, Henry, on the continent. But *you* know that, her secretary and all. I think the gold is for him."

Nell was thinking hard. *What information might she extract from talkative John or his beloved Lydia about Lady Margaret?*

"Do you drive many noblemen to Woking for their audiences with Lady Margaret?"

"Oh, dozens," said John. "I most enjoy the foreigners, for the English are so closemouthed. They reckon their driver will be listening, so they sit in silence the whole way. But the French and the Dutch and the Spaniards, they gibber away merrily. 'Course, I haven't a clue to what they're saying, but I like the way it sounds."

"Who comes most . . . of the foreigners, I mean?"

"Oh, the Spaniards, for sure. Why, the ambassador of the King and Queen of Spain came just last month."

"From the court of Ferdinand and Isabella?"

"Aye. And he was very generous too. Gave me a gold coin, he did, and taught me a Spanish word. *Grass-yes*. That means thank you."

Finally the rain became too heavy for even John to ignore, and on the last leg of the journey south, Nell sat in silence, contemplating her ever more complicated life. There were times the sound of rain on the roof was so heavy it was as if a wave had crashed down on it. The coach lurched as it sank into frequent potholes, and wove crazily along the rutted road to avoid others. Occasionally John would call back that the stream they had just crossed was far over its bank, or the bridge they had just crossed was about to give way.

" 'Tis a mighty storm, this!" he said to her after the first brilliant bolt of lightning illuminated the sky, and just before its deep, roaring thunder rattled the carriage.

"Should we stop, John!" she called out to him.

"No, miss, we're almost there!"

Indeed, it was not twenty minutes later that the soggy vehicle clattered over the two Woking moats and into the manor yard.

When the heavy door was opened for her, Nell was surprised to see Lady Margaret standing just inside with an anticipatory expression. It appeared as if her employer had been *waiting* for her.

"Good evening, Lady Margaret."

"Good evening, Nell. I trust your journey was uneventful."

Nell was perplexed. *Was the woman joking with her? No,* she answered herself, *this was not a jesting woman.*

"The storm has gotten very bad," she said.

"The storm?" Margaret peered out a window. "I see. How long has it been coming down?"

"Half the day," said Nell. "Were you altogether unaware of it?"

"I was in my office." Lady Margaret moved to the window and stared silently out for a great long time, contemplating the tempest.

Nell was unsure what to do or say, so she stood in her place and said nothing. Finally Margaret turned. "Come with me," she said, motioning for a servant to take Nell's bag to her room.

Nell followed her employer through a portrait-lined corridor and the carven door to the warren of rooms where Margaret's offices were. It was a Sunday night—no one worked on Sundays, even Margaret Beaufort—and it was therefore surprising to see someone in the office. Indeed, he was sitting behind Margaret's desk, in her chair, with his back to them. As they entered he turned.

It was Harry Buckingham.

"My lord!" Nell greeted him, altogether flummoxed.

"Good evening, Mistress Caxton."

Nell marveled that the man could imbue the words of her name with such arrogance and disdain.

"Nell," said Lady Margaret in a dispassionate tone. "I wish for you to be present whilst I speak to my nephew."

"Aunt Margaret, is this necessary?"

Buckingham was certainly aware of Nell's dislike for him.

Ignoring him, Margaret Beaufort continued speaking to Nell. "You will not immediately understand why you have been included in this conference, but the reason will be clear when we are finished."

"Yes, madam."

"You may sit," said Margaret. "Pull up a bench."

Nell did as she was told.

"First let me say how appalled we both are about the boys' murders."

"They're dead, then?" Nell whispered, her voice failing her.

"Our dear king—" Margaret began in a sarcastic tone.

Nell glared at Harry Buckingham and grew bold, interrupting her employer. "I understand it was *you,* my lord, who had the children's longtime servants dismissed."

"That is correct," Buckingham answered. His tone had suddenly lost its arrogance. Now there was hurt in his voice. "'Twas done on King Richard's orders just before he left for Yorkshire. They were *his* people sent in to attend the boys when the others were let go." Buckingham looked genuinely stricken.

"I loved Richard. Believed him the rightful king. Believed him a righteous man. But to murder children . . ."

"I don't understand," said Nell, trying to coalesce her thoughts. If Edward was dead——? "I heard in London that you were leading a rebellion to *restore* Edward to the throne."

"That had been my plan," said Buckingham. "I'd gone back to gather my Welsh forces to liberate them, for I hadn't faith that the southern rebels could manage it. I was halfway to Wales when I learned that the princes had been taken."

"What else are they saying in London, Nell?" Lady Margaret seemed genuinely curious.

Nell looked with confusion at Buckingham. "That now Harry Buckingham is leading the revolt to place *himself* on the throne."

"Give me my chair, Harry," said Lady Margaret. Harry vacated the seat behind her desk.

Nell could see that her employer was thinking hard. As soon as Lady Margaret sat, the slender fingers began drumming on the desk. Something shifted in her demeanor and now it was as if Nell were invisible, no longer in the room.

"I need an answer from you, Harry."

Nell could tell Buckingham was annoyed. *No,* she thought, *far worse than annoyed. Furious.* He had somehow been backed into a corner by Margaret Beaufort, and he looked ready to snarl and snap like a wild animal about to have a pack of mastiffs set upon him. This was his aunt Margaret, wielding control over him. He was younger than she, but he was a man, and this balance of power seemed altogether unnatural.

"Strictly by lineage," he began, barely able to get the words out through clenched teeth, "my claim to the throne is better than yours."

*What was Buckingham saying? Was Margaret Beaufort contemplating the English crown for herself?*

"You have bastardy in your bloodline, twice over," he went on. "I am descended directly from Edward the Third and have no such stigma attached to my name."

"True," said Margaret in a sanguine voice. "But my Henry commands fifteen ships and five thousand troops from Brittany. He has Duke Francis's support, and my money behind him."

*Henry Tudor!* Nell was stunned.

"He's already sailed with his invading army and will land on the south coast whether you join him or not." Margaret's spine was straight as a steel blade. "The people of Kent and Devon are more my people than yours, Harry. You must know that. They will fight under Henry's banner before yours."

Nell chanced a look at Harry Buckingham. She enjoyed seeing him humiliated, especially by a woman.

"If you wish to see Richard defeated and a Lancaster king seated on the English throne again," Margaret continued, "the chances would be far greater if you stood at Henry's side and lifted him up, much as you did Richard." Now her tone changed. It was urgent, and Nell could hear a touch of the feminine nature that, in Margaret Beaufort, was so often hidden. "Help place the crown on Henry's head, nephew. Think of it, a kingmaker *twice over!*"

She was persuasive, this small, sly woman, but Harry Buckingham had a sour look on his face. Clearly, he had long dreamt of the crown himself.

"Do you not wish peace in England?" Margaret demanded of him. "Can you not see how the joining of the two houses would seal that peace?"

*The joining of the two houses? What could Margaret mean?*

"You are already married, Harry. But Henry is not. If he marries Elizabeth—"

*What was Margaret saying? That Henry Tudor should marry Elizabeth Woodville? That was lunacy!*

"She's eighteen. Beautiful. And her mother is a broodmare. There's no doubt the girl will give Henry many healthy sons."

*Sweet Jesus,* thought Nell. *She means Princess Elizabeth of York. Bessie!*

"You would be the highest peer in the land," Margaret continued. "Bar none. And we will make you the richest as well. Think of it. All that wealth and all that power, without the responsibility of kingship on your shoulders."

Buckingham's eyes were darting round as he considered the offer.

"Join my son in this invasion, Harry. Crown him king, and Elizabeth of York queen, and you will end this endless War of the Roses to forge the greatest dynasty England will ever know!"

Harry Buckingham sniffed once and lifted his chin haughtily. "Put it in writing," he snapped. "My grants. My titles. My estates."

*Ah,* thought Nell, her brain exploding with the magnitude of the many revelations. *This is why Margaret needed me here. She expected Buckingham's capitulation and knew she would need a trusted scribe.*

"Very well," Margaret agreed, then her voice softened. "You'll not be sorry, my boy. We will see in the golden age of England together—you, Henry the Seventh, and myself." Then Margaret turned and gazed at her secretary.

"Shall I get the writing implements?" Nell said, and stood.

"Writing implements?"

"Do you not wish me to—" She glanced at Harry Buckingham.

"Sit down, Nell," said Lady Margaret.

"I think I should like to remain standing," Nell said defiantly. "And I think I should like you to tell me why I have been party to this extraordinary conversation."

"Because," the older woman replied, "I did not wish to have to repeat it to you verbatim."

"But why did you feel I should know!"

That strange smile twisted Margaret Beaufort's lips.

Then she began to explain.

# BESSIE

WESTMINSTER SANCTUARY had become a dreadful residence. Surrounded as she was by hundreds of King Richard's guards, there was no chance of escaping, or even of Bessie darting out to visit Nell. It was not a place meant for prolonged living, nor for more than a person or two to stay. Yet, for four months, Bessie, her mother, and four sisters had remained in the cramped quarters, squeezed amidst piles of furniture and the royal treasure Elizabeth Woodville had made off with from Westminster Palace. There were no servants willing to come and go, so Bessie and the girls did their best to keep the damp stone rooms clean and tidy. They subsisted on simple fare the friars brought them from the abbey kitchen. There were no diversions for the young children, and barely enough light to read by. The thick walls had at least kept the airless rooms cool in the summer, but now that the weather had changed, cold moisture was seeping through the stone. Even Bessie could feel the chill in her bones.

Worse still was the gut-twisting fear under which all of them lived, for they knew that if Edward and Dickon could be so handily abducted from a fortress as awesome as the Tower of London, they had nary a chance behind Westminster Sanctuary's walls if someone wanted them dead.

Worse yet was the seething anger that flowed from Bessie to her mother, and from Elizabeth Woodville to everyone in the world.

The woman, Bessie felt sure, was possessed by a demon. Small as their living quarters were, her mother managed to pace every inch of them hour after hour, day after day. Dickon had written to Bessie of the African lion in his cage at the Tower menagerie, pacing back and forth, back and forth, with slitted eyes, snarling at anyone who came to stare at him. Her mother snarled at her daughters now, even the youngest, Bridget, whom she made cry with bitter words and insults. They were all "miserable girls," meaningless, with less power than a pawn. To Bessie she raged constantly, over and over again, complaining of the treatment she had received at the hands of ruthless men out to destroy her.

Elizabeth had tried her best to free her sons. The conspiracy for the southern rebellion had been hatched right here in sanctuary, her one last trusted courier carrying messages to her last remaining friends and relatives still at large. For several weeks the little stone rooms had thrummed with hope and excitement. The boys would be freed by rebels, and Edward restored to his throne. There were toasts around their little table with the friars' poor wine in golden goblets, and Elizabeth Woodville had been almost merry. Life for those short weeks had been bearable.

Then, on Friday night past, the courier had come one last time, with horrific news. The boys had been taken from the Tower, but not, as expected, by Elizabeth's southern rebels. Word was that her sons were dead, murdered by King Richard's henchmen. The messenger, terror in his eyes, had apologized, but said he would no longer be able to come.

Bessie had endured the agony of knowing that she had supported Dickon being taken to the Tower to join his brother, and though she knew his going had been inevitable, with or without her blessing, she could not shake the awful feeling of guilt, and complicity in his fate.

By Saturday morning, Sanctuary Tower—indeed, all of Westminster precinct—was aswarm with Richard's guard. Elizabeth had been found out as the grand conspirator of the southern rebellion.

She'd tossed her head with smug disdain. "All those soldiers to guard one little woman." She seemed almost pleased.

That was the limit for Bessie.

"Your sons have disappeared, Mother! They may well be dead. And why? Because of your endless scheming! Have you no pity, no sadness that they're gone? My sweet brothers are lost to me forever because of you!"

Elizabeth held Bessie in a withering gaze. "How do you dare speak to your mother that way?"

"How do I dare? Because I loathe you. Because everything your enemies say about you is true. You're horrible and self-serving. Ice water, not blood, runs through your veins."

Elizabeth crossed the room and came eye to eye with her daughter, then slapped Bessie hard across the face. Bessie hardly flinched, such was the pain she had come to know every hour of every day.

"Would you have had me stand by and do nothing when your father died and left the protectorship in the hands of a man who hated me?" Elizabeth Woodville was glaring at her daughter.

"Perhaps if you'd been more a wife to him while he lived—"

"More a wife to him!"

"If you'd spent less time raising your brothers and sisters to glorying heights and more on Father—"

"You poor, naive girl." Elizabeth, defeated, stood down from

Bessie and sat in a high-backed chair that had once served as a throne. "Do you really believe that if I had been a better wife, your father would have taken no mistresses, swived no whores?" She laughed mirthlessly. "Listen carefully, Bessie. All men are driven by their pricks. All men are unfaithful, but most especially kings. Kings feel 'tis not simply their right to have lovers, but their *duty*. I myself would have been one of Edward's whores if he'd had his way. But I denied him. Told him that I was perhaps not good enough to be his queen, but far too good to be his mistress. Oh, what lust *that* inspired! Enough to make him cross his good friend Warwick and marry me. But not enough," she continued bitterly, "to keep him faithful." Tears formed in Elizabeth Woodville's eyes.

Bessie thought that they were the first she'd ever seen her mother shed.

"From the moment we married, indeed at the first swelling of my belly with you, he went astray. But I knew what I had married, and I knew what rewards were mine as queen, and so I was understanding, even gracious. Tell me, what kind of man shares his favorite mistress with his best friend, and his wife's own son? Yes, I raised my brothers and sisters high. Arranged good marriages for them all. What else could I have done? Let them languish in poverty and obscurity whilst I queened over the land? I would have been equally derided and loathed for that. And yes, I schemed and conspired and protected what was mine, what I had earned. But that was not the true reason I was despised. Shall I tell you, Bessie, the truth of how it has come to this?"

Bessie, perhaps hearing her mother clearly for the first time, nodded silently for her to go on.

"The Duke of Warwick handed your father the throne. 'The

Kingmaker Warwick.' He reveled in the title. In the fame. He'd gone to France to find a proper wife for Edward. A royal princess. But when he returned home he found that the king had married a commoner. A widow with two grown sons. Warwick was livid. He never forgave your father for following his own heart, his own desires. And he despised me. I became the enemy. In his eyes I could do nothing right, even when I proved to be fertile. In short time I'd had you, and was pregnant with Edward when Warwick rebelled, sent your father into exile. Back then, despite his women, Edward still loved me. Trusted me. I was named Regent of England those months of his exile. *I* was.

"Warwick was not the only one who hated me. Clarence loathed me for producing so many healthy children to his one wretched, simpleminded boy. And Hastings. He resented his partner in debauchery stolen away by a beautiful wife, so he lured your father into irresistible liaisons. And Richard, quiet, loyal Richard. He simply loved his brother to distraction. Anyone who siphoned Edward's affections away from him, he despised.

"But there was something that was common to them all, something that bound them in their hatred for me. Now, despite his mistresses and whores, before his brothers, his friends, and even his kingmaker, *I* was Edward's beloved. *I* was his most trusted. *I* was his primary adviser. Every year I produced an heir. Two healthy sons. Five beautiful daughters. I was the very fountain of life. The progenitor of the York bloodline. No one could touch me. No one could harm me. That was why I could be gracious to his mistress Jane Shore. An adored plaything cannot compete with a fecund queen.

"Do you see now, Bessie? *They had lost control of golden Edward*

*York. Lost it to a woman, and a commoner at that.* This they could not abide. So they fought me at every turn. Campaigned so that everyone, noble and common alike, came to perceive me as a cold and grasping harridan, ambitious only for my family, and nothing more. But nothing could touch the real power I wielded. Not until Clarence found the priest Stillington." Elizabeth looked away, unable to meet Bessie's eye.

"You lived up to your reputation *then,* did you not, Mother?"

"Perhaps I did. I was prepared to fight tooth and claw to protect my children's inheritance, their God-given right to rule. That single indiscretion in the past—Eleanor Butler, the only other woman wise enough to demand marriage before she spread her legs—threatened to become my downfall."

"How could you not know that forcing one brother to kill another would, in the end, harm you as well?"

"Perhaps I knew. But what alternative did I have?"

"You might have let the truth be known back then, ridden out the storm," Bessie offered.

Elizabeth nodded slowly, painfully. "If I could have seen the future, had I but seen the destruction that one killing wrought, I think . . . I think I would have taken my chances with the truth." Her laugh was brittle. "I see that those men—your uncles, your father's friends—have succeeded in turning you against me too."

"I needed no help from them," said Bessie, aware that her words, after such a baring of the soul, would cut deeply. "Could you have never spoken like this to me before? Let me understand?"

"Understand *what?* That there was someone other to blame for my ruthlessness? Despite what I've told you about the men that surrounded your father, there is no one else to blame. I've finally become the woman they made me out to be. 'Elizabeth Woodville, bitch queen.' Hard-hearted out of necessity, but hard-hearted all the same.

"But as for my plotting since your father's death, whilst I regret the consequences, I'm not ashamed of the actions. It was a hostile act, Edward naming Gloucester as protector. I think sometimes that he hated me at the end. He knew me very well, and he knew taking my power from me, placing it in Richard's hands, would drive me to acts of desperation. He knew that! But I knew I was the best protector. That down deep in that quiet, smoldering heart of his, Richard of Gloucester was not to be trusted. Now see how my fears have been borne out. The man is a monster!"

"We don't know that, Mother. We don't know that Edward and Dickon are dead."

"We know that my brother and my son are dead at Richard's hand. We know that Hastings is dead on Richard's orders. Why should we not believe he has done away with Edward and Dickon?"

Bessie fought back tears, for her mother's words could hardly be denied. "They might be kidnapped," she said. "Held in a safe place. Shipped off to the continent. But there's no *proof* that they're dead."

"Proof? Proof! You sound like a lawyer, Bessie, not the sister of two murdered brothers." Elizabeth closed her eyes. "Oh, how my head aches. Bring me some wine."

Bessie gazed at her mother, illuminated finally in the light of truth. It was, perhaps, an unbecoming light in many ways, and yet a certain sympathy had been born for the woman. What she'd said about men rang unhappily true.

"All we have is the friars' watered-down claret," said Bessie.

"That will do," her mother said, spent of all energy. "Bessie . . ."

"What is it, Mother?"

"I take heart in knowing that your nature is so different from my own."

Bessie stared down at her mother sitting limp on the discarded throne. "I'll get the wine," she said.

# NELL

THE STORM HAD BECOME a raging monster. True to John's warning, flooded streams and washed-out bridges made for a nightmarish journey back to London. Several times he'd been forced to track backward and find other passages, but all the country roads were axle-deep in water and mud, and a downed tree had killed a family in Oxford. Staunch John never wavered, and Nell silently blessed him for that, for Lady Margaret had been dead determined that her secretary accomplish the task set before her in a timely fashion, the storm be damned. Though it was unspoken, Nell realized, and was humbled by the thought, some part of the fate of England relied on this mission. But the jolting coach had made her plan-making difficult.

Her relief on seeing the tall spire of St. Paul's was short-lived, for once they were in Southwark, it remained for them to cross the Thames, and whilst London Bridge still towered high over the raging waters, the river had overflowed its southern banks and the streets leading to the bridge were beginning to flood.

"We'll make it. Just!" John called back to Nell. "Though I cannot promise your feet will not get wet!"

Indeed, as they approached the bridge, water began seeping into the coach bottom, and Nell could feel the whole vehicle swaying, as if being rocked by a strong current.

"Hold tight, Nell!" John called. "We'll be soon be on dry ground!"

Nell poked her head out the window just as the carriage passed the broad stone gate at London Bridge's south entrance. The tall buildings towering on either side momentarily lessened the force of the storm, but Nell could feel and hear a great rumbling beneath her, the rush of the river sluicing through the bridge's twenty massive pillars of stone. Even in fair weather, Nell knew, this was a wild and dangerous current.

From the towered gate at the middle, Nell could see the River Thames. It was odd to see the great waterway clear of all vessels, for not even the brashest of boatmen were foolish enough to brave this violent storm tide.

Once they'd passed out the bridge's north gate into London City, Nell directed John west toward Westminster precinct. This part of town, whilst puddled and muddy, had been spared from serious flooding. Totehill Street, not entirely deserted, was shorn of its teeming crowds of merchants, shoppers, and roustabouts.

"Slow down, John," she called to the driver, and, holding her hood over her eyes, leaned out the window. Huddled in doorways and under the arch of the church doorway were several faces she recognized.

"John, stop!" She pushed open the coach door and, heedless of the ankle-deep mud, hurried toward two women leaning inside the apothecary's archway.

Nell had found the first of the people she was seeking to help her. God willing, she would find the others.

Once the bedraggled women were safely ensconced in the carriage, Nell opened the hatch to the driver's seat. "Head back toward the Tower of London, John. Take us to Gresham's Haberdasher."

.   .   .

HER FATHER'S HOUSE behind the printshop was the perfect staging area for Nell's covert operation. Nell had instantly taken William Caxton into her confidence, and it was decided between them that Jan de Worde could be trusted as well.

Happily, the streets and alleys adjacent to the shop—Westminster Palace, Abbey, and Sanctuary—were cobbled and well drained, so whilst they were slippery with the downpour, there was neither mud nor flooding thoroughfares to contend with.

In Nell's bedchamber the sisters, Rose and Lily—Totehill Street's prettiest young whores—were preening before the looking glass.

"I like the cut o' this gown," said Rose, tugging an inch more of her plump breast from the low-cut bodice. "And feel this velvet, Lil."

Her sister was too busy rearranging her own conical headdress, deciding whether the chiffon veil should be strapped tightly under her chin or left hanging loose, to admire Rose's new dress.

"Which d'ya like better," Lily demanded, turning to Nell, who sat on her bed, enjoying the girls' obvious pleasure at their windfall. A good washup and Margaret Beaufort's gold had, to the eye at least, transformed these two from gaudy streetwalkers to fine ladies of the court.

"Stick it under yer chin, sis," advised Rose. " 'Twill 'old up the extra."

"I 'aven't got extra!" Lil pushed Rose from the mirror and checked her profile to be sure. "Yer the pudgy one, to be sure. Ain't she, Nell?"

"Neither of you is pudgy. And you've each got the one requisite chin."

"And two fat duckies," Rose added, playfully poking her sister's bosom. Lily slapped her hand away and the two prostitutes laughed uproariously.

"Wish Iris could see us now," said Rose.

"She can see you later," Nell told her. The girls' older sister worked the Tower precinct streets.

"Ya mean we can keep the rags as well as the money?" Rose's tone was incredulous.

"If we're not all caught and thrown in the jail," said Nell.

"Don't ye worry yerself about us, miss," Iris assured her. "We know what our job is, and we'll do it to make you proud."

The sisters appraised each other carefully.

"Yer supposed to be a fine noblewoman, Lil."

"So?"

"Think of a great broom handle stuck up yer arse and ye'll be perfect."

Now they all laughed.

" 'Tis time, ladies," Nell announced.

They trooped down the stairs, out the front door of Caxton's house, into the small garden, and through the printshop's back door. There, Jan de Worde was entertaining a ragged street urchin with a tour of the press room. The ten-year-old cutpurse, Itchy Mitchell, known to be the finest of his trade, was staring openmouthed at the printing press. Jan lifted the handle and extracted a printed sheet.

"So that's how 'tis done?"

"Yes," said Jan. He spread the page before the boy's eyes. "Do you know how to read?"

"Na," Itchy replied. "D'ya know how to do *this*?" From behind his back Itchy produced a small leather pouch, the strings holding it round Jan's waist a moment before neatly snipped.

The apprentice gaped at his purse.

"Yer a little pest, Itchy Mitchell," said Lily. "Give the man back his property."

"Leave off, Lil," he said. "I was just flauntin' me skills." He plopped the purse into Jan's outstretched hand.

"I think it's time to go."

They all turned to see William Caxton standing at the archway into the bookstore with Bessie's old pensioner friend, Tom Wilson.

"All right, then," said Nell. "Lily, Rose, grab your cloaks. We'll leave through the front door. Itchy, the back. Tom . . . ?"

" 'Tis all arranged as you asked."

Caxton's face was tight and hard.

Nell went to him and kissed his cheek. "Don't worry."

"That's right," Rose agreed. "Yer girl'll be fine. She's surrounded by geniuses."

A few moments later the shop was empty, save William Caxton and Jan de Worde, who, despite the assurances, fixed each other with expressions of the deepest concern.

T HE SOLDIER'S PURSE was neatly filched, and with a cry to alert him and the other guards who stood sentry along the abbey's east wall, Itchy Mitchell took off running, zigzagging 'tween men too slow, or slipping on wet cobblestones, to grab him. It was a tease, a great performance, with Itchy jeering and shooting sneers, and bending over to display his small white buttocks and blowing farts through this mouth. The troops, miserable in the pouring rain, enjoyed the show.

It was all the diversion Nell needed to convey Rose and Lily quietly down the narrow street toward the Sanctuary Tower. Just past it was the Westminster wall enclosing the sanctuary and its courtyard. Here stood another company of soldiers, posted three deep round the curved Tower. Clearly, Richard had ordered the strictest security for the devilish Elizabeth Woodville.

Nell and the whores, rain pelting their cloaks, began to move past. They allowed themselves to be seen by the soldiers, no doubt appearing as ladies of the court, keeping their heads down, their faces discreetly shadowed by their hoods.

The barking was faint when it started, but Nell was listening hard and heard it first. She squeezed the girls' hands and they slowed their pace.

The barking grew louder. The soldiers could hear it too, even over the pounding rain. They glanced uneasily at one another. *What were so many barking dogs doing in Westminster's streets?*

The snarling pack, sixteen strong, came racing round the corner into the sanctuary courtyard, amidst Richard's soldiers. All hell broke loose. These were the royal mastiffs, savage, muscular, square-jawed beasts bred to kill bears in the bearbaiting pit. Men scattered, shrieking at the sight of the bloodthirsty animals, who began lunging and snapping at the panicked soldiers.

Now racing round the corner came Hal Wilson, Richard's royal dog keeper, cloakless and drenched, covered in heavy nets, shouting, "Don't harm the king's dogs! Kill one and you're a dead man!" He began heaving nets to the soldiers and barking out orders on how to corner the raging creatures. Everyone obeyed.

*God bless Tom Wilson and his son!* thought Nell as she herded Rose and Lily toward the now unguarded sanctuary door. The old almsman whom Bessie had befriended had retired as the royal dog keeper, but his son Hal had taken his place. Both had been more than willing to help "their princes."

A moment later Nell, Bessie, and Lily had slipped inside. It was dark and gloomy on the wide spiral staircase. Hesitating for the space of a breath, they began climbing the stone stairs, moving stealthily round and round to the top floor, where the sanctuary apartments were. At Nell's signal the girls dropped their cloaks and, with a conspiratorial smile, left Nell behind as they climbed the final turn of stairs.

Nell could hear muffled voices as the veteran prostitutes engaged in seductive banter the two sentries guarding the apartment door. There was laughter—some girlish, some masculine. When all became silent above, Nell began to climb again.

Round the final curve she saw that the girls had done well. The soldiers, both with faces to the wall, were madly humping their gifts of free cunny. Over their shoulders Nell received a smile from Rose and a wink from Lily.

She opened the apartment door and slipped in.

All the York girls were at the slit windows trying to see through the pouring rain the loud chaos of barking dogs and shrieking men below in the sanctuary courtyard.

Little Katherine, four, and as beautiful as a porcelain doll, was the first to turn and see Nell. "Bessie!" she cried. "Look who's come to visit!"

Cecily and Mary spun round. "Thank God!" Cecily cried, and ran to Nell's side. Bridget, three, toddled over too. With the girls gathered thus, Nell looked up to see Elizabeth Woodville, worn and ghostly white, enter from another room.

Bessie appeared behind her. "Nell!"

The friends flew to each other and embraced fiercely. When they pulled apart their faces were wet with tears.

"How did you manage this?" Bessie cried.

"I do not think you'd wish to know." By now Elizabeth had come to their side. Nell curtsied to her, then added, "I would not let your daughters peek outside the door just now." Her expression became earnest. "May I speak with you and Bessie in private?" she said quietly.

"Come." Elizabeth Woodville led Nell and Bessie to the small room she used as her bedchamber. Nell was startled to see the enormous, gorgeously hung Bed of State crammed incongruously into the space. The once-imperious Queen of England bade Nell and Bessie sit on the bed, as there was scarce room for standing. Even now Elizabeth wished to hold the higher ground.

For the entire journey back into London, Nell had rehearsed how she would begin, and in what manner she would choose to present Margaret Beaufort's case to Bessie and her mother. The two women would no doubt respond differently—very differently—so once seated, Nell directed her opening salvo to Elizabeth Woodville.

"I'm most grieved to tell you that your sons are dead . . . on the orders of King Richard."

Elizabeth's face was a stone mask. Nell, unable to meet Bessie's gaze, plowed on. "You must forgive me for dispensing with my sincerest shows of sympathy, Your Majesty, but my time here is necessarily short, and I have much more to say."

"Go on," said Elizabeth.

"Henry Tudor and five thousand of Duke Francis's troops will shortly be landing his fleet on the south shore of England. The Duke of Buckingham, now loyal to Tudor, is already marching southeast with his Welsh army to meet him. These two will join with the rebel forces that you yourself rallied in the south for Edward. King Richard has no fighting men to speak of with him in the north. He's only just left Yorkshire, still two days' ride from London. Once here, he must pull together an army. Tudor and Buckingham are sure they can move on London and take Richard down."

"Lady Margaret is behind this," said Elizabeth, more a statement than a question.

"Yes, madam. That is who sent me."

"But why did she go to such lengths to alert me to her son's
cause?"

Nell hesitated, for this was the most painful moment. "She
wishes for Bessie to marry Henry Tudor and take the throne beside him."

"What are the chances of Tudor's invasion succeeding?" Elizabeth asked, hardly taking time for a breath.

"Mother!"

"Your brothers are dead, Bessie," Elizabeth said, the force returning to her voice. "This is our only chance to keep the York
bloodline alive."

"Uncle Richard is a York!" Bessie cried.

Elizabeth looked at her daughter as if she'd lost her mind.

"'Tis *your* bloodline you mean to keep alive at any cost,"
Bessie accused her mother. "*Any* cost!"

"That's enough," Elizabeth commanded.

"Your Majesty," Nell said, "may I speak privately with Bessie?"

"Yes, do. Perhaps you can talk some sense into her." Elizabeth turned and swept from the room.

Bessie turned on Nell. "How could you?" The hurt in her
eyes was agonizing to behold.

"Forgive me," Nell pleaded. "But if I had not been the messenger, your finding out might have been far more terrible.
Bessie . . ." She drew her friend to her and kissed her cheek.
"I'm so sorry about Edward and Dickon." Misery of her own
forced Nell into silence.

"Do you honestly think they're dead?" Bessie demanded to
know.

"When I heard that they were gone, I went back to the Tower, to their rooms." Nell looked away, remembering. "There'd been a struggle. I cannot say for certain, but my heart tells me they're no longer amongst the living."

"Your heart? What about your mind! You, of all people, Nell. Where is the proof? In *my* heart, I cannot believe that my uncle Richard would harm his brother's sons. You heard him yourself. He did not wish to be king. 'Twas thrust upon him."

"True. And for a time I suspected Harry Buckingham of the deed. But now I can see that once on the throne, Richard came to believe himself the rightful king. Believed he could do good in England. When your mother's rebellion in the south raised the specter of losing the crown—"

"He became a murderous, child-killing fiend?" Bessie finished for her. "I tell you, 'tis not Richard of Gloucester's nature."

"He executed his own brother, Clarence," Nell argued.

"On my father's orders," Bessie countered.

"He had beheaded, on his *own* volition, Lord Hastings, Lord Grey, and Antony—" Nell's voice cracked. "Lord Rivers. Do you not think it possible that to protect against further uprisings in Edward's name he might wish to rid himself of any further claimants to his throne?"

"If he wishes to rid himself of claimants," said Bessie, "then he had better be prepared to spill much more blood than my brothers'. The Duke of Clarence's son would stand in his way, as would the Earl of Lincoln. I know the man's heart, Nell, and he is not capable of this!"

Nell softened, part from pity, part from the good logic of Bessie's words. "You may well be right. But the fact is, whether dead or alive, murdered by Richard's hand or not, your brothers are *gone,* and their chances of returning soon are next to nothing. Someone must be King of England, and it appears Tudor, if his invasion is successful, will be that man. You don't know him.

None of us does. He may be a loathsome creature, and I'm sure that you could never love him as you do your uncle Richard. But one thing is certain. If you marry Henry Tudor and join the York and Lancaster bloodlines, that marriage will once and forever end the war that your two families have been fighting for thirty years! There will be a united England. There will be peace."

Bessie was listening hard. She was dry-eyed and seemed to be gazing into the future.

"You always knew you would have to marry for dynasty," Nell continued, "but you believed 'twould be a foreign prince. Exile in a foreign kingdom. This way, at least your husband would be English. You'd not be forced to leave your home. Your destiny has always been to be a queen, Bessie. This way you would be Queen of *England*."

The door opened and Elizabeth Woodville entered. Nell could see that she meant to command her daughter to consent to the marriage, but Bessie was not about to be commanded or coerced.

She stiffened her spine and lifted her chin. "I'll marry Henry Tudor," she announced, "and I'll be Queen of England. But never, ever, expect me to believe that Uncle Richard murdered my brothers. Now leave me," Bessie said, her beautiful face contorted with grief. "Both of you."

IN HER ENTIRE LIFE, Nell had never experienced such misery as she did now. She was altogether unaware of the ceaseless rain beating on the roof and the violent jolting motion of the coach, such was her despair. Her dearest friend in life hated her now, had dismissed Nell from her presence in the same breath as her despised mother. Worse still was the stunning realization that her dismissal may have been well deserved.

Logic had always driven Nell. Logic and intellect. Logic suggested that as Edward and Dickon had disappeared under King Richard's watch, from his fortress, he and his henchmen were responsible. His motives for the desperate act had seemed clear enough. Much as she loathed Harry Buckingham, she had believed his accusation of his once-respected master's culpability, and so had the sharp and analytical Lady Margaret. 'Twas a tightly woven fabric, this theory of Richard as the boys' murderer. *Have I been unduly influenced by Margaret Beaufort's opinion?* she wondered. She was in awe of the woman, sharp and analytical as any person she'd ever known. *Have I become too malleable? Too easily moved?*

Bessie's intuition, on the other hand, her instinct seen through the eyes of love—that Richard of Gloucester was innocent of any wrongdoing against her brothers, and her refusal to believe they were dead—seemed a flimsy, gossamer web in comparison.

The coach door opening shocked Nell from her ruminations. So deep had her reverie been that she'd not even felt the carriage stop. Now John, his oilcloth dripping wet, came inside and, slamming the door closed behind him, took the seat across from her. He pushed his hood back and she regarded his rugged features, aglow with exertion.

"We'll not be getting back to Woking tonight, I'm afraid," he said. "I've been driving west along the north shore, and we should be able to cross the river at Brentford, but by now the road south will be too treacherous to attempt in the dark. I have an idea, though."

"Tell me."

"Lady Margaret has a house, more a small castle, on the south shore near Brentford. I've been there many times. We're not far. We should stay the night there, and see what we see in the morning."

" 'Tis a sound plan, John," said Nell, relieved for someone capable and trustworthy to be taking charge.

The beating rain had finally let up, but Nell could now hear the roar of the river nearby. John stopped the coach at Brentford Bridge's north side and she let herself out. A rare glimpse of the moon moving between banks of clouds illuminated the scene before them. Another carriage was stopped, its driver silently assessing the safety of a crossing. Brentford was not nearly as grand as London Bridge, just a sturdy span of stone where the Thames's mouth was normally narrow. The waters had reached the apex of its arches. Fallen branches and rubble from collapsed houses were wedged against the western wall, and the roadway itself was awash with spray flying up over the stone sidewall.

Their four horses were skittish and stamping, and rearing away from the bridge's entrance. Even to her untrained eye, Nell could see that the waters had risen just in the time they'd been standing and watching.

"I don't like the look of it!" John shouted over the roar. "But if we don't go now, we may lose our chance altogether!"

Nell hesitated for just a moment, then shouted back, "I say we chance it!"

John smiled. "You're a plucky girl, Nell! I hope the horses are as brave as you! Get in, then, and hold on tight!"

As she climbed inside, Nell could see that the other coach was preparing to follow their lead. She slammed the door closed, then raised the cloth window flap, looking west at the onrushing river. A cloud scuttled over the moon, obliterating it, and with John's encouraging cry to the horses, the coach lurched forward in pitch blackness, with only the tiny lantern lights at the bridge's southern end showing them the way. Nell held her breath, hoping the terrifying passage would at least be brief.

It was not to be so.

They'd gone just a short way when the carriage stopped dead, then jolted backward as the team reared in fright.

Nell opened the window to the driver's seat. "John, what's happened?"

"Huge limb came flying past the horses' heads not five feet in front of 'em! Git up!" he shouted, cracking the whip, but the terrified creatures were paralyzed.

There were frenzied calls from the coach behind for them to move, and move quickly, for the water was rising fast.

But John was having no joy with the animals. "I'll have to get down and lead them!"

A moment later he had disappeared from the driver's seat. Several long moments passed and Nell realized they were still not moving. She flung the door open and jumped down into calf-deep water. A moment more of moonlight allowed her to find John tugging at the left fore horse, who, stubborn as a mule, was not budging from his spot. Nell grabbed the bit of the right fore horse and began urging him ahead.

"Come on, boys!" John shouted. "If a plucky girl can cross this bridge, so can you!"

As if his words had shamed them, the horses finally moved, thankfully forward this time, and with Nell and John leading the horses, the bridge's south lights were growing larger.

Without warning, and with great crashing and shrieking, the bridge jolted beneath them. Nell and John were thrown off their feet. She looked up and saw, to her horror, a whole tree looming over them. By the look of it, it was ancient, with a thick gnarled trunk and limbs still leafy, its great snarl of roots pointing unnaturally skyward.

Another surge of the storm tide forced it farther over the bridge and it teetered, an obscene canopy, over the two coaches.

Wordlessly, John and Nell scrambled to their feet. This time the horses needed no urging, for they were eager to be gone from the terrifying bridge. The coach had just cleared the last suspended branch when another wave lifted the tree from the west wall, but as it flew up and over the top, a stout limb hooked in the harness of the team behind, and to Nell's unbelieving eyes, ripped the horses, driver, and carriage, like a child's toy, toppling it into the river. The waters took the rig but for a brief distance before it sank beneath the churning darkness.

"Come on, Nell!" John cried, but Nell needed no further encouragement. She wished she could take off her heavy, waterlogged skirts. Her thighs burned as she slogged through the now knee-deep water. But finally the bridge's south lights were close, and two men rushed out to help them the final distance to safety.

Nell collapsed on the step of the coach. John stood above her, panting and looking back at the treacherous Thames.

"Those poor people," she said, her teeth chattering.

"Close call for us," he said. "But 'twasn't our time to be taken. Come on, then, get back in. The castle's not far. It wouldn't do to save you from a tree falling on your head to die of a bloody chill."

THE SILHOUETTE OF Barkley Manor in the fitful moonlight proved John right. It was less a manor than a castle, much like Woking, though it was made of old-fashioned timber and plaster rather than stone. Perhaps, thought Nell as they clattered over the moat's drawbridge, Margaret Beaufort chose to call her residences "manors" to draw attention away from what must surely be her astonishing wealth.

The moat guard had been asleep, and now Nell could see that

Barkley was almost altogether dark, even its front lanterns extinguished. Faint light could be seen through the small windows, and when she knocked there was no answer. It took several minutes of pounding with the heavy knocker, Nell shivering miserably, to raise a servant, and when the door was finally opened, the portly steward in his nightclothes wore such a scowl that she thought for a moment he would turn her away.

It took some proving of her identity and circumstances to finally be allowed entry into the house, clearly shut up and manned only by a skeleton staff. Even by torchlight Nell could see that this residence was as grand as Woking, rich tapestries adorning every one of the walls, fine furniture, and portraits of Margaret Beaufort's ancestors hanging proudly in the corridors. Nell was surprised, as the steward led her to the kitchen, to see a heavy carven wood door, much like the one that led to Lady Margaret's offices at Woking, and wondered briefly at what creatures of habit all people were.

By the time John had seen to the horses and come in, Nell was wrapped in a blanket and was gratefully partaking of a slice of warmed-over meat pie and some spiced wine in the servants' kitchen. John joined her at the table, and the cook, who was as dour and unfriendly as any house servant Nell had ever known, provided him with a portion of the same, grumbling the whole time.

The steward and the cook, who listened wide-eyed to John's telling of his and Nell's adventure of Brentford Bridge, were otherwise quite uninterested in them, most eager to put their visitors to bed and get back to their own.

John was sent to the stables, where grooms, stableboys, and drivers lived when the house was open. Nell was given a bedchamber on the upper floor, small but comfortably appointed. The cook had provided her with one of her own nightgowns, which

Nell gratefully donned and fell, instantly, into an exhausted
sleep.

*She was floating on a gilt barge with Antony, colorful banners snap-*
*ping above them. Amidst red silk pillows they reclined, he with his fair*
*head in her lap, she lazily caressing his face with her fingers. The air was*
*soft and warm on their skin, and the only sound was water lapping gently*
*at the hull. They were speaking to each other as lovers do, but the lan-*
*guage was Latin gibberish, which both of them seemed to understand.*
*Nell became aware that the sound of the snapping banners was growing*
*louder, so loud, in fact, that all conversation was drowned out. The*
*sound, now a roar, alarmed her, and when she turned to look upriver, she*
*saw a great wall of water rushing toward them, with houses and trees and*
*the bodies of cows and horses balanced high on its roiling crest.*

*Antony was yet unaware, but when Nell opened her mouth to warn*
*him, no sound emerged. She shook him, but he was fast asleep and alto-*
*gether peaceful. She thought,* I must wake him from so peaceful a
dream.

*Then the wave struck and the barge was lifted high and overturned.*
*Nell hung, for dear life, onto the wooden boat and lay half drowned on*
*her belly in the cook's nightdress. Red pillows floated on the water now,*
*a meat pie, and many of her father's books. She spotted Antony's long*
*yellow hair floating like a tangled mass of golden seaweed, and reached*
*out for it. She pulled with unnatural strength and he came bobbing to*
*the surface, alive, the sweet peaceful smile on his face, altogether unper-*
*turbed at his near drowning. Their hands were clasped now and Nell be-*
*gan tugging him up to the overturned barge with her, but something was*
*holding him down and he could never quite be hoisted aboard.*

*Slowly she began losing him, more and more of his torso, neck, and*
*chin submerged. Still the sweet smile played on his lips, even as he was*
*pulled deeper and his face disappeared under the water, leaving only the*
*golden tresses floating on the surface. Nell clutched his hand desperately,*

*refusing to lose him. With all the strength she had, she gave a great, final tug. To her joy the yellow-haired head surfaced once again, water streaming down the face. But it was not Antony Woodville's face. It was young Edward, gray-skinned and skeletal. Dull eyes were sunken in their sockets, and when he opened his mouth to speak to Nell, the hideous head of a green eel slithered out. Nell shrieked and tore her hand from Edward's.*

*The boy slipped away under the water.*

She came awake with a scream, sitting bolt upright in bed. Confused momentarily by her surroundings and the horrible dream, moonlight and the wispy remnants of storm clouds out the bedroom window brought her to her senses and the present moment. *I am at Barkley Manor,* she told herself. *Antony and Edward are dead, England is at war with itself, and my dearest friend in the world hates me.*

Good cause for a nightmare.

There was no chance for sleep now, so Nell gathered a small coverlet round her shoulders, lit her bedside lamp, and left the room. She was curious about her employer's properties, and now with the probability of Henry Tudor supplanting Richard as king, Margaret Beaufort would become much more than merely a wealthy woman. She would be queen mother and, more importantly, Bessie's mother-in-law. Nell wondered, as she padded quietly down the dark stairway to the first floor, whether her friend would ever forgive her for the part she had played in Margaret and Henry's plan. She'd only been the messenger, but that had been enough for Bessie to feel utterly betrayed. Of course it was more than that, thought Nell. She had dared to believe and say aloud that Bessie's beloved Richard could be a monster. Perhaps a true friend would never have entertained the thought.

It was odd and unnerving wandering round a dark, unattended manor. Nell's candle flickered in the drafty corridors, and its light illuminated but a small area before her. She held the taper high to examine an old portrait, it inscription proclaiming the man as John of Gaunt, fourth and youngest son of King Edward the Third, He was ancestor of both the York and Lancaster lines, and therefore the progenitor of all the familial infighting that, nearly a hundred years after his death, was still creating havoc and mayhem in England.

Farther down was a portrait of Catherine Swynford, Gaunt's mistress and later his wife. Unlike Elizabeth Woodville, who had insisted on marriage before bedding, Catherine had birthed two bastard children by him, legitimized when she'd become his wife. Margaret Beaufort was a grandchild of that union.

A third portrait told of Henry Tudor's paternal lineage, just as flawed and just as eminent as his mother's. Owen Tudor, whose long, severe face stared out from the picture, had been a wardrobe clerk to the triumphant victor of Agincourt, King Henry the Fifth. When the king had died, his widow, Queen Katherine, had taken the rather lowly Welsh servant into her bed and produced three bastard children—one of them Henry Tudor's father—all of whom were made legal by the good graces of the next Lancastrian king.

Suddenly Nell found herself at the carven door so like the one leading to Lady Margaret's Woking offices. Impulsively she reached out and tried the door handle, fully expecting it to be locked. The door opened. Nell shut it quickly, realizing that she was shamelessly snooping in the home of her employer and, perhaps, the mother of the future king. But curiosity quickly overtook good sense, and with a final look behind her, Nell slipped through the doorway.

She was quite unprepared for what she discovered. Here was

an almost exact replica of Margaret Beaufort's warren of offices at Woking Manor. Nell stepped into the hub where Lady Margaret's desk sat facing in precisely the same direction as its counterpart at Woking. Down a short hall to the left she discovered the cartography room with its baskets of rolled maps, and the table map of England and the continent, with its military pieces all neatly set to one side. In other rooms farther down the hall Nell's lamplight revealed the fully stocked armory, and the treasury—though the shelves and chests were here empty. Lady Margaret was too sensible to allow her fortune to be too far from her person at any time. Nell stood in the scribe's chamber staring at its two high desks and stools and the long, broad table where the second correspondence secretary might lay out the incoming and outgoing documents.

It was eerie to see, by a single candle's glow, the twin offices in which, one day when Margaret's yearly progress brought her to Barkley, Nell would likely find herself working. And a stranger thought still: *Did Lady Margaret keep such a warren of offices—each the same as the next—in every one of her residences?*

The squeaking of a door was so unexpected it nearly unhinged Nell. She made to blow out the candle, but thought quickly that the sulfur smoke would give her presence away. Licking her fingers, she extinguished the flame quickly between them and hid herself behind the open scribe's-chamber door and peered out through the crack in the hinged side.

Across the hall a long, heavy tapestry was pulled back and through the faintly illuminated doorway behind it emerged the cook. The woman, in her nightdress, carried a tray in one hand and a lantern in the other, and even in the dim light Nell could see she wore a scowl deeper than she had in the servants' kitchen that evening. Even alone, she was muttering angrily to herself.

Blessedly unaware of Nell's presence so close by, the cook proceeded down the short hall, past Lady Margaret's desk, and out the carven door. Nell sagged with relief, then realized she was standing in pitch blackness with no way to relight her candle. Using the scribe's door to guide her, she moved out into the hallway, then remembered the glimpse of faint light she'd seen behind the cook as she'd emerged from the doorway and tapestry hiding it.

Blind, as if her head were encased in black velvet, Nell managed to grope her way down and across the hall to where she believed the tapestry hung. Her hand struck a small wooden plaque hung on the wall, and before she knew what had happened, it had clattered noisily to the floor.

Nell froze, knowing the cook was still close enough to have heard. She felt her way into the cartography room and slipped inside just as the carven door opened again and the cook stuck her head through.

*Please do not come back in,* Nell prayed. But the woman entered and stood by Lady Margaret's desk, holding up the lantern and peering round her. Too lazy or uninterested to investigate further, the grumbling woman, to Nell's extreme relief, turned and exited.

This time Nell waited, stock-still in the dark, till the cook had had sufficient time to return to the kitchen. Again groping, but much more carefully this time, Nell found the fallen plaque—by the feel of it a wooden coat of arms—and replaced it on the wall. Then, locating the long tapestry, she pushed it back and fumbled for the door behind. The latch clicked too loudly for comfort, and the door squeaked open on its rusty hinges.

Indeed there was light behind the door—a single wall torch burning—and it shone on an ancient and decrepit stairwell that curved down and away into more darkness. Nell's heart began a violent thumping, and a strange terror overwhelmed the intense curiosity that normally drove her forward.

This place had the stench of evil about it. Fear was not a common emotion with her, but Nell's skin was crawling, and even in the chill, she could feel beads of perspiration forming above her lip. The thought passed through her mind that she had gone too far. Eavesdropping on people of importance was one thing. Trespassing here, in Margaret Beaufort's inner sanctum, was another. If she was found out, the consequences of her snooping might cost her more than her job.

Still, she was driven, like the proverbial cat, by her unrelenting curiosity. She lifted the torch from its wall mount and began to descend the well-worn stairs. The smell of mildew and putrefaction was quite overwhelming, and she could see mold and moss growing upon the stone walls, and the carcasses of dead rats pushed to the sides of the steps. The place felt ancient, almost primeval, certainly older than the rest of Barkley Manor, perhaps by a thousand years.

Her suspicions were borne out when at the next turn she noticed a Corinthian pillar on either side of the stairs, joined by a carven stone arch. Barkley had been constructed over the ruins of a Roman building! As she descended deeper, the rockwork appeared to be crumbling and the walls dripped with moisture.

All that was needed here was fire, she thought, to make the place hell on earth.

Finally she reached the bottom, a long dirt-floored corridor. She saw an unlit torch in its mount and lit it with the one she carried. On the opposite wall was illuminated the meaning of this underground chamber—it was a barred cell, a dungeon. Nell's stomach churned as she held her torch closer to see the chains and manacles hewn to the wall, and imagined the human suffering that had here taken place. There were more empty dungeons down the line, and such was her utter shock at the revelation of such a place that, until she noticed a crack of light at the end of the corridor, did she wonder what the cook could have been doing down here with a dinner tray.

The thin line of light drew Nell forward. She could see now it was a crack at the top of a tiny door in the center of a large, heavy wooden door. Near it, a key hung on a nail.

*What monster must be housed in such a place?* she asked herself. *What evil needs keeping so far from the world as this?* She had heard tales of families who had been forced to lock away forever a relative so insane and murderous that even asylums would not have them. Did Margaret Beaufort or Lord Stanley have such a relation? Would that person, when Henry became king, be such an embarrassment or danger that secret imprisonment was the only answer?

Once more, Nell's instinct for discovery drove her. She must know who or what lay behind this door. Slowly she swung open the hinged window, poised at any moment to spring back if the fiend should rear up in her face.

But nothing sprang at her, and she stepped closer to peer in. All she could see in the faint flickering light was a rude pallet, the straw from its mattress falling out in several places, an old blanket crumpled in one corner. There was something poking out from beneath the blanket, something flat and square, and she held her torch up to the window, hoping to cast more light on the object.

It took a moment for her mind to register that the object was familiar to her, and it took an adjustment of the torch to realize, to her horror, exactly what she was seeing.

'Twas the green cover of *Jason and the Argonauts*!

Nell spun away, clapping her hand over her mouth, but she fell to her knees, retching violently in the dirt. She was thus disabled when she heard a familiar voice from inside the door.

"Who is it? Who's there?" came the weak, tiny voice.

It was Dickon. Nell was sure of it. She did not immediately answer, for her mind was chaotic, inundated, frenzied. *How should she announce herself? In what condition would she find the boys? And why was Edward not speaking? Oh God, let him be alive!*

Now there was a small whimper, and Nell's heart broke. She wiped her mouth, stood, and grabbed the key from the nail. She leaned close to the window, which was too high for Dickon to see her, and whispered with as much calm as she could muster in her state of agitation, "Dickon, 'tis Nell, sweetheart."

"Ohh," was the only sound that came from within.

"I'm going to unlock the door and come in, so stand away."

"Nell, is it really you, or am I dreaming?"

"No, Dickon, you're not dreaming. Stand away so that when I open the door—"

"Come in, come in quickly." His voice was desperate now.

Nell tried to turn the old key in the rusty lock, but it jammed halfway to opening.

" 'Tis hard to open," Dickon whispered. "Cook struggles with it every time."

*The old witch!* thought Nell. *Dour-faced jailer of children.* Oh, she prayed it was *children* and not a single child within! She jiggled and finessed the key to no avail.

"Please, please!" Dickon cried.

"Just a moment more," she lied, for the key was now jammed in the ancient lock.

"I tell you, I heard something clatter to the floor."

'Twas the cook! Nell heard the woman's voice echoing down the spiral stairs and along the long dungeon hall.

"We'll have a look," the steward answered irritably.

Nell had to act quickly. The key was jammed in the lock and the torch she'd lit was still burning at the base of the stairs. They would know someone was here!

Footsteps were echoing closer now.

With a great yank she ripped the key from the lock and hung it back on the nail.

"Dickon, stay still!" she whispered. "I'll be back." She closed the tiny door within the door.

"Noo," she heard him moan.

Grabbing her own torch, she hitched her nightdress and raced toward the lit torch at the base of the stairs, but the cook and steward were almost at the bottom. There was no time! Nell extinguished her torch and pushed the closest barred dungeon door, but it was locked. She tried the next. Locked again. And the next! Finally one opened. She dove in and pressed back into the shadows on the wall toward which the cook and steward were coming.

"You left the lower torch burning again, Mary," said the irritated steward. "When will you learn?"

"Just stop your pestering and do your job."

"My job would be easier—"

"Shut your trap, Harold!"

Once they had passed, Nell stealthily pressed up against the bars and looked down the corridor. The steward was placing the key in the lock of the wooden door.

"Damn thing!" he cried, and with a grunt and the shriek of metal on metal, the key pushed through and clicked open. He poked his head in, was quickly satisfied, and slammed the door shut again.

Nell tiptoed to the opposite side of the cell so their torch-light would not illuminate her.

"Now will you leave me in peace, woman?" said the steward.

"You'll be lucky if I leave you in *one* piece," the bad-tempered cook rejoined.

They grumbled and nagged at each other all the way up the

stone staircase, but Nell waited till she heard the latch click shut at the top before she left the fetid hole. With her doused torch she ran to relight it on the one still burning on the wall. She hurried back to the boys' cell. This time when she placed the key in the lock it turned with blessed ease. She pulled the door open and beheld the most piteous sight her eyes had ever seen.

Dickon, his once soft golden hair hanging in brown strings round his grimy face, was kneeling by a second flea-bitten pallet, his arms protectively encircling his elder brother. Edward, lately the King of England, lay limp as rags, his sunken eyes closed, and his face as gray and skeletal as it had been in Nell's nightmare.

Dickon looked up slowly, disbelieving that Nell was not a vision, but flesh and blood come to rescue them.

"Nell, Nell!" He flew to her, arms clutching her waist, and hers cradling his head. He wept and murmured unintelligible exhortations of gratitude. She crooned comfortable words and stroked his hair.

"Is Edward——"

"He is alive, but barely," Dickon answered. "The pain is terrible. I think he wishes to die to be taken out of his misery."

"No!" said Nell, pushing the young boy to arm's length. "He must not die." She went to Edward's side and knelt there. Heat was rising from his body. She had no need to feel his head. He was burning with fever. The pillow beneath him was clotted with gore and pus.

"Edward, can you hear me? Edward, 'tis Nell."

He moaned very faintly, but audibly.

"I am going to get you help. I will get you and your brother out of here to safety."

"No, Nell, you mustn't leave us!" Dickon was tugging at her arm.

She turned to him. "If I am to help you, I must leave you, but I *will* come back here with a rescue party. And very soon."

The boy began to sob, and all Nell could do was hold him to her breast as he wept.

"Think of this," she said, trying to force strength into her voice. "Jason, on his adventures, was tested in trial after trial. Think of all he suffered! But he was a brave warrior, and in the end he prevailed. You and Edward are the bravest boys in England, and if you hold on just a little longer, you will survive this most terrible trial. Can you hold on, Dickon?"

He sniffed. "Yes. But Edward—"

"You will have to be strong for him as well. Do you hear me? You must stay at his side and whisper in his ear constantly that help is on the way. *Help is on the way!*"

"Do you promise?"

"On my soul, Dickon!" She bent and kissed Edward's emaciated cheek, then embraced Dickon once more. She moved to the cell door and looked back at them. "Princes of England," she said, fighting back her tears of outrage, "have courage!"

"Courage," said Dickon.

Nell closed and locked the door behind her, then went to find John.


LONG A MAN OF the world, William Caxton nevertheless found it impossible to disguise his shock and horror at Nell's revelation.

Once leaving the grisly cellar at Barkley, she had dressed in her still-damp clothes, hurrying to the stables to wake John. He'd had a difficult time believing that the princes were indeed alive, but more especially that his employer was capable of both the kidnapping and imprisonment in such ghastly circumstances.

His father, he told Nell, had been a Yorkist sympathizer and had actually fought for Edward during Warwick's rebellion at the battle of Barnet. John himself had celebrated in London when young Edward had ridden through Londongate just six months ago. The driver had trusted Nell's unlikely story as much out of his respect for her as his joy that the little king was still alive and might one day be restored to the throne.

Now sitting at Caxton's dining room table, her father, Jan de Worde, and John learned every detail of the boys' present surroundings, their physical and mental condition. It was obvious to them all that something had to be done quickly, and the urgency was made all the greater with the most recent news from the Westcountry and the south of England.

"The Great Storm," as it was now being called, had managed with its hurricane of winds and torrential rains to essentially change the course of the rebellion against King Richard.

On his first attempt to cross the Channel, Henry Tudor's fleet had been beset by so wild a tempest that he'd been forced to return to Brittany, and whilst he and his fleet were, even now, making a second attempt at landing, Harry Buckingham's army had been thwarted altogether. The Severn River had so extravagantly flooded its banks that the Welshmen had been unable to cross over it into southern England for their rendezvous with Tudor. Waterlogged and dispirited, his troops had dispersed, returning to their homes, leaving Buckingham alone and, if the rumors were to be believed, himself a fugitive on the run.

Whilst Nell and Caxton could not be sure how these events would modify Henry Tudor's invasion, they worried that *any* deviation from Margaret Beaufort's tightly organized operation might somehow affect the plans for her young prisoners, perhaps in a deadly fashion. Edward and Dickon needed to be rescued quickly and quietly from Barkley Manor and transported to safety. What was more, it could not appear that Nell or her father was in any way involved with their liberation.

"You must return immediately to Woking, Nell." Caxton's eyes were vague and unfocused as he spoke, but she knew him well, and this particular gaze was an indication that her father's mind was working with furious intensity. "You will say that on John's advice, you stayed the night at Barkley Manor, but left at dawn before the cook and steward awoke. At Kew you found the road washed out, and 'twas necessary to detour east again to . . ." Caxton hesitated.

"Chiswick," John offered. "We had to detour east again at Chiswick before heading west back to Woking."

Caxton smiled appreciatively at John. "Thus the delay in your return." Caxton turned to his apprentice. "How long ago was Edward Brampton in our shop?"

Jan thought for a moment. "Three days. He bought several volumes and asked that I have them delivered to his London lodgings within the week."

"Good. Edward Brampton is a Portuguese businessman and adventurer," Caxton told him. "A converted Jew and a Yorkist sympathizer. The elder King Edward, in fact, stood as godfather at the man's baptism. When Edward died, Brampton moved back to Lisbon, but not before stopping off in Bruges to visit Edward's sister Duchess Margaret of Burgundy. In mourning together for their lost king, they became close friends, and 'tis well known that their dearest wish is a restoral of the Yorkist bloodline."

"But her brother is a York," Nell reasoned.

"Of all her brothers, Richard was Margaret's least favored. Like young Edward, she chose to believe Gloucester responsible for the death of Clarence, who was, in fact, her *most* beloved sibling."

"Would Margaret not support her own niece as queen?" Nell asked. "After all, Bessie is Edward's natural daughter. Her blood—"

"I know Margaret of Burgundy well," said Caxton. And whilst she is good-hearted in the deepest sense, she is driven first and foremost by her passions and her own strong beliefs. *Of course* 'twas King Edward who was responsible for Clarence's execution. Richard was merely following the orders of his master. *Of course* Bessie's blood is as purely York as her brother Edward's, but Margaret of Burgundy believes, as so many do, that the succession of kings should proceed through the *male* line. In her mind, her nephew Edward is England's only true king."

"So she would do anything to restore and preserve him?"

"I believe she would."

"And Brampton?" Nell asked.

"Luck seems to be with us. You know he returns to England periodically on business and is here right now. I would wager my life that he would happily be Duchess Margaret's instrument in this rescue." Caxton spoke to his apprentice. "Jan, I would like you to be on the first possible ship sailing for Burgundy. You will carry a letter to Duchess Margaret from me. Nell—" He turned to his daughter and grasped her hand. "With great care you will hie to Woking."

"I'll look after her, sir," John offered, his voice thick with loyalty and passion.

"I will go see Brampton myself," Caxton continued. He looked to Nell and John. "When all the plans are in place, I will contact you at Woking. The winds of Fate are very changeable, so whilst a plan is necessary, we must all be prepared to fly where these winds take us."

"I wish for Bessie to know that her brothers are alive," said Nell.

"You cannot risk another meeting in sanctuary," her father objected.

"Bessie must be told, Father. When all had given up hope, Bessie *knew* they lived. Knew Richard was innocent. I shall never doubt her again." Nell thought for a moment. "When Rose and Lily and I left there, the girls had made close friends with two of the door guards. Perhaps 'favor' might be traded for 'favor.' A note—"

"If it fell into the wrong hands—"

"When I wrote to Antony in his prison, I devised a code of sorts. I should be able to convey the information so that no one but Bessie will be the wiser. And I trust that the girls will make it inside sanctuary."

"All right," Caxton relented. "Devise a message and I'll find the sisters."

Nell stood and hugged her father round the shoulders from behind. "I feel an idiot," she said. "And a terrible judge of character. I work for Margaret Beaufort, see her every day. Yet had no inkling."

"Then we are all idiots," he said. "How could we ever have guessed she was capable of such an evil conspiracy?" He shook his head. "True, she is perfectly positioned. Harry Buckingham is her nephew, Constable of England, with access to the Tower, close confidant of the king. And Buckingham is a weakling compared to Lady Margaret, able to be controlled by his aunt. But Henry Tudor has been in exile so long, who would have suspected his mother to be so powerful and so desperate to see him king that she would perpetrate an outrage such as this?"

"How can I look her in the eye and pretend I don't know?" said Nell.

"You must find a way. 'Tis imperative that you return to

Woking before Henry's invasion force lands. You must find out Lady Margaret's plans for the boys."

Nell felt tears welling. "It makes me ill to think of them in that place for even one hour more, suffering. Edward perhaps dying. And poor Dickon, he wondering if anyone will ever return to rescue them."

Caxton stood and fixed his daughter with loving eyes. "You gave him your word. He knows to trust it. And you have my word that we will rescue them."

"Father . . ."

They embraced, neither wishing to let go their hold on the other.

"Keep yourself safe, child," he said. "You are all I have in the world."


N ELL AND JOHN SPOKE hardly a word during the drive to Woking. She could not tell whether her mind or heart was racing faster, and John, bless his soul, was intent on getting them there with the greatest speed and safety.

As they approached the lowered moat bridge, not one but *three* riders galloped out the gate and past the coach. The gate guards, normally friendly, waved John through without even a smile. With a signal that bespoke their collusion, John left Nell at the door and drove off to the stables. Nell, calming herself with a deep breath, entered the manor.

Servants rushed round in silent urgency, none meeting the others' eyes. Many trunks and crates were piled by the door as if waiting to be removed, and more were being hauled down the broad stairs even now. Messengers—at least a dozen of them—milled about, impatiently waiting to be called inside the office.

It took all of Nell's strength to put out of her mind the memory of Edward and Dickon in their hellhole, for otherwise there was no way she could face Margaret Beaufort without reaching out and strangling her. Instead, she directed all thought to the rebellion, the invasion, and the fate of Lady Margaret's nephew and conspirator, Harry Buckingham.

She went immediately through the carven door to the offices. What she had seen without made her sure of what was to be expected within. But the disorder and confusion with which she was confronted was much worse; it was barely controlled chaos.

The central hub was smoky, as a servant stood feeding a huge pile of documents, one by one, into a brazier. The two scribes were even now bringing more from their chamber to pile at his feet. Chests of gold and jewels were being carried by servants from the treasury room, and men of Margaret's personal guard were emptying the armory of its contents.

Lady Margaret sat at her desk, back facing the door, as two messengers stood before her. Both were filthy and mud-splattered, and their faces were pained, both of them having clearly been the bearers of bad tidings to their mistress, who sat silent and ramrod straight in her chair, digesting the indigestible.

Finally she spoke, and Nell heard in her voice a cold fury mingled with disbelief.

"I was led to understand," she said, "that after the tempest pushed Henry's fleet back to Brittany, all fifteen of his ships finally reached the coast of Dorset."

"No, madam," said one of the couriers. "Only your son's flagship and one other reached the harbor at Poole. He sent a small boat ashore to assess the conditions. Soldiers called out from land that all was well, the rebellion flourishing, and that the boatmen should land. But Tudor wisely disbelieved them and evaded the trap. The two ships then sailed westward." The man looked to the other messenger to continue.

"I was in Plymouth when the two ships arrived. They hovered off the coast only long enough to learn that the rebellion had collapsed *entirely,* and that King Richard had traveled unopposed from York all the way south to Exeter. 'Twas more, they said, like a Royal Progress than a war march." This courier looked fearful, as though he believed his dire report would earn him a sword in his throat. But he finished bravely. "Your son sailed back to Brittany on four October."

Margaret dismissed both men with a wave of her hand, as though her voice would betray her. As they hurried out she sat stock-still at her desk. Nell straightened her own back and presented herself to her employer.

"Forgive me for my tardiness, Lady Margaret, but the river—"

"I know all about the rivers and the bridges, the wind and the rain and the fainthearted rebels," she said, her voice flat. "My son's invasion has failed because of them."

"I'm very sorry, madam," Nell lied, she hoped convincingly.

"And my nephew now lies headless in a wood box in Salisbury."

"Harry Buckingham is dead?" Nell was incredulous.

"When Richard reached the town where he had taken refuge, Harry pleaded for an audience with the king."

"Would he not grant it?" Nell asked.

"Richard of Gloucester is a spiteful man," Margaret asserted.

Nell felt compelled to defend him. "Lord Buckingham did betray the king badly."

"I think the king is weak-livered and sentimental. He remembered how strong was Harry Buckingham's influence on him. He'd led Gloucester round by the nose from the moment they met up in Northampton. He single-handedly placed Richard—a most reluctant king—onto the throne. He knew that if he saw Harry face-to-face he would forgive him. Pardon him. And Richard does not wish the world to see him as he really is. Thus, the refusal for an audience. Thus, the execution. Now go and help the scribes bring out the documents to burn."

"Must *everything* be destroyed?"

"Perhaps 'tis not clear to you, Mistress Caxton, but I will shortly be arrested for my part in this insurrection, this 'treason.' The less they have of my plans committed to paper, the greater my chances of surviving with my head intact upon my body."

"I understand." Nell turned to go.

"Wait," said Lady Margaret. Nell turned back. "What said Lady Bessie and her mother to our offer?"

"What *said* they?" Nell replied stupidly. She wondered what it could possibly matter, now that Henry Tudor's rebellion had been stillborn.

"Out with it, girl. I do not pay you to repeat my questions like a silly child."

"Forgive me. Lady Bessie and her mother were amenable to your son's offer of marriage."

It was the first sign of pleasure Nell had seen Margaret display. The woman noticed Nell's quizzical expression. "You wonder why it should matter now," she said.

"I do wonder, Lady Margaret."

"Because this is one small battle lost, and every day one lives and breathes brings new opportunities. My Henry is alive and well in Brittany. And he is destined to be King of England. His time will come, and when it does, the York princess will be his bride . . . Ah, Reggie!"

"My lady."

As Reginald Bray appeared and knelt to kiss Margaret's hand, Nell felt herself summarily dismissed. Four men carrying a huge casket of gold coins blocked her way, allowing her to linger long enough to hear Reggie say, "When do you wish me to leave for Barkley?" and Margaret's reply: "This evening. I wish you to travel at night, arrive before dawn."

The bearers having gone past, Nell was forced to move away and no more could be heard of Lady Margaret and Reginald Bray's conversation. *But much sooner than she expected, Bray was off to Barkley Manor, where no business went on except the captivity of the princes of England. There could be no good end to his trip there.*

Nell moved through the motions of helping the scribes pull documents from the shelves, then carried them out, straining to hear what Margaret and Reggie Bray were saying, but their heads were close and they were whispering now. Nell could see a sinister smile playing about the man's lips, and she imagined he was taking pleasure in the thought of snuffing out the lives of the two young Yorks.

*She must delay his leaving!* It could not be long before she had word from her father of his plans. But if Reginald Bray arrived at Barkley Manor before Caxton's rescue party, Edward and Dickon would surely be murdered. *Please, Father,* Nell silently prayed, *send word. Send it soon. Send it now!*

# BESSIE

H OW BAD CAN the man be, after all?" said Elizabeth
Woodville. She was beginning to lose her patience.

"Spawn of that midget woman, Lady Margaret,"
Bessie replied with disgust. "He might be despicable. He might
look like her!"

"That 'midget woman' is going to be your mother-in-law,
my dear, so you'd best learn to love her and her son."

"I'll marry Henry Tudor, Mother, but if you expect
me to——"

Without warning the sanctuary door flew open and two
ladies, elegantly cloaked in velvet and ermine, hurried inside
and shut the door behind them. They pushed their deep hoods
back to reveal two girls whom Bessie instantly recognized as
prostitutes from Totehill Street.

Bessie stood to greet them. "You're Nell's friends from the
precinct," she said. "Come in, come in."

"What is the meaning of this?" said Elizabeth. "Who are these
people, Bessie?"

"They're whores, Mother."

"That we are," said the dark-haired one with not a little
pride. "I'm Rose and this here's me sister Lily." As if suddenly
remembering, she elbowed Lily, and they both curtsied, first to

Bessie and then to her mother. "But today we're somethin' more, me and me sister. Today we're——"

"But how did you get past the guards?" Elizabeth rudely interrupted.

"Oh, madam, you wouldn't want the gory details," Rose assured her.

"Maybe she would," her sister said with a lascivious grin.

"Shut up, Lil. But the point is, good ladies, we've come from Master Caxton with news."

"News!" Bessie turned excitedly to her mother. "We have had so few messages from outside."

"How goes the rebellion?" Elizabeth had forgotten the lowly status of the couriers and came forward to hear them.

"The rebellion?" said Lily. "Oh, 'tis dead. Dead as Harry Buckin'am, cradlin' his handsome head in his lap."

"Buckingham is executed?" Elizabeth Woodville was trying to understand. "But what of the invasion? All those ships from Brittany?"

"That Tudor fella, he turned tail and sailed home to France," Rose answered.

Bessie could hardly contain her joy.

"But listen now," said Rose. "That ain't the reason we've come."

"Yes it is!" cried Lily.

"The *other* news," Rose reminded her sister. "The *important* news."

"What could be more important than news of the failed invasion?" Elizabeth demanded.

"Well . . ." said Rose, drawing her answer out dramatically. "You might think the young princes bein' alive might be a tad more important."

"My sons are alive?" Elizabeth sought her chair, for her knees had suddenly gone wobbly.

"I knew it," said Bessie, her own body sagging with relief. "Where are they? When can we see them?" She turned to Elizabeth. "Mother, they're alive!"

The woman's eyes were glazed over.

"What's the matter with you?" Bessie shouted at her. "Edward and Dickon are alive!"

"Alive," Elizabeth murmured, "but bastards still. Edward deposed. And Henry Tudor gone, his invasion failed."

Bessie turned on her mother with fury. "And I no longer a queen-to-be? Your precious plans in tatters? Has your heart turned entirely to stone?"

Elizabeth said nothing in reply.

"Go to the devil!" Bessie cried, then turned back to the streetwalkers. She took their hands in hers. "Tell me more," she said. "Tell me all you know!"

# NELL

WAITING FOR WORD from her father seemed an eternity, whilst the hours till Reggie Bray's departure for Barkley flew by. She made an excuse to withdraw and had gone immediately to John. He had a strategy, he told her, but was unable to begin till it was known which vehicle or mount Margaret's henchman would be using to travel north.

Now Lady Margaret was keeping Nell maddeningly busy in the office. The couriers were piling up outside the carven door, and when each, in turn, arrived bringing updates of King Richard's movements, or Henry's journey back across the Channel, their messages needed logging in and recording. Nell shared these duties with the first correspondence secretary, so frantic was the pace, and with Margaret's "secret" revealed, Nell was privy to the contents of the documents received from the rebellions co-conspirators.

Bishop Morton sent word that after Harry Buckingham's execution he was fleeing the country. It became apparent through his letters to Lady Margaret that during his "house arrest" at Buckingham's Welsh estate, Morton had been instrumental in urging "poor Harry" to join forces with Henry Tudor.

"'Twas Bishop Morton who planted the idea of Harry

rebelling in order to take the throne from Richard for *himself*," Margaret muttered cynically. "Now the man would have me think he supported my son from the beginning. Does he really think me that naive?"

"I cannot imagine anyone thinking you naive, madam," said Nell.

"Elizabeth Woodville's kin are fleeing as well," said Margaret offhandedly.

"Should you not attempt to leave yourself?" Nell inquired. "If the charge be treason—"

"My husband has done his job well," Margaret replied with something like pride. "He stayed close to Richard through the entire uprising, always professing his loyalty. I shall be spared the ultimate punishment."

"But how could the king have trusted Lord Stanley during the rebellion?" Nell wanted to know. "'Twas his own stepson, Henry Tudor, trying to usurp Richard's throne . . . with Stanley's wife's backing!"

"My Thomas is a very clever man. Sometimes I think there is magic in his ability to inspire trust where none should be given."

"Mistress Caxton?" The latest messenger to be admitted to the office stood before the desk.

"Yes?" Nell's heart lurched. *Please God, be a message from my father,* she thought.

The young man handed her a folded parchment. It took every mote of control not to sigh with relief to see William Caxton's distinctive wax seal closing it.

Nell looked to Margaret for permission to read it. She nodded her assent.

Nell's hands shook, but as she read aloud—for she was sure Lady Margaret's curiosity would require satisfaction—she calmed. Her father's ruse was so clever. "'Dear Nell, I am writing to you in private, for I do not wish that your father should know of this letter. He would be cross with me. But my master is ill, much more so than he will admit.'"

Nell looked to Margaret with a stricken expression. Margaret too looked alarmed, as she was sincerely fond of William Caxton.

"This is written by my father's apprentice, Jan de Worde," Nell said, then continued reading. "'He would not like you to leave Lady Margaret's service at so difficult a time for her, but I fear that if you do not hurry home quickly'"—Nell paused and clutched her throat before continuing in a wavering voice—"'he may not live long enough for you to see him alive again. Your friend, Jan.'"

Nell quickly glanced at the page bottom to find her further instructions, but looked up quickly and fixed Margaret with pleading eyes.

"Well, of course you must go," she said, barely able to contain her frustration.

"Thank you, Lady Margaret!" Nell began to turn away, then hesitated. "May I have John drive me? He has been—"

"Take whomever you like," Margaret snapped, then added in a more kindly tone, "I will pray to Saint Stephen for your father's recovery."

JUST BEFORE DARK Nell found John in the stables, which were, like the house, in a state of mad confusion, with many more horses and riders and carriages coming and going than could comfortably be accommodated by the stable hands.

"Where have you been, Nell?" John whispered urgently. "I've learned what carriage Reggie Bray will be taking to Barkley, but I need your help to—" He looked round them. "Come on."

She followed him to the coach house, where Lady Margaret's four rigs were in various states of readiness. A smith was pounding noisily on the metal undercarriage of a caravan, and liverymen were busy cleaning and polishing Lady Margaret's conveyances inside and out.

John nodded silently in the direction of the very coach they had arrived in that morning.

"He's taking that one?" she asked quietly.

John nodded. "Pretend we are talking together," he said. He moved to a position in which Nell's skirts were blocking him in case anyone should look in their direction. "Have we received our instructions?" he said, bending over the coach's steel-and-leather harness. A hammer and sharp chisel were suddenly produced, and as he and Nell continued their conversation, she advising him of their instructions, John would watch and wait for the smith to strike at the metal undercarriage, then himself strike at the harness's central shaft in perfect syncopation.

It took six precisely placed blows before the driver stood and smiled at Nell. "Master Bray should make it ten miles or less before the shaft snaps. 'Twill create a goodly delay."

"Brilliant! Now, what coach might *we* take?"

John looked round them. "These are all spoken for."

"Pity we cannot steal one."

"We may have to ride. Are you able, Nell?"

"I do not ride all that well, but I can if I must."

"I swear if I were a lady I would ride badly too, both legs slung over one side of the horse." He thought for a moment. "If I give you a pair of breeches to wear under your skirts, you can ride like a man."

"I like the sound of that," she said. "Anything that will get us to Barkley before Reggie Bray."

. . .

THE WAY NORTH had been so badly damaged that had they used a coach, the trip would have taken days. In many places, crews of men worked with saws and winches removing fallen trees that blocked the road. There were countless funeral processions, and whole villages crushed and leveled by the storm.

It was just before dawn when they reached the manor, but fearful of being spotted, they took the river path from Brentford Bridge, and at the Barkley dock and boathouse—thankfully unattended and set far back from the castle—they waited for the rest of the party to arrive.

Whilst the storm had clearly passed, the Thames was still running high and fast from the Westcountry toward London, and Nell worried that her father's plan to use the river for transportation was ill conceived.

They peered downstream into the dark for hours, and Nell began to despair that the rescue would take place at all. Whilst Reggie Bray would surely have been impeded by John's fouling of the carriage harness and the bad roads, the man, a loyal servant on so vital a mission, would surely find a way round all impediments.

They were startled therefore to hear voices coming from *up-river*. Soon a country barge was approaching the dock. Nell heard a gravelly male voice calling, "Poppet?"

'Twas them! "Poppet" was her father's pet name for Nell as a small child. *Thank Christ!* She and John moved out of the boathouse shadows and helped the hands tie up the barge. There were six of them, two boatmen, a large stocky man who even in the moonlight Nell recognized as Edward Brampton. Three other men under his direction worked quickly without lanterns, to prevent drawing attention to the operation.

With the briefest greeting to Nell, Brampton gestured for John to help his men unload two good-size and rather heavy crates. Another man heaved a sack over his shoulder, and when all conspirators and equipment had been set upon land, Brampton ordered the bargemen to continue downriver.

"How will we escape if they leave us?" Nell asked him. "The tide is against them returning."

"They're only polling out of sight of the manor. They'll tie up near that copse of trees." Brampton pointed downriver a hundred yards. Nell could make out a shadowy cluster of foliage. "It would be easier to load the boys from dock to barge, but if there is even the slightest suspicion of our activity, the river will be the first place they will look."

"Of course," she agreed. Before he turned away, Nell placed her hand on his muscular arm. "Thank you, Master Brampton. I thank you with all my heart."

"There is no need. 'Tis a sacred duty. These children are England's soul, its future. Any Englishman"—he acknowledged her with a smile—"or -woman worth their salt would do the same. But come now, this part is the most dangerous—moving unseen from the dock to the manor. What is your man's name?"

"John. He's there." She pointed to the pair of men carrying the heavier of the two crates. "He will tell you where we can gain entrance."

Brampton hurried ahead, and Nell caught up with the young man toting the sack. He was quiet, and simply acknowledged her with a nod. "Did you all travel upriver in a coach?" she whispered.

"Aye," he answered.

Nell had wrongly assumed from her father's terse instructions that they would be *sailing* upriver from London. "At which town did you acquire the barge?"

The young man stopped in his tracks, reached up, and quite

suddenly pulled off his cap. In the moonlight a great mass of golden hair fell down about his shoulders.

"Good heavens!" Nell was riveted to the spot.

The "young man" turned. It was Bessie, an impish grin crinkling her pretty face. "Oh, Nell!" Bessie dropped the sack and the girls embraced fervently and forgivingly. "You found them, you found them," Bessie murmured gratefully.

"How on earth did you escape sanctuary?" Nell asked.

"I changed clothes with Mistress Lily," Bessie replied, very pleased with herself. "I wish you could have seen my mother's face, realizing she'd be entertaining a streetwalker for the next three days."

"Ladies!" Brampton hissed back at them. "We must hurry!"

Nell grabbed the sack and slung it over her shoulder. "I'm wearing breeches too, under my skirts," she said as they followed the others into the manor's moon shadow. "You would not believe how pleasant they make riding a horse."

Nell's description of the old Roman dungeons had elicited from John the possibility of an outside entrance to Barkley's subterranean world. When found, it was no more than a large rusty grate in the ground, the wooden plank covering it half eaten away by rot. It was a strange artifact he had briefly taken notice of, then quickly forgotten, whilst leading a team round the manor's east—and least used—entrance.

The small party attempted perfect quiet near the house, but the four men carrying the two heavy crates could not help grunting with their exertions. The boxes were set down and all the men, including Brampton, helped in lifting the grate, which, whilst unlocked, was made of such thick metal that moving it took monumental effort. Finally it was set aside, and only then were lanterns removed from one of the crates and, by Brampton's orders, lit.

With him and Nell in the lead, the crates and men following, and Bessie bringing up the rear, they descended a rock stairway similar to the one Nell had taken down from Lady Margaret's offices. This had clearly been abandoned for hundreds of years, perhaps a millennium.

There were rows of Corinthian columns on either side of a long corridor, remnants of its frescoed walls visible, its floor under the filth revealing a colorful mosaic design. They entered, in wonder, a grand, high-ceilinged chamber where even their whispers were magnified, and echoed down the two corridors radiating out from the room. If this followed the design of most Roman villas, thought Nell, those two corridors would soon angle off in a perpendicular fashion, all surrounding a central courtyard.

"Which way to the dungeons?" Brampton asked Nell.

She conferred with John, explaining precisely how she had found the original staircase but that, by her memory, she had climbed many more steps down to reach the dungeon than their party had done to find this chamber.

John took one of the lanterns, then squatted on his haunches. In the thick film of dust he began diagramming Barkley Manor. All stood round him, listening as he reasoned out where the original stairs Nell found would be, where the rescue party stood now, and in which direction they would need to move to reach the dungeons.

Nell could hear in John's voice great confidence and command, and she knew how proud he felt to be part of this operation.

"My guess is another level exists below," he said. "By Nell's reckoning, I would say we move down the western corridor, looking for a second staircase down."

They reassembled and passed through the hallway leading west from the great chamber, off of which were small rooms, clearly bedchambers. Nell's urge to explore this capsule of a lost age, a culture whose language she had studied for so long, was made almost unbearable by inscriptions in Latin painted in the frescoes—perhaps names of the individuals whose portraits graced the halls, a family motto. Who had these Romans been, living in splendor so far from their home on the farthest, wildest outposts of the empire?

But there was no time to waste exploring. Somewhere below were two scared boys—*pray God there were still two living*—who needed a swift rescue.

Now, in the west wing of the villa, it became clear why the Romans had abandoned it. The corridors were, in places, piled so high with river silt that the party was forced to climb over great drifts of it. The Thames, in centuries past, had overflowed its banks and inundated the southern shore one time too many.

"Here!" cried John.

It was a stairway down, and Brampton, wasting no time, urged the party on. Wall torches in their sconces and matching columns joined by a carven stone arch, much like the first she had found, cheered Nell immensely. They could not be far now. She and Bessie, hands tightly clutching, took the treacherous stairs down, bracing each other for safety. A tiny slip now could be disastrous.

But indeed, a small disaster lay at the bottom of the curved stairs. Below the final pair of columns and its arch the doorway had been walled up. It was a dead end, and Nell's heart sank.

But Brampton had come prepared. He was gesturing for his men to pry open one of the boxes. Out came picks and sledge-hammers, enough for each man to be armed. Without another word, they began smashing at the stone and mortar. It was grueling work, but their hearts and souls were behind their efforts.

"The sound is enough to wake the dead," said Bessie.

"It may," Brampton said. "If the cook and the steward find us out, we shall kill them."

The words were spoken with a matter-of-factness born of necessity, and Nell surprised herself with the lack of sympathy for the boys' jailers. They were human beings. Knew right from wrong. And Margaret Beaufort was no queen to be obeyed un-challenged. Still, Nell prayed that their operation might be completed with success and no bloodshed.

"Ha!" One of the wall smashers had finally broken through. With renewed efforts, the others, with violent swings of their sledgehammers, widened the hole and one by one the rescuers stepped through, carrying with them their equipment crates.

The basement tunnels were lined with doorways leading to storage and workrooms, servants' quarters, and even a kitchen, eerie with its hearth and oven, smoke staining its upper arch, evoking in Nell the strangest feeling of communion with those who had once dwelt here, whose baking bread had forever seared its mark into stone.

"Nell!" It was John calling to her. "Could this be it?"

It was a doorway, through which she passed and found her-self standing at the base of the circular stone stairway from Margaret's offices. Holding the torch aloft, she saw the dungeon corridor stretching out before her. They'd found it!

But peering into the dark, she saw no crack of light in the door at the far end of the row of grisly cells.

*Were they too late?*

" 'Tis the place," she said in a hushed voice.

"How *could* she?" she heard Bessie whisper. "They're inno-cent children."

"She is a Lancaster," Nell heard Edward Brampton answer. "To Margaret Beaufort, they are nothing but a threat to her great plan. A true King of England, no matter his age, is never an innocent."

Nell had taken the lead. The quiet was terrible, and though she knew the boys might be sleeping, all she could see were Edward's sunken cheeks, the terror in Dickon's eyes. The pleading that she not leave them. There was no light within. *Jesus help us,* she heard herself pray. How easily it suddenly came to ask for God's grace.

The key was absent from its nail. Nell tried the door latch. It was locked.

Still there was silence within.

"Stand aside, Nell. Princess."

Again sledgehammers were produced. A few moments later the heavy wood door was splintering, the lock shattered. Brampton pulled it open and stepped back. He looked to Nell and Bessie.

Bessie was trembling violently. She clutched her friend's arm for strength, and together they entered the dungeon cell.

Edward, stretched on his pallet, was lying still, but moaning piteously.

Dickon sat in a heap on the floor near his head, perhaps where he had stayed whispering words of hope and encouragement to his brother. He was babbling incoherently, singing snatches of nursery tunes, unaware that the door had been smashed in or that his sister and Nell Caxton were standing over him.

Bessie knelt beside Dickon, who neither acknowledged nor spoke to her. She felt for a pulse at Edward's neck. " 'Tis a weak force"—Bessie's voice cracked—"but his heart beats still." Now she leaned and placed her lips near Dickon's ear. " 'Tis Bessie. We've come for you, baby brother," she crooned gently.

"Come for me come for me baby brother come for me come come come." Dickon chanted the words, a mad song.

"You must step aside now, ladies." Behind them, Brampton was all business. "Outside, if you please."

Nell and Bessie did as they were directed, and as they exited the cell, they saw the second of the two crates pried open by the men who had accompanied Brampton. Nell, till now unflappable and efficient, found herself astonished and unaccountably horrified to see the men lift two stiff corpses from the crate. They were fair-haired children, close in size and age to the Princes of England.

"What is this?" Nell asked.

Bessie, who observed the switching with a surprisingly sanguine expression, answered. "We acquired the poor blessed boys from a Southwark hospital. Brothers." She paused, suddenly losing her composure. "They drowned when a cart pinned them down on a flooded street."

As Bessie and Nell watched, John and Brampton gently carried Edward and Dickon from their foul prison whilst the servants carried the two cadavers in to take their places. The princes were laid carefully side by side in the crate from which the dead children had been taken, and now Brampton's men turned their attention to the tool crate. From within, they pulled several buckets, revealed to be pitch. This, they began dabbing round the boys' cell, down the long hall, and inside the barred dungeons. They returned and smeared the rest on the heavy wooden door.

"What is the meaning of this!" The voice Nell recognized as the steward's echoed down the tunnel. Brampton held up his lantern, and the figure of a man could be seen in nightclothes, holding a torch on the bottom of the stair.

Nell stopped breathing, for the steward was approaching their party quite boldly. In a moment she would surely see him run through by Edward Brampton.

"What have you done here?" said the man, yet unable to see into the crates.

Brampton stepped forward and Nell came to stand by his side.

"We've rescued Edward and Richard of York," she announced proudly. She could feel Brampton bristling next to her. Very subtly she sensed his hand reaching inside his belt for his smallsword.

"Thank Christ!" cried the steward. Even in the torchlight Nell thought she saw sincere relief flooding his face. "God has answered my prayers. Did you come from the riverside?"

"Yes," Brampton answered. "A barge waits a hundred yards downriver."

"You must have come in through the old grate," said the steward. He eyed the splintered door. "Broken through the wall. I know an easier way out."

"Is the cook——?" Nell began.

"The cook will burn in hell," he said. "I may too, for my cowardice in this affair. But Lady Margaret has threatened my family should I not comply with her wishes."

"Show us the way out," Brampton demanded.

"Have you enough pitch to burn the manor house too?"

One of the men shook his head.

"Come with me, then. I'll show you where ours is kept." He turned and started down the dungeon tunnel, but everyone held their ground.

"Do we trust him, Nell?" Brampton whispered. "Or has he laid a trap for us? Reggie Bray may be waiting at the top of the stairs. Perhaps 'twould be safer if we killed him."

Nell's mind clicked off the logic of known facts. The steward had been part of the boys' heinous captivity. Anyone could concoct a story that his partner in crime was solely culpable, and that his own family had been threatened. All Nell had to support the steward's innocence was knowledge that Lady Margaret was indeed capable of making and carrying out such threats . . . and an *instinct* that the steward was telling the truth. And memory of that one instant when joy at hearing of the princes' rescue washed over his face. It had been only a fleeting moment, but she had believed it sincere then. *Could she trust her intuition when so much hung in the balance?*

"You must come with me quickly!" the steward called from the far end of the dreadful corridor.

"What do you say?" Brampton urged.

"Nell . . ." It was Bessie, who'd come up behind and placed a soft hand on her shoulder. She offered no advice nor demanded an answer. She simply stood at her back, a pillar of strength and confidence.

"Follow him," Nell said.

Brampton whispered a few instructions to two of his men, and they strode down the tunnel, then followed the steward up the stairs into Lady Margaret's offices.

Brampton was thinking on his feet. "John," he said, "take Dickon. Nell, pull the door closed. Bessie, the blankets."

Everyone did as they were told, Bessie pulling thick wool blankets from the sack she'd carried off the barge. These they wrapped round Edward and Dickon. Brampton himself threw the tools into one crate and pushed both of them into the nearest barred cell. The near-empty cans of pitch he threw in after them. As gently as he was able, he lifted the emaciated boy who had been king into his arms.

"Take the torches," he directed Nell and Bessie, "and set it ablaze. Start in the boys' room, then follow us down the hall." He looked Nell up and down. "Mind your skirts do not catch fire."

"Let me have your smallsword," she said.

"In my belt," he directed her, and lifted Edward's body clear of his waist.

Nell snatched the blade and began ripping away her skirts to reveal the woolen breeches underneath. She grinned at Bessie.

"A couple of proper young gentlemen," she said. "Go on, then," she added to Brampton and John, who had picked up the still-delirious young Duke of York. "We'll catch you up in a moment."

The two men with their precious cargo started down the long tunnel. Nell and Bessie each grabbed a lit torch from the sconces. Together they entered the boys' prison and discovered the scene set by Brampton. Dickon's double was propped in a macabre parody of the prince, at the bedside of his elder brother.

Bessie, her lovely face contorted with fury, lowered her torch to the pitch-smeared blanket that covered Edward's double.

"Wait!" Nell cried. She stooped and retrieved the boys' well-worn volume of *Jason and the Argonauts* from under the head of the straw pallet. Dickon had, perhaps, read to his brother of courage and the hope of one day returning home, to keep him alive. "Now," she said to Bessie.

Both cots, the walls, and the straw on the floor were set ablaze. Heat seared and singed the girls as they hurried out, closing the door behind, then set it alight as well.

As they ran down the tunnel they touched their torches to the pitch-daubed walls and the straw in the dungeons. Choking smoke was quickly obliterating the corridor.

"This way!" Nell heard Brampton call. The men were at the base of the curved stairs, but when Nell started up them, Brampton stopped her. "No, we go back the way we came!"

*In case my instinct was wrong,* she thought, but did not argue.

The two men carrying the princes, followed closely by Nell and Bessie, stepped through the doorway near the stairs and made their way back through the silt-filled passages, the great Roman hall, and up the stairs to the castle's outer east wall.

John and Brampton laid the boys on the ground whilst the four of them struggled, heaving and grunting, to replace the heavy grate in its place. Hopefully fire would obliterate evidence of their deception, but this was a clue that, to a discerning eye, might spark suspicion.

They ran to the river and splashed through the hundred yards of reedy marsh to the barge. They would wait for the others to return.

The boys were taken to makeshift but comfortable beds that had been readied for them. Bessie, tears coursing down her cheeks, silently held the comatose Edward's hand, and Nell sat with Dickon tucked under her arm, rocking him gently, letting him babble, only occasionally whispering comfortable words in his ear.

*It was taking too long for Brampton's men to return,* Nell thought. Perhaps the steward had betrayed them. Perhaps even now Reggie Bray was setting the dogs on them. Yet no one said a word. Only the river rushing by and the sung words of Dickon's mad ditties unlaced the silence.

"Look." It was John, and he was pointing in the direction of Barkley Manor. An orange glow could be seen above the trees. An explosion rocked the night and a flame—one that had to be a hundred feet high—shot skyward.

A moment later they heard splashing in the reeds. One of Brampton's men, smelling of pitch and smoke, climbed aboard. When he'd caught his breath he told of the steward's energetic assistance. He had considered setting the house ablaze and leaving the cook inside to burn alive—"a fitting end for so vile a creature as she," he'd said. Finally the steward relented, worrying that to his considerable sins, for which he expected to suffer great torments, would be added murder. He instructed Brampton's men as to which chambers upstairs to first set ablaze, leaving him time to fetch the cook and himself to safety, and give the men opportunity to escape unseen by her.

Quickly ascending the central stairs, one had taken the east wing and the other the west wing of the manor to douse it with pitch and oil, and decided to make their way back to the barge separately.

By the time Brampton's man had done his job above and below and was running from the front door, he could hear the cook shrieking with terror. She and the steward descended the stairs, he shouting at her to unhand him, that they would better escape each on their own two feet.

By the time Brampton's man had turned the corner, heading for the river, the house was a raging inferno, flames shooting out windows, the half-timbered walls and chimneys beginning to crumble. He worried that his cousin was not yet back, and requested to return to find him. But a moment later the same splashing was heard in the reeds and the second panting and exhausted fire-starter was hauled aboard. His long hair, eyebrows, and lashes were altogether singed from his body, and his hands were badly burned, his face beginning to blister.

Agonized with pain, he was yet eager to make his report. He'd been forced to delay coming down the stairs until the cook and steward had escaped. By the time it was safe, the staircase was littered with fallen hangings and portraits. He ran up again to find a long-enough staff to clear the steps, as he and his cousin had set fire to all the others in the house. He'd only been able to find a broom, the straw already ablaze. He'd stomped it out and, returning to the stairs, used the broom handle to push debris out of his path. Halfway down, a large burning tapestry had fallen on his head. He'd managed to push it off him, but this was how he'd received his wounds and lost his hair.

His listeners bade him lie down and allow his burns to be tended, but there was more to report, he said. As planned, the steward was keeping the cook from facing the door from which Brampton's men were to escape the house. But as he emerged, a lone man on horseback galloped up and began shouting at the steward. Hiding behind a pillar and wishing desperately to be gone, but worried that he would be spotted and the whole operation exposed, he stayed, trying to get the steward's attention, but avoiding the cook and the man who'd just ridden in.

The rider was angrily demanding an explanation for the fire, and the steward bravely took responsibility, saying that he'd gone to the kitchen for something to soothe a bellyache, and had accidentally set some cooking oil on fire, cooking oil, he said with some glee, that the slovenly cook had let spill all over the floor. The fire had spread with amazing swiftness. He'd just been able to save "the old bat" when the rider arrived, but there'd been no time, he added pointedly, to get to the basement.

Just then the steward had spotted Brampton's man peeking out from behind the pillar and skillfully turned the rider away from the house for the moment needed for the fire-starter to make a run for it.

"I'll see to it that the steward is well taken care of," said Brampton, leading his brave servant to a makeshift bed that his cousin had made for him next to the princes. "He'll no doubt be terminated from Lady Margaret's service."

"I should think we will *all* be terminated from her service," said Nell, "if she is to be arrested for treason. I, for one, will be most happy to be gone from the woman's presence."

# BESSIE

WITH A MODICUM of peace restored to the rescuers and rescued, Bessie had taken a place between her brothers—both of them now asleep—to keep vigil. Nell came and sat beside her on the deck.

There was a silence between them, rare for two girls who, in each other's company, were never short of conversation. Bessie thought Nell had the strangest look on her face. Shy, shamed, and proud.

"Can you forgive me?" Nell finally said.

"For refusing to believe my uncle Richard innocent? For believing my brothers dead?" Bessie smiled at her friend. "Had I been you, I would not have believed me either. All that I held was illogical in the extreme. 'Twas only what my heart was telling me. And for all my surety in Richard's innocence, I would not in a thousand years have guessed the true villain was Margaret Beaufort." She took Nell's hand in hers and kissed it. "So yes, friend, I most assuredly forgive you. And I thank you with all my heart. My mother thanks you. England thanks you."

"The Fates had a hand in it too," said Nell. "The storm. John the driver stopping us for the night at Barkley." She paused, tears welling in her eyes. "A dream that woke me."

"Your father's plan was brilliant," said Bessie. "Rose and Lily.

Your intelligence 'web.' Jan de Worde. Master Brampton. These two brave cousins. And my aunt Maggie, of course."

"Is that where Edward and Dickon will go? To Burgundy?"

" 'Tis unclear. For now, they will be taken to her London house on the river. When they're well enough, they'll be smuggled out of England. More than that I do not know. But they are alive, Nell. Kings or no, they'll grow up to be men. You should be very, very proud."

"What about *your* part in it?" Nell insisted. " 'Tis not every princess that will trade places with a whore, put on a pair of breeches, and set fire to cadavers and a wicked woman's manor house to save her brothers."

Bessie considered Nell's words carefully, as though for the first time. Indeed, since Rose and Lily's visit to the Sanctuary Tower, she'd not had a moment to spare for thought or reflection. She had not been asked, nor required, to take part in the rescue, but her fury had driven her to action. Once her mind had been set—and to the extreme displeasure of her mother—Bessie had set out for the adventure. That her part in it had proven important and its outcome successful was, with Nell's assurances, only now occurring to her.

She looked again at the sleeping princes. "I *am* proud of my myself," she said, "but I'm prouder still to have you as my friend."

"Look ahead!" cried the forward bargeman. "There be the lights of London!"

A ND SO THEY WERE," Queen Bessie told her son. "We had arrived safely home, and no one was the wiser of our adventure."

"If the little princes—my uncles—were not killed by my

great-uncle Richard," said Harry, "then why is it always said that they were? Why did James Tyrell confess to being King Richard's henchman?"

" 'Tis my guess," said Nell, "that many of the couriers Margaret Beaufort sent out into England and abroad before Richard's soldiers came to arrest her were meant especially to perpetuate that story. She was bound and determined to weaken and undermine her son's rival, and what could be more damaging than for a man to be known as a murderer of children, indeed his own nephews?"

"Then my grandmother Margaret believed the ruse? That the two bodies found in the dungeon were Edward and Dickon?"

Nell and Bessie smiled at each other.

"Well, Harry," his mother said, "we did our job so well, and Barkley Manor burned so fiercely, that it collapsed in on itself and the Roman ruins below. There was nothing left but a pile of charred rubble. By that time Lady Margaret—"

"My grandmother!" Harry cried incredulously.

"Your grandmother had been arrested for her part in the invasion conspiracy, her titles and all her properties stripped from her. She was placed under house arrest at Woking, and all her servants were taken. By Reggie Bray's report, the boys were surely dead, and the manor was simply plowed over. Last I heard 'twas pastureland."

"But Grandmother was not executed, as all traitors are," Harry reasoned.

"Do you remember," Nell asked him, "the day she learned that her son's invasion had failed? How she said that Lord Stanley's loyalty to King Richard would save her?"

Harry nodded eagerly.

"She was right. Indeed, Richard was so grateful—"

"And perhaps foolishly naive," Bessie interjected.

"—that he created Lord Stanley his wife's only jailer. All Margaret Beaufort's confiscated properties were forfeited not to the state, but given over to Stanley. In fact, though hard to believe, King Richard named him Constable of England!"

"A blunder he would live to regret," Bessie added.

"How very peculiar," said Harry, sincerely perplexed. "If Henry Tudor's invasion failed"—he looked at his mother—"and your marriage with him never took place, then how is it that he became king and you his wife, and I your child?"

"I'm sure you've heard of the battle of Bosworth Field," said Nell, "and how King Richard the Third was slain and your father took his crown?"

"*Everyone* has heard that story," said Harry. "But what of my other grandmother, Queen Elizabeth Woodville? I don't remember her."

"She died when you were a year old," Bessie answered evenly, "in the nunnery where your father confined her at the end of her life."

"She ended up in a *nunnery?*"

There was a brisk knock on the chamber door and a moment later Lady Margaret swept into the room.

Prince Harry stifled a gasp. Nell and Bessie regarded her with the properly sad smile of women grieving for a lost prince.

"Harry, Nell, 'tis time to take your leave. I must insist. You've been keeping the queen talking for too long. She needs her rest."

"You're quite right, Lady Margaret," Nell agreed. She rose and gave Bessie a kiss on the cheek, whispering, "She won't keep me away so long next time."

Harry was next, embracing his mother so fervently that Lady Margaret's wrinkled old mouth pursed with displeasure. It appeared that Lady Margaret would be taking Harry with her, so when Nell bent to kiss him, she said very quietly, "Next time you will hear about the *second* invasion."

Margaret herded Nell from the room, but not before the two friends exchanged a warm, knowing smile. Then the queen mother, no taller than her ten-year-old grandson, took his hand in hers and led him away. Nell could hear her words fading as they moved down the corridor. "You must learn to be more thoughtful, Harry. 'Tis wicked to tire your mother so." And his obedient reply, "Yes, Grandmother, I will."

Just before they began descending the stairs, Harry turned back and fixed Nell with a conspiratorial smile. She sighed contentedly. The true story of the little princes' disappearance had never been told before. Bessie's and her rendition of it had been quite masterful, she had to admit. If she hadn't cared about living a long, healthy life, Nell thought, she would like to have written it as a book to be published, for it was well that people knew the truth.

But Henry Tudor was king, and Margaret Beaufort the first lady of the land. With such despots at the helm of the ship of state, truth was a rare commodity, and the spreading of it a deadly endeavor.

As usual, Nell would keep her counsel.

WHEN THE ROYAL CARRIAGE clattered across London Bridge, the bridge 'twas all but deserted, the shops long closed, only the lights of the merchants' houses above glittering over the Thames. Nell tried to pay the driver, but Bessie had clearly ordered him to take no money from her friend.

Nell was weary, but there was still work that needed attending to. Inside the dark mercantile it was peaceful, and the smell of the cloth that nearly always evoked sweet memories of early childhood and her father's own mercantile in Bruges this night brought forth memories both bitter and sweet. Her chest tightened at the thought of Antony, for it was in that shop in Burgundy that she had first met him. Nell was swept back in time.

*She was five, and still small enough to be dandled on his knee. She had thought Master Antony the handsomest man in the world, even then, and had told him so. She remembered his laugh at her very serious declaration, and his beautiful smile. Time shifted suddenly and there he was Governor of Wales at Ludlow, a whole royal court revolving round him. How deeply she had fallen in love with him! She knew the memory of those few kisses had to last a lifetime. There'd been promise of so much more in those kisses. There had been promise too in "Edward Quintus," the shining hope of England for three short months.*

*How, if he had reigned, she wondered, would England have been different?*

*England without the wretched Tudors! The soulless mother and son. Perhaps Bessie, after Anne's death, would have married her beloved Richard. Nell would be married still to Antony. Perhaps the potent Woodville blood would have triumphed over her barrenness. She might have had children of her own.*

*But as it had actually come to pass, Bessie was queen of the country she adored. If her fate, like Nell's, was to lose her life's truest love, then even the cost of an unhappy marriage was not too high. Three beautiful children, and a son whose heart was sweet and pure. Prince Harry was a rare gift.*

*Mayhaps the seer had been right. Mayhaps the Tudors would reign glorious for a hundred years. They were a family of mixed blood of Lancaster and York, yet all blood of the same ancestor. They might indeed be destined to produce greatness.*

*But to see them now—the mad king, the wicked mother, the grieving queen in her loveless marriage—such a resplendent future seemed no more than the ravings of a mad, blind prophet.*

Nell climbed the stairs to her apartment. All the maids had retired but one, who offered her mistress a late supper.

"A cold meat pie and some ale," she told the girl. "I'll have it upstairs, if you please."

Nell took one of the lanterns that lit her great room and sought the stairway to the floor above. She'd taken pains to have the heavy oak stairs built well, the banisters sturdy, for halfway up they split—one set of steps leading to her bedchamber above the mercantile, the other to the wing above the haberdashers.

A fresh-faced young man carrying a leather pouch met her coming down. "Mistress Caxton, good evening!"

"Good evening, Will. Are you off to Plymouth, then?"

"Yes, ma'am."

"And has Martin left for Calais?"

"Soon. His ship sails tomorrow evening."

"Ride safely," she said.

"I will. And God protect you, Mistress Caxton." His boots clattered on the stairs.

Will was bright. And his heart was in the right place. She would see to it he went far.

At the landing Nell held the lantern up. Tonight, the sight of the intricately carven wood door made her stop and smile. She could hear John's voice within, calling good-natured orders to her couriers, secretaries, and scribes.

And her spies. Hers and her patron Queen Bessie's spies.

*The invisible web.* Nell, with Bessie's help, had spun it very wide indeed. *Bessie, the weak and powerless queen, and her mercer friend Nell Caxton of London Bridge, had more of a grip on the world than it appeared to the naked eye.* They had, through their intelligence network, treated with many heads of state, from Burgundy to Scotland to Spain, and the great Earls of Ireland, and had a hand in fomenting a rebellion or two. In all, they'd been a sharp thorn in Henry Tudor's side. And he had never, in all these years, been the wiser.

Her dear friend Bessie, Elizabeth of York, would likely go down in history as a cipher, lacking all influence, more a pawn than a queen. But she was stronger than anyone knew, more courageous, and had worked diligently in the shadows for the true blood of England.

Prince Harry, who already knew of his mother's goodness, today had learned of her power. But there was more to know. Much more. 'Twas fitting for the future King of England to hold the truth of history in his hands. Nell and Bessie would, in the coming months, provide it.

With a great sigh of contentment, she pushed open the carven door.

There is no more enduring nor acrimoniously argued mystery in English history than that of the little princes' disappearance from the Tower of London. Since the boys vanished without a trace in 1483, countless books, articles, and novels have been published on the subject. Thanks to William Shakespeare's characterization of Richard in his *Tragedy of King Richard III,* the princes' uncle is remembered by most as the withered-armed, crookbacked monster who murdered his brother's two sons. Today, international organizations such as The Richard III Society passionately defend his innocence.

The debate is stymied by several widely read fifteenth-century chronicles, all of which are seriously flawed by bias, factual error, and incompleteness. Modern-day "traditionalists" line up behind Shakespeare, and "Ricardians" claim as guilty everyone from Henry Tudor to Harry Buckingham. But none of them has fashioned a wholly satisfying conclusion.

A perfect example of the confusion is Sir Thomas More's *History of King Richard III, a* frequently quoted source, the one upon which Shakespeare based his popular play. Universally respected for his integrity, More enjoyed, for centuries, unquestioned authority on the subject. In fact, More's *History* is not even a contemporary account. He was five years old at the time of the princes' disappearance. Further, his credentials are tainted, young Thomas having lived during his formative years as a ward of King Richard's avowed enemy, Bishop Morton.

This clergyman was one of the fifteenth century's greatest Lancastrian plotters and power brokers, an intimate of Lady Margaret Beaufort, and later, high counselor to her son, King Henry the Seventh. Prejudiced as he must have been, Morton was More's primary source. Some even believe that Morton wrote parts of *The History of King Richard III* himself.

More's version, lionizing the ruling Tudor king and naming Richard as the boys' murderer, is in several important ways flawed. Sir Thomas placed long, melodramatic passages of dialogue into the mouths of the main figures, as though they were characters in a play. He never actually *finished* his history of the period, leaving out some of the mystery's most vital information. Most interestingly, More refused to allow his manuscript to be published in his lifetime. Twenty years after his death, his nephew edited the book and had it published. It occurred to me that More might have realized, after beginning the work, that his theory of "Richard as monster" was deeply flawed, even wrong, causing him to shelve the misleading manuscript. This, in itself, is a mystery worth considering.

Neither do the histories speak much about the women who were central to this story. Queen Elizabeth Woodville and her daughter Princess Elizabeth of York (Princess Bessie) rate exactly one book each, and I found none about Anne Neville, King Richard's wife.

Margaret Beaufort's biographers do nothing but exalt "the Venerable Margaret" for her piousness, learning, and charity. With the exception of a brief and inconclusive paragraph in Jeremy Potter's *Good King Richard,* no historians—medieval through modern—for one moment consider the pathologically ambitious Margaret a suspect. Josephine Tey's classic novel on the subject, *Daughter of Time,* diverts the blame from Richard and places it squarely at the feet of Henry the Seventh. A sensible approach on first glance, it falters when one remembers that the exiled Henry Tudor hadn't set foot on English soil for seventeen years at the time of the princes' disappearance. It never occurs to Tey that Henry's mother—the convicted financier and master conspirator in both Buckingham's rebellion and her son's invasion attempts—had both the clearest motive and the greatest opportunity to have the royal boys snatched. Though punished for her treason and placed under close house arrest, Margaret nevertheless launched a *second* invasion, this one so successful that Henry was able to steal the crown and found the great Tudor dynasty.

Margaret as the villain of this story seemed most logical to me.

Nell Caxton was my other most exciting find. William Caxton did have one child—a daughter named Elizabeth, whose nickname might well have been Nell. London records document her divorce from Gerard Croppe, and this was the seed from which her character grew. William Caxton, with his shop steps away from Westminster Palace, held an extraordinary position within the inner circle of the courts of three kings— Edward the Fourth, Richard the Third, and Henry the Seventh, as well as Duchess Margaret of Burgundy. Later, during Henry's reign, Margaret Beaufort became Caxton's greatest patron. Surely this enlightened man would have provided his only child with a stellar education, as well as entrée into his world of royal connections. Beloved as Caxton was by each of these rulers, Nell must have known Princess (and later Queen) Bessie, and a friendship between them would certainly have been smiled upon by all.

The little princes' mysterious disappearance is not so much

a blank in the historical record, or even a wide chasm, as a cosmic-size *black hole* in which one can easily become lost. In fact, *there is no consensus on whether the princes were murdered at all*. In virtually every history on the subject, even the most virulent anti-Richard author admits that the boys may not have died, but simply have been kidnapped out of the Tower by one of the interested factions. It has been variously suggested that they were abducted and locked away in a dungeon, snatched in 1483 and held captive in various castles in England, and only murdered later. Another theory holds that they were smuggled out of England to be raised by their aunt Margaret of Burgundy. In this scenario, Edward eventually died, but Dickon (Prince Richard of York) lived to young manhood, and with the support of most of the heads of state of Europe, led a serious rebellion against Henry Tudor. Most believe the young man in question was not Prince Richard, but an impostor named Perkin Warbeck, though I find the idea of Dickon's survival quite plausible.

Of course there is the question of the bones.

In the year 1674, what amounted to two sets of bones were found under a stairwell in the Tower of London, in a place where Thomas More had suggested the princes' bodies had been interred after their murder by King Richard's henchmen. In 1933 they were exhumed, examined, and determined to be the skeletons of two children, aged approximately nine and twelve. The bones were reinterred in a marble urn, which to this day resides at Westminster Abbey. The problem is, Sir Thomas More also claims in his *History* that the bones were *removed* from the stairwell by Richard's henchmen at a later date. There are actually several other children's skeletons found in excavations of the Tower, one of which has been carbon-dated to the Stone Age.

There has never been a modern, scientific analysis or a DNA study performed on the bones in question, and it has never been conclusively proven that these are the earthly remains of the York brothers. Yet they are often cited as "proof" of Richard's guilt.

My theory of Margaret Beaufort as mastermind of the boys' kidnapping is, as far as I know, altogether original. I hope it provokes further debate in this already spirited controversy.

## Main Sources

*On Richard:*
    *Richard III,* Michael Hicks
    *Richard the Third,* Paul Murray Kendall
    *Richard the Third, England's Black Legend,* Desmond Seward

*On Margaret Beaufort:*
    *The King's Mother,* Michael K. Jones and Malcolm G. Underwood
    *Of Virtue Rare,* Linda Simon

*On the little-princes mystery:*
    *Royal Blood,* Bertram Fields
    *The Princes in the Tower,* Elizabeth Jenkins
    *The Princes in the Tower,* Alison Weir
    *The Perfect Prince,* Ann Wroe

*On William and Elizabeth (Nell) Caxton:*
    *Caxton and his World,* N. F. Blake
    *William Caxton, a Portrait in a Background,* Edmund Childs
    *England in the Age of Caxton,* Geoffrey Hindly

*On Elizabeth Woodville:*

Elizabeth Woodville, Mother of the Princes in the Tower, David Baldwin

*On Henry Tudor:*

The History of the Reign of King Henry VII, Francis Bacon

Henry VII, the First Tudor King, Bryan Bevan

*On Elizabeth (Bessie) of York:*

"Privy Purse Expenses of Elizabeth of York: Wardrobe Accounts of Edward IV, and 'Memoirs' of Elizabeth of York," *The ORB: The On-line Reference Book for Medieval Studies* (www.the-orb.net) and The Richard III Society, American Branch (www.r3.org)

*On Henry the Eighth:*

Great Harry, Carolly Erickson